CORNWALL LIBRARY
D0269652

THE CROWN

THE CROWN

NANCY BILYEAU

First published in Great Britain in 2012 by Orion Books,
an imprint of The Orion Publishing Group Ltd
Orion House, 5 Upper Saint Martin's Lane
London WC2H 9EA

An Hachette UK Company

1 3 5 7 9 10 8 6 4 2

A CIP catalogue record for this book
is available from the British Library.

ISBN (Hardback) 978 1 4091 3306 3
ISBN (Trade Paperback) 978 1 4091 3307 0
ISBN (ebook) 978 1 4091 3308 7

Printed and bound in the UK by CPI Group (UK) Ltd,
Croydon, CRO 4YY

Designed by Akasha Archer

The Orion Publishing Group's policy is to use papers that are natural, renewable and recyclable products and made from wood grown in sustainable forests. The logging and manufacturing processes are expected to conform to the environmental regulations of the country of origin.

www.orionbooks.co.uk

For my husband, who believed

PART
ONE

1

London, May 25, 1537

When a burning is announced, the taverns off Smithfield order extra barrels of ale, but when the person to be executed is a woman and one of noble birth, the ale comes by the cartload. I would ride in one of those carts on Friday of Whitsun week, the twenty-eighth year of the reign of King Henry the Eighth, to offer prayers for the soul of the condemned traitor, Lady Margaret Bulmer.

I heard the cartsman's cry go out as I made my way on Cheapside Street, clutching the London map I'd sketched from a book in secret two nights before. I moved faster now that I'd reached such a wide and cobbled street, but my legs throbbed. I'd spent the morning trudging through mud.

"Smithfield—are ye bound for Smithfield?" It was a cheerful voice, as if the destination were a Saint George's Day fair. Just ahead, in front of a tannery, I saw who had shouted: a burly man flicking the backs of four horses hitched to a large cart. A half-dozen heads peeked above the rails.

"Hold!" I shouted as loudly as I could. "I wish to go to Smithfield."

The cartsman whipped around; his eyes searched the crowd. I waved, and his face split into a wet smile. As I drew nearer, my stomach clenched. I'd vowed I would speak to no one this entire day, seek no assistance. The risk of discovery was too great. But Smithfield lay outside the walls of the city, to the north and west, still a fair distance away.

When I reached him, the cartsman looked me up and down, and his smile sagged. I wore a heavy wool kirtle, the only one available to me for the journey. It was a bodice and skirt made for the dead of winter, not spring, and not a day when bursts of warmth were anchored by sheets of billowing mists. Mud soaked my tangled hem. I could only be grateful no one could see beneath the heavy fabric, to my shift drenched with sweat.

But I knew it wasn't only my dishevelled garments that gave the cartsman pause. To many, I look strange. My hair is black as polished onyx; my eyes are brown with flecks of green. My olive skin neither reddens by Saint Swithin's Day, nor pales by Advent. Mine is the colouring of my Spanish mother. But not her delicate features. No, my face is that of my English father: a wide forehead, high cheekbones, and strong chin. It's as if the mismatch of my parents' marriage fought on the foundation of my face, plain for all to see. In a land of pink-and-white girls, I stand out like a raven. There was a time when that troubled me, but at twenty-six years of age, I was no longer subject to such petty concerns.

"A shilling to ride, mistress," the cartsman said. "Pay up and we'll be off."

His demand took me by surprise, though, of course, it shouldn't have.

"I am without coins," I stammered.

The cartsman barked a laugh. "Do ye think I do this for amusement? I've run low on ale"—he pounded a wooden barrel behind him—"and I must earn enough to pay for the cart." On the far side of the barrel, I could see his passengers craning to get a look at me.

"Wait," I said, and fished for the small cloth purse in the pocket I'd stitched into my dress. Swirling my fingers around the purse, I found a slender ring. I didn't want to give him anything finer. Some important bribes lay ahead.

I held out the ring. "Will this do?" In an instant his scowl turned to delight, and the slight golden ring of my dead mother disappeared into the driver's dirty palm.

When I climbed into the back of his cart, I could see pity and contempt playing across the faces of the other passengers. My ring must be worth more than the ride. I found a clean pile of straw in the corner and looked down, trying to avoid their curious stares, as the cart resumed its journey.

An elbow poked my side. A sturdy woman sidled closer, one of middling years, the only other female in the cart. Smiling, she held out a piece of brown bread. I'd had nothing to eat since last night's supper. Ordinarily, I gloried in the pangs of hunger, the mastery over my weak mortal flesh, but my mission required a certain vigour. I took the bread with a grateful nod. A mouthful of food and a gulp of watery ale from her wooden tankard brought strength to my dazed body.

I leaned back against the railing. We passed a small market that appeared to sell nothing but spices and herbs. Now that the rain had stopped, the sellers threw off the blankets keeping their narrow stalls dry. A rich mix of borage, sage, thyme, rosemary, parsley, and chives surged in the air, and then dissolved as we rumbled on. The urgent smells of the city rose again. A row of four-storey buildings came into view—more prosperous than any I'd seen so far. The sign of the goldsmith hung from a street corner.

A young man sitting across from me grinned and said, loudly, to the whole cart, "We're grateful to King Hal for burning a young beauty at Smithfield. Last person killed was an ugly, old forger."

A knot of swallowed bread rose in my throat, and I covered my mouth.

"But is she a beauty?" demanded someone else.

An elderly man with milky blue eyes twisted a long hair that sprang from the middle of his chin.

"I know someone who has seen Lady Bulmer in the flesh, and yes, she is bonny," he said slowly. "More so than the queen."

"Which queen?" one of the men shouted.

"All three of them," answered another. A nervous laugh raced around the cart. To mock the king's marriages—the divorce of the first wife and the execution of the second to make way for the third—was a crime. Hands and ears had been lopped off for it.

The old man twisted his chin hair harder. "Lady Bulmer must have offended the king grievously for him to burn her out in the open before commoners, not to order the axee for Tower Hill or hang her at Tyburn."

The young man said, "They've dragged all the nobles and gentry down to London, the ones who followed Robert Aske. For king's justice. She's just the first to die."

My breath quickened. What would these Londoners say, what would they do to me, if they knew who I was and where I came from? One thing was certain: I would never reach Smithfield.

I searched my prayers for something to uphold me. *O Lord my*

God, help me to be obedient without reserve, poor without servility, chaste without compromise.

"The Bulmer woman's a foul rebel!" shouted the woman who'd shared with me her bread. "She's a Papist northerner who plotted to overthrow our king."

Humble without pretence, joyful without depravity, serious without affectation, active without frivolity, submissive without bitterness, truthful without duplicity.

The old man said mildly: "In the North, they gave their lives for the old ways. They wanted to protect the monasteries."

Everyone erupted in scorn.

"Those fat monks hide pots of gold while the poor starve outside their walls."

"I heard of a nun who had a priest's brat."

"The sisters are whores. Or else they're cripples—idiots, all cast off by their families."

I heard a ragged noise. It was my own laugh, a bitter, joyless one—and unheeded, for there was a shout just then outside the cart. An urchin ran alongside, so fast he shot ahead of our horses. A panicky look over the shoulder revealed the child to be not a boy but a smudge-faced girl, her hair chopped short.

A clod of dirt sailed through the air and hit her shoulder. "Awww," she howled. "Ye curs!"

Two large boys, scrambling up along the side of the cart, laughed. Within a minute, they'd have her. The men in the cart cheered on the chase.

The boys' prey darted out of the street and toward a row of shops.

Another girl beckoned from a doorway. "This way!" she shouted. The urchin darted inside, and the door slammed shut behind them. The boys reached it seconds later and pounded, but it was locked.

I closed my eyes. A different girl was running. Eight years old, breathless, a stitch in my side, I charged down a narrow path between tall hedges of yew, searching for a way out.

I could hear people calling my name, but I couldn't see them. "Hurry, Joanna, hurry—we're to play tennis next!" shouted my boy cousins, so strong, so hard. "Come now, girl, you can manage it," boomed the careless voice of my uncle, Edward Stafford, third Duke of Buckingham and head of the family. "You must find your own way out. We can't send anyone after you and risk the loss of another child."

I was trapped in my uncle's maze. He'd just had it built—"I hired better monks to design mine than Cardinal Wolsey used," he said again and again. Today, September 4, the annual birthday celebration of the second Duke of Buckingham, my long-dead grandfather, the maze was put to use. We cousins were blindfolded and led to the centre. Then they whipped the cloths off and told us to race out, to see who'd be first. "Tread the maze! Tread the maze!" my uncle cried from outside the tall winding hedges.

I was one of the youngest and immediately fell to the back of the pack. Soon I was alone. I ran this way and that, hoping to see the hedge walls open to the gardens, but my instincts were always wrong and just led me deeper into the maze.

"What's wrong with you, Joanna?"

"Think, girl, think!"

The voices grew louder, more impatient. "Joanna, don't be such a doddypoll," shouted one Stafford boy. An elder hushed him.

I'd become the centre of attention, something I always hated. Had I turned right at this corner, or left? Panic made me forget which paths I'd already tried.

How my head spun with the smell of the roses. Dozens of sternly tamed red bushes dotted the maze. It was almost the end of the season; the rose petals had frayed and loosened. And the hour of the day had passed for peak freshness. But there were so many bushes, and I had passed them so many times. I could almost taste those cloying, dusty, imperious roses.

I turned a corner, fast, and slammed into Margaret.

We both fell down, laughing, the beads of our puffy sleeves hooked together. After we'd disentangled, she helped me up: Margaret was a year older and two inches taller, and always a hundred times cleverer and prettier. My first cousin. My only friend.

"Margaret, where have you gone to?" bellowed the Duke of Buckingham. "You'd better not have slipped back in the maze for Joanna."

"Oh, he's going to be angry with you," I said. "You shouldn't have done it."

Margaret winked. She brushed the dirt off my party finery and hers and led me out, holding my hand the whole way.

At the mouth of the maze, they'd gathered, what looked like the entire Stafford clan and all of our retainers and servants. My uncle the duke, the preeminent peer of England, wore cloth of silver and a long ostrich feather in his hat. His youngest brother, Sir Richard Stafford, my father, stood at his side. A long shadow stretching across the garden almost reached them. It was cast by the square tower that soared above us all. Thornbury Castle, in Gloucestershire, was built to withstand attack. Not from a foreign enemy but from generations of covetous Plantagenet kings.

Margaret walked right up to the duke, unafraid. "See, Father, I found Joanna," she said. "You can play tennis now." He looked us both over, eyebrows raised, as everyone waited, tense.

But the Duke of Buckingham laughed. He kissed his cherished daughter, his bastard, raised alongside the four children of his meek duchess. "I know well that you can do anything, Margaret," he said.

My father hugged me tight, too. He'd been sporting all day, and I remember how he smelled of sweat and soil and dry, flattened grass. I felt so relieved, and so happy.

The London cart lurched and shuddered, throwing me down on the straw. My reverie was finished.

We'd left the city walls and taken a side street. The cart's wheels were trapped in the muck. The cart horses whinnied, the driver cursed, the boisterous men moved to the back of the cart.

"No matter," the woman said to me. "We are almost at Smithfield."

I followed the group to the end of the street and then down another one lined with taverns. It opened into an enormous flat clearing, teeming with people already arrived and awaiting the day's execution. There were hundreds of them: men and women, sailors and seamstresses, children as well. A family pushed ahead of me, the mother carrying a basket of bread, the father with a boy sitting on his shoulders.

Without warning, a foul stench filled my nose, my throat, and my lungs. My eyes watered. It was worse than anything I'd breathed in London so far. With a cry I clutched my burning throat.

"That's the butcher yards to the east," said the woman I had ridden with. "When ye catch the wind, the blood and offal can be rank."

She touched my elbow. "Ye be unused to Smithfield, I can see that. Walk with me, stay close."

I shook my head, blinking. I wouldn't bear witness to the end of Margaret's life with such a heartless creature. She shrugged and melted into the mob. I stood alone.

Trembling, I reached into my pocket once more and removed the letter, the one Margaret wrote to me days before the outbreak of the Northern Rebellion, what we call the Pilgrimage of Grace. I unfolded the tight rectangle of cream-coloured paper and admired, as always, her sloping, delicate script.

My most entirely beloved Joanna:

I have learned from my brother that you plan to enter the Dominican Order at Dartford Priory and take vows to become a bride of Christ. I admire you so much for your choice of a holy life. I lit extra candles at morning Mass to honour you, dear cousin.

I only wish that somehow you would find a way to know my second husband, Sir John. He is a good, honest, true man, Joanna. He loves me. He cherishes me. I have finally found peace in the North, the same peace I hope you will find at Dartford Priory.

I cannot but think these are hard, wretched, frightening times. Those who serve God as our Holy Father ordains are scorned and persecuted. There is heresy everywhere. It is different in the North. Every night I say three prayers. I ask God to protect our monasteries. I seek salvation for the soul of my father. And I pray that someday I will see you again, Joanna, and that you will embrace me and forgive me.

Written at my manor in Lastingham in York, the last Thursday of September
Your cousin and dearest friend for eternity
Margaret Bulmer

I replaced the letter, pulled my hood over my head as far as it could go so that not a single strand of hair showed, and stepped into Smithfield.

2

Standing on the edge of the clearing, filled with people eager for the sport of Margaret's burning, I remembered something my father said about Smithfield. "That was where the Plantagenet court once held their most magnificent jousts, Joanna. That's why they chose it. Not far from the palaces was a 'smooth field.' And it became Smithfield."

My father wasn't a man ready with fine words. But he could describe a joust. He had been a champion in his youth, one of the finest jousters in the kingdom. That was before the execution of my uncle the duke for high treason when I was ten years old, and my parents' banishment from court. Before the fall of the Staffords.

It had been many years since he'd jousted. But the memories were sharp. I'd close my eyes and listen to him tell the story and feel as if I were on horseback: thundering down the course, divided in two by a low wooden fence. Silver armour blazing in the sun. A shield in the left hand, a lance in the right. In the distance, an opponent draws closer . . . closer . . . until the other jouster is a few feet away and down come the lances with a mighty crash.

When I imagined that moment of contact, when a man might die if a lance pierced below armour, I'd shiver and my father would smile. That quick grin was like a boy's, no matter his thick chestnut hair showed a few strands of grey.

I hadn't seen that grin for a very long time. When I told him last year I wished to become a novice and profess vows, he argued with me, tried to change my mind, but not for long. He could see I was sincere in my longing for a higher life, far from the clamour of human voices and the touch of man. My father wrote the necessary letters and, with some difficulty, paid for my endowment at the priory. He did it to make me happy, since he knew no other way to do so.

And for some months at Dartford I *was* happy. In a contemplative life, I found certainty and purpose, the grace I'd longed for, insulated from the selfishness and vanity, the mindless pomp of the world. But it was a fragile happiness. I had come to a religious life that was not just in decline—far fewer people entered monasteries today than in past centuries—but under vigorous attack. Our king had broken from the Holy Father. In the last two years, England's smallest abbeys and priories had been closed, their monks and nuns sent onto the road. Prioress Elizabeth reassured the sisters that the larger religious houses such as ours would not be touched, but the fear of another round of closings haunted the stone passageways, the cloister garden, even the dormitories of Dartford.

It was just a week ago, on my way to Vespers, that I'd heard her name whispered for the first time, ahead of me on the south passageway. "The woman who helped lead the second Northern Rebellion, Lady Margaret Bulmer . . ."

I cried out, "Whom do you speak of?" and the two sisters who'd been walking together stopped and turned around. A novice should never address her superiors in such a way.

"Forgive me, Sister Joan and Sister Agatha." I bowed my head low and clasped my hands and then peered up at their faces. Sister Joan, the *circator*, the enforcer of rules, regarded me with cold disapproval. But Sister Agatha, novice mistress, could not resist sharing her gossip. "The last rebel leaders were brought down to London and tried at Westminster," she said, her voice a quick whisper. "All were found guilty. The men will be hanged, including Sir John Bulmer, but his wife, a lady, will be burned at the stake at Smithfield. It is the king's pleasure."

I tilted and reached out with one hand to grip the damp stone wall to keep from falling.

"Yes, isn't it terrible?" clucked Sister Agatha.

But Sister Joan's shrewd eyes were on me. "Sister Joanna, did you know Lady Bulmer before you came to Dartford?" she asked.

"No, Sister." Just like that, a grievous sin committed.

Sister Agatha continued, "I always wonder what becomes of them . . . afterward. Would the family of Lady Bulmer be allowed to take her poor body for burial, even though the crime is high treason?"

Sister Joan gave her a stern look. "Such matters are not our concern. I'm sure the lady's family has the means to bribe the guards afterward if necessary. It is souls that we attend to, not mortal flesh."

We'd reached the church. Sister Joan and Sister Agatha bowed to the altar and took their assigned places. I followed suit and made my way to the novice stall, at the front. My place, as youngest, was next to the chancel step. My voice rose in song. I made all the correct responses in the chanting of the office.

Yet within my mind I stitched together a plan. I knew that our terrified Stafford relations would have nothing to do with Margaret or her burial. I could not bear the thought of her dying, alone and frightened, without the presence and the prayers of a loved one to ease her suffering, and then having her poor corpse consigned to oblivion. God desired me to bear witness, I was absolutely sure of that.

I'd leave Dartford Priory and travel to London, to Smithfield, and since the Dominican Order observed strict rules of enclosure for novices as well as nuns, I'd have to go without permission.

It frightened me, yes. The consequences for breaking enclosure were so serious, the only greater offence was violation of our chastity. For the next two days I wavered, not sure of my decision. I sought direction in prayer.

At the office of Matins, at midnight, enlightenment came. Dartford novices were abed customarily by nine, ordered to rest, but my eyes never closed that night, I was so troubled. I filed into church with the others, and between the Pater and the Ave, it struck me. All of my doubts and fears and worries fell away, as if I stood in a waterfall, cleansed by the purest streams. I would go to Smithfield. All would be well. I raised my arms and turned up my palms, toward the altar, my cheeks damp with gratitude.

As we shuffled up the stairs, back to the dormitories for a few more hours of sleep until Lauds, Sister Christina, senior novice, nudged me. "Did you find Divine Truth?" she whispered. "It appeared so."

"Perhaps," I said.

"I pray I receive the same blessing," said Sister Christina, her voice fierce. She was remarkably devout and sometimes wore a hair shirt under her novice habit, although she'd been reproved for it.

Novices were discouraged from seeking mortification of the flesh. We weren't ready.

Sister Winifred, the other novice, who had professed three months before me, squeezed my arm. "I am happy for you," she said in her sweet, lilting voice.

I made my preparations to leave in secret. The night before Margaret's execution, I slept but an hour or so. In the thick darkness of our novice dormitory, I dressed myself in the kirtle I'd worn when my father brought me to Dartford last fall. I crept down the stairs and made my way to the kitchens. I knew one of the windows had a broken lock. I eased through it and ran across the grounds, through the barn, past the sleeping stable hand, and out the door. I most feared discovery at the large gatehouse out front, for sometimes our porter assigned a watchman. To stay clear of it, I went over the stone wall that surrounded the priory at a low point. I walked up the slope, the grass damp under my feet, to meet the lane leading through the woods to the main road.

The moon hid behind heavy clouds; it was so very dark on the lane, under the trees. There was just the song of the night creatures. They were not disturbed by my presence. No, it was like passing through the ranks of an undisciplined choir—crickets and other shrill insects took the soprano part while the toads and owls played bass. Their gleeful serenade did not please me. My business was deadly serious, and, as ridiculous as it is to admit, I felt mocked in the woods. I was glad that when I reached the main road, the sky to the east was lightening. Soon the impetuous night choir would fall silent.

With a pair of lady's earrings clinking in his pocket, the sleepy warden for Hedge House Wharf helped me into a boat, but with reluctance. "I pray the young lady knows what she is about," he muttered. I did not answer him. As the boat eased away on the River Darent, past the fishery, I thought I heard the faint peal of the bells of the priory, for first prayers, but I may have imagined it.

Dartford is nearly a day's journey on foot from London, two hours by good horse and more than four hours by water. The River Darent twists and turns before meeting the Thames. It is not the way most would choose to travel to London, but I feared being seen in the village if I tried to hire a conveyance. I must disappear long enough to complete my mission.

Soon after we departed, rain pattered on the river and the oarsman tossed me a long covering to shield my head. The last person to wear the covering had eaten salted fish; I could still smell it. A thick, cool white mist enveloped me on the river. I could see next to nothing. There was just the pinprick of rain on the river and the rhythmic grunts of the man sitting behind me as he pulled his oars out of the grey water. I took out my crucifix and wooden beads from the purse and began to say the Rosary.

Margaret, I am coming. I won't abandon you.

The mist parted to introduce a dull sky. As the river widened on its trek, other boats joined us, large and small. A few oarsmen called out to mine, making rude remarks over his passenger being young and female and unaccompanied. I fingered my beads and ignored their coarse foolishness. The instant we docked, well south of London Bridge, I leaped out of the boat. My greatest fear was that I would reach the appointed place too late.

Now I was here, I had indeed reached Smithfield before the burning, but I had not expected such crowds and confusion. All I could see were common people, milling around, laughing, drinking, or crying out to one another. I walked among them, this way and that, searching for some sign of where the execution would take place.

When I came upon a tight circle of men shouting, my pulse quickened. I pushed my way forward to find an opening.

In the middle of the circle was not a person but a chicken. Misshapen and bloody, its eyes flickering in terror, it had one foot tied to a wooden stake. A pockmarked man across from me held a small wooden bat over his head, readying it for his target.

The man hurled the bat with a loud grunt, and it struck the bird.

"God's wounds, what have ye done, ye stupid arse?" bellowed the man next to me as he wiped a splotch of dripping red liquid from his cheek. The bird had been struck so hard a geyser of blood sprayed him.

Uncaring, the pockmarked man scrambled into the circle. "She's me dinner!" he howled. "And it's not even Shrove Tuesday."

I looked down and saw my own dark skirts spattered with bright fresh blood. "Sweet Mother Mary," I moaned and backed away, slipping into a muddy patch. On the way down, I grabbed the arm of a young woman next to me.

It was a mistake. Red-faced, with a laundress's bag slung over her shoulder, she swatted me away, screaming, "Are ye stealing from me?"

"Madame, I was breaking a fall," I said. "I apologise."

The laundress made a mock curtsy. "No, my lady. Forgive *me*."

Someone laughed. A few heads turned.

A burst of hot foetid breath singed the side of my neck at the same second two thick arms encircled my waist from behind. I tried to pull away and could not.

"Hullo, poppet," growled a voice.

I yanked myself away from the stranger. "Take your hands off me," I ordered him.

He spun me around, and I saw my attacker. He was at least a foot taller than me and barrel-chested. A greasy beard hid his face except for a pair of bulging eyes and a nose bent to the left.

"Don't ye fancy me?" he sneered, pulling me hard against his rough clothes and slobbering on my forehead, too drunk to find my lips.

I fought down my revulsion and said calmly, "Sir, I have come to pray for the poor lady's soul. Will you join me? Shall we pray together?"

His drunken leer sagged. I knew I had touched something. Even the most brutish louts spend mornings on their knees at church, at the pleading of a wife or mother.

But then the laundress screamed: "Have at her! Why do ye wait?"

He grabbed my arm. I twisted and turned; I could see a group gathering around, but no one stopped him. No one helped me. I swung back my right foot and kicked him in the shin, and the crowd laughed.

He slapped me, a sloppy blow, but still strong enough to send me staggering backward into the mud. He threw me the rest of the way down, his huge belly knocking the breath out of my body. One hand gripped both my wrists, holding them over my head. The other felt my waist, then higher, and higher. I struggled as hard as I could but for nothing.

Ten years ago, I realised. *Ten years almost to the day.*

Men and women drew closer, in a circle, nudging one another, laughing. I shut my eyes as I sank deeper and deeper into the mud of Smithfield.

3

I wanted to die, I prayed to die, there was nothing else for me, when I felt a thud, a crash, and the sharp pain of a knee against my thigh, and then nothing. He was no longer atop me. I opened my eyes and saw a tangle of bodies and heard curses.

I struggled to all fours, my limbs shaking, crawled between two people, and rose to my feet. A hand grabbed my arm and started dragging me.

"No! No, stop!" I screamed.

"I must get you away," said a voice, and I looked up. This was not my attacker; he was young and tall, broad-shouldered, with close-cropped light-brown hair.

"Where are your people?" he demanded. "Are you lost?"

"I won't be questioned. Leave me alone."

"Leave you alone?" He burst out laughing. The sound of it took me aback. This was not the laugh of a young brute but of a cynical old man. "I *saved* you. Didn't you see? I pulled that beast from you and thrashed him."

"I saw nothing."

"Then you'll have to take it on faith, mistress. I am here to help you." He took a flask of water from one pocket, a white kerchief from another and dampened it. "You may want to clean your face."

I took the kerchief and pressed it against my cheek. The coolness was like a tonic. I wiped it across my cheeks and forehead, scrubbed off the spit and dirt and sweat and the specks of blood of the dead bird.

"Thank you, sir." I handed him back his kerchief. "I am grateful for your assistance." I waited for the young man to move on, but he just stood there, studying me. He had blue eyes the same colour as the hyacinths my mother had sent for from Spain and nurtured in the gardens. His clothes were respectable but certainly not prosperous; I could see the stitching along the sleeves that meant the garment had been altered and refashioned for him. He had not the money to have something made expressly for him.

"Where are your people?" he asked again.

"I am alone."

"No kinsmen, no servants? You're a . . . gentlewoman?"

He looked at me for confirmation. I did not deny it.

"Then how could you come to Smithfield today? It's madness. You must allow me to take you from here immediately. A woman alone, young, who looks as you do . . ." His voice trailed away.

I shook my head, uneasy.

"Please, there is no need to fear *me*. My name is Geoffrey Scovill, I am a constable for my parish."

Behind us, two old men who had been talking loudly began to brawl.

"You see?" Geoffrey persisted. "The mob is villainous."

"If the crowd is so base, why are *you* drawn here?"

He smiled at my tart question, and faint crinkles appeared around his eyes. Now it was certain—he was not as young as I'd first thought, closer to thirty than twenty. "I was sent by the chief constable to observe and take note of the king's justice. This woman incited rebellion against our sovereign."

Hot anger surged through me. "To see a woman die—that pleases you?"

"Of course not."

"She is a mother," I said. "She has a boy and an infant daughter. Did you know that?"

Geoffrey Scovill rocked back and forth on his heels, uneasy. "It is a great pity that the condemned is a woman. But examples must be made. Lady Margaret Bulmer committed high treason. She is a danger to us all."

"Danger?" My voice rose higher. "She sought to harm no one. She and the others wanted to preserve something, a way of life that has been honoured for centuries. Which gives comfort to the poor and the sick. They rebelled because they felt so passionately about their cause. They never sought to overthrow the king but to bring their grievances to his attention. They wanted the king to hear them."

Again I heard the laugh of a cynical older man. "Oh, he heard them, there's no doubt of that. They received the *full* attention of His Majesty."

I walked away, furious he was mocking me.

He followed, pulling at my sleeve. "Wait, mistress. We are all at the service of the king. If he wishes to make changes in religion, then it is our bound duty to obey, to trust in his legal and spiritual authority to guide us. Do you not agree?"

"I agree that the people owe obedience to their anointed sovereign," I muttered.

He was relieved to hear it. "You must then see—if rebels and traitors are not punished, what sort of message would that send? The monarchy would be weakened; we would all fall into chaos. And yet such a punishment can be harrowing . . ." He squinted at something far away, and then offered me his arm. "Perhaps if you see this, it will change your mind."

"I have no intention of changing my mind. I have come here to see the execution of the prisoner."

"Then allow me to show you where it will take place?"

I could hardly turn away the very help I needed. Geoffrey Scovill skilfully moved us through the dense crowd until we came to a long makeshift fence. There was another fence twenty feet beyond, creating a roadway between.

He pointed to the left and I saw, at the end of this roadway, a large heap of branches and sticks gathered around a tall barrel. A stake rose out of the top of the barrel.

"That's where she will be burned," he said.

I took a deep breath, struggling to hide my fear.

"As a constable, I am familiar with the various forms of execution. This is the slower way to burn. It would be more merciful to bring her here and then heap the branches on top. That is what they did in France when they executed Joan of Arc. Today, Lady Margaret Bulmer will suffer far more than Joan."

"Why are you telling me this?" I demanded.

"Because this is no place for you." He shook my shoulder, desperate to change my mind.

Loud cries rose up from the other end of the roadway. "She comes! She comes!"

"Too late," I told Geoffrey Scovill.

The crowd surged to the right, and I went with them, Geoffrey behind me. It would be hard to lose him now. There was a sea of bobbing heads in the middle of the roadway, more than a dozen soldiers heading toward us. They wore armour and carried pickets on their shoulders.

In the back, a soldier led a black horse, harnessed to something that dragged behind.

Geoffrey made a noise next to me.

"What is it?" I asked.

"She's coming on a hurdle," he groaned.

I didn't know what that meant. The horses came closer, pulling a long wooden board, the bottom dragging in the dirt. Everyone was pointing at the board.

"Burn the papist whore!" screamed an old woman. Others took up the screams. The black horse, riled by the commotion, pivoted toward the other fence. Now I could see the person tied to the frame, facing up, arms pulled straight out, to form a T. My heart hammered in my body as I stared at who was strapped to the hurdle. I'd come to Smithfield for nothing. The woman was not Margaret. This poor condemned creature was far too old and poor. She wore a long, torn grey shift and had a dirty and bruised face, with cropped hair hanging just to her ears.

The soldiers untied her wrists and feet and pulled her off the hurdle. She staggered into the mud and almost fell. One soldier righted her and pointed toward the stake. She stood still for a few seconds, straightened her shoulders, and then began to walk toward the place of her execution. The way she'd straightened her shoulders made me go a little queasy.

Just then, the sun finally pierced the roiling banks of grey clouds and bathed Smithfield in light. A ray danced off the head of the prisoner, picking up a strand of reddish gold.

And I saw my Margaret.

The crowed roared "Traitor!" and "Whore!" and "Papist!" as she came closer. I grabbed the fence and pulled myself along, in front of the people shouting at her. One man hit me as I wriggled in front of him. I barely felt it. I looked over my shoulder; Geoffrey Scovill had been swallowed up by the mob.

I knelt down in the dirt, sticking my head out of an opening in the fence. I shouted: "Margaret! Margaret! Margaret!"

As she limped forward, I could see her eyes were half open. I screamed her name now, so loudly I thought the muscles in my throat would shred. She blinked and looked in the direction of my screams.

Something quickened in her eyes. She came toward me.

The people clustered right around me roared in approval. They'd get a closer look at the prisoner now. Two of the soldiers started over. In seconds they'd have her and pull her away.

Margaret looked right at me. I saw her lips move, but I couldn't hear what she said.

I fished in my dress and took out my Rosary beads. I forced my arm out through the opening in the fence and threw her the beads. They landed in the dirt, at her feet. As she knelt to pick them up, an old woman leaned over the railing and spat on Margaret. The spittle landed on her left breast. "Burn, you papist whore!" she screeched.

The soldiers grabbed Margaret. One of them yelled something at the crone. They had seen only the spitting. I watched Margaret seize the beads and tiny crucifix and make them into a ball, clutched tight to her body.

As the men spun her back toward the stake, she looked over her shoulder, saw me as I waved my arm, sobbing.

"Joanna," she cried. And was led away.

The soldiers called for quiet, and the crowd's jeers died down. The grey-bearded official was reading from a scroll, but I could hear only phrases: "guilty of high treason . . . inciting of rebellion . . . conspiracy to levy war . . . the pleasure of His Majesty." The minute the man had finished and lowered his scroll, soldiers grabbed hold of Margaret.

I got to my feet but flinched at the feel of a hand on my shoulder. It was Geoffrey Scovill. He'd found me again.

We both watched as the soldiers hoisted Margaret on top of the barrel and tied her to the stake, around the top of her chest and her waist. Other men heaped the branches, sticks, and kindling around her feet. She was too far away for me to see her face clearly, but I thought her lips moved in prayer. I hoped she still held the Rosary beads.

"Ahh!" the crowd roared as if one. A second later, I saw why: a short man trotted forward, a blazing torch in his hand. He bowed to the soldiers standing in a semicircle around the stake and then lit the branches surrounding the barrel.

"Christ have mercy, Christ have mercy," I whispered and began the Dominican prayer of salvation, the one I had prepared to say at the moment of her death. At least I could perform that task.

A new cry rippled through the crowd. "What is he doing?"

"Where is he going?"

I turned toward the shouting just in time to see a man run by me, toward Margaret. A tall, fit man in his early fifties, a gentleman, his cheeks ravaged with tears.

For a few seconds I was stunned; I could not take it in. Then I scrambled to the top railing of the fence.

"What are you doing?" Geoffrey grabbed my arm to hold me back.

"Let go of me! Let go!" I tore myself out of his grip. "I must help him."

"Help him? What in God's name for?" Geoffrey demanded.

"Because," I said, my cheeks also wet with tears as I hoisted myself over the railing and landed on the other side, "that man is my father."

By the time I had made it over the fence, my father had almost reached Margaret. But the soldiers surged after him, and I saw one strike his shoulder with a picket.

"No, don't hurt him!" I screamed, and a soldier spun around, shocked at the sight of me.

"Get back! Get back!" he said, waving his own picket at me as if I were a crazed dog. Behind him I could see a whole swarm of soldiers trying to tackle my father.

"Father, no! No!" I screamed again, and his head jerked up. Although there were at least three guards on top of him, he was able to get to his feet. "Joanna, get away from here," he managed to bellow before he was kicked in the chest and fell back again.

Someone grabbed my arm and I tried to pull away, but it was Geoffrey Scovill. He had leaped over the fence to follow me. "Come back," he pleaded.

Three guards charged toward us. I saw a picket raised high before crashing down on Geoffrey's head. The young constable pitched into the mud, unconscious.

I heard an angry scream and turned around. My father had broken free again and was running straight toward Margaret. Just as a soldier caught up with him and hit him in the back with a picket, my father pulled something loose from his doublet. Something small.

As he crashed to his knees before her, I saw him throw a dark bag at the flames crawling up Margaret's writhing body.

A few seconds later there was an enormous explosion, like a dozen thunderstorms striking the ground at one spot. Fiery black coils billowed towards me. And it all went black.

4

I watched the sun slip down behind the church spires of London. There was no more fine drizzle. By late afternoon, the sun had become a fiery orb, shrivelling all the clouds and devouring the clammy mist that clung to feet and wheels and horses' hooves. As that sun now trembled atop the crowded western horizon, my eyes itched and stung, though whether it was because of the sun's rays or the black smoke of Smithfield from hours past, I couldn't tell.

I sat facing backward in a royal river barge, my wrists shackled. I couldn't see where I was going, but I felt the sureness of the four oarsmen's sticks, their deep rowing. These men, wearing the green-and-white livery of the House of Tudor, knew my destination. And the other boats on the Thames River, even the Londoners on the shores, I was sure they knew. Whenever we passed someone, I could feel the curious stares crawling over me, hear the burst of gossip: "Who's that they've got now?" An old woman dumping slop jars into the river watched me for as long as she could, her neck craning while she leaned out so far I expected her to fall in.

All of the time, I sat straight and still, my shoulders as far back and my chin as high up as I had been schooled from the time I could walk. I didn't want to show my fear. And I most definitely didn't want anyone to see the man lying on the bottom of the barge, his bandaged head propped up on my skirts. My calves ached from the pressure of Geoffrey Scovill's head, but I couldn't send him back down onto the wet bottom of the barge. His slack face, his closed eyes, the trickle of dried blood on his right cheek filled me with furious guilt. I had so much to think about, to pray over, to try to understand, before arriving at whatever place they were taking me to, but here was an immediate difficulty thrown into my very lap.

Just as the sun disappeared, and a sickly dusk bathed the river in orange-violet light, Geoffrey woke with a groan.

His wrists were unshackled, and he reached out, feeling the bandage around his head with confusion. Slowly, shakily, he sat up and turned to face me, heaved himself up to find a seat. Uncertain eyes met mine. I dreaded the coming confrontation.

"Do you know where you are?" I asked.

Recognition filled his face. "I appear to be in a king's barge," he said, his voice raspy. "Why?"

I looked forward at one pair of oarsmen at the bow and peered behind at the other. The barge was so long they shouldn't be able to hear us.

"I've been arrested with my father, and I believe you have been as well," I said softly.

He took it much better than I expected. His face stayed calm. "What are the charges?"

"I don't know," I replied. "I told them my name, and my father's name, and then they went away for a long time and left me under guard. They put us both in a wagon, and we went to a building; but then they seemed to change their minds and brought us to the river. We sat in the wagon for two hours before they put us into this boat. I never saw my father again. I know he was injured, much worse than you. But no one would tell me anything."

I took a breath, fought for calm.

"How was he injured?" Geoffrey asked.

I shook my head, frustrated. "I don't know. There was a great deal of smoke after the thunder. When it cleared, I saw him lying on the ground, but from a distance. They moved him soon after, and I didn't see him again."

"The 'thunder'?"

"My father threw something into the fire, at Margaret. A bag. That is what he must have been running towards her to do. It caused a loud noise like thunder and a great deal of smoke."

Geoffrey nodded. "Of course."

"Do you know what it was?"

"Gunpowder," he said with certainty, and I remembered he was a constable, and so must be familiar with such things. "When a criminal is sentenced to burn and the king wishes to show some mercy, he permits the wearing of a bag of gunpowder, tied around the neck. The bag catches fire and explodes. It hastens death, cuts short suffering. But the amount of gunpowder must be precisely measured and mixed. It seems your father used too much."

I swallowed.

Geoffrey peered at me more closely. "You called her 'Margaret.' So you knew the prisoner?"

There no longer seemed any point to concealing things.

"Lady Margaret Bulmer was my cousin," I said. "I came to pray for her. I didn't know my father would be at Smithfield as well."

"You're not from the North?" he demanded, his voice grown strong. "You took no part in the rebellion against the king?"

"No, of course not. Margaret went to live in the North about four years ago, and married Sir John. I haven't seen her since then; it's too far to travel. Only letters, and just one since last year. I know nothing of the rebellion. I don't understand why Margaret involved herself."

Geoffrey frowned. "Then why would you and your father risk attending the burning and behaving this way, why risk so much? It doesn't make sense."

I didn't answer. There was the sound of the oars slapping into the river. And the faint tinkle of women's laughter as our boat glided past a manor built close to shore. On the other side of the manor walls, as impossible as it seemed, people were making merry.

Geoffrey's next words flew out of his mouth as sharp as a slap.

"If I am to be taken to the Tower of London because I intervened on your behalf, mistress, then I am entitled to know all."

"The Tower?" I whispered.

"Yes, of course—where else?" he asked impatiently. "That is why they delayed so long before setting out on the Thames. They have to wait until the tide is just right to shoot the bridge to River Gate. But now we are almost there, if I remember the bend of the river. So tell me."

Somewhere deep inside, I had known, too, that that was where the barge was taking me. I wasn't surprised, truly. But hearing the name of the ancient castle still sent a cold rush through me. I remembered a game that my boy cousins played, with toy swords. "To the

Tower, the Tower," they'd shout at the loser of the swordplay. "Chop off his head!"

Dusk had deepened. It was that uncertain time after the sun vanishes but the stars haven't yet found their places in the sky. In the middle of the Thames River, away from the freshly lit torches on the shore, the air was thick and dark. I could not see Geoffrey's face clearly, and that made it easier to try to explain.

"She was more than a cousin, she was my only friend when I was a child," I said. "I couldn't let her face this horrible death alone. Not after everything she has done for me. There was something in particular I wanted to do for her, after her death, but I never had the chance. As to my father's reasons, I don't know them. We haven't spoken in some months. But I can assure you he is not a man of politics. He hates and fears all matters political."

I took a breath, and continued.

"Does the name Stafford mean anything to you?"

He thought a moment. "Wasn't that the family name of the Duke of Buckingham?"

"Yes," I said. And then: "He was my father's oldest brother."

Geoffrey's voice went flat and careful. "The third Duke of Buckingham was tried and executed for high treason fifteen years ago."

"Sixteen years ago," I corrected him. As if it mattered.

"And he was arrested for plotting to overthrow the king because of his nearness in blood, to take the throne for himself. Some thought he had a better claim to it than Henry Tudor."

"I don't suppose this is the time or the place to say that we know my uncle to be completely innocent of all charges?" I asked.

Geoffrey grunted. "No."

Then came the question I was waiting for. "So you are close kin to the king as well?"

"I am not a woman of the court," I said defensively. "I was last in the presence of the king ten years ago."

He repeated, "You are kin to King Henry the Eighth?"

I sighed. "My grandmother and King Henry's grandmother were sisters."

"And your cousin Margaret?"

"My uncle the duke's daughter." I swallowed and pressed on. "The duke's illegitimate daughter."

Now it was his turn to go quiet, to look out the side of the barge.

"Thank you," he finally said. "I begin to understand."

"But you don't understand everything," I said in a low voice.

I could feel the oars begin to pull in a different way. We were slowing down, and I needed to make Geoffrey aware before it was too late.

"I am a novice at Dartford Priory in Kent," I said in a rush. "I left my order in secret before dawn to reach London. I don't expect to be allowed to return, but if so, I intend to take my final vows by the end of next year."

There was silence from Geoffrey. And then I heard something from him. At first I thought with horror that he was crying. But no, it was more like choking.

Anger singed my veins as I finally realised what it was. Laughter. He was doubled over, shaking with it.

"How dare you make a mockery of me?" I said.

He shook his head and slapped his knee, hard, as if he were trying to stop the laughter, but couldn't.

"I come to London to represent my master at a state execution," he said, more to the river than to me. "I save a young woman from harm, then linger for a pair of fine brown eyes, and see what happens? Ah, Geoffrey . . ."

His words were a shock. "So much for your show of chivalry," I hissed. "I told you at Smithfield to leave me alone, and you wouldn't. What happens to you now is—"

Suddenly, Geoffrey sprang forward and gripped me by my shoulders. "Close your eyes and don't turn around," he whispered, his warm breath curling into my ear.

I couldn't believe he would touch me. Using my manacled hands like a club, I pushed him away and he fell into the bottom of the boat, hitting his head with a yelp of pain.

And then, as if compelled to do so, I turned around.

Our boat had slowed as it approached a large bridge. Every twenty feet or so a torch blazed, creating a string of soaring lights across the wide dark river.

Between the torches were severed heads on spikes.

There must have been a dozen of them, although I only saw one clearly, the one closest to me. The head's rotting flesh was black. The flicker of a nearby torch filled its hollow eye sockets and leaped into its gaping mouth. It made it seem as if the head were coming alive and smiling down at me in delight.

A loud noise filled my ears, and sweat curdled on my skin. I shut my eyes tight, trying to erase the horrific vision. But it was too late. My stomach heaved, as if an unruly animal leaped inside me. I bent over and gripped the side of the boat with my manacled hands. "Help me, Mother Mary," I gurgled.

For what seemed like an eternity, I fought it. But I lost. Doubled over, I vomited into the boat, a sour string, hardly anything, for I'd eaten not a bite since riding in the cart to Smithfield all those hours ago. Coughing, I dashed the spittle off my chin with the back of my trembling hand.

The oarsmen rowed the boat under the bridge. The water slapped against the dank stone arches. I shuddered, knowing that right above me stretched the heads of the executed.

My eyes flew open at the gentle touch of a hand on my shoulder. I took Geoffrey's cloth, the same one he'd offered at Smithfield. I ran it over my face.

I looked at Geoffrey. "I'm sorry this is happening to you," I said.

"I know." A smile curved his lips, but not a mocking or angry one. He peered over my shoulder; the smile vanished. I watched his whole body tense.

Our boat was turning. We entered a narrow waterway, with high walls on each side. A huge, square blackness loomed over us, swallowing up the low-lying stars and faint grey clouds; it was, most certainly, the Tower.

"It's the crown or the cross," Geoffrey Scovill said, in so low a voice I barely heard him above the loud slap of the oars.

"Pardon?"

"We must all choose which comes first, which we owe primary allegiance to," he said. "The rebels of the North chose the cross." He jerked his head back toward the fearful bridge. "You saw where that leads."

I didn't need to ask Geoffrey Scovill where his loyalties rested. For him, the choice was simple. As for myself, I couldn't help but think of Sir Thomas More, the brilliant, brave soul who said on the scaffold, "I die the king's good servant, but God's first." *Had it been simple for him,* I wondered, *to embrace martyrdom?*

In those few minutes left before we arrived at the River Gate of the Tower, I did nothing but pray. I prayed for the soul of Margaret, for the recovery of my father, for the freedom of Geoffrey Scovill. I prayed for the strength and wisdom to guide my words and actions. I prayed for grace.

Two groups of men stood waiting for us at a narrow stone landing carved into a massive brick wall. Lit torches were affixed to the sides of an arched doorway, the gated entrance yawning open.

The larger group, all wearing bright uniforms of red and gold, helped the oarsmen of our boat bring it around, parallel to the landing. When the boat was tied to, a man leaned down and stretched out a hand to me, careful not to meet my eyes.

As soon as my feet touched the landing, one of the men from the smaller group stepped forward. He was young, with a well-trimmed beard and bright, nervous eyes. "Mistress Joanna Stafford, you are admitted to the custody of the Tower," he called out, more loudly than seemed necessary. It was such a small area. "Yeomen warders, take them in."

I heard a loud thump behind me and turned. Geoffrey lay at the feet of a yeoman warder on the landing.

"Has he fainted?" demanded the young official.

"Yes he has, Lieutenant," the yeoman warder answered, disgusted.

"He was hurt at Smithfield," I told them. "He took a heavy blow to the head. He is innocent of any crime; his name is Geoffrey Scovill."

Everyone acted as if I had not spoken.

The yeomen warders bent down and picked up Geoffrey and roughly heaved him through the archway, carrying him in feet first. As they passed, I could see fresh blood spreading under Geoffrey's bandage. He must have hit his head again on the stone landing.

"He needs a healer, surely you can see that," I said to the lieutenant.

"You are not here to issue orders to us, mistress," he said, his lips pressing thin with anger. "You are under arrest."

"And what are the charges?" I snapped back. "By whose authority am I arrested?"

A movement on the far end of the landing caught my eye. Another man stepped forward. He was much older, about sixty, and as he came closer to me, into the circle of torchlight, I saw he was dressed in expensive deep-green velvets, his puffy sleeves fully slashed. A thick gold chain hung round his neck. Such attire was appropriate for a high court function, a celebration. The ludicrousness of his attire was made even greater by a joyless, sour face.

"I am Sir William Kingston, the constable of the Tower," he said tonelessly. "You are here by express command of His Majesty."

"How can that be?" I asked.

Sir William stepped closer still and I saw the deep wrinkles of exhaustion creasing his face. "After the disturbance at Smithfield, a messenger rode to Greenwich, where the king and queen are in residence," he said. "The king was apprised of the situation, and it was his pleasure that you, your father, and the third party involved be brought to the Tower pending a complete and thorough investigation."

"Is my father here now, in the Tower?" I asked. "What is his condition?"

Sir William did not answer. Instead, he reached out and, with a long velvet-clad arm, pointed at the dark archway.

"It is time to go inside now, Mistress Stafford," he said.

They waited to see what I would do, the constable and the lieutenant. I'd heard stories of prisoners dragged screaming into the Tower. I would not become one of them.

I bowed and turned toward the archway, and, with yeomen warders marching in front of me and the rest of the men behind, I entered the Tower of London.

5

Stafford Castle, April 1527

"I don't want to be married."

Margaret was seventeen, and I was sixteen. It was late at night, in my bedchamber. We were lying next to each other in bed, in our nightclothes, huddled together for warmth. It was spring, but my room was cold. It was forbidden to light a fire at night after Easter, one of the many economies we practised at Stafford Castle.

I pulled a blanket higher, up to our chins, as I searched for the right thing to say. I'd been pained to hear of Margaret's marriage plans earlier that day, because it meant I would see even less of her, but it was selfish to say as much. Now that she'd confessed she didn't even want to be a wife, I was at a loss.

Something came to me.

"I don't want to be maid of honour to the queen," I said.

Margaret shook her head. "I can't blame you for that."

Our respective fates had been discussed at dinner that day, in the great hall. It was a room rarely used for meals any more, but an effort was made because of the occasion. My cousin Elizabeth, the Duchess of Norfolk, had come to visit for a fortnight, without her husband, of course. She'd brought not only her favourite companion, Margaret, but her eight-year-old daughter, Mary, and, oddly, her brother-in-law, Charles Howard. I had never much liked Elizabeth, who was older than me and quite haughty, and I had no use for any Howard, but this visit was most welcome for bringing Margaret back to me.

The Staffords and the Howards had once been the two greatest ducal families in England. The marriage of Thomas Howard, heir to the dukedom of Norfolk, to Elizabeth, the daughter of the Duke of

Buckingham, was a glorious match. Her fiancé was much older, and a widower, but he was a rising man of the court, a commander on the battlefields of France, Scotland, and Ireland. She took his hand and promised God to honour and obey him.

What a blessing she could not see into her future, see the execution of her father, the ruin of the Stafford family, and the wretchedness of her marriage.

After the Duke of Buckingham was put to death in 1521, his estates, all of his castles and lands and income, were seized by the king, with one exception: Stafford Castle, the family seat, built on a hill in the reign of William the Conqueror. I had lived there most of my life. The duke's oldest son, my cousin Henry, was permitted to hold it and draw income from the land surrounding. He settled in the crumbling castle with his family, joined by my father, mother, and myself. The rest of the Stafford clan, the cousins and aunts and uncles, dispersed, including Margaret. Elizabeth insisted that Margaret come live with her, to keep her company. And so she did. Our many letters went back and forth, but I saw Margaret only when they came back to Stafford Castle for visits. My father travelled to London once a year, to maintain the small house he'd been able to hold on to, but my mother and I always stayed behind. We no longer had money for travelling.

I didn't understand Margaret's marriage. Not only did she seem glum at the prospect, but at dinner Elizabeth was actually distraught about it.

"He's one of my husband's retainers, this William Cheyne," said Elizabeth, angry patches of red flaring in her hollow white cheeks. "He's asked for Margaret, and the duke agreed, without consulting me. He's quite happy that Cheyne will take her without dowry."

"Then it's a love match?" asked Ursula Pole Stafford, my cousin Henry's wife. She was heavy with child, her third pregnancy in five years.

"Margaret hasn't spoken more than a few words to him!" Elizabeth cried. "Oh, I can't bear the thought of losing her to a rough young husband. How could I sleep at night, knowing what crimes he might be committing against an innocent girl?"

Margaret got up and stroked Elizabeth's shoulder. "Hush, do not be troubled," she said. As always, Margaret worried more about her fragile older half sister than herself.

All might have been well if it weren't for the seventeen-year-old sitting on Elizabeth's other side, Charles Howard. "Come now, Duchess," he drawled, "don't some ladies relish crimes in the night?"

Elizabeth drew back from him, her lower lip trembling. Then, to everyone's surprise, she jumped to her feet and began pulling on her long sleeves.

"Do you see this?" she cried. And after a moment, as she pulled the sleeve higher, we did see it, a long, faint, yellowish-purple bruise mottling her thin right arm. "I saw my husband, and the duke told me to cease my oppositions, that I must live with him and sleep beside him again. I asked him where would he put his whore, and he did this to me."

We sat there, aghast, as the duchess turned to the right and to the left, holding up her arm to us with some sort of strange, terrible pride I couldn't understand. Of course, if her father the Duke of Buckingham were alive, Norfolk wouldn't dare beat and humiliate his wife so. We all knew that.

Little Mary Howard looked down at her plate, and I wondered what she thought of her father.

"Sister, calm yourself," pleaded my cousin Henry. The most important thing to Henry and Ursula was to keep the family safe, to avoid all controversy and criticism, so that there would never again be grounds for suspicion.

Now, for the first time, my mother spoke, in her heavily accented English. "Duchess, we are grateful for your help in gaining a position for Joanna with the queen."

All eyes turned on me, as I shifted, uncomfortable, in my seat.

Elizabeth nodded. "Despite everything, the queen is still devoted to you," she said to my mother, who smiled triumphantly.

When my mother was younger than I, only fourteen, she had left her country as a maid of honour to Princess Katherine of Spain, who was bound to marry Prince Arthur of England and be queen of his island kingdom. Katherine wed Arthur, who died young, and then his brother, Henry, and finally became queen. My mother Isabella served her devotedly through it all, and six months after Katherine was crowned, she married the king's handsome cousin, my father, Sir Richard Stafford, one of the finest athletes in the land. Another marriage that began with the highest of hopes.

I was born less than two years later, and shipped to Stafford Castle, to be cared for by governesses and tutors and maids. My mother's place was with the queen, and I saw her only a few times a year. It was not an unusual arrangement.

The Duke of Buckingham was arrested, tried, and beheaded when I was ten years old, and everything changed. All Staffords were unwelcome at court; one of my older uncles was imprisoned along with Buckingham but later released. My parents were never charged with any crime, but they were banished. My mother was forced into the country, away from the queen, who meant everything to her. The size of the staff at Stafford Castle was severely reduced, and so she took me in hand herself. My faraway, glamorous mother was now close at hand, unhappy—and paying close attention to me.

Elizabeth wrinkled her nose at her plate. "This venison is fine enough, but aren't we to have a fish course?" she complained.

We who lived in Stafford Castle winced. My father had spent two days hunting from dawn to dusk to ensure fresh game for our company. He was not as unhappy as my mother with a life in the country; he took a vigorous interest in managing the properties and farms and animals. The more time he was out of doors, the less he saw of my mother, who found endless fault with him. Her litany of complaints filled both my father and me with misery.

"This isn't Arundel Castle, Sister," Cousin Henry said morosely.

Elizabeth sighed and turned back to my mother: "I hope you've instructed Joanna well. The court is more permissive than when you were there. Not the household of the queen herself, she is a saint, but—"

My father, sitting next to me, threw his arm around my shoulders and squeezed. "Joanna is the best girl in the whole world," he said firmly. "No one need ever fear for her virtue."

My cheeks reddened. This was the most embarrassing dinner conversation imaginable. Across the table, Margaret smiled with sympathy.

Charles Howard snickered. "It's not the ladies of easy virtue the queen needs to fear, we know that."

Elizabeth shot him a look of warning, and her brother-in-law shut up. His words made absolutely no sense to me.

I couldn't wait to commiserate later with Margaret, in my room, and to ask her questions about her fiancé. Once we were alone, I asked her if it was true she barely knew the man she was meant to marry.

"I've only spoken to him once," she said. "But he looks at me all the time. It makes me feel strange." A faint line creased between her eyes. "Tell me about entering service for the queen," she said, anxious to change the topic.

"That's all my mother's talked about for years. Training me, drilling me. Embroidery, dancing, music, wardrobe, deportment, four languages. I have to be absolutely perfect—everything depends on it." My stomach churned.

Margaret threw back the blanket.

"I don't care about the rules, I'm lighting a fire," she announced. "And then we'll brush each other's hair."

She used a candle to light the old kindling in the fireplace, and ten minutes later, Margaret was sitting in front of it, as I ran a brush through the thick reddish-gold hair that hung to her waist. I knew it was a treat for her to be waited on, since day and night it was her task to wait on Elizabeth.

"Your father is so very kind to you," she said softly.

"Yes," I agreed.

"I miss mine very much," said Margaret.

I thought frantically of something that would give her comfort, but nothing came to me. Margaret's mother, a servant at another of the duke's castles, had died long ago.

She said quietly: "If my father were here, I think I would be allowed to take vows."

"Is that what you want?" I'd never thought of taking vows. Margaret and I were both pious; it was one of the things that separated us from the other cousins. Still, to me, nuns were mysterious, sad creatures, tinged with scandal. Years ago, one of our aunts had been dragged to a nunnery by her husband—with the Duke of Buckingham's approval—because she had behaved scandalously at court. There were even rumours she'd dallied with the king. She'd returned to her husband after a short time.

Margaret took my hands in hers, excited. "Last spring, I travelled to Durham with my sister, to make a pilgrimage." I remembered this trip, my mother had said the duke beat his wife very badly at their London house, and she had run away to the shrine of Saint Cuthbert, to seek relief and succour from her miseries. "It was such a glorious shrine; you would have been as impressed as I was, Joanna. But even though Elizabeth is one of the highest women in the land, we could not approach the shrine too closely, being female. It troubled my sister. So the next week, the duchess received permission for us to visit a small convent nearby, to meet the prioress. We were with them on Good Friday, Joanna. We crept to the cross with the nuns, on our bare knees, and it was so . . . beautiful. So inspiring. To be among women who were devout and kind to one another. Oh, they had joy on their faces, they looked peaceful fulfilling God's mission. And Joanna, some sisters are very learned. They love to read as you do—they study Latin and holy manuscripts. To be one of them, to be saved from all temptation—"

"Temptation?" I asked wonderingly. "What tempts you?"

She looked at me for a moment. "Do you want to be married, Joanna?"

"No," I answered, surprised at my own vehemence. "I have met no man who I would wish to marry. Every man I see is so lacking in quality, so far away from . . . from . . ."

Smiling, Margaret picked up *Le Morte d'Arthur*, lying on a stool by the fire. "From Sir Galahad and the knights?"

"Is it wrong to hope for a man who is courageous and virtuous?" I asked.

My bedchamber door burst open, and Charles Howard leaped in the room. With a wooden sword in his hand—doubtless taken from one of my young cousins—he parlayed as he made his way toward us. "Not at all!"

I jumped back into the bed and scrambled under a blanket.

"Listening at the door again, Charles?" Margaret sighed. "Have you nothing more worthwhile to do?"

"In truth, I don't. This is a very dull house." Charles bowed low, and when he came back up, he had a glint in his eyes. "You are in need of my company."

I expected him to turn his attention to Margaret. She was so ravishing; men ogled her wherever she went. But instead he veered toward my bed, running his hand up the bedpost.

"I could help prepare you for the men of the court," he offered. "You'll need to learn a few tricks to make the important marriage your mother is counting on."

"Leave now!" I shrieked, burying myself deeper under blankets. "Or I will call for my father."

Charles laughed, bowed again, and backed away toward the corridor. "You've missed your best chance," he said, with a final flourish. "Good night."

After the door closed behind him, I emerged from the blankets. "He is loathsome," I said.

"Oh, he is not as bad as that." Margaret shrugged. "Charles is the youngest son in a very large family. It's not an easy position."

"How can you say that? He is *vile*."

Margaret was quiet for a long moment. She nibbled her lower lip—I knew what that meant. She'd devised a plan. And once my cousin had an idea in her head, it was very difficult to dissuade her.

"Joanna, I want to give you something." She lifted from her throat a delicate necklace strung to a medal. "You know this?"

"Of course. Your father gave it to you. It's from the shrine of Saint Thomas Becket."

"Let's look at it by the fire," she said.

Calmer now, I followed her. "I always think of the story of his death," she said, holding the medal up to the fire so we could see it better. Four men wearing knights' armour stood under a flowing tree. "Archbishop Becket was hated by King Henry the Second. He cried out, 'Will no one rid me of this turbulent priest?' These four men answered his call." I knew the story; every child in England was taught it, but as I listened to Margaret tell it once more, it appeared to have special meaning for her. "The men went to Canterbury and hid their swords under a sycamore tree outside the church. They went inside and told Saint Thomas to come out with them, but he refused. So they went out and retrieved their swords and reentered the church and hacked him to bits. They martyred him and violated a sacred space."

I shivered, even though the crackling fire was hot on my skin.

She pressed the medal into my palm. "I want you to have this."

"Margaret, I can't take your medal, it's too dear to you."

My cousin hesitated, as if she were afraid to put something into words. "I want you to be protected at court," she said.

I knew how much Margaret loathed the king who had destroyed her father. She never accompanied her sister to court.

"I will be with Queen Katherine at all times," I reminded her. "My mother trusts the queen completely. Absolutely nothing can hurt me while I am in her service."

"Yes, Joanna, the queen is a pure and noble woman. But will you take this medal?"

The way the dying flames reflected in her large eyes made me nervous.

I pulled the delicate necklace with its Saint Thomas medal over my head. "I will wear it, cousin. And now, will you stop worrying about me?"

Margaret threw her arms around me. "Thank you," she whispered, and to my shock, I could feel her cool tears on my cheek.

6

The Tower of London, May 1537

I knew something was wrong, for the bed was too wide.

Every morning, just before sunrise, the subsacrist would ring the bell, and I'd sit up and cross myself, then grope for the side of my straw-stuffed pallet. It rested on the floor against the wall of the novice dormitory, next to Sister Winifred's pallet and, on the other side, Sister Christina's.

In our pitch-black room, we would find the habits folded and placed at the side of our pallets hours before, and dress quickly. Within minutes, a yellow light would seep under the wooden door: the approach of the lighted lantern. The twenty-four nuns of Dartford would walk past our room, two by two, on the way to Lauds. We'd wait for the last pair to pass before taking our ordained place at the end of the line and walking down the stone stairs to church.

But this morning, the bed was deep and wide as my fingers reached for the edge. And not just that. A thick, warm light weighed on my eyelids. The sun had already risen, yet that was impossible. No nun or novice of Dartford Priory ever slept through Lauds. If we were sick to our bellies, if our throats were on fire, if our loins cramped with the courses of the moon, we still walked the stone passageway to first prayers. Otherwise, we'd face the sternest of punishments at chapter.

I wanted to rise, to learn what had gone amiss, to make amends, but a strange heaviness held me. I could not open my eyes. It was as if the bed itself were pulling me in. Part of me fought it, but mostly I longed to submit to this sweet black nothingness.

After a time, the nothingness parted, and people on a dirty field, shoving and laughing and cursing, their faces red with drink, surrounded me. I was at Smithfield again. "You are dreaming," I said out loud. "Nothing can hurt you." And indeed, this time my feet seemed to float above the mud. I was drifting, darting. Unobserved.

Then I saw her, and it pulled me to the ground. She moved ahead, but I knew that proud walk so well, her way of pulling back and squaring her shoulders when displeased. I wanted to see her, to touch her, but I was terrified, too. I no longer felt safe in a dream. This had become real.

I called for her, but she didn't hear.

"Mama, help me," I screamed. "Don't let them take me to the Tower."

My mother turned around; her gaze settled on me. "You promised," she said, unsmiling. "You promised her you'd never tell anyone the secret."

I tensed. "Who do you mean?"

My mother's black eyes flashed. "You *know* who, Juana. *Era una promesa sagrada*."

Now I was the one to shake my head. "No, Mama, no. You couldn't know about that. You weren't there. You were already dead!"

It was as if by saying those words I cast a spell to send her away, for she melted into the crowd, replaced by Sir William Kingston.

"I don't want to go back to the Tower," I said.

"You're not."

More hands on me, and then I was being thrust to the top of a small hill of branches, with a stake soaring in the middle. They tied me to it, circling my waist with scratchy ropes. Soon the men were gone, and orange flames licked at the twigs below my feet. A circle of jeering people surrounded me, cheering my death as they'd cheered Margaret's.

I pulled against the ropes, but they were too tight. The smoke rose to form a column around me. In seconds I would be in agony.

"God, please help me!" I screamed. "I beseech you—forgive me, save me."

The smoke parted. A figure floated down: a beautiful man, wearing a breastplate of silver armour. He glided closer. He had curly blonde hair and porcelain skin and blue eyes. Atop those curls was a golden crown. With a shock, I knew him. The Archangel Gabriel, God's messenger, had come down to fetch me.

"You won't feel any pain," he said.

The flames crawled all over me. My arms and my legs, even my hair, were consumed, but it was nothing to me. I laughed, my relief was so great. I knew that was impertinent, to laugh in the presence of the mightiest archangel, he who laid waste to Sodom, but Gabriel laughed, too. My ropes fell off, and I floated up. We began to twirl together; we danced in the sky.

Someone else shook me. I couldn't see the hands, but I felt them.

The luminous blue sky I twirled in began to darken, the Archangel Gabriel to tremble. "No," I cried. But everything broke apart, like a ship dashed to pieces on the rocks. My angel left me; the last glimmer was of his golden crown.

And then I woke.

I shrank from the woman's face but two feet from mine. She was as base and ugly as Gabriel was gossamer beauty. She glared at me with eyes set deep under thick brows, as baleful as a demon.

"Don't hurt me." My voice sounded so hoarse. My limbs felt weak and heavy.

"Of course I won't hurt you," she said. "I was simply trying to wake you. You must eat something. It's been too long."

Slowly, it all fell into place. I had seen Margaret burned at Smithfield; my father caused a disturbance, injured himself, and was taken away; I'd been arrested with poor Geoffrey Scovill and brought to the Tower of London. I must have slept for some time, awakened by this woman, who, I now perceived, having gained distance from my dream, was not a hideous demon but an ordinary woman in her middle years, albeit one dressed in rich brocades and an elabourate French hood.

"Who are you?" I asked.

"I am Lady Kingston. And now you will eat. Bess?"

She beckoned, and a second woman, younger and heavier, carried over a wooden tray. The pungent smell of thick fish broth hit me like cannon fire; every sinew of my body craved food.

"We tried to give you something to eat yesterday," Lady Kingston said as the serving woman named Bess set the tray on my bed and withdrew.

"Yesterday?"

"Don't you recall it? You have slept for two nights and a day. We tried to wake you yesterday. You took some wine, and then fell back asleep. Your dress was changed, the one you had on was too dirty to rest in." I realised I wore a long cotton shift. Lady Kingston pointed at a drab grey dress folded at the foot of the bed. "I know it is not appropriate to your station, but I am kept much occupied."

"It doesn't matter," I said as I drank my first spoonful. Lady Kingston pursed her lips and watched me eat. It occurred to me that a woman wearing such elabourate clothing while doing her husband's business in a prison cell would not approve of my indifference to fashion. But I couldn't care about that. All that mattered was the broth. Every steaming mouthful sent strength back into me.

When I'd finished the soup, I looked around the room. I was being held in an enormous space—it looked about forty feet long—with a cracked wooden floor and high stone walls. Sunlight poured in through a series of barred windows halfway up one wall. The only pieces of furniture were my bed, a small table, and Lady Kingston's chair.

My face must have posed the question.

"We do not usually keep prisoners here," she said, shrugging. "But there are few empty rooms, and we didn't want to put you among all the men."

I sat up straighter. "Is my father in the Tower?"

Lady Kingston picked up the tray and carefully placed it on the table. She gave me a steady look as she sat back down.

"You said some things before I roused you," she said. "You called for your mother, but there were others you called for as well. I heard of an angel?"

"I was dreaming."

"Were you?"

The serving woman, Bess, appeared at her side. "Sir William says you're required in the Lieutenant's Lodging, my lady," she murmured.

"Very well." Lady Kingston stiffly rose to her feet. "Bess, prepare her."

As Lady Kingston swept across the long room, I bit my lip. What were they preparing me for? As the last vestiges of my strange dream faded, an icy dread took hold.

The instant the door shut behind Lady Kingston, Bess grabbed my hand. "Don't tell her anything, I beg you."

I studied her more closely. She looked about thirty. The deep pockmarks in her cheeks and chin meant that she'd had a strong bout of the disease and that it had nearly killed her. Yet what struck me most were her eyes. They gleamed, they shone, they even sparkled. My presence seemed to enthral her.

"Why?" I asked, trying to pull my hand loose from her clammy grip.

"She's a spy for *him*." The words came in a feverish rush. "Lady Kingston calms the women and feeds them, and she asks questions, and they sound very innocent, but she writes it all down for her husband, everything they say, and then Sir William writes to Cromwell."

"Is that so surprising?" I asked.

"You should have heard her with Queen Anne. She went mad here, the queen, when the king had her arrested. She screamed and cried, and she laughed. Yes, she rocked with laughter. She couldn't stop. Lady Kingston sat with her night and day and calmed her. And she wrote down every word. I heard they used it all against her at trial."

I swung out of bed and wrenched free of Bess. "Never speak to me of Anne Boleyn," I said. I backed away from her and hit my head against something. It was a huge ring fastened to the wall.

"What's that?" I rubbed my head.

Bess smiled, following me over. "It was to chain the elephant."

"What did you say?"

"The elephant."

I shook my head, edging away from her again. "You're the one who's mad."

"No, no, no," she said. "I'm telling you the truth. This isn't the White Tower. You're not being kept with the rebels from the North or any other prisoner. They didn't know where to put you, so they had a bed brought to the West Tower. This is the menagerie."

"What?"

"Don't you know of the royal beasts? In this room they kept the elephant that Louis of France gave King Henry the Third. It was just the one elephant. After it died, there was never another. But he was proud of it, and he built this room for it to live in."

It dawned on me that Bess could be speaking the truth.

"There were women kept in this room later," she continued. "That could be why they chose it for you. When King Edward the First needed money for war, he had the women Jews brought to the Tower, and their fathers or husbands had to pay to free them. If they couldn't bring enough money, the Jewesses were starved to death."

"That is sinful."

Bess looked surprised. "They weren't Christians. And they were foreigners."

She was the sort of Englishwoman my Spanish mother had most despised.

The sound of men shouting came through the windows. Bess glanced over and then back at me. "You must trust me, I believe in the old ways, what you believe in," she said anxiously. "You are a servant of Christ, and I will help you as much as I am able." She started to pull on a delicate chain around her thick neck. "I need to show you something."

"You don't need to show me anything."

She pulled the chain all the way out. It was attached to a locket, and she opened it. "Look at this." She panted with excitement.

I glimpsed a lock of dark-brown hair. "It's hers," she breathed. "Sister Barton's. She was in the Tower three years ago."

I stared at it, at the evidence of Sister Elizabeth Barton, who experienced such prophecies that the whole of Christendom marveled.

Bess asked, "Did you know her?"

"No, she was a Benedictine, I am a Dominican," I said carefully. "She was executed before I even entered my priory."

"I knew her. I spoke to her three times in her prison cell." Bess glowed with pride. "She was the holiest woman in England and the bravest, don't you think? To speak publicly against the king's divorce?"

I bowed my head. "She paid a terrible price."

"Yes, they hanged her. I saw." Bess laid her hand on my shoulder. "That's what they're wondering about you. If you see visions about the king. If that's why you went to Smithfield. Remember, Lady Kingston was very interested in your dream."

I shook off her hand. "I don't have visions, I am not used by God in that way."

More men shouted. I hurried to the windows, but they were a foot too high for me to see from.

"Bring me the chair," I called to Bess. "This could be my father, or Geoffrey Scovill."

"Oh, no, you can't look out the window dressed in a shift," she said.

"Only my face will be visible."

Bess looked at me, fearful, and then made her choice. She dragged the chair over to the window.

My room faced a well-kept green and a group of buildings. The largest by far was an ancient square white castle. On the green a line of six men shuffled by, their hands chained. Yeomen warders, all shouting, surrounded them.

"Some prisoners are being led away," I said.

"Yes, more northern rebels are to be transferred to Tyburn for execution," Bess said, standing next to me. "Do you see Sir William and Lady Kingston?"

My eyes scanned the green until I spotted the tall, officious pair. "Oh, yes."

"He was a yeoman of the guard in his youth, did you know?" Bess said. "The king has promoted him a dozen times. He'll do anything that is required. Sir William cried on the day they executed Sir Thomas More. He was his friend. But he led him to the axe all the same."

My attention was on the prisoners. "Do you know these men?" I asked. "Could any of them be Sir John Bulmer?"

"I don't know, mistress. But Sir John is a tall man with a white beard."

I scanned the line. A man with just that description stood near the end. But I was surprised—he looked to be almost sixty years old. Twice Margaret's age. Still, this was the husband she loved so much. Soon they would be reunited, in God's mercy.

A horse whinnied on the other side of the Kingstons. I could see Lady Kingston curtsy. The horse trotted along the line of prisoners, and as I looked at the man riding it, a sickness rose in my belly. He was an old man, older than Sir William Kingston and Sir John Bulmer, but he rode his horse like a young buck. The yeomen warders bowed low.

Suddenly, the horseman looked over. Although he was a fair distance away, his gaze met mine, and he started with recognition. He wheeled and kicked the sides of his horse as I stumbled down from the chair.

"Who else did you see?" Bess asked.

I saw the man who had led the king's army to defeat the rebels in the North, who was wretchedly married to my cousin Elizabeth, who was the highest-ranking peer of the kingdom.

"It is the Duke of Norfolk," I said. "And I expect he's coming to see me."

7

Thomas Howard, third Duke of Norfolk, was angry before he even looked at me.

I heard the rapid stomp of footsteps outside my prison cell, and then he came through the door, pushing aside the yeoman warder who'd unlocked it for him. "What is she doing in here, Kingston?" the duke said over his shoulder, his voice a raspy growl.

Sir William and Lady Kingston hurried in after him, but paused near the doorway, hesitant to get too close, to overstep.

"Your Grace, at present there are very few unoccupied rooms in any part of the Tower," Sir William offered from his safe distance.

"I had to walk past a damned lion pit to get here," the duke retorted. "I don't care who you had to remove or where you had to put them, Mistress Stafford should never have been locked inside a bloody menagerie."

I knew him, all England knew him, as a man of high colour, subject to rages. To my shame, a quick temper was one of my most grievous faults, too. My mother had chastised me for it; at Dartford, our prioress had prayed with me over it. "Humble and faithful, humble and faithful," I whispered, eyes cast down, clinging to the words of holy Catherine of Siena.

The duke walked to the middle of the vast room. Nervous, uncertain, I remained where I was, by the wall of windows. The chair that had helped me peer out onto the green was now shoved back by the table.

I took in his plain riding clothes, his muddy boots. Something quivered in his right hand. It was a horsewhip, I realised. He'd brought it inside. I finally looked up, into the Duke of Norfolk's face. He was scowling; his eyes scanned the walls, the bare floor, the bed in the corner, until finally, they came to rest on me.

Not sure what else to do, I slowly slid into a full court curtsy, sitting for a second on my bent left leg, bowing my head until my chin touched my breastbone.

When I came back up, the duke had closed in. He looked much older than when I'd last seen him: dark hair thickly salted with white, narrow face scored with wrinkles. His eyes, moving up and down my form, were younger than the rest of his countenance. It was an unsettling sight, those flickering black eyes, set deep in a worn parchment of a face.

There was recognition, of course; we had been in each other's presence a half-dozen times. I saw disapproval, too. I was sorely conscious of my shabby grey kirtle; my mismatched bodice, too big for me, showing another woman's stains under the arms, and barely laced by Bess before she scrambled out of my cell. There'd been no time to dress my hair, and my wavy black tresses spilled everywhere—onto my shoulders, down my back.

"She could be taken for a chambermaid," the duke hissed. "Kingston, what is your purpose in this? She's been locked up for two days. Why does she look such a slattern? This girl descends from King Edward the Third!"

Sir William apologised and bowed before the duke, and his wife dropped a curtsy, but not before shooting me a resentful glare. I was the cause of embarrassment for my jailers. No doubt it would make everything all the worse for me.

With a muttered oath, the duke lowered himself into the chair. "So let us hear it, Mistress Stafford. What were you about at Smithfield?"

I clasped my hands before me. "Your Grace, I deeply regret the trouble I have caused. I only wished to be present at the execution of my cousin, Lady Bulmer."

"Ah, Lady Bulmer, Lady Bulmer. My saintly sister-in-law." His thin lips stretched in a smile. "You know that Margaret had no right to call herself that, eh? She wasn't married to Bulmer."

I blinked in shock. "That is not true."

The duke exchanged a look with Sir William, who by now had come over to us, accompanied by his wife. "You think I lie to you, mistress?" The first edge of a threat crept into his voice.

I bit my lip. "No, Your Grace."

"Her real husband, William Cheyne, the man I arranged for her to marry ten years ago, he was still alive when Margaret began to live with Bulmer up in the North. You weren't aware of that?"

"Master Cheyne died," I insisted.

"He went and died of the French pox in April of 1535. The worthless whoremonger. But the fact is, Cheyne was her legal husband and he was still alive in 1534, when she took up residence with Sir John Bulmer. That cankered rebel. My people have not unearthed any record of her remarriage up there."

"I am sure one exists," I said, trying my best not to sound quarrelsome.

"Well, they may have married after 1535, but by that time she'd already given birth to Bulmer's son." He waited for this to sink in. "You seem quite unaware of your cousin's corrupt behaviour. You were still at Stafford Castle, correct? You were not professed yet at Dartford Priory, were you?"

I shook my head.

"So you didn't know the details of her recent life, we see. Could not have been a close companion. Regardless, you left your Dominican Order, without the permission of the prioress, I'm told, and you came to London and made a spectacle of yourself at her execution, you and your father. Interfered with the administration of king's justice, which is a crime."

"I felt it necessary, Your Grace."

"But why, Mistress Stafford?" he demanded, his voice louder. "Why was it necessary?"

No words came out. It was impossible for this hardened courtier and commander to understand me, what I had sought to do for Margaret, the importance of my sacrifice.

"And your father?" pressed the duke. "Why was it necessary for him?"

"I don't know," I stammered. "We did not communicate with each other before the . . . the burning. Or afterward. I was surprised to see him at Smithfield. And he to see me."

He leaned forward in his chair, his hand clutching his whip so tight the skin of the knuckles stretched white. "Your father nearly blew himself up with gunpowder. Why the hell would he do that for his dead brother's bastard?"

I flinched at the ugly words.

"If your father did not order you to Smithfield, then did anyone else?"

"No, Your Grace."

"You experienced no visions directing you?" The duke glanced over at the Kingstons. She must have swiftly shared our conversation with Sir William, just as Bess told me she would.

"My decision was one made with the benefit of prayer, but I am not receiving any sort of holy visions, no."

The duke shook his head. "This doesn't make any sense to me or to anyone else. Unless there is another purpose to your actions, a political purpose. You and your father were trying to make a statement about the rebellion, to incite disaffection?"

"No, Your Grace, that was not my intent," I said firmly. "I am a loyal subject. I was guided by private concerns."

The duke remained silent for a long moment. A bird squawked outside the window, on the green. Another answered. Then a third. There were quite a few birds. Someone must be feeding them close by.

When the Duke of Norfolk spoke again, his words were careful and measured: "I don't think you forthcoming, Mistress Stafford. It would be far better for you to disclose everything to me, now, your kinsman by marriage. The next man to ask the questions may not be so considerate of your birth and station."

I twisted the fabric of my dress in my hands. What was it they imagined me guilty of? "I have told you everything there is to know, Your Grace," I said.

It happened very fast. He sprang out of the chair, his arm raised high, in a streaking blur. *Whack.* The whip hit the wooden table a few feet from where I stood.

"God's blood, I don't have time for this!"

I did not move. The Kingstons did not move. The duke stood there, quivering. "Very well, Kingston, we shall proceed as planned," he said finally.

My heart beat faster as the Kingstons hustled out of the room. I heard men's voices in the passageway, a chain of orders being given. But the duke did not leave. Nor did any yeomen warders remain behind. It was just the two of us. He paced back and forth by the windows, frowning, as if thinking of something else. Something unpleasant.

Keeping my voice as humble as possible, I said, "Your Grace, may I ask you something?"

His gaze returned to me, but unwillingly, annoyed.

"You spoke of my father," I pressed on. "Have you seen him?"

He grunted. "I have."

"And what is his condition?"

"His condition?" The duke considered his answer, and then a smile twisted his gaunt features. "Let's just say he's not the handsomest Stafford any more."

At first I felt pain, as if I'd been kicked, and hard. But then came the anger, flooding my heart, my mind, every inch of me. I could hardly breathe or see or hear. My fingertips were numbed by it.

From a muffled distance, I heard the door swing open, and Sir William returned, without his wife, carrying something. The duke held out his hand for it.

"Mistress Stafford, I show you this," he said curtly.

The duke set down on the table before me Margaret's letter, the one I had carried with me to Smithfield. Yes, of course, they had searched my dress.

The duke read Margaret's letter aloud. His harsh voice made a mockery of her words, the way she congratulated me for seeking to become a nun and lamented the suppression of the monasteries and priories of the North.

As he read it, I thought of the hunt. When my father tracked boar in the forest, a group of young menservants followed. Boars are hard to kill. So after my father sighted one, the servants would chase, harry and confuse it, one after another, in stages, until, weakened and frightened, the animal stumbled into a thicket and met with sharpened weapons, the spears and knives.

Silence thickened in the Tower room. I realised the duke had stopped reading, and he and Kingston waited for me to respond.

"Yes, I brought my cousin's last letter to Smithfield," I said coldly.

The duke dangled something else in his fingers; it was the necklace with the Thomas Becket pendant that Margaret had given me years ago. I'd stitched it into the lining of the purse, to keep it safe, the day before I came to Smithfield.

"What is the significance of this?" he asked.

I shook my head, aching to rip the pendant from his worn fingers.

The duke roared: "You will tell me why you brought this to Smithfield."

Now, instead of being a sin and a hindrance, my anger was a helpmate. I would not cringe before Thomas Howard, no matter his actions. I said, "The pendant was her gift to me ten years ago. I thought that after she died, if I could lay claim to her body as her kinswoman, I would see Margaret buried with it."

"That's very touching. But we suspect it has another meaning."

The duke began to pace: a half-dozen steps away, then back around toward me, while Kingston watched, tense. "Thomas Becket defied his king. He put pope before king, just as Margaret and all the other rebels did, and just as you are doing now. You brought this to Smithfield as a symbol of your defiance."

I shook my head, but he didn't notice. His pacing grew quicker; his words came faster. They rang off the long walls of my cell. "When the king ordered me to lead his army to the North, to defeat the wicked traitors who took up arms against their sovereign, he gave me a special charge, Mistress Stafford. Do you know what his letter commanded? 'To cause such dreadful execution to be done on a good number of the inhabitants of every town, village, and hamlet that have offended that they may be a *fearful spectacle*.'"

His last two words hung in the air.

"The crows are busy in the North, mistress. They make a feast of the men—and the women, too, aye, the women, too—who hang from the trees and the gibbets we raised along the road. Those stupid peasants, at the end they begged me to spare them. They were wrong, they cried. Couldn't the king forgive? I showed no mercy to a single one, mistress, not a one."

The spit had gathered in the corners of the duke's mouth, and I watched it slide down his chin as he ranted.

"Why did they do it? Why did they defy His Majesty, their anointed monarch?"

He rounded on me. "They did it for *you*, Joanna Stafford. They did it for all the nuns and the monks and the friars. They wanted their abbeys restored and their feast days reinstated. They never accepted the king's divorce from Katherine of Aragon or his new queen. They would not swear oath to him as head of the Church of England. They went into battle with banners of Jesus on His Cross—the soldiers wore badges of the five wounds of Christ. A holy pilgrimage, they said. A Pilgrimage of Grace. How *dare* these vermin take on holy airs? Their leader . . . Robert Aske. That foul lawyer—he will hang in chains in York while I stand watch, Mistress Stafford. But they had other leaders from the northern gentry, like Sir John Bulmer and his 'wife.' My damned sister-in-law. I heard the evidence at her trial. She encouraged her husband to lead men in rebellion against the king. She said to him, 'The Commons want but a head.' And that if the Commons did not rise, the family must flee to Scotland. She said she'd rather be torn to pieces than go back down to London."

Such desperate words did not sound like Margaret. I suspected false testimony. And there was something else I wondered as well.

"I observed Margaret at Smithfield, and it was obvious she had been roughly handled," I said.

"She wasn't tortured, if that is what you suggest," the duke said quickly. "And these statements of hers were made in the North, before her chaplain and others, men who freely gave testimony at trial. Do you know what she said about me?" He bared his yellow teeth. "She said not once but twice she wanted my head off. What family loyalty. Ah, but she paid for her crimes. She died a terrible death. You saw it with your own eyes."

I flinched at his cruelty but refused to cower. "Yes," I said, "and even if this 'evidence' is true, if it constitutes the worst of her offences, I still don't understand why her punishment was so severe, why she alone, of all the wives of the northern rebel leaders, was condemned to be burned at the stake before a mob."

Something moved in the duke's eyes, and I knew at once there was more to Margaret's arrest and execution, another set of truths behind the ones I'd been told.

But before I could say anything more, he bore down on me, his black eyes smoking, his narrow chest rising and falling. "Your beloved cousin is gone now. *You* are now our concern, Joanna Stafford.

And you want me to believe that a novice at a priory, a girl raised in a noble family that's a nest of traitors to the crown, could be a loyal subject to King Henry the Eighth?"

I stood mute.

"Look at this girl, Kingston," he called out. "They say Howard women are troublesome, but it's the Stafford females, like my accursed wife and this girl here, who are the worst in the land."

He leaned in even closer. "I could horsewhip you now, and no one would blame me. No one would stop me. You know that, don't you?"

The words came out before I could stop them. "And I know you would enjoy it."

Seconds later, I was lying flat on the floor, face down, my ears ringing, a burning pain in my jaw. The duke had hit me with his fist. I waited for more blows to rain down on me, for him to employ the whip. Would he kill me with his bare hands, here in the Tower, while Kingston watched?

Nothing came. I looked up, and Sir William Kingston had moved between us. He said nothing, raised no hand against the duke or hand to help me, but simply stood there, his face grave and pale. Norfolk had turned his back to me, his shoulders quaking.

Slowly, I stood back up, without assistance.

"Kingston, bring him in now," the duke said in a low voice. His back was still to me, and I realised for the first time he was not a tall man. Kingston topped him by a head.

Nodding, Sir William went to the door and knocked twice. It swung open and the lieutenant walked in the room, the man who had received me at the Water Gate. He gripped another young man by the arm, half pulling him inside.

It was Geoffrey Scovill.

8

Geoffrey looked far better than when I had last seen him, carried away, unconscious, from the landing gate of the Tower. A proper bandage had replaced my makeshift one. He'd obviously been cleaned up and fed during his imprisonment. He stood tall, his hands unbound, before us.

But he wouldn't meet my gaze. He stared down and away, toward the corner of the room.

What a grave mistake he'd made by coming to my aid, I thought. He was one of them, after all; he'd gone to Smithfield to observe the administration of the king's justice. Geoffrey Scovill would be a fool if he did not distance himself from me now. He had not struck me as a fool.

His arrival blew new purpose into the duke, who pointed at him with his whip and asked me, "What is your connection to this man?"

"There is no connection," I said quickly.

"Wasn't he by your side at the burning, as you rushed to interfere with the execution?" Norfolk pressed. "What conspiracy did you form?"

"None, Your Grace. A short time previous, I met Master Scovill when he came to my aid. Another man, a ruffian, attempted to harm me, and he put a stop to it. He was trying to persuade me to leave Smithfield when Lady Bulmer was brought to the stake. He was only concerned for my safety. When he was struck down by the soldier of the guard, Master Scovill was trying to pull me back into the crowd, to protect me."

"How chivalrous." The duke smiled. I hated that thin-lipped leer. I preferred his rage, even his blows, to that. "So you attracted a strapping young protector at Smithfield. That doesn't seem the way a nun should conduct herself."

Geoffrey's head snapped up. He finally looked right at me, and his mouth fell open. With my dishevelled clothing and hair, and the bruise sprouting on my jaw, I was doubtless a pitiful sight.

The duke sneered. "But then you weren't a nun yet, were you, Joanna? Still a novice, eh? And this could have been your last chance at a man. He seems a fine enough candidate for the honour."

Geoffrey Scovill yanked his arm out of the lieutenant's grip and moved in the direction of the duke, his blue eyes sparking with rage. He was rising to the bait. In a moment he would defy the Duke of Norfolk, and for someone of his station, the error would be irrevocable.

"Your Grace is most mistaken," I said in my hardest voice, turning toward the duke to cut off Geoffrey's approach. "I had no significant dealings with this man. How could it be otherwise? You must know enough of him to be aware he is a base commoner. I would never form a personal connection with such a person. You yourself say I am of noble family, descended from Plantagenet kings. He is an insect."

I turned back toward Geoffrey. He stood frozen in place, his eyes glistening. But I couldn't say or do anything, couldn't send him a signal, no matter how subtle, to let him know I was doing this to absolve him.

"Take him away, Lieutenant, and discharge him from the Tower," said Norfolk with a shrug, as if calling for a bundle of clothes to be pitched into the river. A minute later, Geoffrey Scovill was gone. I felt relief, but the victory was a heavy one. My false words had caused pain, and I'd never be able to explain to him, to atone.

A strange scratching sound filled the room, and I looked around, confused. It was the Duke of Norfolk's wheezing laugh.

"It was worth a try, eh, Kingston?" he asked.

"Yes, Your Grace," Sir William said.

I gasped as the truth hit me. "You knew that Geoffrey Scovill had nothing to do with any crime before bringing him into this room. You just wanted to see how we would react to rude questions."

Kingston looked away, uncomfortable. The duke, anything but apologetic, said, "I'd already had him investigated, yes. There was but minor fault in his actions."

My face flushed hot. As calmly as possible, I said, "I have done nothing wrong. I am guilty of no treason, Your Grace, no conspiracy. It may have shown poor judgement to go to Smithfield and to reach out to my father, but nothing more. You are not entitled to harass or harm me or anyone else connected with me. I know something of the laws of this land. You must bring me to trial, or you must free me."

The duke's face turned sour, but he did not raise his whip or storm about the room again. It was possible, just possible, that I had won and would follow Geoffrey Scovill out of the Tower.

A sharp rap sounded at the door.

Kingston let in the lieutenant, who rushed to Norfolk with what looked to be a bundle of letters. The three of them huddled in the corner, passing papers back and forth.

When the Duke of Norfolk turned toward me again, his eyes blazed with new life.

"After I heard you were arrested at Smithfield, Mistress Stafford, I remembered my wife talking about you. Ten years ago, as a matter of fact. She told me that you were to be a maid of honour to Katherine of Aragon, that since your mother came over from Spain in her entourage, it was only right and fitting that you, the only daughter, carry on this tradition. And you were approved to occupy court lodgings. Am I correct?"

My mouth dry as dust, I could only nod.

"So what happened, mistress?"

I said nothing. There was no amount of abuse, no device of torture, that would ever make me disclose what had happened on the single day that I spent in royal service ten years ago.

"You were deemed not good enough, weren't you? You didn't please the court for some reason. So you returned to Stafford Castle, correct?"

I nodded, awash in relief that he was moving on.

"And what happened to you then?"

"I took care of my mother. She was often ill." Two sentences that did not begin to capture my life during those years: the darkened rooms, the herb-soaked poultices, the tinctures and teas, and the bloodlettings that never, ever helped.

The duke continued, speaking more to Sir William and the lieutenant than to me. "When Katherine of Aragon was divorced and exiled, her favourite ladies were not permitted to attend her. But at the end, when she was dying, the King's Majesty was magnanimous. Her two Spanish ladies were recalled to wait on her. Maria de Salinas, who married an Englishman and became the Countess of Willoughby, and Isabella Montagna, who did the same and became Lady Stafford."

The duke glanced down at another one of the letters.

"Here is the report from the Spanish ambassador. This was one of Chapuys's letters intercepted and copied before it left England." A sneering grin from the duke. "The letter to Emperor Charles said, 'The queen your blessed aunt died in the arms of her ladies, the Countess of Willoughby and Mistress Stafford.' I thought it was an error of writing then, that he meant Lady Stafford. Nothing more."

The duke took a deep breath.

"I'm a man of detail, Mistress Stafford. Whether it be preparing for battle or for questioning a prisoner of the state. I requested the recent papers having to do with the family in residence at Stafford Castle, and this is what I received just a moment ago." He held up a letter; I could not read its signature. "It says, 'Isabella, Lady Stafford, died on November 5, 1535.' Which I find very interesting, because Katherine of Aragon died on January 7, 1536. Two months later."

He wasn't shouting any more. His voice was calm, almost gentle. "It was you, Joanna Stafford, who went to Katherine of Aragon in Kimbolton Castle, and cared for her in the last weeks of her life, wasn't it?"

I met his steady gaze with one just as steady. "Yes," I said. "It was. The summons came one week after she died, and I went in her place. It is what my mother would have wanted."

Norfolk nodded slowly. "You personally served the woman who has been the cause of so much contention. How many people have died for her? Cardinal Fisher. Thomas More. Do you know where I was this morning, before the Tower? Newgate. There are seven Carthusian monks chained up, Mistress Stafford, and I approved the orders to give them no more food. They have refused to take the Oath of Supremacy to Henry the Eighth as head of the church, above the pope. And so they will starve."

Pointing a finger at me, he said, "Katherine of Aragon died in *your* arms, and afterward *you* decided to take holy vows, to follow the old ways that she loved. And you expect anyone to believe that you came to Smithfield without a shred of any treasonous intent?"

He did not seem to expect an answer, and I did not give him one.

"There shall now begin a deep investigation of you, Joanna Stafford. 'Bring me to trial,' you commanded, as if I were your damn page. Rest assured, mistress, you shall have one."

The duke fingered his horsewhip. "My work is finished here, Kingston, and we must now move with all possible speed." He stalked to the door, the other two men in his wake. As it swung open, he paused, casting one more look back at me, of pure gloating.

"Today is a most happy day for the king, our master."

The door slammed behind them, and I was, for the first time since waking that morning, alone in my Tower cell. I sank to the floor, to my knees, and bowed my head.

The Lord God knew of my innocence. I had never planned conspiracy nor plotted treason. Like all members of the Stafford family, I'd sworn the Oath of Supremacy to the king two years ago. My cousin Henry, eager to prove our utter loyalty, had insisted we be the first of the old families to do so. And then, when called upon, I nursed a weak and abandoned woman whom my mother—and much of Christendom—revered, but there had been no political agenda. I was not a political person.

Perhaps I was being tested by Him for some purpose I couldn't grasp. If so, I could accept that, but I longed for a sign of grace. When I'd prayed over my decision to go to Smithfield, I'd been filled with the conviction of purpose. That rushing, splendid sense of order blooming out of chaos. I had followed my soul's calling, but it took me to the vicious mob at Smithfield and then to the Tower of London, to men who sought to trap and torment me. Where had I erred—where was my offence to God? The throbbing in my knees sharpened to fiery pain, and still I prayed, pleading to be filled with, if not purpose, at least a feeling of calm, that I was in the hands of the Lord.

I don't have any idea how long I knelt, but when the sound of footsteps came again, my prayers were unanswered. I got to my feet just before the young lieutenant and maidservant Bess came through the door.

"You are to be moved to Beauchamp Tower," he said.

Outside, on the green, I could see ragged clouds chase one another across a blue sky. A warm breeze stirred my hair. I followed the lieutenant down a well-trimmed path, Bess a step behind, towards a three-storey stone building, just west of the square, white keep. A string of mulberry trees stretched along the path, their branches thick with pale-green leaves. Under one of them, a boy shook a branch, hard. White berries fell in a rain of gentle plops onto a dark blanket he'd spread on the ground.

Where on Tower Green did they perform the executions? Brave men had met death here—More and Fisher—as well as infamous criminals. The witch Anne Boleyn was executed on the green one year ago, as well as her infamous brother, George Boleyn. He was one of five men convicted of adultery with the queen.

But I could not think of George and Anne Boleyn now if I wanted to keep hold of my sanity.

Clang. Clang. Clang. Clang.

The sound of bells rippled across the green. I looked to find the church it came from, to draw strength from it, but there was nothing. "Those are the bells of Saint Paul's," Bess said.

"Is it so close?" I asked.

"No, but the sound carries in the wind, and today all the bells must be—"

The lieutenant whipped around to silence her with a look.

Once inside Beauchamp Tower, I was led to a circular stone staircase, its steps worn smooth. On the second floor, we turned down a narrow passage. At regular intervals the walls were marked with wooden doors, bars built into the top half. I didn't look inside any of them as we passed. I heard no voices, no sounds at all, but I was certain that each cell contained a prisoner.

At the end of the passage, the lieutenant beckoned for me to follow him through an archway and down another, even longer passage. As I passed one door, I heard a man's sob, low and broken.

It was that pitiful sound that robbed me of courage. My head swam, and I reached out to the wall to steady myself.

"Mistress Stafford?" called out the lieutenant, at the end of the passage, his hard young face empty of sympathy.

Bess squeezed my elbow. I thought about my uncle, the Duke of Buckingham. He'd impressed all with the dignity shown when imprisoned here, in the Tower. I forced myself to walk the rest of the way.

This cell was smaller and dimmer than my former quarters: rectangular, with a pointed-arched recess at the end, two narrow windows carved in the stone. A bare fireplace along one wall, a bed against the other. My nose and eyes burned from a strong smell. It was lye, used within the hour to scrub the floor and walls—they gleamed with damp patches.

"I will bring you dinner," Bess murmured and left.

I peered out the window. My view was of a raised outer walkway along the top of the castle wall, an allure running between this tower structure and another. Beyond it, the massive stone wall, William the Conqueror's wall, blocked out all. I could see nothing of the green.

"I have a request," I said to the lieutenant, who stood near the door, impatient.

"Yes?"

"May I have papers and pen, to inform my family and the prioress of my order that I am confined here?"

"Sir William Kingston was clear that you should have no means of correspondence. He will see that all are informed."

He turned to leave.

"Wait," I said, my voice breaking. "May I not have books? I thought that prisoners were allowed books."

The lieutenant hesitated.

"The writing of Thomas Aquinas?" I said quickly, before he made up his mind to deny me. "How could there be harm in that?"

"I can make no promises," he said. "I will pass the request to Sir William." And he left.

Moments later, Bess reappeared with a tray of food: bread and a large chunk of cheese.

That is when the singing came. It was faint but lovely: many voices, at least a hundred, raised in common song.

"Bess, is that a Te Deum?" I asked, wonderingly.

"Yes," she said. "It is the court. The king ordered the Te Deum sung. That is where Lady Kingston and Sir William have gone. All those who serve the king were summoned to Saint Paul's."

"Why?"

She looked at me for a moment. "It is Queen Jane," Bess said. "The child has quickened in her womb, and all must celebrate. The king is certain that this time he will have his son and heir. This wife will succeed . . ." her voice trailed off.

Where the others had failed. That was what I thought, what anyone would think. His first wife, Katherine of Aragon, discarded after she could bear only a daughter. His second, the witch Boleyn, put to death when she could do no better.

Aloud, I said cautiously, "A prince would be a source of great joy for our kingdom."

Bess nodded, but her eyes stayed troubled. Her shoulders sagged. That nervous, gossipy spirit of this morning had vanished. "Were you punished for allowing me to look out the window?" I asked.

"Oh, no. Lady Kingston cared only about the royal summons to Saint Paul's. She was afraid Sir William would be held back here too late and they would miss it."

"Then why are you so troubled?"

She shook her head. "I cannot tell you."

"Please, Bess."

She peered over her shoulder at the door, and then sidled close to me, to speak into my ear. "I heard what Sir William said to my mistress before they left for Saint Paul's. The Duke of Norfolk told him that to catch you and your father in treason would be of great value to the king. That in so doing all the Staffords might finally be crushed and the crown made safer from challenge. If they could succeed in breaking you . . ." Bess fell silent.

"Go on."

"Then there would be reward in it for the duke and for Sir William. The king would be grateful and be bound to give them lands."

The voices of the court trilled higher on the final chorus of the Te Deum, the Latin words that give humblest thanks to God. The music slowly died away.

"Thank you, Bess," I whispered. "I will say nothing. Please take the food away."

As she picked up the tray, I saw a tear trickle down her cheek.

I fell onto the narrow straw bed and turned to face the wall. I did not close my eyes or move a muscle. I stared at the stone wall and watched the light grow dimmer against it. Night closed in. The Tower yeomen warders shouted to one another, conveying orders on the castle allure and in the passageway. I heard the word *bonfires*.

After a time, the men fired cannon to salute the king in his time of joy: once, twice, three times, more. It was very loud. A faint acrid smell drifted in through the window, perhaps from the celebratory bonfires, perhaps from the cannon. But through it all the walls of my prison cell never trembled. The walls of the Tower are the thickest in the land, and they never, ever tremble.

9

That first night in Beauchamp Tower, I couldn't know it was to be the first of many. I was rigid with terror all night, until the blackness shifted to dawn. The next day, I lapsed in and out of wakefulness, but rarely rose from bed. I ignored the periodic openings of the cell door, the trays of food shoved inside by a yeoman warder, then reclaimed, untouched. I kept thinking of those Carthusian monks and how they would die by slow starvation at Newgate for their beliefs. How could I take food while they suffered? And why would I even wish to live? I was to be questioned, taunted, and disbelieved—over and over—by the Duke of Norfolk and other hateful men, until they'd gathered facts deemed sufficient to destroy me, my father, and every other member of the Stafford family.

But on the second morning, when the door swung open, and a woman lowered a wooden tray of food, I staggered toward it. The woman was not Bess. She was older and taller, with a long face and black hair nearly covered by a white hood. I fell on the food, the hard chunk of cheese, like an animal. I felt shame over my weakness. But I couldn't deny this wish to live, even if the rest of my existence was to be frightening—and short. After eating I fell back onto the bed and slept for hours, untroubled by dreams.

I awoke later that day physically strengthened but consumed with dread. Would this be a day of more questioning? The day that they determined to "break" me? I prayed and waited, listening for an approach on the passageway. But no one appeared besides the yeomen guards and servants.

This continued, one day after the next. In the morning came the serving woman in her white cap, who I later learned was named Susanna. And in the late afternoon came one of two yeomen warders who worked in Beauchamp, Henry or Ambrose, with dinner. The food bordered on rancid; the ale tasted sour. I ate and drank very little.

After one week, the yeoman warder named Ambrose explained my situation. "If you want decent food, or some furniture, or wood for your fireplace, anything at all, you must pay," he said. "Those are the rules."

After a moment, I couldn't help but laugh. "Do you see any coins or jewels here, sir?" I asked.

"Your family," he said patiently. "I will help with conveying the letters back and forth and making the arrangements. It's the families that pay."

I shook my head violently. "I will not contact anyone. It would not be fitting."

He blinked in surprise. "I thought you were of a noble house," he said.

"No more," I muttered. "No more." I turned away from the yeoman warder. I heard him walk down the passageway and, a moment later, tell another of my refusal to better my situation. I could hear snatches of talk outside my cell, but after that day it never pertained to myself—or to my father. One morning, the prisoner down the passageway who wept was taken away. His tears had been a terrible trial for me, but I discovered there was something worse than listening to a man weep, and that was no longer listening to it. Where else could he have gone but to his death?

I lay half asleep, listless, on my bed, early one afternoon when the door swung open and there was Lady Kingston, dressed in her finery. On this occasion, she wore a gabled headdress beaded with tiny jewels.

"Are you well, Mistress Stafford?" she asked.

I shrugged. The question seemed more than slightly ridiculous.

"You look ill." Her face filled with worry, and I wondered if this were one of her guises, assumed to draw out confidences, so I said nothing.

She pressed something into my hands. To my surprise, it was several heavy books. On each cover was engraved *The Summa Theologica of Thomas Aquinas*.

"Thank you," I whispered, stroking the covers.

"What else do you require?" she asked.

"Now that I have this, nothing, Lady Kingston."

She looked at me for a minute. "How unusual, for a lady to have no demands of me," she said, a strange vehemence to her words.

She swept out of the room, and if it were not for the books in my hands, I would have thought this a dream, the encounter so strange. Within the hour, I had another visitor. The lieutenant came to my cell and, with his usual curtness, bade me follow him. I felt a wave of fear, mixed with bitterness. To give me books on the eve of my destruction seemed cruel, even for the Tower.

He led me a different way than the one I'd come, out onto the castle allure. I blinked hard in the sun when I stepped outside; I was unused to brightness. We walked its length, about thirty feet, and then he paused. I waited for him to open the door, but instead he turned and led me back to where we started. He paused again.

"What are we doing?" I asked.

"You are to take exercise, Mistress Stafford," he said. "Sir William and Lady Kingston order it."

"Why?"

He did not answer, merely jerked his head forward, and I had no choice but to accompany him, back and forth along the allure. If I craned my neck at the far end, I could see the mulberry trees on the green, more thickly leaved.

"Can you tell me anything about my father?" I asked.

"No, and if you persist with inquiry, I will return you to your cell," he said sharply.

It was the least congenial walk I had ever taken. Still, I had no wish to hurry back to confinement; I held back any other questions until the lieutenant was poised to leave me: "How long have I been here in the Tower?"

I expected him to refuse an answer or to hazard a guess. But he said, "Twenty-three days." It was odd how he'd had the number ready.

In the next week, my prison conditions improved dramatically. Susanna or the yeomen warders delivered mutton stewed with potage, boiled beef, roasted capons, or larks. All served on pewter, with ale. Furniture materialised, a chair and a table. My cell was cleaned more frequently. Fresh rushes were laid down on the stone floor. I was even supplied with clean linens.

"Who bears the cost of this?" I asked Ambrose.

He shrugged and spread his hands. "Someone with means," he grunted.

I spent most of my days reading, working on my Latin, absorbing the wisdom of Thomas Aquinas. I studied his interpretation of the four cardinal virtues: prudence, temperance, justice, and fortitude. I found special significance in the beliefs about personal resolve. In the absence of Mass, the denial of the Blessed Sacraments, his teachings comforted me beyond measure.

Once a week, the lieutenant appeared for silent walks along the allure. I was grateful for any release from my cell, which was often hot and airless. Anyone could tell the lieutenant disliked this duty. I yearned to know why the Kingstons insisted I get exercise, who paid for my food, and why no one ever interrogated me. But his stiff shoulders as he stalked ahead made it clear I would get no answers.

I was shocked when he broke the silence one day with a question.

"What did you *do* all day, shut up in a priory?" he asked.

I sought ecstatic union with a merciful, wise, and loving God. Aloud I said, "Religious observances."

"But why isn't Mass enough—worshipping in a church?" the lieutenant asked. "What could possibly be accomplished by all of those nuns and monks, shut away?"

"We gather in community to seek grace through prayer and obedience," I said patiently. "At Dartford, we follow the same Rules of Saint Benedict as at all the other nunneries and the monasteries—the sisters gather at eight fixed hours: Matins, Lauds, Prime, Terce, Sext, None, Vespers, and Compline. There is Mass as well. We chant and we sing. We pray for the souls of the dead."

He narrowed his eyes. "And if someone pays the priory enough money, they receive extra prayers for salvation—or forgiveness for sins not even committed?"

Now I understood his hostility. These were the ideas of those who sought to destroy the Catholic Church, who swore salvation should be received through faith alone.

With a sneer, he said, "Someone once told me that nuns learn Latin and study and write books."

"That's true," I said through gritted teeth.

The lieutenant stopped walking. "All these years, the rich monks and nuns sit in their abbeys and sing and write and chant their Latin, and what does it all do? What does it accomplish? Purgatory is but superstition: that is what the new learning says. All the intercessional chanting at all the monasteries to shorten the pains of purgatory—" His face was twisted with contempt. "When we die, our souls immediately appear before God the creator and judge."

I backed away from the lieutenant, from his hate and his heresy. These were the words of a Lutheran.

The lieutenant took note of my reaction. A smile spread across his face as he leaned closer to me. "I know what you're thinking. I am no Lutheran, but he did have the correct view on women. Martin Luther said, 'Females should remain at home, sit still, keep house, and bear and bring up children.' That is their only purpose, in my opinion."

"And now that I've heard your opinion," I said hoarsely, "I would like to return to my cell."

With a bow, he complied.

One evening the sky opened and sheets of rain beat down on the Tower. Thunder cracked. I stood pressed to the windows, catching the cool stinging drops on my face, when the door flew open and Bess stood there, with my tray. I gave a cry of excitement, and her wide pockmarked face split into a smile.

Duty rosters had kept her from me, she explained while I ate. Susanna's charge was the prisoners of Beauchamp and hers was those of the White Tower and to be at the beck and call of Lady Kingston. "We've been kept so busy with Lady Douglas, I've never worked so hard in my life."

"Lady Douglas?"

"The king's Scottish niece. Didn't you know? She's been here for months. She became engaged to a gentleman of the court without permission of the king, so he sent them both here. It is treason for a member of the royal family to arrange her own marriage because of the succession." Bess sighed. "She's very difficult to please because of—"

Another crack of thunder drowned her out, and a gust of wind blew inside. "Why aren't you drenched from the rain?" I asked, curious, looking at Bess's dry dress.

"Underground tunnels connect the buildings," she said. "But I can't stay long. It would look suspicious. I could only come now because it's Susanna's day to visit her family in Southwark."

"But what of my situation? What have you heard?"

"Not a word," she said. "I listen every day, but Lady Kingston hasn't mentioned you, nor has anyone else."

Two weeks later, Bess managed to visit me, and again, she had nothing to report. "It's so strange, it's as if you aren't even here," she said.

That was it. *I don't exist any more,* I thought, not listening as Bess prattled on about Lady Douglas and her crying fits.

The heat of the summer passed. The nights grew cooler. One day, on an afternoon walk with the lieutenant, I saw a spattering of gold leaves in the mulberry trees. It made me unbearably sad, to see proof of time passing. What had happened to my father? What was going on at Dartford Priory? My throat ached, and tears ran down my cheeks. The lieutenant pretended not to see.

That day I entered my most difficult period in the Tower. A dull sorrow weighed me down, body and mind. I could no longer concentrate on Thomas Aquinas. Some days I never rose from my bed. At night, always the time my fears were most urgent, I abandoned myself to weeping. I thought of my mother a great deal. In the last years of her life, her health was broken, yes, but also her spirits frayed. She slept in darkened rooms. I could still feel the dread in my heart as I'd walk down the passageway of Stafford Castle, carrying her tray, knowing that I'd push open her door to see her once again slumped in bed, listless and despairing. I felt a dark kinship with her now.

Everything changed when, one cool evening, past the time when my dinner tray was removed, I was surprised to hear a jingle of keys at the door.

Bess burst in, her eyes bulging.

"Your father is in the Tower," she said, breathless.

"What?" I shot towards her.

"I heard that Sir Richard Stafford is being kept in the White

Tower, on the lower level. They brought him in two days ago. Something is happening to you tomorrow."

I took Bess's hands in mine. "Bess, I want you to tell me exactly what you heard. Leave out nothing."

"I came in to clear the table, and Lady Kingston said, 'Is it true he's coming to examine Joanna Stafford tomorrow?' And Sir William said, 'Yes, that's why they sent over her father two days ago. Norfolk brought him in to deal with the Staffords. He's the only man Norfolk pays heed to, save the king.'"

"That's all?"

"Yes. There was nothing else. But I heard one of the warders say earlier that there was a new man, a nobleman, on the lower level of the White Tower. It must be your father."

All my lassitude, my despair, and my fear disappeared, replaced by a fierce, raging purpose. *My father is alive. My father is here. I must find a way to see him.*

Bess said gravely, "Mistress Stafford, I could be whipped and branded for it, but I've brought paper and quill with me. If you write him a message, I will take it to him and ask him for reply."

As I stared at her, the plan slipped into my mind, fully formed.

"No, Bess," I said. "You're going to take me to my father tonight. And I know a way to do it."

10

"Bess, stop trembling." The candlelight leaped and shook against the dark walls, because of her unsteady grip.

"I'm sorry, Mistress Stafford, I can't help it." Bess's loud voice echoed down the long tunnel.

"Don't use my true name, *please*."

She ducked her head, and I regretted having to scold her. But Bess risked her life for me, and I had to do everything in my power to protect her.

Scratch. Scratch. Scratch.

The sound came from behind me, like long ragged fingernails clawing a wooden stake. This time I didn't turn around. Bess had warned me that vermin overran the underground tunnel. "We keep setting loose more cats, but it's the cats that disappear, not the rats."

Ever since I'd set foot in this dank tunnel, I'd heard them: mostly behind us, but sometimes I'd catch a glimpse of one ahead, a long shiny tail whipping across the narrow passage, on the edge of our quivering circle of candlelight.

"Rats and ravens," Bess muttered. "My sister's friends think I put on airs. Humph. It's rats and ravens everywhere. Not the sort of royal palace they expect."

I let her go on. Nervous grumbling could help settle her nerves.

Not more than an hour ago, I'd managed to persuade her to help me on my mission. Wearing a makeshift white hood, I posed as Susanna, carrying a bundle of clean bedsheets. The male prisoner who faced questioning the next day by the Duke of Norfolk needed new bedding—that was what we would tell anyone who made inquiry. Susanna and I were of similar height and figure, with the same black hair. She was some five years older, but at night, with my eyes cast down, wearing her trademark hood, I hoped to pass for her, scuttling after Bess. She was a maid of the prison, while Bess served Lady Kingston. It was to be expected that Susanna would walk behind.

We'd come across only one yeoman warder so far, checking some papers on the main floor of Beauchamp Tower. I'd held my bundle of sheets as high as I could, so that my face was nearly obscured. It worked as well as I'd prayed. The warder glanced at Bess and me and then returned to his papers. Within minutes Bess had unlocked the door to the underground tunnel and we were down the steps.

At the other end was the White Tower . . . and my father.

I'd thought of him so often, it felt unreal that I would finally come face-to-face with him, speak to him, gain his counsel on what I should do when interrogated tomorrow. Bess said we dared stay only a few minutes. Would there be time, I fretted, would it be possible for me to ask the question pressing on my mind for months. It was, unfortunately, the same question that the Duke of Norfolk tossed at me in such a crude fashion: "Your father almost blew himself up with gunpowder—why would he do that for his dead brother's bastard?" I simply did not know. My darkest fear was that, without the company of wife or child, my father had gone a little mad at Stafford Castle. If through some miracle he and I were to be freed from the Tower, I'd already vowed to make him the centre of my life. There was no question of returning to Dartford. My offences against the Dominican Order were too serious. But if I could look after my father, at Stafford Castle or anywhere else he deemed best, I would never stop thanking Christ for His mercies. I cherished a picture in my mind, of ladling soup into a bowl for my father as he smiled at me, restored to hale health, his hounds at his feet, a fire roaring.

Bess suddenly stopped short, and I bumped into her. She nearly dropped her ring of keys.

Two enormous rats squatted in front of us, in the centre of the tunnel floor. They didn't scuttle away like all the others. They half turned to face us, the candlelight reflected in their fiery red eyes.

"Lord keep us," whispered Bess. "They're like demons, aren't they? It's a bad omen, I know."

I needed to vanquish these rats, or Bess could lose courage.

Slowly, I edged around her to get out in front. My heart pounding, I took one step forward, then another.

The rats did not budge.

"Be gone!" I cried, and stomped my right foot hard, just a few inches from their heads.

This, at last, drove them back. Both rats scampered to a hole at the bottom of the tunnel wall and pushed their swollen bodies through it. The second rat paused halfway through, as if stuck, then, turning sideways, squeezed the rest of the way, its thick tail twirling and slapping the side of the hole like a whip before disappearing.

"Thank you," Bess said. In the candlelight she was pale as ivory, beads of perspiration bubbling on her upper lip.

"Are we almost there?" I asked.

"Yes—look." She held up her candle to toss the light farther and show me the steps that appeared at the end. As she did so, her hand shook again, and she looked at me, her face an apology. We both knew that it was within the White Tower that we ran the greatest risk of discovery.

I shifted my bundle to my left hip and laid my right hand on her shoulder.

"'Behold, now bless ye the Lord, all ye servants of the Lord. In the night lift up your hands to the holy places, and bless ye the Lord. I have cried to thee, O Lord, hear me; hearken to my voice when I cry to thee. And protect me ever after. Amen.'"

"That was beautiful," Bess whispered.

I smiled sadly. "The words of Saint Dominic, the founder of my order."

"Mistress, I pray I don't fail you."

"You have already done more for me than anyone else since . . ." My voice trailed away as Geoffrey Scovill's young face flashed in front of me, his eyes brimming with pain over my insult, the last words he'd heard from me. There was no point to this now. I shoved him out of my thoughts.

"Let us go forward, Bess."

We climbed the steps, and when we reached the top, Bess unlocked the door to the White Tower.

We stepped into an enormous hall. The light from Bess's candle didn't even reach the back wall of it. There was not a sound. I knew that Sir William and Lady Kingston kept apartments in the White Tower, as did the king's disgraced niece, Lady Margaret Douglas, and perhaps others down below, too, besides my father. Yet now, in this eerily silent space, we seemed quite alone.

Bess and I hurried across the stone floor. The air felt much cooler than in the dank tunnel; a faint breeze fingered my bare neck, though I couldn't make out any windows. I realised from the jutting shape of one stone wall that it was a massive bulwark. With a chill, I felt the strength of the keep's creator: the greatness but also the fear and greed of William the Conqueror. He'd fashioned this citadel five hundred years ago to house his Norman pride and crush the Saxeons. This must have been an enormous banquet or reception hall for early kings. I fought down an absurd fear that the conqueror himself would stalk towards me from the shadows, his chain-mail armour clanking on the smooth floor.

We passed through a series of vaulted rooms. Larger windows shed more moonlight. I could see a faint gold and scarlet light shimmer at the other side of one of the rooms. It wasn't from the moon or from candlelight; it was something else entirely. I tugged on Bess's arm. "It's the chapel," she said hurriedly, without stopping. So those were stained-glass windows. I longed to go there, to pray for divine assistance, but of course there was no time.

After a few more minutes, I saw another light flickering in the distance, stronger than a candle. It was a torch fixed to a wall. Bess straightened her shoulders in front of me, and I knew this was our destination. My heart beat faster as I followed her.

Below the torch sat an empty chair and a table. I heard a footfall, another, and then a yeoman warder came into sight, a tall one with a long black beard.

"Hello, Tom," called out Bess.

I raised the bundle higher, so that it covered the lower half of my face, even though doing so made my arms ache.

"Bess, what are you about? I never see you down here." Tom's voice was friendly.

"We need to get fresh bedding to the nobleman on the south passage," she said.

"Tonight?"

"His Grace, the Duke of Norfolk, will be questioning him tomorrow. He doesn't like it when the lords and ladies reek, you know that."

Tom didn't say anything. My heart pounded even faster. I stayed fixed on the empty chair; I didn't want to meet his eyes.

"By dogfish, is that Susanna?" he burst out, his voice excited.

I could not breathe nor move a muscle.

Bess's voice sounded strained now. "I didn't know you were friend to Susanna."

"I haven't seen you in more than a year; you keep yourself close at Beauchamp, don't you, woman?"

Still I said and did nothing. I felt frozen.

"Why won't you speak to me?" Tom took a heavy step towards me. "Are you still angry over May Day?"

I lowered my bundle. The warmth from the torch's flame danced on my cheeks.

"No," I said in a low voice.

I looked into his face, felt his brown eyes boring into mine. I moved my lips into a smile.

Remarkably, he smiled back. Two teeth were missing. "You're looking bonny, Susanna."

Bess said, her voice turning shrill, "We have our work to do, Tom."

"Yes, I'll take you down to the cell myself," he said, picking up a set of keys.

"No," Bess said quickly. "Just give me that key."

"It's dark down there," he said. "I haven't lit the torches. Why shouldn't you want my help?"

There was nothing I could think of to say, nor Bess. Silently, we followed him down a series of passageways. His red-and-gold uniform was stained and even slightly ripped, I saw when he paused to light the first torch. He was more unkempt than other warders I'd seen. I wondered if the men assigned to nights at the Tower were of lesser stuff.

Tom hummed a song as he walked to my father's cell, turning around every so often to smile at me, as if I'd recognise the tune. I would always nod back. I was braced for him to squint a little harder, to realise I wasn't the woman he thought. But he did not.

After what seemed like an eternity, Tom stopped and lit a torch fixed to the wall with his own. He pounded on the wooden door next to it. "Prisoner, attend!" he thundered. "You have company."

Tom opened the door with his key. It yawned open into a black space. Bess nudged in behind me with her short candle. I could make out a bed in the corner with a long inert body on top.

"You're right, it does reek in here," Tom said. "You need help?"

"This is woman's work," Bess said firmly. "Leave us with him. It will take but ten minutes."

Tom grunted. "Right. I shouldn't leave my post for that long." He backed away and closed the door. I heard the key turn.

Bess placed her candle on the floor next to the door and grabbed my sheets. "I'll do the work while you talk," she said.

I sprinted across the room. "Father, wake up, it's me. Joanna. Please, wake up."

He lay face down under a blanket, and I shook his shoulder. It felt sharp and bony; he'd lost weight.

He didn't awaken, and fear surged through me. Had my father died in his cell? I reached up and felt for his thick hair; I could hardly see him in the faint candlelight. His head stirred at last under my fingers; he turned and opened his eyes.

The man was not my father.

"No!" I howled. "This can't be."

Bess flew to my side. "What's wrong?"

"He's not my father."

"But he has to be," she insisted. "Unless . . ."

"What?"

"We didn't say 'Stafford.' There must be a second nobleman on this passageway, and he assumed this was the man we meant would be questioned by Norfolk. Oh, *no*."

I pounded my thigh with my fist. "We have to get Tom to take us to my father."

"No, no, mistress." Bess shook her head. "We can't. It will seem too strange. I fear he's half suspected something's amiss already."

A croaking sound interrupted us. With a start, we realised it was the man on the bed, listening while we talked.

"I know you," he said hoarsely. "Joanna. Stafford. What are you doing here?"

I looked down. There was nothing familiar about him: a pair of huge dark eyes in a gaunt face. His cheekbones stuck out of his face; his lips were cracked and white. "It's Charles." His voice was broken, gasping. "Charles Howard."

Bess gasped. "The man who tried to marry Lady Margaret Douglas!"

I couldn't believe it. The rash, swaggering young Howard who'd mocked me years ago at Stafford Castle bore no resemblance to this skeleton.

"Charles, was it you? You wooed the king's niece?" I asked.

He closed his eyes and nodded.

"Does your brother know you are this ill? Has the Duke of Norfolk been informed?"

He shuddered, and I feared he was convulsing. But he was laughing. The way his mouth twisted, I finally recognised him as Charles.

"Stop," I patted his quaking shoulder. "You'll make yourself worse."

"I am dying of lung rot, Joanna. It's what my brother wants. It's what everyone wants. Best way to solve it."

"Solve what?"

"My treason." He struggled to gain his breath. "Our treason. But how she loved *me*. The poems she wrote . . ." His voice dissolved into sputtering coughs.

Bess stirred next to me. "And she loves you, too, sir. I know. I've waited on her." I wondered at that. Bess had told me stories only of a peevish girl, raging against her royal uncle's punishment. But I silently thanked her for her kindness.

Indeed, Charles seemed to draw strength from what Bess said. "Does she love me still?" His words came faster now. "I've thought she wanted me dead, too. Then she could marry someone else with the king's permission." He blinked, looked us over with more alertness. "But why are you here?"

Bess said, "You tell him, mistress, while I change the bedding. We'll have to lift him out first."

The two of us lifted his poor body out of the bed, an easy task as he had wasted away almost to nothing. We settled him in the room's chair, and I told him of Margaret's burning, our arrests, the Duke of

Norfolk's questioning, and the news Bess had heard that led us mistakenly to his cell.

"A man my brother pays heed to besides the king?" Charles wondered. "He thinks everyone's a fool."

I shook my head. "I was hoping my father would know."

Bess asked, "Could it be Archbishop Cranmer? Or Cromwell? They've both been here to question prisoners."

Charles thought about it. "Aye, those are the two most important men in the land. But my brother hates the Archbishop of Canterbury and the Lord Privy Seal with all his soul. He pays no heed to them, nor ever would."

"He hates them?" I asked, surprised.

"His Grace, my loving brother, despises men of common birth raised up by the king. And they are both enemies of the old faith. So he is not aligned with them."

"But the duke doesn't care for the old faith—he led the armies against the rebellion." I said, confused. "He had every rebel hanged."

"My brother would never say no to the king's commission, but he prefers the old ways." Charles shrugged. "He's like Gardiner."

"The Bishop of Winchester?" Bess asked.

"Aye, that's the one. Wily Winchester. If there's any man my brother pays heed to, it's him. But he's in France. King got angry with him and made him permanent ambassador. Couldn't be Gardiner coming to see you." He started coughing again, a horrible ripping noise. When he took his hand away from his mouth, I saw fresh blood on it.

There was a pounding on the door. "Are you ready?" Tom called from the passageway.

"Give us a minute," Bess shouted. To Charles Howard, she said, "Sir, we need to get you back into bed."

He nodded. "Good luck to you," he whispered as we laid him back on his fresh sheets.

I kissed his frail, hot cheek. "Good-bye."

Bess was by the door, waiting. I grabbed her sleeve. "Let me try to persuade Tom to take me to my father," I pleaded. "We can say he needs his bedding changed as well. We've come all this way."

She shook her head. "Mistress, it won't work. I feel it. We will be revealed when—"

The door swung open, and Tom stuck his head in. "All finished?"

"Yes," Bess said. "We have only to take the old sheets to be burned."

"Leave them in the passageway," he said. "I'll see it's done."

We shuffled out; he closed the door behind us, locked it, and then stood there. He didn't lead us away. I opened my mouth to make my plea, but closed it. There was something odd in Tom's eyes when he looked down at me. And I didn't have my bundle to hide behind any more.

"I checked with the officer of the watch," he said slowly. "He knew of no orders to clean Lord Howard's cell or anyone else's this late at night. It can always be done in the morning. I didn't think that made much sense."

My throat tightened.

"We had the orders," Bess said. "You'll see."

Tom sneered at her. "Perhaps you took him a love letter from Lady Douglas?"

"Of course not," Bess said indignantly. "Check the cell yourself."

"I don't think I will," Tom said, his eyes lingering on me.

I heard a faint rushing in my ears.

He jerked his head forward. "Let's go."

We followed him down the passageway. I glanced at the wooden doors along the way. Was my father behind one of them? I'd lost all in my gamble to find him. And not only that. I'd brought Bess down with me. Frantically, I tried to think of some way to save her, to excuse her involvement, but nothing seemed plausible.

We reached Tom's station. I expected him to call for a fellow warder and march us to our fate.

He did not.

Tom grabbed my arm and pulled me close. His rough beard scratched my forehead. "Come with me, Susanna." I tried to pull away but couldn't.

Bess demanded: "What are you doing, Tom?"

"You two lasses are up to no good, but I won't say a word. All that's required is a bit of time alone with Susanna, and then I'll take you both to maids' quarters for the night, and no one's the wiser."

"No," I said.

"Come, Susanna, it's not like we haven't done it before. Course I was sore drunk that night. But I remember your sweet mouth. And I'm dead sober now, sweetheart."

"I won't let you take her away from me," Bess howled.

"You can watch if you like, Bess, I don't mind," Tom said.

It happened in a flash. Bess stamped on the inside of Tom's right foot. He let go of me, yelping and hunched over in pain, and then Bess made her two fists into a club and hit him on the back of the neck. His stomach hit the floor, hard.

"Run!" Bess grabbed me, and we sprinted into the darkness of the White Tower.

11

Bess and I ran back through the vaulted rooms. We went so fast that my lungs burned. I'd never run like that in my life. We had no candle now, but there was enough moonlight from the windows to guide us. And Bess, thank the Lord, knew this castle keep well.

We hurtled around a corner. Bess flew up against the stone wall, grabbing bricks with both hands to cling there. At first I thought her winded, stopping to catch her breath, but she shook her head at me to be silent.

I bent over, a pain clawing at my side.

"Do you hear?" she mouthed at me.

After a few seconds, there it was: heavy steps, coming quickly. Frightened, I nodded.

She grimaced.

"Chapel," she whispered.

We crept quietly now, looking behind us, braced for the tall, fearful shadow of Tom. Was he coming after us alone? I wondered why he hadn't alerted anyone else, or called out to us to stop.

In a few minutes we'd reached an arched doorway, and Bess pulled me in after her.

This was a place of aching beauty: the graceful stone columns bordering the long pews, the soaring ceiling, the three stained-glass windows filtering the sweetly coloured moonlight. It had been so long since I had heard Mass; I almost swooned as I gripped the first pew we reached. We crept to the middle of a pew halfway to the altar and knelt on the floor, next to each other. I could see Bess gnawing her lip, and I knew she was trying to think of what to do as we hid.

I heard something. It was so faint that I wasn't sure of my senses. I looked over at Bess; she seemed unaware. It must have been my own nervousness.

Another minute crawled by; I peered up at the nearest stained-glass window. I could see only a face of a beautiful blonde young woman. The Virgin Mary, I was sure of that. Yet this woman had a proud, vain tilt to her head. She looked like someone whose portrait I'd admired. A fresh young Plantagenet queen, who'd served as the artist's inspiration.

I heard the noise again. This time Bess reacted. She grabbed my wrist and held it tight. Her nails dug into the flesh, but I endured it without flinching.

"Susanna? Bess?" Tom's voice was no more than a loud whisper, coming from behind us, just outside the chapel.

I closed my eyes.

"You're in there, aren't you, girls?"

Bess stiffened.

"I'm sorry, I know I frightened you," Tom said, his voice conciliatory. "I was wrong. Lost my head. Come out and nothing more will be said."

Bess's nails eased out of my arm as if she were getting ready to stand up, and my eyes flew open.

"Bess, no!" I mouthed at her.

I felt something cold on my hand. It was her ring of keys.

She pressed her mouth to my ear to whisper. "Mistress, I'll go out and draw him away from you. I'll say you went ahead of me, but I wanted to pray. He'll take me back to maids' quarters and look for you on the way. He'd never expect you to go to Beauchamp now. It's the opposite direction."

I shook my head violently. "I can't make it back to my cell without you."

"Yes, you can. Use the tunnel; you won't be able to get into Beauchamp from the outside, this time of night." She pushed the keys harder into my hand. "Leave these in your cell, under your bed. I'll find a way to get there tomorrow."

Before I could say anything else or pull her back down, Bess had shot to her feet and hurried to the end of the pew.

"Are you yourself now, Tom?" she demanded. "You'll not be a beast to me, or I won't come out."

"Where's Susanna?" His voice was harder than before.

"I was all affright and needed to come to chapel, but she ran straight for her bed in maids' quarters. You know she isn't one for praying."

"Is that so?"

My fingers shook around the key ring. He didn't believe Bess. In a minute it would all be over.

A second man's voice rang out, deeper in the Tower. "Who's there? Declare yourself."

"It's Tom Sharard here, Sir. Escorting out Bess from night duty."

I heard Bess's quick steps as she hurried out of the chapel; then two sets of footsteps headed away. There were male voices, then Bess's, though I couldn't make out what they were saying. They didn't sound agitated or angry; somehow Bess was managing it. The trio of voices grew dimmer, and I realised they were walking away. After a few more minutes, I heard nothing at all.

When I tried to rise up, my knees buckled, and I sprawled onto the pew, terrified. How could I manage this secret journey back to Beauchamp if I couldn't even stand up in the chapel? I thought about remaining in the White Tower all night and taking my chances at dawn. But my Beauchamp Tower cell was always checked just after sunrise on rounds. I couldn't possibly get there in time, past all of the warders, in daylight, still posing as Susanna.

I had to leave now—tonight. And I had to do it alone.

I retraced my steps through the vaulted rooms. One led into another in a straight line—that was not hard for me. I found my way back to the great hall and hurried across it. My eyes had adjusted to the darkness; I could make out the stone walls and battlements. And it was surprisingly easy to locate the wooden door to the underground tunnel. Ten keys hung on Bess's ring; the second one I tried opened the door.

That same foul tunnel smell oozed over me. It was completely black down the steps, and I had no candle.

Trembling, I went forward, closed the door behind me, and edged down the steps, feeling the brick wall as I went. My foot touched the bottom, but it was too dreadful. I scrambled back up. I couldn't bear to leave the steps. As I hovered there, I heard the scratching of the rats. So many of them. I could almost feel their whiskered breath on my legs.

"Mary, mother of God, protect me," I said aloud. But my voice broke. I was a small and puny woman, standing on the threshold of evil.

I took a deep breath. Nonsense. These were mere animals and must be told their place.

I cried, "You will not interfere with me. I am Joanna Stafford, and I will not be stopped!"

I leaped onto the tunnel floor with both feet and willed myself forward, into the blackness, running one hand along the damp, crumbling stone wall, the other stretching forward.

Over and over I said it: "I am Joanna Stafford, and I will *not* be stopped." I'd sickened of the running and hiding and cowering. A new recklessness coursed through my veins.

Three times, running down the black tunnel, my foot touched something alive, a quivering warm body. In each case, I kicked it aside and kept going.

I stumbled onto a step. I didn't even mind the sharp pain in my shin from the fall. It meant I'd reached the end.

I found the correct key and eased the door open a crack. It had to be midnight at least, but warders made rounds all night long. Bess had told me that.

I saw a light shining in the Beauchamp passageway. I pushed open the door a little more. A different man sat in the exact same spot as one had hours earlier—about twenty feet away—with his legs stretched out before him. Between the yeoman warder and me was the stone stairway leading up to my cell. I didn't see how I could make it to those stairs unseen.

I waited, thinking, my fingers pressed to the door, when a sputtering sound made me jump. The door bounced open with a loud creak. I yanked it back and waited, shivering.

But the warder didn't react. I realised why: he was snoring.

I licked my lips and then eased all the way out into the passageway, walking as quietly as I could. One step, then another. He snored again, a deep, wet sound. The man must be ill, snoring like that. His feet shook from the sheer force of it.

I made it to the stairs. My ordeal was almost over.

The winding steps were worn smooth, as I remembered when I

was first brought to Beauchamp Tower. And that was the problem. I'd walked the stairs only once since that May afternoon, and it was trudging behind Bess, not paying close attention to our route. I was concentrating on holding up the bedsheets, trying to pass as Susanna, not on needing to retrace my steps.

Now I didn't know where to go.

Remember, I ordered myself. Remember how many flights you took, where to turn. I shut my eyes tight, then opened them and peered at the circular staircase, going up three levels. My cell was on the second floor, but going in which direction? Each floor had two archways.

I selected the archway on the left of the second-floor landing. Based on everything I could recall, this seemed right.

But it wasn't.

It took me a while to realise, walking down the length of one dimly lit passageway, and then another, that this was wrong. At first I tried to convince myself that I was going the correct way. But a newly painted huge rectangular arch forced me to admit it—I had never seen it before. I doubled back, looking for the circular stairway to begin again. Yet even that was impossible to locate.

I leaned against a wall and pressed my forehead to the stone. My body ached with fatigue; I couldn't remember the last time I'd had something to eat or drink.

But I didn't dare rest for long. A snatch of prayer, and I pushed off from the wall, determined to search again. I walked down a few more dark and silent passageways, fighting down my frustration. I could translate tomes of Latin, speak Spanish and French, do flawless needlework, play music, ride the fields, manage sums, but I'd never possessed a sense of direction. I hadn't had one when I became lost in my uncle's maze long ago, and it was missing now.

I found myself at the end of a long passageway and yanked open the wide door.

The night swooped down to cradle me in its hand.

12

I had stepped outside, onto the castle wall allure that I'd walked every week with the lieutenant.

A thousand stars throbbed in the clear October sky, performing their sombre little dances across the heavens, dances whose design only God could fathom. I took a few steps farther out, turned this way and that, shivering in the cool night breeze. It had been a long time since I saw stars. I took a deep breath—in rushed the damp marshy smell of the Thames, and something acrid, too. What was it? Not a nice smell but familiar, having to do with the river. Finally, I had it: burning eel. Someone had caught eel in nets and cooked them on the riverbank. An enormous fire, too, for the odour to hang in the air this late at night. I never thought I'd savour such a smell; I'd always disliked eel. My throat ached as I realised that this could be my last night sky. More and more, my freedom seemed unlikely.

I found the will to walk back to the door. With a start, I realised it had eased shut behind me without my noticing. And was now locked. I pulled at it, hard. Nothing.

Fighting for calm, I tried the keys one by one. None worked. I ran to the other end, only to find it, too, was locked. Bess had not given me the keys to the allure; no doubt she'd assumed we would never need them.

I was trapped outside on this narrow walkway, hundreds of feet above the ground.

I felt such rage with myself, with my stupidity. I collapsed onto the brick floor of the allure and wrapped my arms around my knees, rocking back and forth, sobbing.

For the first time ever, I flirted with the thought of taking my own life. Of course I recoiled from the greatest mortal sin, as would any Christian. Unforgivable. A purgatory without end. And a disgrace no family could recover from. But my mind kept returning to the possibility. The pain would be brief. I'd finally be free of terror and persecution. Bess would be safe.

In just a few hours, men were coming to break me. And here I was, already broken in spirit. I might as well spare the Duke of Norfolk and his unknown companion the trouble of breaking me in body. I cowered down on the floor for hours, not daring to get back to my feet, for fear I'd hurl myself over the side.

Of course I prayed. But they were feeble pleas. And as with every other desperate prayer I'd murmured since Smithfield, they were met with silence. After the long bout of sobbing finally ended, I slipped into a dull haze. It was too cold and hard there for sleep, although every bone in my body ached with exhaustion.

Out of my haze I heard a volley of soft, sweet cries. It was the river birds greeting one another. I pulled myself up and looked to the east. Yes, the sky was greying toward dawn. More birds called out; they flew overhead. Their wings beat with a rapid *thud, thud, thud.* It touched something in me, these happy creatures, coasting over a prison wall.

I wasn't ready to give up.

My only hope, and it a slim one, was in hiding behind the door. I remembered now that when the lieutenant walked me back and forth, the doors were often propped open on the outside. If that happened today, I could wait until an opportunity presented to slip around and dart to my cell.

I took my position next to the door, on the side I knew it would swing open to. The grey sky turned a sickly orange. The boiling sun was hovering on the edge of the eastern horizon. Already, I felt the chill lessen.

I heard voices, two men coming from the other side of the passageway. I flattened myself. The voices grew louder; keys rattled; the door flew open.

"My wife whelped in three hours," a man said. "It may happen before dinner."

The door slammed into my belly; I covered my mouth to stifle the cry.

A foot kicked something into the bottom of the door. It didn't close.

"Aye, but it doesn't always go so quick," said another man, just inches away. "We could be in for a long wait."

They kept walking. I heard the other door open and shut. And then silence. This was my only chance.

I edged around the door: no one in sight. I ran down the passageway. I could hear the prisoners stirring in their cells. I stalked by a sleepy-eyed servant carrying a basket down one passageway. He didn't say anything to me as I hurried past, looking at the floor.

In a matter of minutes, I'd reached my cell. My hands shook as I searched for the right key. Bess must have supplied this one. At last I found it. I locked the door behind me, and then staggered to my bed. The room spun as I tore off the hood and shoved it under the pallet, next to the keys.

I plunged into nothingness—no dreams, no fear—until I was wakened by a voice. And a pair of hands, shaking me hard.

I opened my eyes to the face of Lady Kingston, in a panic.

"What's wrong, Mistress Stafford?" she pleaded. "Are you ill?"

I shook my head; it was too hard to speak.

"You're so cold, and I swear your dress is damp—how is this possible? Jesu, help us." The pale blue gown she wore did not flatter; it made her look years older than when I'd last seen her.

She whirled around. "Bess, get the food and wine in her quick." My own Bess came forward, her eyes shining with relief.

Bess silently pressed food on me while Lady Kingston cleaned my face with a warm cloth and then hurried me into a fresh kirtle and brushed my hair. "Why must it be today that they come here, when Queen Jane is brought to bed?" she muttered.

"Oh, it's the queen who is having her child?" I blurted.

"Who else?" Lady Kingston snapped. "Her pains began early yesterday. They say her suffering is profound."

I heard a burst of voices outside. Men approached, a group of them. Strangely, I felt little apprehension. My being able to hurtle from the castle allure to my room this morning without discovery: it was a sign of something. The horse master at Stafford Castle was a gambling man—famous for it. Any sort of card game. "My luck is set to turn," he'd always tell me with a broad wink. Could it be my luck was turning?

The door to my cell swung open, and Sir William Kingston stepped inside. He and his wife caught each other's gaze, and some sort of grimly intricate message hovered between them. She nodded and hurried to his side.

Next to enter the small room was the Duke of Norfolk, dressed not in riding gear this time but in furs, his fingers sparkling with jewelled rings. He barely glanced in my direction; his face was drawn, tense.

My pulse quickened as the third man strode into my cell. He was perhaps forty years old. He wore long, spotless white robes and a black cap on his dark hair, neatly trimmed and tinged with grey. His light-hazel eyes gleamed under dark brows; his nose was long, and his lips were full. A man neither tall nor short, not handsome nor ugly.

The man looked at me as if there was no one else in the room. Something quivered under his placid features; if I had to define it, I would say *excitement.*

The Duke of Norfolk cleared his throat.

"Mistress Stafford, this is the Bishop of Winchester," he said. "He has questions to put before you."

I dropped a grave curtsy.

The bishop turned to Norfolk and, to my amazement, patted him on the arm. "No need to stay, Thomas," he said in a low, pleasant voice. "I know you have urgent business to attend to." Norfolk nodded and left. The bishop gestured—a touch imperiously, I thought—toward the Kingstons, and Bess in the corner. "All of you may go. I will proceed alone. It will be more efficient."

One by one, they shuffled out.

He turned and smiled at me—a quick, cool smile. "My given name is Stephen Gardiner, Sister Joanna," he said. "I attended court for years, but I do not believe we have ever met."

I shook my head. It was such a relief to hear my priory name once more. Perhaps because I was only a novice, no one had used it in the Tower.

Bishop Gardiner took a step closer, examining me. "You do appear quite weary, Sister. You're not ill, I hope? There is sweating sickness in the city. If you've been exposed to any sort of contagion, after all of my instructions, there will be consequences."

He hadn't raised his voice. Yet that very reasonableness—the calm, measured way he spoke—gave me pause.

"I am well enough," I said.

"I realise this has not been easy for you in the Tower." He sighed. "There wasn't any way around it. I could not get to London before now. Only the birth of the king's heir was an important enough reason for me to beg leave from my duties in France."

"So I have been kept here, all these months, without anyone else questioning me, because we must wait for you to return to England?" I asked, confused.

He didn't answer.

"Were you the one who paid for my food all these months?"

The Bishop of Winchester closed his eyes and nodded, very slightly. Just once.

I felt my knees buckle, and I knelt before him, my hands clasped. "Bishop Gardiner, please believe me. I am not guilty of any crime against the king. I loved my cousin, Margaret Bulmer, and only sought to honour our bond of family by attending her execution. I have never plotted against His Highness. I took the Oath of Supremacy. I am a true, loyal subject."

The bishop leaned down, and I felt his hands, cool and smooth, rest on my shoulders. "I know that," he said.

His hands moved to my hair; he stroked my black tresses, fastened at the nape of my neck. Though there was no lechery to it, I felt my skin crawl. He touched me like a sportsman petting his prized greyhound.

"I wonder," he mused, "will you be the snare that pulls me down?"

13

I sat on the chair of my cell, where I had been told to sit. Bishop Gardiner stood over me, his hands cupped. I couldn't help but stare—I'd never seen such long fingers on a man. He began to tap his two forefingers against each other. He didn't say anything. Simply kept tapping.

"Bishop Gardiner?" I ventured.

"You'd like to see your father, Sir Richard Stafford."

It was as if he'd plucked the thought from my head.

"Oh, yes, yes, I would, I—very much," I stammered. "Would it be possible, Bishop?"

"When you see him and in what manner, that depends on you, Sister Joanna," he said. "It all depends on you." Again, I noticed beneath his placid demeanour an excitement, tightly harnessed.

He tapped his fingers three more times. "Tell me everything that you know about myself."

That was unexpected . . . and difficult. If only I'd listened to more of the gossip at Stafford Castle about the men of the king's council. They all blurred for me, whether they be men of the cloth or noblemen, soldiers or secretaries. I knew that Gardiner was ordained when the true faith was unpolluted in England; he was not a heretical bishop. But still, he was the king's trusted adviser and an ally of the Duke of Norfolk. There was every reason for caution.

"You were Cardinal Wolsey's man in the beginning. You served under him, and after the cardinal was . . ." I struggled to remember the sequence of events.

"Banished by the king, stripped of power, and arrested for treason?" offered Bishop Gardiner, his voice cool.

"Yes, yes, after the cardinal was . . . gone, then you became important to the king." I felt my face redden; I couldn't recall the details, and I hated sounding so ignorant. "The king made you Bishop of Winchester and a member of his council. And now you are his principal ambassador in France."

The bishop flashed a tight smile. "That is all you know of me? I confess to being somewhat surprised."

"I'm not a political person," I muttered.

"But I am, Sister Joanna. I was at Cambridge, you see. I'd been there for seven years when I left to become Wolsey's new secretary. I still remember the night before he arrived, to interview the men who qualified for the position. I wanted to be selected so badly. I did not sleep for even an hour. And then . . . it came about. Cardinal Wolsey saw at once the promise in me. He knew I could go far."

Emotion crept into his voice. The words were proud, but there was something else. Could it be a trace of shame? I felt as if I were eavesdropping on him in the confessional.

"I rose very quickly in the cardinal's service," he continued. "It was because of my knowledge of the law. I was a lawyer and a teacher, a respected legal scholar. In that capacity, I travelled to Paris and to Rome. I have been to Rome five times since, spent many hours in the papal archives."

He paused, as if to let the significance of that fact sink in. I shifted in my chair, uneasy. I could not imagine how his past travel—or anything of his background—could pertain to my interrogation.

"No one in England has a deeper knowledge of canon and civil law than I do. That's why I proved so useful. The king wanted a divorce from Katherine of Aragon and the pope denied him. So His Majesty turned to the law of the land. I was the one who could supply him with legal . . . solutions. I argued the king's case before Pope Clement himself."

Now a chill rippled through me. The king's divorce from Katherine of Aragon was what sent our country hurtling down its path to chaos, and I was in the presence of one of its architects.

"How easy your face is to read, Sister Joanna. You look at me as if I were Lucifer himself."

Embarrassed, I stared at the floor.

"I know that you served Katherine of Aragon after the divorce, in the last month of her life, as one of her ladies." He sighed. "No, you could never understand my actions. It's unfair of me to expect it. Let us just leave it at this: I serve the House of Tudor." There was a ferocious edge to the way he said *Tudor*.

Bishop Gardiner tapped those long fingers, three times, more rapidly than before.

"You are not terribly knowledgeable about events of the day, so let's talk about the past, shall we? Do you know history? English history?"

I nodded.

"Do you know of Edward the Third? His son, the Black Prince? How about Richard the Lionhearted? Or our king's dead brother, Prince Arthur?"

Hearing this list, I wondered, for the first time, about Bishop Gardiner's state of mind.

"Do you know of those men, Sister Joanna?" he repeated, enunciating each word as if I were slow-witted. "Please answer me."

"Yes. But what bearing have they?"

"Edward the Third founded your priory almost two hundred years ago—surely you are aware of that."

"Yes, Bishop," I said.

"It was of vital importance to him that an order of nuns be founded close to London, near the court. And not just any order. They must be Dominicans. Why did he wish to found the first Dominican convent in England?"

I tried to remember what I'd been told at Dartford. "Because the Dominicans are a very holy order, dedicated to spreading God's word and living in commitment."

Bishop Gardiner smiled. "Some things do not change, even now. The young novices at a Dominican Order are instilled with such pride."

I flushed. Pride was a sin. "Forgive me, Bishop Gardiner."

"No, no, it does your prioress credit." He continued with his saga. "Queen Eleanor of Castile, wife of the first Edward, sought to establish a nunnery at Dartford. But it was not until her grandson, Edward the Third, took up the cause that ground was broken. He paid for the construction from his own privy purse. He insisted that four senior

Dominican nuns be brought from France to be the founding sisters of Dartford. The intensity of his involvement was thought peculiar at the time. His oldest son and heir, Prince Edward, the Black Prince, was dying. England had just lost a war with France. Parliament had refused a bill of taxeation. And yet he was interested in establishing Dartford Priory. More than 'interested.' Obsessed with it. Foreign ambassadors made note of it in their posts home. Can you explain this?"

"No."

"Many of our monasteries and priories house holy relics, Sister Joanna. Yet Dartford does not, neither for the comfort of its sisters nor for the public to make pilgrimages to. Is that correct?"

"Yes, that is correct." I rubbed my eyes, weary and confused.

"Sister Joanna, you have heard of nothing that exists at Dartford that is of great value, that was housed at the priory at the time of its founding by Edward the Third?"

"No."

Bishop Gardiner bent down, closer to me, his eyes searching mine. "Are you sure? Absolutely sure there is nothing the priory has that is special?"

Again, I groped for an answer. "Dartford is famous for its tapestries. The sisters have done exceptionally fine work for generations."

Bishop Gardiner's mouth quivered. In just a few seconds, his entire face turned deep red. A vein bulged on the side of his neck. Grabbing my forearms with both hands, he said in a completely different voice, a rough one: "Do you think that I have come all this way and gone to all this trouble for *tapestries*?"

I was too shocked by his transformation to answer.

He tightened his grip on me and hissed, "Sister Joanna, have you seen the Athelstan crown?"

My stomach clenched. I tried to force a blank expression onto my face, but I could tell from his excitement that it was too late.

He let go of my arm and laughed—a high-pitched, triumphant whoop. "You *have* seen it; you know about it. I was right. I was *right.* The crown's hidden at Dartford. Oh, thank Christ in His mercy, I was right."

He rubbed his hands with glee. "When I heard that a Dartford novice had been taken to the Tower, a Stafford who served Katherine of Aragon—a girl who withstood blows from Norfolk and then asked for the works of Saint Thomas Aquinas—I knew it. I knew I'd found my instrument."

Bishop Gardiner dropped to his knees and folded his hands in prayer. "I thank you, O Lord, for your mercy and your forgiveness. All will be restored and made right in your sight."

He opened his eyes and got back on his feet, meticulously brushing the floor's dirt from his white robes.

"Now, Sister Joanna, you will tell me where to find the Athelstan crown."

"I'm sorry," I said calmly. "But I don't know anything about it."

"Yes, you do," he countered. "It's quite obvious you do. Remember, I was trained as a lawyer. I perceive when people are lying to me, particularly those unpractised in deceit, such as you."

I shook my head.

His expression of triumph faded. "Sister Joanna, I am doing this to help you, to help all of you."

No you are not, I said to myself. *I will never tell you anything.*

"Where is the Athelstan crown?" he repeated.

"I don't know."

"Who spoke of it at Dartford Priory?"

"No one."

He took a deep breath; I could tell he was fighting for calm. "Sister Joanna, I ask you again, where is the Athelstan crown?"

I raised my chin to look right at him. "Bishop, I swear I don't know, and I swear that no one at Dartford has spoken of it to me. That is the truth."

"Sister Joanna, I cannot spend days at this, when I know that my enemies watch where I go. For the last time, what do you know of the crown at Dartford?"

I stayed mute.

Bishop Gardiner turned his back on me and stalked to the door of my cell. "Let me out!" he shouted. Still facing the door, he said to me, "Remember, what happens to you now is of your own doing."

My stomach clenched again.

The bishop left my cell without a backward glance.

I didn't know who would come for me next nor where I would be taken. But I prayed it would be soon. I sensed a fragmenting within; I feared I could not withstand the spiritual trials of another period of imprisonment. The dark lethargy would claim me forever.

My prayers to God had not been answered for a long time. But in this matter, there was deliverance. Sir William Kingston returned to my cell, alone, within the hour, and said, "Come with me, Sister Joanna."

I followed him without a word. Down the stone staircase, out the door of Beauchamp, and onto the green. The sun was so bright I half stumbled on the front steps, unused to the glare.

Kingston led me to another square stone building at the south end, smaller than the White Tower or Beauchamp.

Once inside, we took steps leading straight down. They opened to a long passageway. At the far end of it stood Bishop Gardiner, his arms folded. He fixed me with a hard, angry stare.

Sir William walked me to my interrogator and bowed before him. "Bishop, I am not comfortable with this course of action," he said in a low voice.

"My authority is high enough for it," said the bishop, annoyed. He thought for a moment, and then shrugged. "If you harbour any doubts, you are free to go. I know it's not your delicate sensibilities but because you fear being blamed for any error in procedure."

Sir William Kingston winced, stung by the barb. His footsteps were quick going back up the stairs, as if he could not get away fast enough.

"Welcome to Bell Tower, Sister Joanna," Bishop Gardiner said harshly. He shoved open a wooden door and beckoned for me to follow. My heart hammering in my chest, I stepped over the threshold.

The room was dim. Two weak candles flickered at the far end. The sun shone outside, but in here it was as dark as the White Tower rooms I'd run through at midnight. I heard a steady dripping, although from where or what, I couldn't tell.

Bishop Gardiner took me by the arm and pulled me farther inside, not gently. My stomach heaved at the smell. No one had bothered to scrub down this chamber with lye before my arrival. It reeked of an overflowing privy and of sickness. As my eyes adjusted, I could make out strange shapes in the room: two long tables and a thick column, wrapped in chains, in the middle.

"It's not a pretty room, is it, Tobias?" asked the bishop. "But one gets used to it."

Something moved to my right. It was a man. He was not tall, and to my horror, he was only half dressed. He wore a pair of dark hose, tied around his waist with a rope, and no shirt. Muscular arms gleamed in the faint light.

"How is our . . . guest?" asked the bishop.

"He's out." Tobias's voice sounded like gravel.

"Ah. Well. You know what to do."

The bishop yanked me toward Tobias, who stood in front of an odd table. The closer I got, I saw it resembled a platform with ropes and pulleys strung across the top.

I stepped even closer—and froze. Behind Tobias, an unconscious man lay on top of the table. His arms were stretched taut above him, tied to one end with straps. His feet were tied to the other. Underneath his back, pushing his midsection up a few inches, were large wooden rollers. I knew this to be a device of torture: the rack.

Tobias picked up a bucket and threw water in the man's face.

He gasped, choked, and turned his head toward us. It was my father, Sir Richard Stafford, tied to the rack.

I heard a long, terrible scream. A woman's scream.

My father looked at me—the scream was mine. A bright purple mark covered the right side of his face, below his cheekbone. He'd been disfigured by the gunpowder explosion at Smithfield.

"Joanna, my God," he cried. "*No. No.*" He struggled to free himself, but his arms and legs moved not an inch. He was strapped in tight.

Bishop Gardiner seized both my arms from behind and pinned them together, holding me close. Pain shot through to the tops of my shoulders. "Sister Joanna, will you tell me what I want to know?" he asked.

Tears poured down my face.

"Get her out of here, you bastards!" shouted my father.

The Bishop of Gardiner held up one finger. "Tobias?"

Tobias reached for a lever and, grunting, pulled it down. The crisscrossed ropes tightened and strained, pulling my father's arms in one direction and his feet in the opposite. His eyes bulged; his mouth flew open in a silent scream.

"Stop, no, stop," I pleaded, wriggling in the bishop's grasp. "I will tell you, but please, I beg you, don't hurt him again."

Bishop Gardiner dragged me toward the door, out of earshot of Tobias. He said: "Tell me about the Athelstan crown now. Or by God, we will tear your father into pieces." Even in this light, I could see his face suffused with scarlet again.

God, forgive me for what I am about to do.

"It was the queen," I blubbered.

"*What?*" the bishop cried.

"Katherine of Aragon. She told me about the Athelstan crown before she died."

Bishop Gardiner's hands dropped to his sides. His face slackened in shock. "Tobias," he choked out, "unstrap her father now."

14

"Drink this wine," Bishop Gardiner ordered.

He had moved me to a room on the main floor of the Bell Tower, one furnished with tables, chairs, and shelves of books.

The vision of my father, disfigured and terrified, stretched taut on the rack, came back to me in searing detail. I felt something nudge my hand. The bishop tried to offer me a goblet. I shrank from him, shuddering.

He sighed and put the wine on the table. I could feel his impatience.

"I will tell you all of it," I whispered. "But I feel sick."

"Close your eyes. Take three deep breaths."

I did as he said; I had no choice.

"Now, Sister Joanna Stafford, start at the beginning. The day you arrived at Kimbolton Castle to wait upon Katherine of Aragon. When was this?"

"The second week of December in 1535," I said. "It rained all that day. My father brought me. The roads were impossible because of the mud. Our horses stopped again and again. If we'd come by wagon or litter, we would have never made it. There was a village nearby, a poor one, and an old woman gave me her blessing when we asked which road to take to the castle. 'God bless our poor Queen Katherine.' I was surprised by that. We'd been told that by the king's orders no one was to address her as queen since the divorce. But the common folk always loved her."

"Quite so," the bishop said dryly. "Continue."

I opened my eyes and went on: "I was surprised, too, by how small Kimbolton Castle was. Just a manor house, not a castle, and built on low ground. It was hard to believe that a queen resided there." I stopped short, afraid that I had erred by giving her that title. But Bishop Gardiner waved me on, to continue.

"The owner of Kimbolton, her keeper Sir Edmund Bedingfield, came out to meet us. We were expected. My father had sent a messenger on ahead that I was coming in my mother's place. Sir Edmund took me to the door that connected his home to the apartments of the queen, and then he withdrew. She would not allow him into her rooms because he addressed her as princess dowager and not queen."

"How many people were with her?"

"She had two ladies-in-waiting, two serving women, her confessor, and her doctor, Don Miguel de la Sa. That's all. The furniture was old. The plates and bowls were cracked. She didn't even have a tapestry on the wall. The queen was in bed and very weak, although she said she was happy to see me. But it was hard. I knew that she was dying—that is why she was permitted to have Spanish attendants again. Her appearance was so altered I would not have known her."

"How so?"

"All of the weight she had lost. Her bones stood out from her body. She was in pain most of the time. Sometimes just drawing breath seemed to hurt . . ."

I faltered at the memory of her sufferings, but a glance at Bishop Gardiner's hard face pushed me on.

"I tried to make the queen as comfortable as I could. It was very cold. No snow. But a damp wind came through the windows, off the fens. We tried to block the cracks around windows and keep the fire high. But it never felt completely dry in that room. I was told there was no help for it.

"One day the Spanish ambassador, Eustace Chapuys, came to visit her. We knew he had been given permission by the king to see her a last time after many months of his pleading. We made her bedchamber as presentable as we could and dressed the queen with all of our care. She didn't have any jewels. They had all been taken from her, given to Anne Boleyn, years before. But we did our best.

"When the ambassador came into the room, she was so happy that she wept. She said, 'Now I can die in your arms, not like a beast alone in a field.' That made me feel ashamed, because I had worked so hard to make her comfortable. But I tried to be happy for her, that someone who had worked so long in her interests had come to visit."

"Were you there during any of their conversations?"

"The first day we were all present. She wanted it made plain that she had nothing to hide from the king's majesty. Even Sir Edmund was asked to attend. The second day only a couple of us were within the distance that they could be heard."

"What did they talk about?" The bishop was very curious.

"Her daughter, the Lady Mary. She was frantic about the princess, about what the king would do to her for refusing to accept the divorce. The ambassador swore that he would do everything in his power to protect her, that the Emperor Charles, his master and her nephew, would keep her safe. He would not stand by to see the princess who was a cousin mistreated."

"And yet she *has* been mistreated, and for years," Bishop Gardiner said in a strange voice.

"Yes, Dr. de la Sa told me that when we were alone. He said that Ambassador Chapuys was not honest about the dangers that the Lady Mary had to face. The anger of the king is death; nothing has ever been more truly said. But the doctor could not blame Ambassador Chapuys, because fear for her daughter tormented the queen. And what could the queen do for her now . . . when she was dying?"

"Continue."

"The ambassador stayed with us for four days. The first two days she seemed stronger, but talking to him drained her, perhaps, for the third day he was with her only a short time. That was the night I spent with her alone."

I stopped, kneading my hands, and glanced up at the bishop again. His eyes gleamed. He knew I neared the telling of the secret.

"After the ambassador bade her farewell the third day, that was when she drifted in her mind. She spoke about her brother, Prince Juan, who died so long ago. She spoke as if he were there with her, doing his lessons as a child. It worried me. I gave her some broth, and she was quiet for a time. And then she began to talk about coming to England when she was fifteen years old, to be married to the Prince of Wales."

He leaned forward. "Leave nothing out. Tell me exactly what happened."

I swallowed. "It was the night Dr. de la Sa overslept. The two of us usually tended her together after nightfall. She spoke Spanish at night, and we were the only ones who understood her. That was when she was the most . . ." I searched for the right word.

"Vulnerable?" he asked.

Again, the bishop had pulled the thought from my mind.

"After I came to Kimbolton, Dr. de la Sa said that one of the two of us must be with the queen at all times. So even though I was weary myself, I sat by the queen's bed and didn't call for anyone else. He slept on and on. I was afraid that if one of the other ladies saw my fatigue, she would insist that I go to bed. I couldn't allow that."

"Why did one of the two of you have to be by her side at all times?"

I was surprised that the bishop needed to ask. "Poison," I answered. "Dr. de la Sa said all of Europe knew the Boleyns were trying to poison the queen. They already tried to poison Fisher, her greatest champion. Not a drop of food or drink could touch the queen's lips that had not been tested in his presence or mine."

"But why did he trust you over the others? Hadn't some of them served the queen far longer than you?"

"Because of my mother—my Spanish blood," I said.

The bishop's eyebrows shot up. "All English are potential poisoners?"

I shrugged. "That is how he felt. That is how my mother felt, too. That the English could never be fully trusted."

"And did you see any sign of poison?" he asked.

"None," I admitted. "And she ate very little anyway."

He nodded. "Tell me about this night when you were alone with her."

"She spoke of King Henry the Seventh, her father-in-law, at first." I paused. "The things she said were not pleasant. It was the first time I ever heard her criticise anyone."

"Don't leave anything out. Do you hear me?"

"I didn't realise she was referring to old King Henry for a time. She spoke of a beggar. She said, 'He was a beggar, a beggar in exile.'

She was quiet, then said, 'No one thought a Tudor could be King of England.' The queen said this three times: 'A beggar cannot be a kind king.'

"She told me that every day he was on the throne he feared losing his riches. Her exact words were: 'He was so cruel and suspicious. He was cruel to his wife and to his sons. Inside, he was twisted. And he twisted his son.'"

"Which son was she referring to?" As we both knew very well, Katherine of Aragon was sent by her parents to marry England's Prince of Wales, to form a dynastic alliance. First she wed Prince Arthur, but he died five months later. Then she married his younger brother, who became Henry the Eighth.

"It was Arthur. She said: 'The prince could not lie with me after we married. He was so afraid of his father. Terrified. He wanted to be a man. That is why he took me to Dartford Priory.'"

I heard Bishop Gardiner's sharp intake of breath. "Those were her words?"

"Yes."

"Then what did the queen say?"

"Not much more. She said, 'The legend was true. Poor Arthur.' She was quiet for a long time; I thought she'd fallen asleep. But she moaned, and then she said so loudly I thought it would wake the ladies in the next room, 'I was wrong. He is worse than the father. Sweet Jesu, protect my daughter.'"

"She spoke of King Henry the Eighth then?"

"I'm not sure. After that she fell asleep."

Bishop Gardiner thought for a moment, his brows creased. "But when did she speak of the Athelstan crown?"

"The night she died. Right after the ambassador left for good, her lady-in-waiting Maria de Salinas finally arrived. She had come to England with her from Spain, as my mother did, and was very close to the queen. But it was then that the queen grew much, much worse. It was almost as if she had been waiting for Maria. Just after midnight, she asked if it was dawn yet. She knew she was dying and wanted to hear a last Mass. Her confessor said we could have a Mass immediately, for her. But she said, 'No, we must wait until dawn.' She quoted scripture to us, about how Mass could never be heard before dawn. The queen was so devout. She wore a hair shirt under her nightdress, from the Order of Saint Francis.

"Those were the longest hours of my life. We prayed together the whole time. We were weeping, although we tried to hide it from her. It was still hours before dawn when she asked me, 'Juana, are you pious?' I said, 'Your Highness, I try to be.' Then she said, 'You are unmarried?' I said, 'Yes.' She was quiet, and then she said, 'You should take vows at Dartford Priory.' She looked at me so intently, and everyone else looked at me, the doctor, Maria de Salinas, her confessor. I said, 'Yes, Madame.' That seemed to give her peace."

Bishop Gardiner stared at me. "So Katherine of Aragon gave you the idea?"

I nodded defiantly. "Yes, she did."

"But the Athelstan crown? You still haven't got to that, Sister."

"It was about an hour later. The queen turned her head a bit, she could hardly move, and she looked at me. I bent down, and she whispered, 'Arthur. Mary. Dartford. The Athelstan crown. Protect my daughter. Promise me, Juana. Protect the secret of the crown for her sake. And tell no one. If you love me, tell no one.'"

I looked at the floor, flooded with anguish.

Bishop Gardiner repeated it: "Arthur. Mary. Dartford. The Athelstan crown. Protect my daughter." He bit his lip, thinking. "No one else heard the queen?"

"They may have, but she spoke in Spanish. The doctor was not close by at that moment, and neither was Maria."

The bishop took a deep breath. "So Katherine of Aragon sent you to Dartford Priory."

"No, she did not *send* me," I said, my voice thick. "She suggested I take vows there. When I returned to Stafford Castle, I began to consider it in seriousness, as a way to find purpose. After a few weeks of prayer, it seemed the right thing to do."

"Did you ever tell your prioress about the Athelstan crown?"

"Of course not."

His questions flew at me.

"Did you never wonder why she wanted you to profess at Dartford in particular?" he demanded.

"I knew that Eleanor of Castile first promoted our existence.

Queen Katherine's mother was Castilian. It made perfect sense to me—the Dominicans originated in Spain, and Queen Katherine was of Spain. Dartford is the only Dominican nunnery in England."

"What did the prioress make of the queen's desire for you to take vows at Dartford?"

"I never told her," I answered.

"Why not?"

I paused, searching for the right words. "To parlay my conversation with the queen in that fashion, with a dying woman, it would seem as if I were trying to draw attention to myself, to put myself in a special light. I wanted to be accepted on my own merits."

Bishop Gardiner stared at me. "You are an unusual person, Sister Joanna."

I had no response to that.

Fatigue was returning; my eyelids felt heavy. From a distance I heard him say, "It is a moment worth recording for posterity, when a question like this one is answered."

"Answered?" I asked dully.

"Yes, I know now that the Athelstan crown exists. And it is at Dartford Priory."

I struggled against my fatigue. "But the queen must have been confused. It's not there. I don't even know what it is. I've never heard anyone there say the words *Athelstan crown.* And I was at Dartford for seven months."

"Katherine of Aragon was an astute and formidable woman, even at the hour of her death. The crown exists. It is carefully hidden and has been for generations. But it won't be for much longer."

"Why do you say that?" I asked, full of dread. "Are you going to Dartford Priory?"

A grim laugh from Bishop Gardiner. "With Cromwell's spies everywhere, watching everything I do? I think not."

His eyes settled on me.

"No, Sister Joanna, I'm not going to find the Athelstan crown. You are."

15

It's not prudent to laugh at a man. And most assuredly not prudent to laugh at Stephen Gardiner, the Bishop of Winchester, who had demonstrated within the past hour that he was no stranger to torture. But what he had said was so absurd, I couldn't help it.

"Do you think that I can walk into Dartford Priory and start opening drawers—peer into the dark corners?" I asked, breathless. "I broke my vows to go to Smithfield; I have been imprisoned here in the Tower since May. I'm forever disgraced."

The bishop did not take offence.

"Don't you want to return . . . to be a novice again?" he asked quietly.

"Even if I did, it would not be possible."

"Sister Joanna, you insist on underestimating me. I am the Bishop of Winchester. I have only to write the letter to your prioress, and you will be restored without question."

I shook my head. "The Dominican Order does not answer to an English bishop."

Now it was his turn to laugh. "All of you, including your prioress, took an Oath of Supremacy, to obey King Henry the Eighth, as head of the Church in England. I am his representative. The Prioress of Dartford has no choice but to submit to me."

Excitement stirred in my belly at the thought of resuming my life at Dartford. *One heart and one soul seeking God.* Those were the words of Saint Augustine, so many centuries ago, when he founded the first religious community. Prioress Elizabeth repeated them to me that first afternoon, when I sat, nervous, in her office. It was such a simple creed and so true. I heard the singing, smelled the incense clouds, felt the silks in my fingers at the tapestry loom. It was hard to fight down the longing to experience those sensations again.

"I could never do anything to harm my order," I muttered.

Bishop Gardiner slapped the table. "You still distrust me?"

"There can never be trust between us," I said. "You had my father *tortured*."

"I don't want to hurt anyone," he said. "You are the one who forced that encounter. I am doing what I have to do in order to save the monasteries from destruction. I am responsible for thousands of souls."

"But the king is not proceeding any further," I said, bewildered. "He suppressed the smaller abbeys and priories, or the ones that had fallen into disarray. But the larger houses—they are safe. My prioress told us that they could *never* be closed down. It's not possible."

Bishop Gardiner's smile was bitter. "Do you think, Sister Joanna, that having added the income of the sale of those small houses, those worth two hundred pounds or less, to the royal treasury, that Master Cromwell will halt? That he does not hunger for the destruction of the larger houses? To gain centuries' worth of riches at a time when the royal treasury is close to empty?"

I swallowed. Such evil lay beyond my imagination. "But how could finding a crown stop Cromwell and the king, if they be so determined? I don't even know what it is. A crown of the king's?"

"No Tudor has ever worn this crown—nor any Plantagenet, for that matter."

"Is it a relic?" I asked.

Bishop Gardiner smiled, though it was closer to a grimace. "You have a nimble mind, Sister Joanna." He walked over to the other end of the room. The sunlight pouring through the mullioned window bathed his face.

"It is more than a relic," he said softly.

"More?" I didn't understand.

"Cromwell and his minion Richard Rich and the other heretics—they sit in their chambers and make mockery of the holy relics, the shrines, the saints' days. They call it superstition and work day and night to sweep the Catholic Church away. But the Athelstan crown could not be swept away. It could not be denied. If I had it in my possession, I could put pressure on Cromwell to stop his destruction."

The bishop tapped his long fingers. I waited. I saw he was struggling with how much to tell me, and I would not hurry him. Near me stood a shelf of newly bound books. I studied the words on their bindings. A handsome new crimson one was engraved with the words *The Prince.*

"There is more to the Athelstan crown than its place in history," he said finally. "Recall what Katherine of Aragon said."

"'The legend is true,'" I whispered. "So there is a legend to it?"

The bishop's face went white. "Yes. And there is prophecy. A prophecy of great reward but not without great risk. It is both blessing and curse. It has a power, Sister Joanna, that has never been unleashed, for if it were, it would change the lives of every man, woman, and child living in England—and beyond."

My skin prickled with fear.

"Is that why it must be hidden?" I asked.

A sharp banging at the door made us both jump. The bishop laughed a little, laid a hand on my shoulder, as if to steady us both. The touch of his hand made me shudder. He did not notice.

The young lieutenant was at the door.

"Bishop Gardiner, your secretary is here with two friars," he said.

"Ah, yes!" He turned toward me. "There is much to do. Wait here."

He shut the door behind him.

For months I'd seen not a single friar, monk, or nun. Curious, I peered outside the window. Bishop Gardiner talked to three men on the green. One, a young priest, clutched documents; I assumed he was the secretary. The two other men wore belted white gowns, covered by black cloaks, hoods gathered at their shoulders: the habit of the Dominican Order. One friar was tall, thin, and fair; the other was stouter and much darker. They both looked to be about thirty years of age—far younger than the decrepit friars I was accustomed to seeing at Dartford Priory. While Bishop Gardiner talked animatedly, his teeth flashing in the sun, they listened, hands folded, heads tilted with respect.

After a time the bishop ushered the friars inside Bell Tower, to the room where I waited.

"This is Sister Joanna Stafford, novice at Dartford Priory," he said with a grand gesture, as if I were a new painting he'd commissioned.

The two friars looked at me doubtfully. I wore no novice habit.

The bishop said, "I present to you Brother Edmund." The fair one bowed his head, with grace. "And Brother Richard." The dark one bowed slightly. His eyes were cold, speculative.

"You will leave in an hour," Bishop Gardiner told them. "I am having food brought in for you first. You must eat before the journey."

The bishop turned toward me. "Dartford is blessed to have the services of these brothers."

"Dartford?" I cried.

"They have been valued members of the Dominican community at Cambridge, which Cromwell has ordered to be suppressed." Brother Richard winced at the word *suppressed*. Brother Edmund's pale face showed no reaction. Gardiner continued: "It has been in the works for some months now, to transfer them to Dartford. Up to now, your priory has housed a few friars from Kings Langley Abbey to officiate over Mass, to manage the sisters' finances, and to perform other administrative duties. One of the brothers is sick with dropsy, correct?"

I nodded, taken aback that poor old Brother George's ailment was so widely known.

"He has been recalled to Kings Langley, to Hertfordshire. Brother Richard will take his place as president and steward. Brother Edmund has skills as an apothecary. Your village infirmary will be transformed by him."

The door behind Bishop Gardiner swung open, and Bess appeared with another maid, carrying trays of food.

"Excellent." The bishop beamed. "Sister Joanna, it is essential that you eat, too. I calculate your arrival at Dartford at just after sunset, and you can't be sure of a late meal there."

I gripped the chair I stood behind. "I am going to Dartford tonight?"

"All three of you are."

"But the prioress does not know of this." I sounded panicked.

"A message went by fastest horse ten minutes ago, informing her of your release and that you would be accompanying these good friars," he said smoothly. "The roads are dry. The message will precede you by two hours. Now, please sit."

I fell into the chair pulled up to a table.

Bess laid out food: platters of meat tiles, strips of dried cod, and bread. The rich smell of the tiles—made of chicken, crawfish tail, and almonds—filled the room. Brother Richard fell on it as if it were the first meal he'd consumed in days, while Brother Edmund ate little.

Bess looked around to make sure no one was watching her, and then flashed me an excited smile. To her, this must be joyous news—not only was I being released but I was also being restored to my former life. I wondered what she'd think if she knew I'd broken a deathbed promise of silence to Queen Katherine of Aragon and agreed to go to Dartford in order to betray a prioress's trust.

But wait—when had I agreed to anything?

My thoughts churning, I sipped the warm spiced wine Bess had poured and ate a piece of meat tile—I hadn't tasted anything like this in many months. We had meat only on feast days at Dartford, and then it was meat pudding.

Bishop Gardiner stood at the head of the table and nibbled a cod strip while talking to the friars of Cambridge. He asked for details of a new printing press, then for news of the head of the university. After Brother Richard told a long gossipy story, the bishop threw back his head and laughed, "Ah, how I've missed Dominican arrogance." Brother Richard smiled up at him. Bishop Gardiner seemed very much at ease with the friars. "He favours the old ways," Charles Howard had told me. No one seeing this would argue it.

I felt someone watching me watch Bishop Gardiner. It was Brother Edmund: his large brown eyes made for an odd contrast with his ash-blonde hair. Suddenly, I had a curious feeling of recognition. Had I seen him somewhere before?

Gardiner held up a lettuce leaf and announced, "When I was a boy student, boarded in Paris, Erasmus stayed in the same house for a week. I took it upon myself to help serve him his food. He favoured lettuce—how I slaved over it, dressing it with butter and sour wine. He said he had never enjoyed a dish more daintily served."

Brother Richard drew back in his chair. "And you have no regrets, waiting on Erasmus with such solicitous care?"

Gardiner shook his head. "I know what you're about to say—that

Erasmus lit the torch that Luther made to blaze. But it's much more complicated than that."

There was a noise in the doorway. The lieutenant stood there, glaring at all of us. His eyes lingered on the tonsured heads of the friars. To him, this convivial gathering was something repulsive.

He walked in the room, reluctantly, and thrust a parcel in my hand, then turned on his heel and left. Bishop Gardiner's narrowed eyes tracked his every move.

The parcel contained the books I'd been given, the tomes of Thomas Aquinas. Something else fell out, too: the purse I'd brought with me to Smithfield, with my small jewels and trinkets. My heart in my throat, I fished out the pendant of Thomas Becket and wrapped it around my wrist.

Bishop Gardiner's secretary reappeared, and they spoke in low tones, at the other corner of the room, as the friars finished their meal.

Bess was clearing dishes from the table, placing them on her wooden tray, when I pulled on her sleeve. I slipped the purse containing the jewels onto her tray. Bess looked at it and then at me, her face a question.

"Remember me," I whispered.

"The Virgin Mary will protect you," Bess whispered back. I watched her strong, solid back retreat from the room and knew I could never forget her.

Bishop Gardiner took charge. The friars were ushered out by his secretary, to be taken to a waiting wagon. I would follow, he said, after a few final words. He drew me into the corner of the room where he'd whispered with his secretary.

"Be careful how you proceed, Sister Joanna," he said. "You must use subtlety to ascertain location. Do not draw attention to yourself with obvious searching. It is very important you tell no one of my charge. Not your prioress, nor the sisters, nor the friars I send you with. Absolutely no one. Once you learn where the Athelstan crown is located, communicate that to me alone, in writing. You must *not* touch it yourself, not even for an instant. You understand?"

I frowned and said, "We are not permitted to write letters or receive them except by permission of the prioress, who may read all correspondence."

"I am aware of that. Arrangements have been made. Adjoining Dartford land, to the northwest, is a leper hospital, one that was abandoned years ago, correct?"

"Yes."

"Next to the main door is a window, facing east. You will find along its side an opening, a stone cavity where letters can be safely concealed."

I was stunned at his detailed knowledge of this obscure building. Someone familiar with Dartford Priory—the land and properties—must have fed him information, I realised. They knew exactly what lay outside Dartford, but evidently could not get inside. Not without me.

"I must return to France directly after the christening of the king's heir, should the child survive. The queen suffers greatly and seems no closer to delivery, poor woman." He grimaced.

I hadn't thought him capable of sympathy for a woman's pain. My surprise must have registered on my face. He said, "I performed the wedding ceremony for His Majesty and the Lady Jane Seymour. She is a good Christian woman. Now . . . to business. I will expect correspondence from you every fortnight, Sister, apprising me of your progress. We don't have much time. I just learned that Cromwell's commissioners are set to begin another round of visitations of the remaining priories and abbeys. They start in Wales and work their way east. They aren't expected in Dartford until after the new year. We must find the crown before they arrive."

I shook my head. "But Cromwell's men visited Dartford before I came, two years ago. The prioress told them nothing of any crown then, I am certain. Why would she do different this time?"

"Cromwell's commissioners have been very thorough in their inventory of monastic property, mistress. It is assumed they make such record for reasons of greed—so the Lord Privy Seal knows where the opportunities for ripest plunder are. But there could be another agenda."

After a few seconds I made the connection and was filled with horror. "The visitations of the monasteries—are they but a pretext for Cromwell to have the monasteries searched for the crown?"

Gardiner winced. "The purposes of King Henry are hidden within each other, one feeding another—and yet another. No one understands Henry Tudor, and absolutely no one can predict his actions. Not even Cromwell."

"And the king knows about the existence of the crown and that it contains a mystical power?"

"It is possible. His Majesty couldn't know it is in Dartford, or else he would have brought down the priory years ago, every single brick." I shuddered. "He may know that it exists, but not where it is kept. Still, just as I have secured the ways and means to quietly search for it"—he gestured toward me—"Cromwell may have, too. In fact, I've received a disquieting report that he is up to something at Dartford. That is why I *must* be first. You cannot disappoint me, Sister Joanna."

"And if I do?" I swallowed. "You won't hurt my father again?"

"Your father will be released from the Tower of London on the day I learn from you the location of the crown," he said quickly.

I took a step closer, peered into the bishop's light-hazel eyes. "But if I fail . . . you won't hurt him?"

"You may have success before All Souls' Day—that's just over a fortnight from now. I have heard that each Prioress of Dartford writes a letter for her successor, to be read by that successor alone. Your prioress is very old. She must have already written her letter, and within it there must be indication of the crown's location."

My voice steady, I said, "Bishop, I must ask you again, and this time I require an answer. Is my father safe from further harm at your hands?"

His eyes locked into mine.

"Make sure your first letter is in place by All Souls' Day," he said. And with that he brushed past me, to Sir William Kingston, waiting outside the room.

At that moment, I hated Stephen Gardiner, Bishop of Winchester, and during my life I'd already had good cause for hate. But he took precedence above all. My body trembled with the violent, impotent force of it.

Across the room, Sir William, his face a careful mask, handed Gardiner a paper, and the bishop signed it, saying, "I see Thomas has already signed. Where is Norfolk?"

"He is kept busy, Bishop. His youngest brother died in the White Tower this very morning, and arrangements must be made."

I couldn't stop it. A noise escaped me, a low moan of grief. No one heard me, no one cared about dead Charles Howard.

Kingston beckoned to me and held open the door.

"Joanna Stafford," he said, "I release you from the Tower."

With my Thomas Aquinas tucked under my arm and my Thomas Becket pendant wrapped around my wrist, I left Bell Tower and walked onto the green, where the late-afternoon sun slanted through the branches of the mulberry trees.

PART TWO

16

"Friar, won't you buy an apple?"

The boy, no more than seven years old, stood in the middle of Watling Street, holding up his apple to Brother Richard. Even in the gathering dusk, the piece of fruit gleamed; it was a deep, luscious red.

London lay safely behind us. It was past Michaelmas; the wheat and barley fields were stripped of harvest. Apple trees hugged the west side of the road to Dartford, the road that stretched from London all the way to Dover. I sucked in the scent of their heavy sweetness. It all felt unreal, a dream of delirium, that I rode free through the countryside, hours after being imprisoned in the Tower of London.

The trees' branches were skimpy of fruit close to the ground, but higher up, where a nimble boy could climb, the red globes hung more thickly. I saw the boy sitting under the largest tree, his feet sticking out into the road, when our wagon rounded a bend. He scrambled out to Brother Richard to peddle his wares.

The child's eyes, though, were not on the man but on his horse. At the Tower, when I'd been led to the waiting friars and a wagon, Brother Richard already sat tall on one of the finest horses I'd ever seen: a slim dappled grey, with a glossy coat and bright eyes. Brother Richard made it clear that not only did the mare belong to him, but he would not tie her to our wagon, pulled by less aristocratic steeds. Sweeping his black Dominican cape to the side, he'd vaulted into the saddle and seized the reins, ready to ride to Dartford. Brother Edmund and I, it seemed, would follow, sitting in the back of the wagon, driven by a rotund Tower servant.

The boy said eagerly, "We grow the best apples in Kent, Friar—I'll sell you a basket for three farthings."

"Be off with you!" snapped Brother Richard, untempted.

The boy's thin shoulders sagged, and he shuffled back to his place under the tree. Certainly, this was not the time to buy fruit, but Brother Richard's rebuff seemed to me over rude. I sneaked a sideways glance at Brother Edmund, who hadn't spoken since we left the Tower of London.

The fair-haired friar nodded, as if he'd heard my thought.

"This is a very hard thing for Brother Richard, the suppression of our friary," he said quietly.

"But he has a place to go to," I pointed out.

"Yes, and we are both grateful for the arrangements made by Bishop Gardiner, to have us transferred to Dartford Priory." He paused, weighing his next words. "But what you must understand is that some day Brother Richard was expected to make prior at Cambridge. He boarded there as a child, professed as soon as he came of age, and was extremely dedicated. He's a true theologian; he's published works read on the Continent."

I looked at Brother Richard doubtfully. A sharp tongue did not always lead to a sharp mind, in my experience.

And then there was the trunk.

Two trunks rode in the back of the wagon. One was small and weather-beaten—it contained Brother Edmund's apothecary supplies. The other was large and burgundy, with a gold-plated lock and trimming. It belonged to Brother Richard, but I couldn't imagine what was inside. The rules of Dominican conduct were chastity, humility, obedience, and *poverty*. Perhaps in Cambridge they'd followed different rules.

"And for you, Brother Edmund, is this . . . difficult?" I asked.

"I am a friar, I serve God wherever I go," he replied. "And it means I will share a roof again with my younger sister, Winifred."

That is why he looked familiar. He shared the same unusual colouring—ash-blonde hair and brown eyes—as my fellow novice and friend, Sister Winifred. "She will be very pleased to see you," I said. "She once told me that she had a brother who was a friar and that she missed him."

"I have missed her, too," he said. "Though I hoped to one day make her proud of what I had achieved in the eyes of God, not to come crawling to her priory as a supplicant."

The words were bitter. Yet Brother Edmund's face was calm. In fact, his large dark eyes looked positively serene. It was impressive—though a trifle strange—how the friar managed to control himself.

"In any case," he continued, "if we need be sent to a nunnery, Dartford is a prestigious one. Brother Richard's administrative skills will be put to use managing the priory's wealth."

"Wealth?"

"It is the seventh richest establishment in all of England—you didn't know that?"

I shook my head no.

"Brother Richard says it is because of the original charter granted by Edward the Third. The priory is exempt from all taxees *and* is granted one hundred pounds a year. He told me Dartford is a substantial landholder in Kent. Not just open farmland but income from mills, businesses, manors, even quarries. The priory has holdings in London, too. He said he'd never in his life seen such care taken by a king to ensure financial security for a religious house."

"We are most fortunate," I muttered.

Our road curved, and I caught a glimpse of the River Darent. Our wagon rumbled on, and a large black building came into view—it was the Lowfield Almshouse for the poor, which our prioress oversaw and visited at least once a week. We'd reached the outskirts of the town of Dartford.

Even though the evening air had turned cool, my palms felt hot, itchy and moist. This was happening so fast. I'd be face-to-face with Prioress Elizabeth and all the sisters within minutes. What would I say to them? What had Bishop Gardiner already told them in the letter that preceded me?

When she was angry or dismayed, Prioress Elizabeth would look away from the object of her disappointment, as if the sight of that person was too painful. She'd purse her lips, fold her hands. She never stayed angry for long. How long before she would look at me again with those wise, kind eyes? I longed for her forgiveness, even though I had no right to expect it.

I thought of the sisters, too—of the gossipy novice mistress, Sister Agatha, and the silent tapestry mistress, Sister Helen. I was closest to the other novices, naturally. Sister Winifred, whose brother

I sat next to, was one of the kindest people I'd ever known, as selfless as my cousin Margaret. Sister Christina, the senior novice of the three of us, had her turbulent moments. For that very reason, I felt even closer to her; we shared certain unspoken understandings. She, too, came from an old family. Her father, Lord Chester, was a wealthy Kent landowner who had for years been a favoured hunting companion of the king's; her mother was a Neville, a family as respected as the Staffords.

Brother Richard turned around on his horse, smiling. "Pilgrims ahead!" he called out.

Along the side of the road, three figures walked single file, dressed in long coarse robes. As we grew closer, I could see they were barefoot.

Brother Edmund looked at me inquiringly.

I said, "There are many pilgrims who stop at Dartford on their way to the shrines at Rochester and Canterbury." I pointed to a distant line of treetops, above which peeked a row of tall, whitewashed buildings. "Those are the inns where they stay."

Brother Richard called out to the pilgrims, addressing the tallest. But the man did not answer. The second pilgrim turned to make explanation: "Brother, I'm sorry, but my father does not speak," he said in a high, polite voice, that of a boy no older than twelve. "We are on the road to the shrine of Saint William of Rochester, he will speak there, to beg for forgiveness for his sins."

Brother Richard cocked his head. "Sins?"

"We lost our mother to plague this year, and the harvest was so poor we may lose our farm. My father fears he sinned greatly to have earned God's displeasure."

"I pray you find the blessed mercies you seek," said Brother Richard. He turned back on his horse and said to Brother Edmund, excitedly, "Did you hear that? They do believe in the shrines. Christ still moves among the people!"

Brother Edmund nodded, his large brown eyes so placid yet impenetrable they looked like gemstones.

The friars puzzled me. I wondered why Bishop Gardiner plucked these two from Cambridge for salvation. Could it be a coincidence that he chose Dartford as their destination? It was true that we were the only Dominican nunnery in England, and other abbeys were likely full to bursting with friars. Dominicans could serve only next to their own kind. I had been ordered not to discuss the Athelstan crown with either of them, and I had no intention of doing so. But how could I be sure they didn't know something—even if it were an inkling—of my mission?

My mission. It felt impossible. The bishop instructed me to use "subtlety." I wasn't a particularly subtle woman. My emotions always showed on my face, and even when I was a child, I'd never been good at deception. I once read a story about a female spy in Rome, during the time of the Borgias. After failing to break the secret codes contained in a letter she'd stolen from a wicked cardinal, she was about to drink a vial of poison—only to be rescued by a husband who'd escaped from prison. This silly book was the extent of my knowledge of spy craft. Real spies existed, I was aware of that. Privy Seal Thomas Cromwell was notorious for his network of operatives. It was said that one of the reasons he looted the monasteries was for the gold needed to bind all men to him. From lowly pages to foreign ambassadors, they secretly worked in his service. As I secretly worked for Bishop Gardiner. I bowed my head. *But not for money*, I told myself fiercely. *For the life of my father.*

The wagon slowed. Ahead lay the centre of the village: the inns, the tall parish church, a thriving market, dozens of shops—bakers, tanners, butchers, tailors—and a few small shipping firms. But we wouldn't be going into the village. Dartford Priory lay just north of the village. The narrow road I knew so well emerged from between two graceful elm trees.

Just as the driver pulled on the reins to turn, I heard bells. Very faint. I hardly paid them any mind. But they kept pealing . . . and pealing. I'd never heard bells ring that long. Our wagon had started up the priory road, and still the bells pealed. Brother Richard noticed it, too, and held up his hand. We halted . . . and listened. After a minute there were yet more bells, and louder, layered onto the first set. It was as if the orders to ring started far away, and then other churches, ones that were closer to Dartford, pulled the ropes to their bells, too.

"The bells mean it's a son," Brother Richard cried.

We all crossed ourselves, even the wagon driver.

"It's a sign from God that He blesses *this* marriage, don't you see?" Brother Richard exulted. "The queen will be able to help us now!"

He kicked his horse, to hurry up the road to Dartford. I looked to Brother Edmund for an explanation. He glanced at the cart driver and then said in a low voice, "The queen favours the old ways; she supports the monasteries. But when she tried to intervene late last year, to ask that we be spared, the king ordered her to be silent. With a prince on her lap, she could become a respected adviser."

I nodded, though it all seemed unlikely. Would this king listen to any woman, for any reason? I spared a quiet prayer for Katherine of Aragon's daughter, the Lady Mary. She was five years younger than me, motherless, declared illegitimate by her father, and now officially displaced by a prince. The king might not consider Mary—or Anne Boleyn's girl, Elizabeth—a fit heir. But in Spain, women could rule in their own right. Katherine of Aragon's mother, Queen Isabella, was but one example. On this island, sadly, a female still meant very little.

Our wagon resumed its journey up the lane to the priory. The sun had just fallen in the sky. It was high dusk: violet light bathed the open fields to our left. I craned my neck, anxious to see the priory, but a grove of trees blocked my line of sight.

Brother Richard, out front, glimpsed Dartford first. I saw him freeze in the saddle. Yes, even he would be impressed.

The wagon cleared the grove of trees, and, rising above the stone walls encircling it, I saw my home.

The first thing that always struck me was the priory's size: the tall, square front walls. It wasn't grim or imposing, though. The walls were a creamy light grey, made of Kentish ragstone. But what always moved me was the symmetry of the design, its confident elegance. Four large carved crests of the Dominican Order stood out along the top of the wall. There wasn't quite enough light to decipher their faces now, but I knew the design by heart. Black-and-white shields represented joy and penance. On those shields bloomed lilies, the symbols of our faith.

The cruciform church rose from behind the front wall, from the centre; the last dying rays of light reflected off the triangles of stained glass. Smaller buildings spread behind: the friars' quarters, the stables and brewery. All perfectly balanced. It would always be the most beautiful place I'd ever seen.

"Sister Joanna?" someone was saying.

"Yes, what is it?" I gasped, dashing the tears from my cheeks.

Brother Richard pointed at a distant hill to the left of us. "Is that where Lord Chester's property begins?" he asked. "I've met his younger brother, the Bishop of Dover."

I nodded, still not able to manage myself. Brother Edmund examined me with his usual expression of distant calm. I turned away from the friars, irritated.

We reached the large gatehouse in front of the priory—it was dark and empty. The driver of the wagon looked back at us, unsure of what to do.

"There should be someone out front to greet us," Brother Richard said.

"The priory has a porter," I told him—my voice had thankfully returned to normal. "Sometimes he's in the gatehouse, but after dark, he's most often inside the front priory."

"Without lighting torches outside for us?" Brother Richard asked accusingly, as if I were responsible.

Brother Edmund said, "It will be an easy matter to make him aware we've arrived." We climbed out of the wagon. With a loud sigh, Brother Richard dismounted and handed the reins of his horse to the wagon driver.

The entrance to Dartford Priory struck most people dumb. Even the two friars seemed impressed.

One entered the priory through a soaring, near-pointed archway. On each side the statue of a king stared forward—our founder, King Edward the Third. Across the top of the archway was a stone carving celebrating the ascension of the Virgin.

Brother Richard knocked on the thick wooden door. He waited less than a minute, and knocked again. No one answered.

"I can think of no excuse for this," Brother Richard said.

Finally, the door creaked open. To my relief, Jacob, the elderly porter, shuffled outside. He frowned as he looked at the friars; when he saw me, his expression changed to shock. "Sister Joanna, is that you?" he quavered.

"Yes, Jacob," I answered.

"Didn't your prioress inform you of our arrival?" demanded Brother Richard.

Jacob shook his head.

Brother Edmund said in his gentler voice: "Was there no messenger from London today?"

"Yes, Brother, there was a messenger."

"What did the prioress say to you after reading it?"

Jacob looked at Brother Richard, and his eyes widened. His mouth flapped open and shut. I'd never seen our porter like this—so at a loss.

"Jacob, what is wrong?" I asked.

But he would not answer me, either.

"Take us to your prioress," said Brother Richard.

Jacob backed away from him. "No, no."

"Take us to your prioress—now!" the friar thundered.

With a final flap of his mouth, Jacob turned and led us into the priory.

The ivory statue of the Virgin Mary on her throne gleamed in the front antechamber. I expected Jacob to bear left and take us to the *locutorium,* the room where nuns could meet with visitors, while he fetched Prioress Elizabeth. The men were Dominican friars, yes, but chapter rules dictated that no men, religious or otherwise, were allowed access to where the sisters served, unless it was sanctioned in advance by a prioress.

But to my shock, Jacob turned away from the *locutorium* and the other rooms where outsiders were permitted—the prioress's front office chamber, the lodging rooms for boarders and overnight guests—and headed for the heart of the priory.

He took out his keys at the door leading to the cloister, chapter house, church, refectory, kitchens and dormitories.

"Jacob, what are you doing?" I asked.

He opened the door without answering.

"So far I have seen rules broken—first of hospitality, and now the strictest one of all, enclosure," Brother Richard fumed. "The good report I had of this priory was much mistaken."

I glanced at Brother Edmund, hoping he would calm his agitated fellow friar. But he stayed silent, wrapped in his own thoughts.

Jacob looked only at me. "Go to the church," he whispered, holding open the door.

The three of us stepped over the threshold, and Jacob locked the door behind us.

It must be time for Compline, a sacred Dominican office, a deeply inappropriate moment to reappear, and with two friars in tow. But I didn't know what else to do—Jacob had plainly lost his senses. He had always been so dedicated to the prioress. I couldn't imagine what had happened to him.

"Follow me," I said.

We moved towards the cloister: the open courtyard and garden in the centre of the priory. Columned passageways squared off on each side. In moments we reached the far corridor leading to the church. My joy at being in the priory again was tamped down by confusion. I couldn't hear a thing: neither singing nor chanting nor spoken responses. Compline was not a silent gathering.

From the minute we'd arrived I sensed something was wrong. Now I was overwhelmed by fear.

We reached the archway opening to Dartford's exquisite church. We bowed, and then dipped our fingers in the holy water in the stoup and made the sign of the cross. But I couldn't see much of anything. A burst of thick incense enveloped me, filling my nose, throat, eyes. I'd never smelled so much at one time. It was not just lavender, either; I detected rosemary afloat in the air. Candles flickered at the apse, creating points of light that shimmered through the fragrant cloud. I felt slightly woozy.

The sisters of Dartford were indeed all there. The two dozen women stood in their assigned stalls. And now that I was in the same room as them, I realised they were not silent. They were weeping.

I looked again. On the side of the apse stretched a long platform draped in black cloth.

As the incense cloud thinned, a white face came into view. A person was laid out on the platform. Those weren't drapes, but a long black cape.

I took a step closer, then another. And another. I knew that profile, those wrinkled cheeks. It was Prioress Elizabeth Croessner lying on the platform.

17

Sister Joan Vane saw me first. She eased out of her stall and rushed down the centre aisle.

"Why are you in here?" she asked, her voice sharp. "You should be in the *locutorium*. And to bring these friars in here?" She frowned at the sight of Brother Richard and Brother Edmund.

I was too full of shock at the sight of the prioress to answer her. I couldn't take it in. I had been thinking of what I would say to Prioress Elizabeth, imagined her words to me, heard her soft, cultured voice.

Sister Joan grabbed my arm and propelled me toward the friars, who were waiting at the back of the chapel. It did not surprise me that Sister Joan had taken charge. She was always a diligent *circator*, ensuring that rules were followed.

Brother Richard asked her: "Is that your prioress?"

"Yes," said Sister Joan. "God has taken her to Him."

The friars crossed themselves. I did the same, my right hand shaking.

"When?" asked Brother Edmund.

"This morning," she said. "I knew of your arrival, but I did not think you'd come so soon after the messenger from London. I have not had an opportunity to tell the sisters anything. I wanted to give them time with Prioress Elizabeth before she is taken for burial."

At the mention of burial, a low moan escaped from my lips. Tears bubbled up and coursed down my cheeks. Sister Joan ignored me.

"It is good that I am here," announced Brother Richard, "for there is much to do. I am familiar with the procedure for selection of a new prioress. Letters must be written and sent at once."

Sister Joan raised her pointed chin. She was already a tall woman—suddenly, she seemed even taller. "There is no need for that."

"No need?" he repeated.

"I am the next Prioress of Dartford," she said proudly.

Brother Richard stared at her as if she were mad. "On whose authority?" he finally asked.

There was a stir behind us. A trio of nuns stood a few feet away, staring. It was my fellow novices, Sister Winifred and Sister Christina, and between them the stout novice mistress, Sister Agatha. Other nuns clustered behind, straining to see us.

"Edmund, is that you?" quavered Sister Winifred, blinking with confusion.

Brother Edmund took a step toward her, his face lit up with a gentle smile. How much they resembled each other. "Yes, dear sister," he said.

Sister Winifred's eyes flitted uncertainly from his face to mine. "And Sister Joanna?" she gasped. "We were told you were in the Tower."

"Enough!" said Sister Joan. "We will speak outside of the church. Sister Agatha, come with us." She raised her voice so she could be heard by all the nuns. "Please, Sisters, the rest of you remain here. You have your turns assigned to you, for the nightly vigil of watching over our leader. At dawn, she will be cleaned and wound in her sheet."

A fresh burst of sobs erupted.

Her voice rising louder, Sister Joan cried, "I will return shortly. For now, you must respect our beloved prioress, even if others do not." She glared at me.

I saw Sister Winifred turn to her fellow novice, upset and overwhelmed. Sister Christina hugged her; over the smaller woman's shoulders, she shot me a furious, suspicious look.

I followed Sister Joan and Sister Agatha out of the chapel, the friars coming last. I wiped the tears from my cheeks.

In a moment we were all inside the chapter house, next to the church. Sister Agatha nervously lit candles.

Brother Richard spoke first. "I need to know on whose authority you have assumed the position of prioress," he said briskly. "Was it the Bishop of Rochester?"

Her eyes narrowed. "What is your name?" she asked.

"I am Brother Richard."

"Then, Brother Richard, I must tell you first that I am not answerable to you in any way," she said smoothly. "But neither do I wish to conceal anything, for all has been done properly. The members of the priory elected me this day, following a recommendation. And no, it was not from the Bishop of Rochester, though arguably we do fall under his jurisdiction. As you must be aware, I did not approach your patron, either—the Bishop of Winchester. My authority comes direct from the second man in the land, from the Lord Privy Seal and Vice Regent of Spiritual Affairs, Thomas Cromwell."

Brother Richard shrank from her, as if she had conjured up Satan. His voice hoarse, he stammered, "But . . . but . . . Cromwell is the man who seeks to destroy the monasteries."

A flush spread over Prioress Joan's face. "While monasteries stand in this land—and, Brother, we all pray that the dissolution will proceed no further—Cromwell is the authority we report to. That is according to the Oath of Supremacy."

"How did he even become aware that a new prioress would be needed here?" Brother Richard demanded.

"My predecessor, Prioress Elizabeth, took ill this summer. By September it was clear she would not recover. I wrote to Cromwell personally and made him aware of the situation and of my qualifications for the position. His approval was sent by letter last week. You may examine it if you wish."

Brother Richard and Brother Edmund exchanged a look of dismay. I knew little of the procedures involved in selecting a new prioress while one lay dying, and whether she had flouted any rules. But I suspected their alarm had more to do with the direct involvement of Cromwell.

"Now, on to the business at hand," she said briskly. "Bishop Gardiner has arranged for the two of you to be transferred from the Cambridge friary to Dartford. I have no objection. Brother Richard, I will see that all of the account books are passed to you tomorrow." She glanced at the fair-haired friar. "You must be Brother Edmund."

He bowed his head.

"The priory's infirmary in the hamlet of Stanham has been lacking for many years, and the one here, within our walls, is inadequate as well. If you possess half the skills that Bishop Gardiner claims, then it will be worth the cost of feeding and sheltering you."

Brother Richard grimaced. It was not the most gracious way to welcome new members to a religious house. But Brother Edmund himself showed no emotion.

"Yes, Prioress," he said.

Brother Richard said, "I have a trunk that needs to be brought to the friars' quarters and a horse that requires stabling. Our party came by wagon; those horses need to be fed and watered before the return journey, and the driver given sup as well."

Prioress Joan shrugged. "Those are matters for the porter to arrange."

"Your porter proved himself inept when we arrived."

She rolled her eyes. "Yes, he was indulged by Prioress Elizabeth for years and is now next to useless. One of my first actions after her burial will be to pension him off and get a younger man."

I felt chilled by the prioress's judgement, but I detected a glint of grudging respect in Brother Richard's eyes.

"As for you, Joanna Stafford."

My insides churned.

"I am ordered by Bishop Gardiner to accept you back into the priory. He said the investigation against you has been dropped and you are not guilty of any crime."

She paused for a moment.

"But in my eyes, you are guilty of a great deal. You broke your vows of obedience and honesty and violated the sacred rule of enclosure. You brought censure and suspicion upon us—that a novice of Dartford would behave such—at a critical time for all English nuns. Bishop Gardiner says that you are not to be questioned about your confinement in the Tower, that it is to be put into the past. But I tell you, I shall never put my trust and faith in you. As you stand before me today, I question whether you should be allowed to profess your full vows and become a bride of Christ."

I stared at the floor. My whole body ached, as if I were a dog that had been kicked and whipped.

"Sister Agatha, take her to be changed into a habit before she is permitted inside the novice dormitory."

"Yes, Prioress," said Sister Agatha meekly.

My face burning, I followed Sister Agatha out into the passageway. I longed to break away from her, to run from Dartford Priory. I couldn't face the novices or nuns; it was impossible to remain here, so loathed. Begging my bread on the open road would be preferable.

We reached the closet room, and she found me a novice's habit. I put it on, felt the rough cloth on my arms and legs again. It had been so long; now, finally, I wore the white habit and brown belt of a Dominican novice.

But I felt so unworthy. I covered my face with my hands.

Sister Agatha patted my arm, awkwardly. "It must have been a shock to you, the death of Prioress Elizabeth. You were close to her, weren't you?"

I nodded, grateful for sympathetic words.

"I am glad you have returned to us well and safe," she said.

My throat tightened. "I fear that Prioress Joan is not glad."

"Our prioress is a determined woman, but she comes into her new responsibilities at a difficult time," Sister Agatha said. "She is beset by challenges. And she does not even have the letter of Prioress Elizabeth to guide her."

"Letter?" I gasped.

"Yes, it is a sacred tradition at Dartford Priory that each prioress write a letter of instruction and pass it on to her successor, for her eyes alone. Prioress Elizabeth wrote a letter. I saw her composing it myself. But this morning, when it was first discovered that our holy leader had passed into God's hands, the letter was nowhere to be found. Prioress Joan ordered the room searched repeatedly. But the letter was gone."

18

I had been back at Dartford for twelve days when the Westerly children begged me to marry their father.

On Thursday, at the end of dinner, I stepped forward to take the basket of leftover food to the Westerlys. For a week I'd volunteered to perform the task. It gave me a chance to talk to the children; I'd always been fond of them. And it took me away from the nuns and their blatant disapproval. In the Bell Tower, when Bishop Gardiner spoke to me of returning, I had longed to serve God at Dartford Priory, to be part of something again, something fine and beautiful. It hadn't occurred to me that the acceptance I'd felt there was built on trust. Now that trust was gone, as dead and buried as Prioress Elizabeth, laid to rest below the chancel of the church, next to the other prioresses of Dartford.

This very morning, after High Mass, I'd made confession with the others. Doing so filled me with anguish. The day after my return I'd confessed to all sins committed at Smithfield and in the Tower except for agreeing to Gardiner's charge, which I still hadn't voiced. Although I knew I'd be damned for this omission, I couldn't disclose my search. I had sworn to speak of it to no one, and that included poor old Brother Philip, our friar chaplain and confessor, on the other side of the confessional. Only the fear for my father's life could have driven me to commit this sin. I could not hope to experience grace at Dartford without the cleansing act of true confession.

Carrying the basket, my throat tight with grief, I shoved open the pantry door. It led to the vegetable garden and orchards and, beyond that, the barn and friars' brewery.

The children's mother, Lettice Westerly, the priory's head laundress, was a good-tempered and tireless woman who had, one month before my return to Dartford, collapsed with a pain in her head. She grew steadily worse and now lay in the infirmary, near senseless. Before her ailment struck, the children had been favourites at the priory, permitted visits by the sisters. Now they were here every day. No one had the heart to discourage it.

"Children?" I called out.

"Sister Joanna—here we are!"

The Westerlys' small forms materialised before me. It was as if they were sprites grown from the very shrubbery.

I held up the basket of food. The first to reach me was Harold, a sturdy, compact boy. Then came the littlest one, the scamp, Martha, no more than four, clutching her doll. Last to join us was nine-year-old Ethel, darkened by a surliness I couldn't fault. She was old enough to grasp the likely fate of her family.

As their eager fingers seized the food, I took stock of them: dirtier than usual and more dishevelled. Martha's matted hair even sported a broken twig.

"Ethel, when was the last time you were home?" I asked. I suspected they were sleeping in one of the outlying priory buildings, to be close to their mother. They couldn't be sleeping outside—it was too cold, and I remembered that last night it had rained. They didn't look wet.

Ethel shrugged as she crammed the largest crust into her mouth.

"It's not safe or proper," I reminded her. "You must stay in the village, with your father."

Harold piped up: "He's never home, Sister."

I glanced at Ethel for confirmation. "He's gone to London again," she muttered. "He says there's not enough work in Dartford for a rag-and-bone man."

I sat on a stump, pulled Martha onto my lap, and tried to tug the twig from her hair. She did not flinch from the pain, even though I could feel the roots of her hair arching from her scalp. She held her smiling rag doll with one hand and with the other stroked the rough cloth of my habit. When I'd finally extricated the twig, she turned and looked up at me. "Will ye be our mother when she's gone?" she asked in her sweet singsong.

"Yes, yes!" Harold clapped his hands. "We wanted to ask ye. Ye are our favourite. Marry our father. *Please.*"

I patted Martha's little shoulder. "No, children," I said as gently as I could. "You know I will help you, but I can't do that. I'm a novice here at Dartford."

"I told ye she wouldn't do it," said Ethel. But her lower lip trembled, and I realised that she, too, might have hoped for this.

"I'm sure your father is a fine man, but I will never be anyone's wife or mother," I told her.

Ethel squinted at me. "Is there going to be a priory much longer?" she demanded.

Even the children of our servants doubted the future of Dartford. That left me shaken. At times, while I was performing my daily duties, or raising my voice in song or prayer, the threat to the monasteries receded from my thoughts. Of all people, I should know how very real it was. But when following in the faithful footsteps of the novices and nuns who had gone before me, lived and died by the Rules of Saint Benedict for centuries, it felt impossible that this way of life could end. Now, sitting with the children on the grounds of Dartford, panic clawed inside me. The ground itself seemed to rise and tilt—unsafe for me, for all of us. Cromwell's soulless army advanced each day.

I murmured to the children, "Eat your food, I must return the basket." After they'd finished, I hugged each of them to soften the blow of my rejection. Ethel was like a scratchy twig in my arms.

Inside, all was quiet. Everyone was occupied. Much of the work of the priory, from gardening to baking and brewing to studying Latin, took place between noon and five. There was more cleaning expected than ever before. Prioress Elizabeth had run an orderly priory, but her successor immediately laid down additional requirements for scrubbing and sweeping. I doubt there was a more spotless convent in England. The sisters who worked as teachers were not excluded from manual labour, either. Girls from good local families attended afternoon lessons on the upper floors of the front rooms. Only eight students appeared these days, when once it had been three times that, but teaching was still a priority.

My afternoon responsibility was tapestry work. I hurried down the south passageway to the tapestry room, near the Dartford library. The library door stood slightly ajar. It was a room carefully supervised because of some of the manuscripts' fragility. This was the home of the priory's cherished private book collection, to be used for study in a connecting room. This library was a source of great joy to me from the moment of my profession. Few Englishwomen could read, apart from the ladies of the court. And even for them, reading was an accomplishment mastered so that the men of the family would be duly impressed and honoured. In the convents, reading and study was a way to honour Christ, yes, but it was also a path to greater understanding of the spiritual world, to the improvement of our minds, which were not neglected here but respected.

It was a wondrous privilege for me to study the books of the Dartford library, but rarely was it unlocked and unattended. I had never seen the library door hang open midday.

I peered inside and saw no one, although candles burned on a table in the middle of the room, far from any books for chance of fire. Someone must have lit the tapers and then stepped out. Taking a deep breath, I slipped inside.

Since the evening of my return, I'd learned absolutely nothing of the crown, not a scrap of information that could be of interest to Bishop Gardiner. Whenever I was not under direct scrutiny by the other sisters—which was seldom—I searched the priory for clues. I found an opportunity to examine the precious objects gathered in a large ornate chest behind the altar, but there was nothing resembling a crown among them. I had looked in every room for something significant, except for the prioress's own chamber. Nothing. In less than a week I'd reach the date the bishop set—All Saints' Day—and the only finding I had to report was that Prioress Elizabeth's letter to her successor had gone missing. To an outsider it might appear the letter was stolen, but only a nun could have entered the private room of the dying prioress, and the thought of a sister of Dartford committing such an act . . . I recoiled from it. And yet how could such a letter be misplaced?

It was highly unlikely I'd find it wedged among the manuscripts. But perhaps I'd learn more of Dartford's origin and background, anything that could help explain why a king would hide a mysterious object here—and where to find it now.

I scanned the covers of the books. Most were devotional, of course, such as *The Mirror of Our Lady* and *The Book of Vice and Vir-*

tues. We owned three illuminated manuscripts, exquisitely rendered by monks and of great value. But the cornerstones of the collection were the books written by spiritual women of the Dominican Order: Saint Catherine of Siena, Saint Margaret of Hungary, and more.

There was nothing to be found about the origins of Dartford Priory.

The last place to look was a small section on general topics. Impatiently, I examined them. One was on legal contracts, another on the reigns of the early Plantagenets. And then I saw it. A slender book, dark brown, with the title: *From Caractacus to Athelstan.* I blinked several times; I couldn't believe I was looking at the word.

I pulled the volume out and opened it, my hands quivering. A quick skim revealed it to be a history of early England, beginning at the time of the Romans and Emperor Claudius's conquest of our isle. Caractacus was a Celtic ruler who defied Rome. Chapters followed of life under Roman occupation, the decline of the Caesars and their withdrawal from England, the Saxeon invasions, the conflicts with the Danes. The book seemed straightforward, even ordinary. I leafed through to the last chapter, titled "Athelstan the One King."

> *After the death of Ethelward, his half brother, Athelstan, succeeded in 925, although born of a concubine. Many kingdoms opposed Athelstan. The Danes were not idle. They sent boats to take York once more, and plotted to drive south. They raided many villages and committed grievous atrocities, as was their wont. The Scots planned their invasions as well.*
>
> *In the first year the Saxeon nobles were discontent with their new king. Athelstan's younger brother Edwin was said to plot against him with the nobles and was condemned. Edwin protested his innocence and took a sacred oath before priests. But Athelstan set Edwin to sea in a boat with no sail and neither food nor water. The boat was never seen again.*

I shivered a little, thinking of that young man on the boat, cast out. Frightened. Starving. How pitiless King Athelstan was. Then I resumed my reading.

Athelstan later made penance for his brother's death. He was a monarch who showed a ruthless spirit to his enemies but was pious and virtuous above all others. He heard Mass three times each day. He founded many monasteries and was known throughout Christendom as a collector of holy relics.

"You are a lover of books?"

I gave a cry and dropped what I was reading. It hit the floor with a loud *clap*.

Brother Richard stood inches away from me. I had been so absorbed I hadn't heard him come in.

"Did I startle you?" he asked

"Yes, Brother." To my horror, my voice broke.

"I'm pleased to see the works amassed in nearly two centuries; this is a fine little collection at Dartford," he said in his patronising way.

"Yes, Brother." My voice had calmed. I bent down to pick up the book.

"May I see what you were reading?" he asked.

I held it out to him.

"Ah, this is not a time that much is known about," he said, leafing a few pages. "Rome . . . the Celts . . . the Saxeons . . . Alfred the Great." He paused. "And his grandson, King Athelstan."

He closed the book but did not give it back to me. "You have curious interests, Sister Joanna."

I bowed my head slightly, turned, and left the library, my heart pounding. I could feel his eyes burning into my back.

Tapestry work was well under way when I hurried in to join my fellow novices. Sister Christina and Sister Winifred paused in their weaving as I rushed over to my place on the bench before the large wooden loom. Ours was the only such loom at a priory in all of England; most tapestries were woven in Brussels. At the turn of the century, a farsighted Dartford prioress had arranged for the loom to be brought here, and a special room made to accommodate it: large windows allowed more light into this room than reached any other. It took a year for three weavers, sitting side by side, to make one tapestry that reached five feet in length.

I sat between the other novices. They looked nothing alike. Sister Christina was tall, with piercing eyes and high cheekbones. Her piety was profound. Beneath her formidable exterior, though, was a perceptive spirit. She noticed things others missed. As for Sister Winifred, she was much smaller than either Sister Christina or myself. With her large liquid eyes and heart-shaped face, she seemed childlike, and the older nuns tended to coddle her. But I had seen her push herself to accomplish difficult tasks. Her determination could never be discounted.

This afternoon, my arrival drew only a cold stare from Sister Christina, who had given no sign of ever forgiving me for my crimes against Dartford, but Sister Winifred flashed me a smile. Perhaps, for that friendship, there was hope.

I braced myself for reproof from Sister Agatha, sitting at the head of the room to supervise the novices. But her face was creased with worry, her eyes cloudy. She didn't comment on my lateness. Behind her, Sister Helen, our tapestry mistress, small and elegant, sorting out her silks, didn't say anything, either, but since she hadn't spoken to a soul in three years, it was no surprise.

Prioress Elizabeth received special dispensation from the Continent for Sister Helen to remain with us, even though she did not sing, chant, nor pray aloud. It had been that way since her older brother, a monk, was hanged in chains in Tyburn for refusing to take the Oath of Supremacy to the king. In the beginning, when the king first attacked our way of life, some brave monks and friars and nuns and abbots chose to oppose him. They were punished with stunning savagery. Following that, most took the oath.

Sister Helen, perhaps to compensate for silence, put great effort into the tapestries, her domain for some twenty years. They were original, exquisite, haunting. I arrived at Dartford an adept seamstress; under my mother's tutelage, I'd mastered the most complicated stitches. But we did not stitch these tapestries, we wove them, with a bobbin, in and out, through the warp threads. Sister Helen taught me how to weave quickly yet carefully, and when to push the pedals beneath our feet. Most remarkably of all, it was Sister Helen who came up with the design of each tapestry, what story it would tell. A talented artist, she drew the picture to be followed and then painted the life-size cartoon. Before beginning each tapestry, the cartoon was cut into vertical shreds and fastened beneath, to show patterns. We were more than halfway finished with this latest one.

As my bobbin went in and out, I thought not of my work but of the book I'd discovered. Athelstan was a real person, a king in the time of the Saxeons. He would indeed have possessed a crown. But why would it be hidden at Dartford? Monasteries had existed in England during that dark, turbulent time; he himself founded them. So why did Edward the Third not use one for hiding the crown instead of building Dartford Priory from the ground up, as Bishop Gardiner had suggested?

I thought about Brother Richard's reaction to finding me with the book, how his fingers had closed tightly on the volume. He'd known at once the identity of Athelstan, even though he was an obscure ruler, born in the last years of the first millennium.

A low moan from the front of the room jarred me from my thoughts. It was Sister Agatha. Tears glittered in her close-set eyes.

We novices looked at one another, unsure what to do.

It was Sister Christina who spoke up, as was usual. She was the senior. "Are you well today, Sister?" she called out.

Sister Agatha shook her head, as if angry. "It isn't fair—you are young; you have prosperous families who could take you in. I have nowhere to go. My family is dead, and I've no money of my own."

"What do you mean?" Sister Christina asked.

She shook her head. "I should not speak so. But I heard this morning that Cromwell's commissioners have started another round of visitations. Of the larger monasteries. I had hoped it was all over, that we were safe. But the new reports from London say otherwise."

Sister Winifred looked at me, frightened. I made a face of surprise, though it was anything but news to me. Whispered fears must be racing up and down the passageways of all the large houses, from Syon to Glastonbury.

"God will protect us." Sister Christina's voice rang out. "And, Sister Agatha, never think us more fortunate than you. I myself will never leave Dartford, no matter what occurs. If I must, I will do the Lord's work in the rubble."

I looked sideways at Sister Christina. She'd stopped weaving; her jaw tightened with resolution.

Sister Agatha seemed heartened by such conviction: "Yes, it is quite impossible to believe the king could ever suppress Dartford. We are a priory favoured by the nobility." She glanced at us—not angry any more, but with hope. "The king's own aunt was a nun here, before I professed."

"Wasn't her name Sister Bridget?" asked Sister Winifred.

"Yes, Sister Bridget," said our novice mistress. "She was the youngest sister of Queen Elizabeth. The old queen visited her on occasion—once she brought along her son, Prince Arthur."

A sharp pain pierced my left palm. I had scissors in my lap. I looked down: a perfect circle of blood bloomed on my skin. I'd jabbed myself at the name "Arthur."

I grabbed a scrap of cloth and pressed it into the heel of my palm. "When was that, Sister?" I asked quickly. "When did they visit Dartford?"

Sister Agatha thought for a moment. "I believe it was just after Prince Arthur married Katherine of Aragon. I'm told Queen Elizabeth wanted Sister Bridget to meet Arthur's wife, so they travelled down one day."

Struggling to keep my voice casual, I said, "Katherine of Aragon was at Dartford?" The throb in my palm grew worse; I pressed the cloth harder.

"Yes, yes, that's right. Blessed Queen Katherine was just a girl then. So long ago. Before my time." She calculated in her head. A minute crawled by. She was not quick with sums. "More than thirty years ago. Yes, that's it. You see? We have direct ties to the *royal family*. How could the king ever suppress Dartford and turn us out onto the road?"

So that was no deathbed hallucination of Queen Katherine's. She did come here with her young first husband.

I looked down—I could not staunch the blood flow, and so weaving must stop. I mustn't drench these delicate light blue and white silk threads with blood.

Sister Winifred started coughing. A rasping cough with a ragged wetness to it.

Sister Christina and I both knew what that meant, and we jumped to our feet.

"Loosen her habit," I suggested.

"No, it's too late for that," Sister Christina said.

Sister Winifred's white face flushed scarlet as she fell back on the bench, gasping and coughing.

"This is your fault," Sister Christina called out accusingly to Sister Agatha. "You upset her with talk of being turned out into the road. We are supposed to work in *silence* here."

Sister Agatha sputtered with indignation. "I am your novice mistress—you cannot criticise me."

Lifting up Sister Winifred, I announced, "I am taking her to Brother Edmund."

After I'd ferried Sister Winifred to the door, I paused, but no one tried to stop me. Our novice mistress was caught up in her quarrel with Sister Christina.

I glanced over at Sister Helen, in the corner, sorting through her silks as always. But she was far from indifferent. I saw a long tear drip off her cheek.

19

I could hear the man screaming from the cloister garden.

The infirmary came off the east side of the cloister, at the end of that passageway. To shorten the distance, I pulled Sister Winifred straight across the garden, minding that we kept to the paths. She staggered alongside me, and I had to be careful she didn't overturn the baskets full of harvested valerian or bump her head against the branch of a quince tree. The sound of screaming made her shudder, but I tightened a grip around her heaving shoulders. "All will be well," I said.

When we came through the infirmary doors, I saw Brother Edmund bending over someone, his hands running across the man's collarbone and shoulder. It was John, one of our stable hands, slumped forward on a pallet, his shirt loosened, his eyes bulging. I was relieved that this was Brother Edmund's time to work in our infirmary, and not in the one he managed in Stanham, which was nearby.

"It hurts, Brother. Christ's blood, it hurts."

"Do not blaspheme," Brother Edmund murmured. His fingers halted their exploration. "I will adjust your shoulder now. The pain will be sharp, but then it will ease. Prepare yourself."

John made a wild sign of the cross with his one hand, the other dangling at his side. Just as he'd finished, Brother Edmund threw himself onto the man's damaged shoulder, his black friar's cape whipping into the air as he attacked.

"Brother, no!" I cried out. But I was unheard, drowned out by John's agonised screech. He collapsed onto the pallet.

As Brother Edmund stepped back to straighten his robes, he spotted us standing in the corner.

"Sister Winifred is having another fit," I said.

Brother Edmund hurried to his oak cabinet, a key gleaming in his hand. "Set her down anywhere," he said over his shoulder.

I helped Sister Winifred, whose choking had settled into bursts of wheezing, onto another pallet. A tendril of blonde hair hung down in her face, and I tucked it back under her novice cap.

"When did it begin?" Brother Edmund asked me as he briskly ground a dark plant in a bowl with mortar and pestle.

"Just ten minutes or so," I said. "She was agitated, then began the choking."

"What agitated her?" Brother Edmund stooped before the low fire with his bowl.

I told him of Sister Agatha's laments over the future of the priory.

"I see." He stopped grinding. "I am going to apply the remedy. Step away, Sister Joanna. It is best you do not inhale it as well."

I backed into the corner, watching as he propped her up and placed the smoking bowl under her face. I had been in the infirmary last week when he administered the same remedy. He had brought many new medicines and potions—and new skills—to this position. Sister Rachel, a sharp-tongued nun, had been in charge of the infirmary when he arrived and was furious to be ousted. But even she had to admit that Brother Edmund was an apothecary to be respected. And it was a simple matter for him to move between the priory infirmary and the small one in town, skimpily attended since the death last year of Brother Matthew. Friars were accustomed to moving among outsiders. They were not monks or nuns, living in retreat from the world.

"Breathe," he commanded. "Again. Again."

Sister Winifred took a final deep breath and groped for his hand. "Thank you," she moaned. He lifted her hand to his lips and kissed it lightly, then eased her back down to rest. Seeing them together, I was struck by the siblings' resemblance. The same brown eyes, pale eyelashes, and wide mouth with thin lips. But I also noticed that Brother Edmund did not look well today. His skin had a yellowish tint, and lines crinkled around his eyes.

I crept toward the smouldering bowl. "What is this cure?" I asked.

"*Ephedra helvetica* is a remedy, not a cure," he said. "The leaf of a plant grown in Italy. A Swiss brother travelling to Cambridge had a supply for himself and told me of it. I send for it every six months. I'll need a greater supply now. Dartford is not the best climate for Sister Winifred—there are so many marshes nearby—but there's no help for that. So I must redouble my course of remedy."

John stirred behind us. To my amazement, he smiled.

"Brother, it's better, ye're right," he said. "When can I return to my work?"

"Do not lift or pull anything heavy for two weeks," Brother Edmund said.

Jumping off the pallet, John said, "A one-armed stable hand is useless. The new porter is a hard man—he'll dock my wages or even dismiss me. There are ten men in town that could take my place tomorrow. The priory is the best place to draw a wage. Could you speak for me? Please, Brother, I have a wife five months with child."

He was beginning to babble. Brother Edmund held up his hand. "I can't promise you anything, but I will put in a word."

"Thank you, Brother," John said fervently. "It was a good day for us when you came to Dartford."

After John left, I said, "He shows you true gratitude."

Brother Edmund sighed. "Just because I know of a few treatments, a few potions, doesn't mean I can work miracles. There is very little that I can do to help anyone. It's all in God's hands." He gestured toward the far corner of the infirmary, next to its tiny chapel. A blanket was strung across two poles. At the far end I could see two stockinged feet peeking out.

"Lettice Westerly?" I whispered.

Brother Edmund was back at his cabinet, to replace his leaf potion. I watched him remove a small velvet purse from another drawer.

"All I can do is ease her suffering," he said as he approached Lettice's corner.

"May I see her?" I asked.

He pulled back the blanket. For a second I thought I looked upon a corpse. Her skin was ashen; her mouth hung open; her tongue was coated with a frightening dark slime. Then I saw her chest rise and fall.

Brother Edmund removed a gleaming black bead from his bag. He lifted Lettice Westerly's head to push the bead back into her throat. "Get me some ale to wash it down, Sister Joanna," he said. "I must make her swallow."

I poured the ale for him. "What is that potion's name?" I asked.

"It has no Latin name," he said. "It comes from the East. It has been called the stones of immortality."

My skin prickled at the name; it had an eerie power.

"Come, Lettice, swallow. Yes, there we go." He eased her head back down.

"Brother Edmund, how much longer will she live?"

He felt her forehead, and then touched her wrist. "A week. Perhaps two."

My throat tightened as I pictured the three Westerly children bounding toward me for food.

Suddenly, Brother Edmund had my own hand in his. I flinched, knocking him away in fright.

"Sister Joanna, you are bleeding," he said patiently, pointing at my left palm. The cloth I had wrapped around it had fallen off, and the blood still trickled.

"It's nothing," I said. "I pierced myself with scissors, but not deeply."

Brother Edmund smiled. "Then my sister was not the only one agitated by the talk of the monasteries' fate?"

"That is not what agitated me," I muttered.

He looked at me more closely. "But something else did?"

I said nothing. He bore a solicitous attitude, but, as with Brother Richard, I sensed a deeper purpose to his questions.

"Come, Sister Joanna, let me clean it. I've seen terrible festering diseases caused by a prick smaller than that one, if left unattended."

He turned my wrist over to look more closely, then wiped the blood away with a dampened cloth. His large bony hands were amazingly deft.

"Sister Joanna!"

I jumped away from Brother Edmund to face Sister Eleanor, the priory's new *circator*. She was just thirty years old, and yet the new prioress had chosen her for this important task, the enforcer of rules. It might have something to do with the fact that she was the niece of Prioress Elizabeth. The departed prioress had loved her but also gently remonstrated with Sister Eleanor for her burning zeal to serve God, fearing at times for her health. Sister Eleanor fasted more days than anyone else, refused sleep in order to redouble her prayers to the Virgin Mary, and whipped her back with cords. I wondered if Prioress Joan now cautioned Sister Eleanor—or if it was the opposite.

"Why are you here, Sister?" she demanded, her dark eyes blazing in her thin face. "This is your time for tapestry work."

Brother Edmund stepped forward. "Sister Joanna pierced her skin in the tapestry room."

Sister Eleanor's scowl deepened at the sight of Sister Winifred, who was sitting up at the end of her pallet.

"And what of her?" she asked. "Another fit?"

Brother Edmund nodded.

"Sister Winifred, are you well enough to return to the tapestry room alone?" Sister Eleanor asked, in a manner that suggested disagreement would be unwise.

The novice nodded.

"Good. Because I came here for Brother Edmund and was going to fetch Sister Joanna next. You're both wanted in the prioress's chamber immediately. Follow me."

Brother Edmund and I exchanged a look of puzzlement, and then we followed Sister Eleanor out of the infirmary. I couldn't imagine why we were being summoned. I wondered if it had something to do with Brother Richard's finding me in the library, reading the book on King Athelstan. But no matter the reason, I'd finally make my way into the last unexamined room of the priory.

Less than a minute after Sister Eleanor rapped on the door connecting the cloister to the front of the priory, Gregory, the new porter, unlocked it. Jacob had been swiftly pensioned off, as the prioress had planned, and now lived in a small house in the town of Dartford. Gregory was one-third his age, a tall man with a well-trimmed beard. He nodded with respect at the sight of Sister Eleanor and ignored the friar and me.

The prioress's chamber lay at the east end of the front passageway. Sister Eleanor bade us wait in the antechamber, on the bench, and then hurried off to complete her inspection.

There were voices on the other side of the prioress's door. At first they were low and indistinguishable. After a moment, they grew louder, and I knew one was a woman and the other a man. And after they grew louder still, I could tell it was Prioress Joan and Brother Richard—and the conversation was a furious one.

"Whatever makes you think you could trust Cromwell?" Brother Richard shouted. "Because he took your bribe? Do you think that will save the priory? He is the sort of man who will take a bribe with a smile and *still* dissolve us. You will live to regret your dealings with him, be assured."

"And you think Gardiner will save us?" Prioress Joan screeched. "Then you're the greater fool. Everyone knows where they are with Cromwell. He makes no secret of his policy. But Wily Winchester has betrayed everyone who put trust in him."

Brother Edmund leaped to the door and pounded on it.

It flew open to a wild-eyed Brother Richard. He stared at Brother Edmund, and some sort of silent message passed between them. Brother Richard glanced over at me, took a breath, and then beckoned for us both to come inside.

20

I followed Brother Edmund inside, and we both bowed to the prioress, sitting behind the large oak trestle table that dominated her chamber. I furtively glanced around the room. I had not been inside it since Prioress Elizabeth was alive. Besides the table and a few chairs, it was bare of other furniture; there were no bookshelves or chests. No place where a valuable object could be hidden away.

"The reason I have summoned both of you is to tell you we are to have guests at Dartford Priory," said the prioress.

Brother Richard made a strange sort of noise, as if he could not bear to listen, and he walked to the window facing the sweeping lawns. The prioress's lips tightened.

"Lord Chester, our neighbour, is coming to the priory in nine day's time," she said.

"Sister Christina's father?" asked Brother Edmund.

"That is correct." I heard a faint *click, click, click* from under the desk. I knew what it was. The prioress wore a delicate chain around her waist attached to a silver pomander ball. It was stuffed with sweet-smelling, exotic spices. Sister Agatha told me the spices were specially delivered from the Far East. With nervous fingers, the prioress often clicked the pomander ball against the chain.

"Lord Chester wishes to come to Dartford on All Souls' Day," she said. "That evening we will be holding the usual special Mass, the honouring of the departed. That is, of course, only for members of the priory. But in the afternoon, before the Mass . . . She raised her chin. "Before the Mass we will have a requiem feast, to which Lord Chester and his wife are invited."

I could not believe I had heard her correctly. A feast . . . *inside* the priory?

"What sort of feast, Prioress?" I asked.

"The usual sort," she snapped. "Food. Drink. Music."

Brother Edmund and I were shocked into silence. The clicking of the pomander ball quickened.

After a moment, Brother Edmund said, "May I inquire as to the reason we are holding this feast?"

"Ha!" Brother Richard turned from the window. "Because Lord Chester has asked us to, that's why. And we must curry favour with a courtier in high favour with the king."

The prioress said, "Brother Richard, the next such criticism will lead to your transfer out of Dartford Priory forthwith. Bishop Gardiner will simply have to find another place of refuge for you."

The prioress's cheeks flamed scarlet as she glared at Brother Richard. He met her gaze for a full moment, and then looked down, in submission.

"Since Lord Chester is the father of our senior novice, it is only natural for him to wish to visit her," she continued, much calmer. "I believe his choice of day has to do with his other child, his son, who died a year ago."

I remembered that last November, Sister Christina had received special permission to leave the priory for the funeral. She had come back very pensive; it took her a few weeks to return to her usual forceful self.

"How can Sister Joanna and I be of service?" Brother Edmund asked.

The prioress answered, "For the performing of music at the requiem feast. You play the lute, I am told. Sister Joanna is quite skilled on the Spanish *vihuela*."

I was stunned the prioress knew of my passion for music. I had played my *vihuela* only a few times at the priory. It was a prized possession; my mother had sent to Spain for the instrument when I was twelve years old and had taught me to play it herself. I brought it with me, and Prioress Elizabeth had encouraged my practising, but I hadn't touched it since my return. I was moved that the new prioress had taken note of my small talent.

Brother Edmund asked in the same mild voice: "Wouldn't Lord Chester be better served by employing musicians familiar with songs of the court?"

The prioress answered irritably, "No, Brother, he would *not* be better served. He's specifically requested that members of the priory play for him."

The friars began to discuss the plan for music with the prioress, along with other details of the feast. These plans included me, yet my interest was drawn elsewhere. A large portrait hung on the back wall, behind the prioress. It had been there every time I entered this chamber. But I had never taken close note of it until today.

The wooden frame was carved in the shape of intertwined branches sprouting leaves. The frame's brown colour gleamed, as if the leaves and branches had been painted gold more than a century ago and gradually faded. But it was the man who drew me in. He was solemn, neither old nor young, with brown hair parted in the middle and hanging just past his ears. He did not resemble a saint, nor any of the great Catholic princes revered by the Dominicans. He looked more like a knight of high chivalry, perhaps one of Chaucer's heroes. A dark patterned tunic stretched across broad shoulders; a simple medallion hung down his chest. His face was handsome, with a thin nose and high cheekbones, but there was a severity to his expression, a cold haughtiness. It went beyond the stiff sameness of men painted by artists in past centuries, before the innovations of Master Hans Holbein.

I heard myself say, "Who is the man in the portrait?"

Prioress Jane stopped in the middle of her sentence, surprised, and turned around.

"Isn't it Edward the Third, founder of this priory?" asked Brother Richard.

The prioress shook her head. "No, it is Edward the Third's oldest son, the Prince of Wales. King Edward commanded that this portrait be hung here."

"Why would he have wanted a portrait of the Black Prince in this room?" asked Brother Richard.

The Black Prince. I'd heard someone speak of him recently, but not at the priory. An anxious memory gnawed at me.

The prioress opened her mouth to answer Brother Richard when a knock sounded at the door. The porter told her that a messenger had arrived from London.

"Very well, Gregory, show him in. Brother Edmund, you may as well remain, but Sister Joanna, you may go. Sext prayers will be soon."

I bowed and hurried out. I had almost reached the church when it came to me who had spoken of the Black Prince. I heard again the voice of Bishop Gardiner in my Tower prison cell: *"Do you know of Edward the Third? His son, the Black Prince? What of Richard the Lion-hearted? Or our king's dead brother, Prince Arthur?"*

There was a reason Bishop Gardiner had spoken of the Black Prince; there was a reason for everything he said. I struggled to make sense of the mention of those men's names. Edward the Third founded Dartford Priory. The Black Prince was heir to the throne but died before his father. Prince Arthur, the brother of our King Henry the Eighth, visited Dartford months before he himself died. What the significance of Richard the Lionhearted was, I couldn't see. He lived and died centuries before Edward the Third—but centuries *after* King Athelstan. My head spun. What connection could there possibly be between them all?

The two dozen nuns of Dartford Priory had assembled in the chapel when I joined them, taking my place with my fellow novices.

Sister Winifred leaned over to whisper, "Thank you for helping me, Sister Joanna." On the other side of her, Sister Christina looked my way, in a kinder fashion than any time since my return. Relief coursed through me. With time, both my friendships might flourish again.

I heard a *whoosh* as the prioress strode up the centre aisle to the front of the church, and smelled a whiff of her pomander ball. As with Prioress Elizabeth, she did not enter the church until we were all seated and prepared. But in many other ways, she carried out her duties as spiritual leader very differently than the serene dead prioress. It was hard to accustom myself.

When she turned around to face us, I saw something had happened.

"Sisters, before we begin, I must share some grievous news with you," she said in her clear, sure voice.

I felt my body tense.

"Our queen has died. The king's most beloved consort, Jane,

passed from a fever contracted in her childbed. We shall now sing the office of the dead. For the next month we shall hold special vigils for Her Majesty."

I looked over at the iron grate hung with black cloth that separated the nuns from the friars in church. I couldn't see Brother Richard or Brother Edmund, but I wondered at their response to this sorry news. They'd pinned their hopes on the woman whose body now lay cold in a royal chapel. Queen Jane was twenty-eight years old, one year older than I. She must have had the most highly trained physicians in the land when her time came. Yet she had suffered and died, in a haze of blood and fever, all the same.

I have heard that some outsiders believe we take the veil because we loathe men and fear bearing children. If only it were possible to make others understand. Becoming a nun has nothing to do with fear and hate; it is the opposite. I thought of Saint Catherine of Siena's famous words: "Everything comes from love." Love of God, love of one another, and devotion to those who've come before. When I sat in this stall, I could feel the presence of decade upon decade of eager young novices, learning prayers and songs. In merging my soul with theirs in our holy observances, I came the closest a person could to embracing eternity. Dartford was the only place I'd ever found spiritual peace or feeling of true worth. Again, I felt the claw of panic. How could God in His mercy allow this way of life to end?

Forcing down my fears, I folded my hands and prayed for the young dead queen, that the soul of Jane Seymour would move swiftly through the perils of purgatory and on to the kingdom of heaven.

21

As All Souls' Day drew close, we prepared for the requiem feast for Lord Chester. Chairs had to be covered with cloth, made comfortable for the head table, since the only chairs we possessed were bare wood. Tankards and fine plates, tablecloth and embroidered linens—all were foreign to a Dominican Order but must now be obtained. I heard Brother Richard discussing with Gregory which farm animals would be slain. Extra kitchen help was hired, principally a woman knowledgeable in how to prepare rich dishes. A feast for a nobleman must offer meat courses, but at Dartford we ate no meat, except an occasional pudding, and very little fowl.

In the midafternoons, instead of tapestry work, I met with Brother Edmund in the chapter house to practise our music. We were never completely alone. Under the supervision of the porter, workmen moved in and out, preparing the room for noble company. It was unsettling to see our chapter house converted into a hall for a lord's company, but it was the only space large enough.

The songs of the priory could not be adapted to a lute and *vihuela*. But the friar and I knew some secular tunes and played them together in the corner, his lute melodies dancing above the deep, gentle strumming of my *vihuela*. At times, because we lacked other instruments, an improvisation was called for, to fill gaps in the songs. His ideas always impressed me.

"You have a true gift, Brother," I said on our third day of practice, as I waited for him to replace a string on his instrument. His lute had fifteen strings, and he was ever vigilant of their strengths.

He smiled without looking up from his work. "I enjoy honouring God with my music. At my friary, I was known for three things: my work as an apothecary, my humble skill with the lute, and my interest in history."

I watched him finish tightening the new string. "Whose history? That of the Dominican Order or of England itself?"

"I would say both."

I bit my lip. "Then may I ask you something, Brother?"

He looked up, and as always I was struck by the flatness of his large brown eyes. One summer day, in the gardens at Stafford Castle, I had seen a long lizard sunning itself on a rock—I was frightened when it stared at me, unafraid and unblinking. Brother Edmund's gaze unnerved me in the same way.

I shook off my apprehension. The private library of Dartford had been locked to me ever since my discovery of the Athelstan book, and there was still so much I needed to learn.

"The Prince of Wales whose portrait hangs in the prioress's office—why is he called the Black Prince?" I asked.

"Yes, I remember that portrait interested you," he said. "Hmm. He was not always called that. It is something of a new name. It could have to do with his armour—he wore black armour into battle."

"He was a soldier prince?"

"Yes, he led the armies of his father the king into France. We engaged in a long war during the reign of Edward the Third. You are aware of that?"

I nodded.

"The Black Prince—his name was Edward, too—he took many towns, won many battles, over a period of years. But he was not always a merciful prince." A shadow passed over Brother Edmund's face. "There was one act he committed that was so cruel, it could be the reason for this name."

I saw again the prince's supercilious eyes. "What did he do, Brother?"

"It's not a pretty story; I would rather not say."

I looked at the friar. "Do you think that I can only hear pretty stories? I've heard and seen much ugliness in my life already." The shadow of the Tower of London fell between us.

He sighed and began. "It was the siege of Limoges. A city in the South of France that the prince conquered returned to French control after his army had moved on. He went into a terrible rage. He laid siege to its walls, and when the city fell to him, he would not spare a single citizen. They say he had three thousand people put to death.

All were massacred as they begged for their lives. Even the children were killed."

I stroked the smooth side of my *vihuela*, trying not to show how sick I felt.

Brother Edmund said, "Those were different times. In most chronicles of the day, he was praised as a great man. He founded the Order of the Garter, after all. Such strength was valuable."

"It surprises me then that he died before his father. It was not from wounds in battle?"

"Oh, no. He became ill in France, not long before the siege. They say he was carried by litter to the walls of Limoges. After he'd retaken the city, he went back to England. His was a very slow decline. It took years. All the leading physicians in Christendom were sent for by his father the king. Every cure was attempted. I read some of the correspondence about it; I have always been interested in mysteries of medicine. The Prince of Wales was in the prime of his life, but he was gradually wasting away, and they could not find a sure and recognisable symptom of illness. It was neither plague nor lung rot nor the pox. They thought it dropsy for a time, but then decided not. There was one passage I remember . . ."

Brother Edmund pursed his lips, trying to recall it. "The Italian physician wrote, 'It is as if the force of his mortal existence were being drained away, and no man can stop it.'"

A shiver raced up my spine.

Brother Edmund smiled down at me. "Sister Joanna, you have lost your colour. Come, let's try another song."

I picked up my *vihuela*, and we resumed our practice. We had completed two of the songs in our planned repertoire when the other novices appeared in the chapter house.

"Thank you for joining us, Sisters," Brother Edmund said. He half turned to me to explain. "I believe it would be better to have two more musicians join us to play at the feast. I could not ask any of the senior sisters—I fear their dignity might be offended—but perhaps I could employ the two of you? Brother Richard helped me obtain two citterns. They are easier to play."

Sister Christina had begun shaking her head while the friar still spoke.

"No, Brother Edmund, not this," she said.

"I can teach you how to play a simple melody," he said reassuringly.

"I *know* how to play," Sister Christina said. Her forehead creased. "I cannot perform for my father. Do not ask it of me, please."

She turned and ran out of the room.

Brother Edmund said, "I erred in my request. I did not know that Sister Christina disliked her father."

"Dislike her father?" His words appalled me. "That is not true."

He bowed his head. "I've erred again. Forgive my words, Sister Joanna. And now, shall we attempt some music? Sister, may I show you? I think I remember our mother teaching us both to play a few songs. The knowledge will come back to you."

Sister Winifred sat down. "Before we begin, I need to ask you a question, Brother."

"Of course." He smiled. "Today seems to be a day of questions."

She leaned forward, her eyes as serious as I'd ever seen them. "When a priory or an abbey is dissolved by the king's commissioners, what happens?"

Brother Edmund went very still. "I don't think this is a prudent topic to discuss."

"May I ask why?"

He reached out and gently cupped her hands in his. "I don't want to upset you, for the sake of your health."

"But I am not a child," she said evenly. "I am a novice pledged to service at Dartford, and I should know what the future could bring."

He took a breath. "When an abbey is ordered dissolved by the king, all must leave within the month. There are pensions. Some are adequate, others less so. I know of friars who've left England, to live in faithful countries. There are not many openings to be found, so they travel from abbey to abbey, in strange lands, searching. Should they remain here, they can turn to the priesthood if they are willing to adapt to the new services. Or leave religion altogether and seek out new professions . . . marry, even."

"That is the men, but what of the women?" she persisted. "They have fewer possibilities, I think."

Brother Edmund and I glanced at each other.

Sister Winifred said, a trace of resentment in her voice: "If Sister Joanna may know these things, if she is fit to discuss matters of the world with you, then so should I."

Brother Edmund smiled ruefully. "Yes. You are right. And they *do* have fewer possibilities. Women can travel to the Continent in hopes of a European convent taking them in—though I have not heard of anyone doing so. They can seek shelter with their families. Or they can turn from the religious life and marry, bear children."

Sister Winifred took it in.

"And what of the priories themselves?" she asked. "What happens to them?"

"They are commonly awarded to courtiers favoured by the king and Cromwell," he said. "Some priories are converted into homes, just as they are; others are demolished by the owners, for their value. The buildings are pulled down stone by stone; any gold or silver or valuable stones are melted down; the tapestries and sculptures and books, even the vestments, are taken away; even the lead is stripped off, for what monies it could bring."

Sister Winifred's eyes widened; her lower lip trembled ever so slightly. But she looked at the two of us without flinching.

"Thank you, Brother. And now, I'm ready to learn the songs."

22

At the last meal of the day in the refectory, I heard bits of conversation among the sisters. I saw the resentment in their faces about the requiem feast in three days' time.

Sitting next to me at the novices' table, closest to the door, Sister Christina barely touched her soup or bread. I felt protective of her; I believed she was embarrassed by her father's request. I knew that many novices and even nuns struggled with the desire of parents to remain in our lives, even though we must be shut up to the outside world. We did not wish to hurt them, we loved and honoured them, but our lives must part from theirs.

Contemplating Sister Christina's father made me think of my own. The bread turned to dust in my mouth. No matter whether we lived together or apart, he was my only family. I so feared for him in the pitiless Tower, the place that haunted my dreams. But his liberation was nowhere near. The next day I had to deliver my letter to Bishop Gardiner, but I had little to report. I had failed my father.

Sister Agatha may have thought she kept her words low enough so as not to be overheard, but our novice mistress's grating voice carried over several tables.

"No, we've never had a feast in the priory before now," she said, "but we *have* been visited by members of the royal family. When the king's mother visited Sister Bridget here, many years ago, she might well have been served food and drink. A precedent could exist."

I could see Sister Anne shake her head. Our senior member sat across from Sister Agatha at their long wooden table. She said something to the novice mistress, but her voice was much softer, and all I could make out was "Prince Arthur."

I sat up straighter on my hard wooden bench. *Of course—Sis-*

ter Anne! I made a mental calculation of her age against the year of Prince Arthur's visit with his mother and his bride, Katherine of Aragon. Yes, it was just possible she had lived in Dartford in 1501.

The instant Sister Anne rose from her place, I jumped to my feet and made my way over to her. A few of the other senior sisters drew back at the sight of my approach—novices were expected to keep to themselves—but I didn't see how I could get another opportunity to talk to her tonight.

"Sister Anne?" I asked, with a respectful bow.

She was bent over with age, her face sagged with wrinkles, but Sister Anne smiled at me. "Oh, Sister Joanna, are you well?"

"Yes, Sister. May I walk with you to Vespers? It would be much appreciated."

She thought for a moment, and glanced around us, taking in the stares of the other nuns. I noticed her habit was made of linen, not the coarse wool everyone else wore. When nuns grew very old, they could receive permission to wear fabric softer to the skin.

Finally, she smiled at me again. "Of course, Sister Joanna. Walk with me."

As soon as we reached the passageway, out of the earshot of the others, I said, "Sister Anne, I am very interested in learning about the earlier days of our priory. I heard Sister Agatha mention the visit to Dartford of Prince Arthur. Were you at Dartford then?"

"I was here, yes." A sadness flitted across her face. "I am now the only one alive from that time. He came with his mother, Queen Elizabeth, at the end of 1501. He was only fifteen."

"Did you see the prince yourself?"

"Oh, no. The old queen always met with Sister Bridget in the *locutorium*. When she brought her son and daughter-in-law to visit with Sister Bridget, they remained in that room. They would never enter the cloister."

My spirits sank. We continued along the passageway, past the lavatory; I could hear the shuffle of the other sisters' feet behind us.

Sister Anne continued, "There was another sister then who was most anxious to see the prince with her own eyes. What was her name?" She thought for a moment. "Ah, Sister Isabel. She was perhaps unsuited to priory life. She was quite . . . lively. She persuaded the porter to allow her into the front rooms of the priory. She told me that she saw only the back of Prince Arthur as he walked away, toward the front door. He had blonde hair, she told me, and his wife, Princess Katherine, had red hair."

Sister Anne laughed softly. I tried to force a smile.

"Sister Isabel had foolish ideas," she reminisced. "There was something else she said about Prince Arthur's visit. Something about his disappearing."

"What?" My voice rang out in the stone passageway. I recovered, and in a lower voice, said, "I would be most interested, Sister Anne, to hear everything about it."

"I dislike passing on foolishness," she said. "Especially when it revolves around incorrect behaviour."

With great difficulty, I kept myself from begging her for the story. I did not want to frighten her. We passed the cloister garden; the quince trees bristled in the evening breeze.

To my relief, she picked up the memory again. "Sister Isabel said she was so determined, she made her way to one of the front rooms with windows facing the front lawns and gatehouse, so she would be able to see the royal party leave. She watched the old queen appear, with her ladies-in-waiting. They were taken to their horses and attendants. But the prince and princess did not join her. Sister Isabel saw the queen wave in the direction of the doorway and then depart, so she thought that meant Prince Arthur had decided to stay longer. After a few minutes, Sister Isabel came out to the passageway to find where he was, but she couldn't. Not the prince or the princess. She said she checked every room in the front of the priory. The porter said he hadn't seen the royal couple. They hadn't entered the cloister area, he was certain of that. And during this time, he hadn't seen Prioress Elizabeth, either."

Sister Anne and I had reached the archway to the church. The other sisters glanced at us, curious, as they passed. I asked quickly, "So she never saw the prince again?"

"No, but she heard him. She heard him leave. About an hour later, she heard the orders called outside, in the front, for the royal horses. By the time she found a window, the prince and princess were riding away."

Most of the nuns had filed into the church, and Sister Anne plainly wanted to follow them. Sister Rachel scowled at me as she walked in, followed by Sister Helen and Sister Agatha. But I had to know it all—now.

"So where was Prince Arthur that day?" I persisted, reaching out for her arm.

Sister Anne pulled away from me, puzzled by my vehemence.

"Please, I beg you, tell me the rest of the story," I whispered.

With a final shrug, she said, "Sister Isabel told this story to us many times, and she always said the same thing at the end. That there must be a secret room in Dartford. You see? She was very foolish."

A secret room in Dartford.

"And Prince Arthur has been dead oh so many years now," she mused. "So young to die only a few months after coming to Dartford. And of such a strange sickness." She shook herself out of her reverie, and we took our places in church, she with the oldest, most senior nuns, and myself with the novices.

I missed two of the responses in prayers that night because I was so distracted. If some sort of secret chamber existed, where could it be located? I knew the row of rooms in the front of the priory; they were orderly and sparely furnished. Between the walls? It didn't seem likely, the prioress squeezing into a narrow hidden chamber, followed by a royal couple. And what happened in that secret room? Did it have something to do with the Athelstan crown? Katherine of Aragon's dying words rumbled in my head: *"The legend is true. The Athelstan crown. Poor Arthur."*

More and more, I was convinced that to discover the hiding place of the crown I must learn more about King Athelstan. After Vespers, I murmured excuses to Sister Winifred and Sister Christina and darted out of the church.

I scuttled in the opposite direction of the rest of the sisters, toward the passageway leading off the cloister garden to the library. The last light of dusk filtered down. A taper fixed to the stone wall flickered outside the infirmary, but I saw no sign of activity within. Brother Edmund must have retired to the friars' quarters.

I turned the handle to the library door. To my amazement, it opened. Inside, the room was dark, so I removed the wall taper to better see.

I hurried to the section holding the books of general interest. Again, I saw the history of the Plantagenets, a collection of maps. But where I had found the dark-brown *From Caractacus to Athelstan*, there was now just a gap. Brother Richard might not have known its correct place, so I searched the entire library, checked every single book.

I couldn't find it. The book was gone, just like the letter from Prioress Elizabeth to her successor.

It was as if someone knew what I searched for, and was able to move things just out of my reach, moments before.

At that moment, I heard something. Whispering. Right outside the door. I blew out the taper and stood still. The whispering died down. I took a step to the door and heard something else. The patter of feet running along the passageway. Then silence again.

My breaths came fast; I quivered with fear. I had learned just hours ago of a secret room, and now I heard furtive movements. But I couldn't hide in the library much longer. Sister Eleanor always checked the novice's room before retiring to her bed. If I were not in my bed, an alarm would be called.

I turned the knob on the door, oh so slowly, and pushed it open a crack. Nothing. The passageway was dark and silent. I crept out of the library and made my way toward the cloister.

Behind me, in the infirmary, I heard it once more. A burst of whispers. And then a girl's giggle.

The Westerly children!

I stormed into the infirmary, and there they were, huddled near the fire that was no more than dying embers. Harold saw me first and gave a frightened cry, jumping to his feet. Martha threw her little arms around him but broke into giggles when she saw me.

"Hello, Sister Joanna," said Ethel, the only one who kept calm.

"Children, what are you doing here?" I said. "I know you wish to be near your mother, but to hide in the cloister after dark? It's completely forbidden." I looked around the infirmary. "Do you sleep here?"

"Cook lets us sleep in the pantry," piped up Martha. "As soon as dawn comes, we hide in the—"

"Shhhhh," ordered Ethel.

There was a bundle in front of Harold. He tried to edge it out of my sight.

"What's that you have?" I demanded.

The trio said nothing.

I reached down and uncovered the bundle. To my surprise, it was a heap of fresh yellow cakes.

"Where did you get these?" I asked.

"Cook made them for us," said Harold.

Ethel said, "They're soul cakes. We're going to give them away in the village tomorrow, on All Hallows' Eve."

I winced at her pronouncement of a pagan holiday.

Ethel said defiantly, "When you get a soul cake on All Hallows' Eve, you are supposed to pray for someone's soul. It's the day of the year when the wall is thinnest between the living and the dead. We'll get lots of villagers to pray for our mother, that she doesn't die."

"No, no, no," I said, upset over her knowledge of druid practices. "In the priory, *we* will pray for your mother, as we always do. God will look after her."

Little Martha's lip quivered. "You won't take our soul cakes away, Sister? You won't stop us from saving Mother?"

I groaned. How to make them understand?

"Is your father still in London?" I asked.

"He's still in Southwark," Harold said.

I heard a faint wheezing breath from the corner. It thickened to a gurgle. Their mother sounded even worse. Harold looked at his sisters and at me, his eyes filling with tears.

I made my decision.

"It's dark now; you couldn't make your way safely to town anyway. Get to the pantry, children."

"You won't tell on us?" begged Harold.

"Not tonight, but this is *not* a fit solution. I will pray on what to do and say."

I led the Westerlys out of the infirmary and toward the kitchen pantry. Martha slipped her hand in mine as we walked. Her warm, stubby little fingers gripped mine with surprising force.

I settled them in their forlorn corner, which I now realised was the children's usual sleeping quarters. They pulled torn blankets out from behind baskets. "Eat the cakes yourselves," I pleaded. "Don't use them for prayers. It's against God's wishes."

Martha threw her arms around my neck. A wet kiss covered my cheek.

"I love you, Sister Joanna," she said in her singsong voice.

"I love all of you," I said. My voice broke.

Ethel looked at me, startled.

I pulled Martha's arms off my shoulders and backed away. With a final awkward little wave, I left the children behind in the pantry, to make my way to my own novice bed.

23

The next day we lost the sun.

It had been pleasant, this last October week. The afternoon sun warmed the gardens and grounds, caressed the red and orange leaves heaped everywhere. The sisters filled baskets with light-green quince fruit that had ripened in the cloister trees. Most mornings, the sour yet pleasing smell of bonfires drifted in through the windows.

But a cold, fierce wind came before dawn on All Hallows' Eve. It brought sheets of rain that ripped the last loose leaves from the trees. On an ordinary day at the priory, I would be inside, oblivious of the tempest. But this morning I tucked my letter to Bishop Gardiner into my habit's sleeve and, with muttered excuses, made my way to the barn. After making sure no one was watching, I trudged to the leper hospital on the northwest edge of priory property, just beyond a hill fringed with tall trees.

I had donned a cloak so my habit would not be soaked through. I could have pulled its hood over my head, but I scorned such protection. I wanted to feel the cold rain on my face. I longed for the wind to sting my eyes.

My mood was wretched. I had written and sealed my letter to the Bishop of Winchester, and it was lamentably short. I relayed that Prioress Elizabeth had died on the morning of my return and that her last communication had gone missing. A story told by our oldest nun suggested that a secret room might exist at Dartford and that, when he visited the priory in 1501, Prince Arthur may have gone to this room. I had no precise knowledge of its location, but the room must be in the front part of the priory, not the cloister. There could be hidden the Athelstan crown. "Suggested . . . may have . . . might . . . could." I pictured a clerk handing him my letter, and the bishop breaking the seal, impatient for news, his face darkening with rage after he'd raced through my few sentences.

I reached the top of the hill and paused to take shelter under the trees. A red squirrel darted away from me, upset that I'd penetrated his dry domain within the bushes.

Just below, in a hollow, stood the leper hospital. It had been abandoned before I came to Dartford; I didn't know when exactly. Twenty years ago? Fifty? One hundred? Half the roof had collapsed. I could see the brown field through a ragged gap in the back wall. Green ivy choked every yawning window; the vines had long ago crawled inside, eager to claim the rooms once denied them.

But what of the lepers, those poor despised souls? Had they gone to another hospital to be cared for, or were they driven to find corners of London to hide in, frightened and sick? There was no one to ask.

Looking down on the hospital, the tears on my cheeks mingled with the raindrops. Fifty years hence, some girl might look at an abandoned Dartford Priory and wonder: *What happened to the nuns once sheltered there? Why did they leave their parents and forsake marriage and motherhood to live in such a place?* There'd be no one to tell the girl who we were or what we believed in: humble service to Christ, support of one another, learning, and contemplation.

Halfway down the hill to the hospital, I stumbled and fell to my knees. Heavy rains had turned the countryside to mud. I recovered and walked a more careful path to the front archway. The door was long ago torn off its hinges—for firewood, no doubt. Carved in stone over the arch were the words LEPER HOSPITAL OF SAINT MARY MAGDALENE AND ST. LAUDUS. Below, in smaller words, was THE ORDER OF SAINT LAZARUS OF JERUSALEM. I knew a little of this order: a medical one created by the Knights Templar. The Crusades. My boy cousins loved playing crusaders at Stafford Castle. They'd storm down the wide halls, brandishing wooden swords and shouting, "God wills it!"

I quickly found the window described to me. I felt along its sides. Yes, a wide opening existed. I took out my letter, which I'd sealed with waxe this very morning. I removed the loose panel, slipped it inside, and replaced the panel. This hiding place had been well researched and prepared. For the first time, I wondered who would come for my letter and convey it over the channel to Bishop Gardiner. Some local man paid well for his trouble?

I had no wish to linger in this forlorn place and left through the archway.

I'd climbed halfway up the hill when something made me turn around and read the words over the archway again: The Order of Saint Lazarus of Jerusalem. The Crusades. And then I remembered.

Richard the Lionhearted. King of England, leader of the Third Crusade. The other man mentioned by Bishop Gardiner in the Tower. *Do you know of Edward the Third's son, the Black Prince? What of Richard the Lionhearted? Or our king's dead brother, Prince Arthur?*

Although he had lived two centuries earlier, I knew more of Richard's life than of the Black Prince's. I'd always been interested in the Crusades. Richard, the Coeur de Lion, who fought the Muslims with tremendous bravery. He was imprisoned by another king on his way home from Jerusalem, and freed himself to reclaim his throne from his treacherous brother John. I remembered he married but had no children before he died in his middle years in the South of France.

The South of France.

How odd. King Richard died in the same part of the world where the Black Prince first took ill with the sickness that would kill him.

My thoughts raced as I reached the trees again. This was not unlike working on one of Sister Helen's tapestries. At first only she knew the meaning of the pattern; we wove where the cartoon bade us but didn't know what world we created until certain things took shape: men and women, deities and beasts, forests and seas.

I was beginning to see an outline to Bishop Gardiner's strange pattern. With more perseverance, I might yet learn the secret of the crown.

I moved just a few feet out of the shelter of the trees, back to the priory. Something caught my eye to the far right. I squinted in the rain.

This ridge continued for a ways, then widened to a more circular, flat hill, bare of trees. A woman walked away from me on the hill, dressed in a plain novice habit, her hood down around her shoulders, like mine. It was Sister Christina.

I made my way toward her, clinging to branches where I could.

The scratchy bark hurt, but I had to keep from falling down the slippery hill.

"Sister Christina!" I shouted as soon as I emerged from the trees. She had stopped walking but didn't turn to face me; the wind must be carrying my voice away. It blew harder and colder now, though the rain had lessened.

When I was almost upon her, I called her name again. This time she jumped in surprise. I saw her face was ravaged by tears, as mine must be.

"What troubles you?" I asked.

She shook her head. I didn't pry; I shared her grief over the shadowed future of Dartford Priory. Her wide forehead crinkled with lines, as if she were an old woman. Her nose was red from the cold—or from weeping. Her slate-blue eyes looked tired.

Suddenly, she grabbed my hand and squeezed it, hard. "Oh, Sister Joanna, forgive me for my anger with you."

"I deserve all of the censure that I have received," I said. "But thank you, Sister Christina. I've missed your friendship."

We embraced, and I laughed a little; we were both so wet and cold.

She looked at me thoughtfully. "You were willing to sacrifice everything—your place as a novice, even your life—to honour your cousin, who died because she rebelled against heresy. I now think that what you did was very brave."

I couldn't bear her praise, minutes after hiding my spy's letter.

"No, no, no." I shook my head. "It was wrong of me."

With a sweeping gesture, she turned around on the hill. "Do you know this place?"

I shook my head.

Now she pointed down, just to the side of her right foot. A grey stone was embedded deep in the ground.

"There was a nunnery here, on the hill, centuries ago," she told me. "This is the foundation. You can find most of it if you look hard; it forms a giant square. Walk it with me, please."

I followed Sister Christina, my eyes fixed to the wet ground. I could make out the intermittent stones peeking below the grass, in too straight a line to be of nature.

"It's said that King Edward selected this land for Dartford Priory because of the existence of an earlier nunnery," she said. "But I doubt he knew what became of it."

"Why . . . what happened?"

Her back to me, she said, "The sisters were members of the cult of Saint Juliana. Do you know it?"

"I know Juliana was a martyr."

"She converted to Christianity and wished to live as a virgin, but her father was a pagan. He ordered her to marry a Roman like himself. They say the devil even appeared to try to persuade Juliana, but she stayed strong. She wouldn't deny her faith, and she was killed for it. The Romans beheaded her."

I shivered in the wind. I felt so exposed here, with Sister Christina. Below, at the priory, we could be visible. The prioress's windows faced the hills. It was permitted to walk on priory property, as long as we did not leave the grounds. On such a day as this, though, a walk would prompt questions.

But Sister Christina seemed bent on telling me of this lost nunnery, and I found her tale intriguing.

"When was it built, this nunnery?" I asked.

"I don't know when it was built, but it was destroyed in the eighth century."

A century earlier than King Athelstan's reign, I thought. Aloud, I asked, "Why was it destroyed?"

She whipped around, her face fierce. "*Norsemen,* Sister Joanna. That was when they were at the height of their power. The Norsemen invaded here and there, killing Christians. They stole our goods and burned our farms. But their favourite sport was the violation of nuns."

I flinched. "Sister Christina, that's terrible. Don't speak of it."

She went on as if she hadn't heard me.

"The sisters must have hoped that their nunnery was far enough from the coast and close enough to London to be safe, but it wasn't. A party of Norsemen found this nunnery—it was very small, perhaps eight women. They tried to get inside, to rape the sisters."

I put my hands in front of my eyes, as if to shield myself from a horror happening here, now.

"The nuns got word that the Norsemen were on their way. They bolted all the doors. That wouldn't stop the men for long—they had axees. But do you know what the nuns did?"

"Sister Christina, I can't hear this. I beg you. Any story of a woman being violated, I can't—"

She grabbed me by my shoulders and shouted, "*They burned themselves to death!* When the fire died down, the door was hacked to bits, but all they found was burned flesh. The Norsemen were so angry, they destroyed the nunnery; every brick was scattered across the field."

The rough grey sky spun around me, and my knees weakened. I knelt, gagging.

In a much different voice, Sister Christina said, "Oh, Sister Joanna, I didn't mean to do this to you. Forgive me."

She squatted down and patted my heaving back. "I didn't think you would be so upset. You've been in prison, in the Tower of London. *Interrogated.* I thought that I could tell you of this, that you could bear the tale. People of the village of Dartford know it; it's been carried down for centuries. I heard it before I came to the priory."

She helped me back up to my feet. I took a deep breath. "I simply can't hear stories like that, but you had no way of knowing it, Sister."

"I'm sorry," she said again. "I can see that you would not have the same view as I on the deaths of the nuns."

"I grieve for them. What other view could there be?"

"In their deaths, they shared in the suffering of Christ in a special, most holy, way," said Sister Christina. "The flames were purifying; they were a form of"—she searched for the right words—"a form of divine ravishment. Do you see?"

"Not entirely," I admitted.

Movement at the priory entrance cut short our conversation. The prioress, Sister Eleanor, and Sister Rachel walked out into the cold, wet courtyard without their black cloaks to protect them, carrying baskets.

"Look." Sister Christina pointed at the priory lane emerging from the woods. A line of people approached. I recognised the man leading them. The poorest people of Dartford had come to receive alms from the priory, as they did twice a month. It was a tradition established generations ago. The head of our priory would make the distribution of food and coins on the other side of the gatehouse.

Unnoticed, Sister Christina and I made our way to the priory. Beholding the majestic entrance of Dartford was a comfort, after seeing the crumbled walls of the leper hospital and the fragments of the ancient nunnery.

So many times I'd hurried past them, but now I paused to examine the stone statues of the king on either side of the door. Someone had told me when I came to Dartford that they were two versions of King Edward the Third: one young and one old. The statue on the left was bearded and wore long robes. The figure on the right was clean-shaven and wore chain-mail, armour, and carried a sword.

I took a closer look at the stone warrior on the right. "Wait," I said. "Before we go in, do you know the histories of these statues?"

"The old one is King Edward the Third; the young one is his son, the Black Prince. The prince died before the priory doors opened."

I was taken aback. "You are quite familiar with the era."

She shrugged. "I grew up in Dartford, remember? I came here for lessons as a child. I know everything about the priory."

She pointed at the tableau of stone carvings over the entrance. "I prefer the story of the Virgin to that of the kings."

I looked at the figures, all genuflecting before Jesus and Mary. The figure of Christ stretched His hands over her head as His mother bowed before him. Above her head, carved deep in the back of the stone wall, nearly covered by lilies, was the outline of a crown. I had never noticed it before. It hovered over the exact centre of the pointed archway that welcomed all to Dartford Priory.

Sister Christina followed my startled gaze and beamed as she, too, studied the carvings.

"Sister Joanna, you love the coronation of the Virgin, as well? Isn't it wonderful? Her son is crowning her as the queen of heaven."

24

Between the pagan holiday of All Hallows' Eve and the sacred celebration of All Souls' Day fell All Saints' Day. I'd always looked forward to it as a child. At Mass, huddled with my cousin Margaret in our family chapel, listening to the priest, we'd be frightened but also thrilled by details of the martyrs' deaths. Our favourite was Saint Agnes, who at the age of twelve was devoured by lions as the crowd roared in the great coliseum of Rome. Martyrdom was but a ghoulish game to us.

Now, at the All Saints' Day Mass at Dartford Priory, I honoured the women and men who endured pain and terror and untimely death for our faith. Cromwell and the heretics who followed him were terribly scornful of our saints. I could not understand it.

"It is this day more than any other that we celebrate the martyrs," intoned Brother Philip, at the apse of the church. "And we revere their sacred bodies, who have become our blessed relics in monasteries and churches across Christendom. How can we, the low and the miserable, comprehend the sacrifices of those who shed their own blood for the Lord God and the Virgin Mary? I call on Saint Jerome to shed the light for us today. For it was he who said, 'We venerate the relics of the martyrs in order to better adore Him whose martyrs they are.'"

I thought of touching those bricks the previous day, the foundation bricks for the Saint Juliana nunnery on the hill. I shivered as I prayed for the women, they who chose to end their lives just outside our thick limestone walls. Next to me, Sister Christina moaned and swayed in the pew. We shared the same intensity of devotion.

After Sext prayers, everyone scattered in different directions to prepare for the next day's feast. I met Brother Edmund and Sister

Winifred for a last session of music practice in the chapter house. But my fingers were nervous on the *vihuela;* I kept missing notes. It was a relief when Gregory and two servants trudged in, carrying a rolled-up tapestry. We all stopped playing to watch them hang it behind the head table.

The tapestry was Dartford's most recently completed one, borrowed from its owners, a local shipbuilding family. They were more than willing to lend it for the occasion. Everyone wanted to honour Lord Chester, the town's most prominent citizen.

"How wondrous," Brother Edmund said when they unfurled the five-foot-long tapestry. Sister Winifred and I looked at each other, proud. We'd both worked on *The Myth of Daphne;* it had been finished just before Lent.

The tapestry tableau was based on a Greek story: a river god turns his beautiful daughter, Daphne, a nymph, into a tree. Sister Helen always completed the human figures herself, and in this case she had outdone herself: a lovely blonde girl pauses midflight, her white limbs sprouting branches and leaves as a group of men watch. Sister Helen had worked in more than twenty different shades of green for the forest alone. I know she had not only used silks imported from Brussels but had dyed some of the threads herself. Beautiful flowers sprouted on the banks of the river: daffodils and roses and violets. In the lower right-hand corner, through a burst of water lilies and weeds, poked the grey-haired head of Daphne's father.

Gregory shouted at the servants, "Be careful, fools!" as they struggled to hang the tapestry evenly on the back wall, behind the centre of the dais.

"Music is at an end, don't you agree, Brother?" Sister Winifred said. I'd already put down my *vihuela*.

Brother Edmund did not answer. He could not take his eyes off the tapestry.

"It is a beautiful sight, agreed?" I asked.

"Yes, certainly," he said slowly, "but the story of Daphne is a strange choice of subject for a priory. Not just for you to create, but to be displayed tomorrow at a requiem feast."

I nodded. "I used to feel that way about such stories. But Prioress

Elizabeth assured us that the classics displayed in art are not blasphemy."

Brother Edmund opened his mouth, as if to say something else. He glanced at his sister, and me, and then appeared to think better of it. His usual serene expression returned.

Brother Richard beckoned to him from the doorway. "You're needed in the infirmary," he called out to his fellow friar.

Brother Edmund handed his lute to his sister and hurried off. I, too, left the chapter house, to continue my other work. In the passageway loomed Sister Eleanor, even more serious than usual. I saw why in a moment: six nuns followed her, carrying the treasures of our church. They bore chalices, plates, and, most precious of all, our reliquary. It had been brought out for the Mass of All Saints' Day and now was being moved to the chapter house for display before our guests. A priory's precious objects were the pride of the house.

I flattened myself against the wall to make room for the procession. Sister Rachel carried the reliquary as if it were a newborn infant. The Dartford Priory reliquary was a pale life-size carving of a woman's hand that sprouted from a cylindrical gold-gilded base, encrusted with diamonds and small rubies. It was more than two centuries old, a founding gift of Edward the Third's. I had held it myself; it looked delicate but was surprisingly solid. Reliquaries are meant to contain relics—a lock of hair, a fingernail, some fragment of a saint's body—but this one came to us empty. Still, we revered its intent and its beauty. My pulse quickened as Sister Rachel carried it past me. The reliquary was beautiful—and yet I found it frightening. Sometimes it seemed as if the two fingers pointing straightest would grab hold of me.

Sister Eleanor called out to the last nun in the group: "Sister Agatha, when you've brought in the chalice, don't forget to go to the library for our *Life of Saint Matilda*."

I quickly stepped forward. "Sister Agatha, may I assist you?"

The novice mistress brightened at my offer. "Yes, Sister Joanna, why don't you open the library and wait for me? I will be there in a moment." She fished in her pocket and removed a key from a ring.

It was all I could do not to sprint to the library. My hand trembled as I unlocked the door. Once again, I went straight to where I'd once found the book on Athelstan. But there was nothing but a gap. It still hadn't been replaced.

Above it, though, my eyes settled on *The History of the Plantagenets*. I wondered if it would touch on the life of Richard the Lionhearted. My hand was on the cover when Sister Agatha bustled in. I jumped back to face her, but she hadn't noticed what I was about.

"Oh, thank you, Sister Joanna. This is such a delicate manuscript, and Sister Eleanor gets so angry if I make any mistakes."

We turned to *The Life of Saint Matilda*, one of the priory's five illuminated manuscripts. Each colourful drawing that faced a page of words must have taken the monks many weeks to complete.

As she fumbled to undo the bindings that tied the manuscript to a stand, Sister Agatha said, "Lord Chester has never struck *me* as a man of books and learning, but then my opinion is not solicited or listened to."

"You have been in the presence of Lord Chester?" I asked, surprised.

"Haven't you?"

I thought for a moment and then shook my head.

Sister Agatha pursed her lips. "He was a frequent visitor for a time; not surprising, I suppose, since he is our neighbour. But now that I think on it, he has not been to the priory more than once in the last two years. Not since his daughter professed."

She finally managed to free the manuscript from its stand. I moved closer, to help with the carrying.

Sister Agatha's mouth twitched; she had something else to say.

"Young blood is good for any priory, of course. Our prioress is forty-one years of age; she still has the strength to accomplish much. But a thirty-year-old *circator*? It is not easy to bear. Not that I mind Sister Eleanor being so much younger than Sister Rachel and myself and having a higher rank. *That* is not the difficulty."

While Sister Agatha kept on her stream of talk, we bore the heavy book out of the library. With my free hand I closed the door behind us. She did not ask me to lock it.

In the chapter house, I helped her place *The Life of Saint Matilda* on the long table, next to the reliquary, mounted on a plaster pillar. At the sight of the Daphne tapestry, now evenly hanging, she brightened and joined the other sisters who stood rapt before it.

"Yes, this one is our greatest accomplishment," she announced, and then pursed her lips. "Oh but wait, the girl in the middle. Her face looks familiar to me. Who is it?"

With a bow, I eased away from the sisters, backing toward the door. I paused, waiting for Sister Agatha to call out, Sister Joanna, I must have my key back.

She did not.

This was, if anything, a sin of omission, I told myself as I hurried down the passageway. By Vespers, I'd make sure that Sister Agatha had her key again.

Back in the library, a fresh candle on the table, the door closed, I pulled down the Plantagenet book.

I quickly found a chapter on Richard the Lionhearted, the second Plantagenet king of England, and leafed to the end:

In the last year of his reign, after his return from the Holy Lands and release from imprisonment, Richard was much preoccupied with his quarrels with the French king over territory. Richard's Château Gaillard, on the bank of the Seine, was a mighty fortress, completed in the year 1198. But it had required much money to build, taken from the treasury of England and from Richard's kingdom of Aquitaine, granted to him by his mother, Queen Eleanor.

In the spring of the year 1199, Richard held state in his court of the Aquitaine when he received word that treasure had been discovered deep in the ground, near the Château of Châlus-Chabrol, not far from his residence. It was in the territory of the Viscount of Limoges, who was bound to be Richard's vassal but who had many dealings with the French king and thus was not trusted.

Richard journeyed to Châlus-Chabrol and claimed the treasure, for he had sore need of money. It had been dug up by a peasant. Richard said after he examined the treasure, which was gold coins and objects of royal value, that it was of English origin.

Lord Montbrun of the Château of Châlus-Chabrol, who was a relative and ally of the Viscount of Limoges, was much offended and said that the treasure could not have come from so far away. He publicly charged that Richard had stolen it. This was a belief many held. But it was a grave insult that no sovereign could let stand. Richard called for his armies to fight the French lord, and the château prepared for a siege. It took one month for the soldiers to assemble with the necessary siege works.

On the evening of March 25, Richard walked around the walls of the Château of Châlus-Chabrol. His men begged him to wear his armour because French soldiers on the walls still had many arrows. Richard refused to do so. He called out to one crossbowman on the wall and laughed and bade him fire, and the man complied. His second arrow hit King Richard in the left shoulder. The king returned to his tent and removed the arrow himself, but it broke off and part of it remained inside his body. The king would accept no treatment for the wound.

He began a fever and after a few days it was feared that he would die. But Richard, as his final command, directed that the crossbowman must be pardoned and never harmed. Richard said he was not worthy to be king and had already become weak before he was struck with the arrow. His words caused his nobles much grief, and they protested that he was the most valorous man they ever served.

When he died on April 6, in the Year of Our Lord 1199, his men disobeyed his command. The château was taken. The crossbowman was found, and the English lords flayed him alive.

All Christendom mourned the death of such a mighty sovereign. He was forty-two years of age. He had reigned for ten years.

The book slipped from my fingers. For a long time my thoughts whirled around the strange death of Richard Coeur de Lion. Why would the most experienced battle commander of his time invite a shot from a crossbowman who held a position on top of a castle wall? *Richard said he was not worthy to be king and had already become weak before he was struck with the arrow.* It made no sense.

Finally, I resumed my reading. I leafed through the book, until I found the story of the life of the Black Prince. The treasure was found in land belonging to the Viscount of Limoges; the Black Prince laid siege to the town of Limoges. There must be a connection.

But there was not much written about the terrible siege that I hadn't already learned from Brother Edmund. The Black Prince grew sicker after the town's citizens had been slain, and he returned home. The book said: "He had delivered to England a shipload of great treasure."

I raced ahead to the description of his death:

> *The Prince of Wales bore all his sufferings patiently. In the last moments he was attended by the Bishop of Bangor, who urged him to ask forgiveness of God and of all those whom he had injured. For a time he would not do this, but at last joined his hands and prayed that God and man would grant him pardon and so died in the Royal Palace of Westminster in his forty-sixth year.*

The library door swung open, and Sister Eleanor hurtled inside.

"Sister Joanna!" she cried. Behind her stood Sister Agatha, just as shocked as the *circator.*

I placed my book back in its place on the shelf. Sister Eleanor didn't look at the book, only at me. Her eyes danced with rage. "Once again you violate our trust and our rules. We all knew of your crimes against the Dominican Order. But we were assured that you had committed yourself to redemption."

I felt my face turn hot. "Sister Eleanor, I lost myself to reading. I beg forgiveness. I realise there was work to be performed, but—"

"Lettice Westerly died one hour ago," she said, interrupting me. Her children became hysterical. We couldn't calm them, no matter what we said or did. They asked for you—the littlest one begged for you. No one could find you."

I rushed past her, to the door. "Where are the children now, Sister?"

"Gone," she said. "They ran away. We all went looking for you, and when we came back, they'd disappeared."

"But their father is in London; he's not at their house in town," I said, frantic.

She nodded. "That's correct. So, Sister, whatever befalls the Westerly children, let it be on *your* conscience."

I swallowed.

Sister Agatha edged forward. "I'll take the key back, Sister Joanna."

I handed it to her.

Sister Eleanor said, "Your crimes will be read before all the sisters, in chapter, the week after our requiem feast. Your punishments will be up to Prioress Joan. There are some sisters who believe you should never have been restored to Dartford Priory. Perhaps now they will be listened to."

I joined the search for the children. I cornered Elene the cook; she of all people would know their whereabouts. But between the frenzied preparation for the feast and her grief over losing her closest friend, Elene was useless.

The motherless Westerly children had gone, and no one knew where.

At the evening meal, the whispers in the room encircled me like a storm. There was no worse choice of nun to know the details of my latest disgrace than Sister Agatha. Everyone with a pair of ears must know all by now.

We ate in silence at the novice table. I kept my head down, not wishing to meet the gaze of Sister Winifred, sitting across from me, or Sister Christina, to my left.

Near the end of the sorry meal, I could bear it no longer. I looked up, straight at Sister Winifred. She looked close to tears.

"There is something you wish to say to me?" I said.

"Oh, Sister Joanna, what *happened* to you?" she whispered.

My bitter response was out before I could stop it: "A very great deal."

Sister Christina leaned toward me. "Tell us," she said urgently. "You must."

I shook my head. "No."

"We are your closest of friends," she pressed. "Why will you not tell us what happened to you in the Tower, so that we can be of support to you?"

I closed my eyes.

"I'm sorry," I said. "I can't."

In bed that night I staggered from one nightmare to the next. I searched for the Westerly children, my chest heaving with sobs. But then the scene changed, and I was running, frightened, through the thick forests with my cousin Margaret. We fled a demonic creature that sought to devour us, but every time we thought ourselves well concealed, it discovered us once more.

There was a scream, and for the first few seconds I thought it part of my nightmare. But then it came again, the scream: so frightened, so agonised. I opened my eyes and knew the sound was real. It came in through the small window, high in our room.

"What is that?" groaned Sister Winifred next to me, sitting up.

"I don't know," I said, just as hoarse.

"It's a pig," said Sister Christina. Her voice was clear, as if she had been awake for quite a time. She didn't sit up; she lay on her back, on her pallet against the opposite wall. I could just make out her profile in the grey dimness. The night was beginning to lighten; it would be dawn within the hour.

"Pig?" I asked.

"They're killing it for my father to eat today."

There was one more scream and then nothing. I lay there, rigid, breathless, waiting for more, but it never came. They must have slit the pig's throat.

25

I sat in the chapter house, between Brother Edmund and Sister Winifred, my *vihuela* in my lap, and waited for Lord and Lady Chester to arrive. It was midafternoon. For reasons I didn't dare ask, the requiem banquet was set to begin hours later than our usual dinnertime of eleven in the morning. Perhaps it was to accommodate a request of our neighbours'. Or perhaps it was to allow enough time for the cooking of the dishes. All morning the smells of roasting meats travelled the passageways, so strong you could not escape them. There was pork, of course; the young pig slaughtered that morning turned on a spit in the kitchen fire, terror seared into its dead eyes. But there was more on the menu: venison, roast beef, lark, rabbit, and capon. All were foreign to our priory, to our senses. When I passed Sister Rachel in the south passageway off the cloister, she pressed a cloth to her nose, her eyes brimming with fury. She pulled the cloth away to spit the word "Defilement," and then clamped it back down on her nose and mouth.

Now Sister Rachel sat in the same room as the rest of the nuns, her sallow face a shield of resentment. Every space was taken on the stone benches that lined three of the four walls. Sister Christina waited among them, not at the head table. Whether that was at her own request or because of a novice's low ranking, no one said. She clenched her hands in her lap, a stance of hers that I recognised: it meant she'd turned within herself to pray.

I sat apart, with my fellow musicians, on a narrow stool. Cool air streamed in through the cracks in the mullioned windows behind my head. We'd been placed off to the side of the long head table. I was closest to it, with Brother Edmund in the centre and Sister Winifred on his other side.

Only two people sat at the head table: Prioress Joan and Brother Richard. They were far apart, with two empty chairs between them. Brother Philip was not present. At the first Mass of the day for All Souls he'd said a few impassioned things about purgatory. But then he'd pleaded indisposition for the banquet. He was the only who dared.

The appointed time for Lord Chester's arrival came . . . and went. The minutes crawled by.

Gregory, the porter, rushed in, bowing, and whispered something in Prioress Joan's ear. Whatever she learned displeased her. She shook her head and whispered something back. The porter scurried out. Brother Richard shot a look at Brother Edmund and then, the ghost of a smile on his lips, raised his goblet of wine for another long sip.

It was possible Lord Chester would not come, even though the feast had been arranged specifically for him. Some gentry lived by whim. It was nothing to them to overturn the plans of those they considered unimportant. All the preparations and expense? Worthy of a shrug. The only reason that I expected Lord and Lady Chester to materialise was not for the prioress's or the nuns' sake but for that of their daughter. She was their only living child. Even in times of fear and greed and dissolution, the ties of family exerted their pull.

No one spoke; we all waited, filled with our own unhappy thoughts. I hated sitting here, waiting to perform music for a spoiled lord, while the Westerly children remained missing. I was also wasting valuable time that could be spent searching for the Athelstan crown. How much had my father's health suffered since I left the Tower? I twitched in my seat as the question tormented me.

My stool's position afforded me a close view of our prioress. She didn't touch her goblet or pick from the plates of radishes and salt set before her. Her jaw was tight, and her eyes were wary. She had determined that this requiem banquet would be of help to the priory, and so it had been organised, despite all feelings of disapproval. I admired women of strong character, and the truth was I admired Prioress Joan Vane. She suddenly glanced over, as if she could hear my thoughts, and I was doused with the usual cold suspicion. My esteem for the prioress was not reciprocated.

Weary of her dislike, I gazed up, up at the ceiling of the chapter house. I examined the stone carvings that encircled the top of the four thick pillars. The carvings resembled lilies, the symbol of the Dominicans, conveying the purity and dedication of those who professed our vows. King Edward the Third must have employed the finest artisans in his kingdom to create these stone lilies. They bloomed all over the priory: above the entranceway to Dartford; in the crests in the front wall; along the border running along the cloister passageways; and here, in the chapter house. It was not easy to make out the floral details, both because of the height of the columns and the shadows cast by the afternoon light. It did look as if something else peeked above the lilies: swooping lines that reached a point. I squinted, trying to determine the lines' direction, when it struck me with such force that I cowered on my stool.

Behind the lilies was the carved outline of a crown.

They were intertwined, the lilies and the crown. Why did King Edward the Third order it? The location of the crown was a dread secret, yet its very presence was proclaimed in the walls. There must be a purpose. Did the lilies signify protection? The Dominican Order, considered the most vigilant of all, was powerful enough to keep the crown safe from violation.

But something gnawed at me, some fault in that logic. What did Bishop Gardiner say? "*And there is prophecy. A prophecy of great reward but not without great risk. It is both blessing and curse.*"

There was a faint rushing in my ears as I seized the different strands and wove them together.

The crown was extremely dangerous. It didn't require protection from the people. People required protection from it.

The treasure in the ground in Limoges included objects of "royal value." What was more royal than a crown? It was Richard the Lion-hearted who first encountered the Athelstan crown, hidden in the earth until a peasant dug it up. He spoke the truth. The treasure *was* English, sent to France for unknown reasons. When the king lay dying, Richard not only pardoned the crossbowman but also must have ordered the crown concealed again. Still, someone must have known of it, rumours must have lived on, for two centuries later, an arrogant soldier prince, the oldest son of Edward the Third, came looking for it—and found it. "He had delivered to England a shipload of great treasure," the book had said. *The Black Prince brought the crown back to England.* Too frightened of its power to destroy it, his father the king must have decided to place the Athelstan crown in a holy place. He had an entire Dominican priory built for concealment. And still, someone must have known and told, for a Tudor boy came thirty-six years ago, and, for a third time, the crown felled a prince of the blood.

"Once you learn where the Athelstan crown is located, communicate that to me alone, in writing," Bishop Gardiner had insisted. "You must not touch it yourself, not even for an instant. You understand?"

Touch. That was it. To touch the crown was to trigger death, a death that could not be stopped no matter what remedies were applied, what physicians were found. And it was here, somewhere, within the priory. Locked away, inside our walls, or perhaps beneath our feet.

Bishop Gardiner had found out about the crown and sought to gain hold of it. But why? Did he crave it as a weapon, as a means to fatally weaken our sovereign, King Henry? The bishop said he wanted to save the monasteries, but he'd also said, with great passion, "*I serve the House of Tudor.*" I recalled the bishop's nickname—"Wily Winchester"—and his reputation for betrayal. I'd glimpsed the darkness within him. Was it possible his plan was to obtain the crown and present it to the king to shore up his faltering status, to ingratiate himself with Henry Tudor? Or did he really want to serve the king, I wondered. How could a man with such a crown bow down before another man who wears a crown?

An elbow nudged my rib, and I jumped on my stool. It was Brother Edmund. He pointed at the doorway with his chin.

A couple, dressed entirely in black, stood just over the threshold of the chapter house. Lord and Lady Chester had arrived at last. I had no choice but to push aside my thoughts of the crown and to endure the requiem feast.

Lord Chester entered the room first. He appeared a handsome man, just past his prime. He towered a full head's length above the porter, who now backed away, deferential, from our guest of honour. He wore a long black doublet elabourately stitched with silver thread, a costly piece of fashion. As he came closer, I noticed the doublet strained at its buttons because it was too small for him; he was just starting to spread to fat and either did not know it or did not wish to know it. Our neighbour had lost half his hair; his pate shone beneath the thinning chestnut strands. Large jewelled rings gleamed on both hands.

His steps were heavy; it took a long time for him to reach the centre of the table and the chair that he assumed—correctly—was reserved for him.

Prioress Joan rose to her feet. "Dartford Priory welcomes you to our requiem feast in honour of All Souls' Day, Lord Chester," she said.

He bowed and said in a deep voice, "I thank you, Prioress." Without looking back, he beckoned carelessly with one hand. "My lady, attend."

Lady Chester, pale, thin, and short in stature, made her way to the chair next to his. Her black bodice and skirt, her gable hood, made for an ensemble so severe she looked more like one of us than a lady. Not a single jewel, not even a slender ring, adorned her body. These were the clothes of strict mourning, which I realised was only fitting, since Queen Jane died a week ago and her husband served the king.

Lord Chester turned to examine my corner of the room. Now that he was closer, he appeared not so hale. His eyes were bloodshot; his neck was loose. A faint spider's web of broken red veins mottled his nose.

He smiled with approval at the sight of the musical instruments: my *vihuela* and the others' lutes. Lord Chester had requested music; we were ready to perform it.

And then he belched. The stench of wine hit me like a puff of wind.

Lord Chester, it seemed, was quite drunk.

26

"Where's my daughter?" asked Lord Chester loudly. He squinted as he examined the nuns sitting on their stone benches carved from the walls.

My eyes found Sister Christina, across the room. The late-afternoon light stretched across her lap; her face was in shadow. Unreadable.

"Ah, there she is," Lord Chester said. "Have you no greeting for me, child?"

Sister Christina did not move or speak.

Lady Chester leaned forward in her chair. "Sister Christina, I greet you on this day of remembrance," she called out, nervous.

"I greet you, Lady Chester," Sister Christina responded formally. A few seconds later, she added: "And you, sir."

Prioress Joan broke in: "We *all* greet you, Lord and Lady Chester. We are honoured to have you as our guests at Dartford Priory."

"Ah, that's what I like to have said." Lord Chester nodded at all the nuns, novices, and friars assembled before him. "That's what I like. Yes. Very good. The beginning of a new era."

He held up his goblet of wine, as if toasting the prioress, and then took a long, thirsty sip, as if he'd drunk nothing before it this day.

"Prioress, we are behind the appointed time, and for that I apologise," Lady Chester said. "We first paid a visit to the grave of our son."

Lord Chester slammed down his goblet and glared at his wife. She looked away. One of the sisters coughed, then another. The air hummed with nervous tension.

Prioress Joan spoke up again.

"Lord and Lady Chester, you have not met our new friar, who

comes to us from the Dominican friary of Cambridge. I give you Brother Richard, our new president." She gestured toward the friar who sat at the end of the table. "In the absence of Brother Philip, I've asked him to say a few words before our feast commences."

Brother Richard got to his feet, and I sat up straighter on my stool.

"We are here," he began, "to think about the faithfully departed, those who have gone on before us, to enjoy eternal life."

Lord Chester folded his arms across his chest. His stare was sceptical, and might have given another friar pause.

But Brother Richard showed no sign of intimidation.

"Is it not the Blessed Virgin who makes stronger each day our faith in such eternal life?" he asked, turning directly toward the sisters of Dartford, his hands outstretched. "We are all linked to one another in the faith. Every deed, good or bad, influences us all. And each time one of us prays for a departed soul, it helps not only that soul but also all the others who must purify on their journey to Heaven in order to find eternal rest and peace. And so today I beseech you to pray not just for the loved ones in your life but for all who travel on before you. And do not mourn. Be happy for them, for they are now in the kingdom of Heaven. And be thus strengthened and sustained in your faith in God and the Virgin."

I thought of my mother. Yes, I prayed she had found peace in God's kingdom, the peace that had eluded her in life. Next to me, Brother Edmund took a deep breath, and I wondered which departed souls he contemplated.

"And so we bless this meal, which will be laid before you," Brother Richard concluded, and sat down.

Prioress Joan smiled with pride and, I thought, a touch of surprise.

"That's very eloquent, Brother," said Lord Chester, his arms still folded. "Very nicely said. I haven't heard such a graceful sermon since Bishop Gardiner addressed the court at Saint Paul's last year, before he was packed off to France."

Brother Richard, startled, looked at Brother Edmund and then at me. I wondered at Lord Chester's picking that bishop to form his comparison. Did he know Bishop Gardiner sent us here? We were all three wondering the same thing, I was sure of it—and then realised with a start that in my thoughts I was more bound to these two friars than to the nuns who filled the room.

Lord Chester clapped his hands. "And now it's time for music."

I lost track of how many times we played the songs we knew. In no time we worked through the four prepared for the occasion and had to begin again. And again. No one took issue with it. Every time he looked over, Lord Chester would smile approvingly at our playing. His eyes always lingered on my *vihuela*, an unfamiliar instrument to Englishmen.

The conversation at the head table was dominated by Lord Chester. It had nothing to do with All Souls' Day. The talk revolved around his newest appointment at court: keeper of the king's hounds. He spoke of land spaniels and water spaniels, harriers and greyhounds. Because of my music playing, I followed few of the specifics. Lady Chester nodded as he spoke, as a wife should. I saw little of Sister Christina in her, neither in physical form nor attitude. My fellow novice more closely resembled her father, it must be said.

About halfway through the feast, conversation died down. Lord Chester devoted himself entirely to his food. Course after course had appeared, borne into the room on huge silver trays. He enjoyed the roast beef, the rabbit, and the capon. But it was the pork that he devoured with the most gusto. It seemed impossible he could be so hungry. Yet he picked up each and every sliver of pork and tucked it into his mouth, leaving nothing on the plate. His fingers shone with pork grease; it dripped from his mouth and spattered the fine tablecloth. And then there was the wine. I lost count of how many times his goblet was refilled.

No one else at the head table showed nearly as much appetite for food or drink. Lady Chester picked at her meal. The prioress and the friar discreetly avoided the meat courses, eating only bread, cheese, and fruit. The rest of us had nothing, of course. We'd all had bread and broth earlier in the day, and that would be all. It was no hardship. We were accustomed to going for many hours, even a day, without food. We welcomed it.

The room had lost all natural light when Lord Chester finally reached his fill. Servants lit candlesticks, including a huge candelabra at the head table. The priory's Mass for All Souls' Day was supposed to commence before nightfall but would plainly have to be delayed. The rules of hospitality meant we could not rush our guests from the table.

With another of his belches, Lord Chester made a show of pushing back his plate. We laid down our instruments, grateful. It was almost over.

Lord Chester turned to the prioress. "This has been a fine feast." His words were slurred.

"I am glad you enjoyed it, sir," she said.

He sighed and tilted back in his chair. "It will be such a tragedy," he said, "when the rest of the abbeys and priories are dissolved."

One of the sisters gasped, I couldn't tell who. Brother Edmund bowed his head, and on the other side of him, Sister Winifred reached for his arm.

But no one was as stricken as Prioress Joan. She blinked and swallowed, as if she could not believe what had been said.

"It won't be like before," said Lord Chester. "When the commissioners come, they're not rooting around for evidence of any laxeness in the orders, any sins committed, or any monies hidden away." His words were less slurred now as he warmed to his topic. "They're coming to tell the heads of all the houses in person what the king wants them to do: Resign. Go quietly. Dissolve of your own free will. If you do, every person in the house will be pensioned, every monk and friar and nun. The king's not going to go so rough this time. He doesn't want his courtiers stripping the monasteries with such base and obvious greed. Doesn't look good. They'll be given the monasteries as royal gifts, but it must be done quietly. And he doesn't want any more martyrs. No more monks and friars starving themselves to death or getting themselves hanged at Tyburn because they won't take the Oath of Supremacy. Too provocative."

Brother Richard's face had turned red. He held on to the edge of the head table with both hands. I could hear the rapid clicking of the prioress's pomander ball.

But Lord Chester paid no heed to the offence—the pain—his words caused anyone. "Nobody wants another rebellion, eh?" He chortled. "There are enough heads on Tower Bridge."

While we all watched, he rose to his feet.

"You'll all get a pension; no one will starve," he called out to the room, swaying a little.

Lady Chester tugged on his black taffeta arm. "My lord, enough."

He shook her off and moved the other way, past Brother Richard, who recoiled, his face twisted with loathing. Lord Chester didn't notice, didn't care. He lumbered toward the long table that bore the prized possessions of Dartford.

"Ah, look at all of this," he bellowed. "Just *look* at it. Worth a fortune. Believe me, there are lords of the court lined up outside Cromwell's chamber, right now, clamouring for Dartford Priory."

He thumped his chest with one hand. "Not me. I'm rich enough. I don't have to sack the religious houses. But for some of the others, a thing like that"—he pointed at the jewel-studded reliquary—"is just too tempting."

He swayed back and forth, and I thought for a moment Lord Chester would fall. But then he steadied himself.

"I will know tonight what's inside it," he announced.

I saw a nun rise off the bench. It was his daughter, Sister Christina. Her eyes blazed in the candlelight. "Father, you cannot touch our reliquary," she said.

"Can't I?" He turned on her. "You can't tell me what to do, daughter. No one can. Not you, not the old bitch who used to be prioress here, not the one up there now." He pointed at Prioress Joan. "I want to see what's inside it, and I shall."

The prioress jumped to her feet. "It is empty, Lord Chester. It came to us that way—everyone knows that. It was the will of the king who founded us, Edward the Third."

"'Everyone knows that,'" he mimicked the prioress. "That's what *you* say. But what if I don't believe you? The king does not believe you. He does not trust the monasteries. People say it's all to get money for the treasury, or because he's still in a rage that the abbeys opposed his divorce. That's why he's dissolving the houses. But I know better. He's said it to me, more than once." Lord Chester's voice rose an octave as he now mimicked the king: "'They have their secrets in the monasteries, their devious purposes. Their first loyalty is not to me.'"

Lord Chester narrowed his eyes at the prioress. "And I *know* you have secrets. No one knows better than I do about the secrets of Dartford Priory. " He laughed. "Tonight I will learn another of them."

Before anyone could say or do anything more, Lord Chester charged for the reliquary. He grabbed it with his grease-drenched fingers and turned it around, looking for the delicate little door.

I felt light-headed. *What if,* I thought frantically, *it wasn't empty—what if inside the reliquary was part of the Athelstan crown? Who will be hurt, if not killed, because of what he's doing?*

"Ah, I've got it." He wrenched open the door in the base of the reliquary and stuck his hand inside.

All over the room, the nuns wailed at the desecration. Sister Christina started for her father, as if to stop him herself, but Sister Agatha and Sister Rachel restrained her, one on each side. Brother Richard, on his feet, called out something to Prioress Joan, but I couldn't make out what he said above the sound of weeping. Lady Chester, crouched in her chair, had her face buried in her hands.

"There's nothing," Lord Chester said angrily. "Empty."

Prioress Joan made her way around the table, toward the man she had invited to a requiem feast. "Lord Chester, I ask you to put our sacred reliquary back on the table."

Lord Chester put it down. "I was simply curious. Don't worry. I don't want your gold, your treasure. I've never wanted that."

He swung back toward the head table and started laughing again. "I always prefer *human* treasure."

He turned, away from the prioress and Brother Richard, both approaching him.

Lord Chester, to my terror, staggered toward me.

"You, there," he shouted. "Novice! What's your name?"

I jumped up from my stool.

He came closer. "What's your name?" he repeated.

Brother Edmund rose to step in front of me.

"Get out of my way, Friar," roared Lord Chester. "Don't you know who I am? I am a member of the king's household, and I will be told the name of this novice."

I backed away from him, against the wall, the back of my head hitting the window panel.

"Joanna Stafford," I spat at him.

"Stafford?" he reared back like a spooked horse. "Oh, that's not a good name. No, no, no. That's a very bad name. The king hates the Staffords; he hates all of the old nobility. Like the family of my blessed wife." He gave a mock bow to Lady Chester, still hiding her face.

He cocked his head at me. "It's not only that. You're *dark*, aren't you? I don't like them dark. I prefer them fair . . . like this one."

He lunged for Sister Winifred and had her in seconds. He tore off her novice cap and her ash-blonde hair tumbled down over her shoulders. She screeched in fear, struggling in his arms.

It happened so fast, I barely saw it. One minute Lord Chester was attacking Sister Winifred, the next he was on the floor on his belly.

Brother Edmund stood over him, his fist raised high.

27

Lord Chester sprawled across the floor of the chapter house, rubbing his jaw.

Brother Richard ran over to his fellow friar and grabbed Brother Edmund by the arm, yanking him back. “No more, Brother, you can’t,” he pleaded.

Lord Chester got up on all fours.

“I’ll make you pay, Friar.” He lumbered to his feet, his left cheek bruised and a trickle of blood on his jaw. “I’ll have you whipped for this. I’ll have you hanged at Tyburn.”

He faced the prioress and Brother Richard, standing in front of the head table. All of us looked at one another, frightened and repulsed, waiting for his next move. It felt like a bear baiting, with all of us surrounding a strong, crazed, enraged animal.

But that is the moment when Lord Chester froze. He stared over the left shoulder of Prioress Joan. His mouth hung open as he looked at the tapestry that hung on the wall behind the head table, where he had sat for hours. The flickering candlelight illuminated the silken threads of Daphne, transformed in the deep forest.

His head moved back and forth as he scrutinised the tableau, each figure depicted.

“How could you do this?” he finally asked. “How?”

He turned to look at the nuns, half of them on their feet, the other half cowering on the benches. All of his leering rage had gone. He seemed unsure, even cowed.

“Who did this?” he asked.

There was a noise at the door, and it was Gregory, the porter, along with a trio of male servants. John, the stable hand, carried a long stick in his right hand, his face fearful.

"Prioress, what do you want us to do?" called out Gregory.

She held up a hand, ordering him to wait. "Lord Chester," she said, "I would prefer if you would leave the priory now of your own will, rather than have my men compel you. Will you do so?"

I heard a wheezing cough. It was Winifred, her hair still down around her shoulders. She was going into a fit. Brother Edmund moved her away from our stools and loosened her collar. I was the closest one to him now.

Lord Chester gave no sign he'd heard the prioress's question. He spoke in a hoarse whisper, one only I could hear.

"How could you know?" he asked. "How could you know about her?"

His knees buckled and Lord Chester collapsed to the floor, unconscious.

"Is he dead?" Brother Richard hissed. "Brother Edmund, go!"

The blonde friar carefully placed his sister down on a stone bench and went to Lord Chester. He knelt beside the man he'd struck minutes before.

"Do not hurt my husband," Lady Chester pleaded. She had pushed past the nuns and servants to get to him. Her face was puffy from weeping.

"Brother Edmund is an apothecary, as good as a physician," the prioress said.

With no sign of anything but medical interest, he felt the lord's wrists and lifted his eyelids.

"Lord Chester is alive," Brother Edmund said, matter-of-fact. "It is the wine that did this. He will recover."

"Yes, he has reached this state before," Lady Chester said. "He will sleep for many hours, impossible to rouse, and then he'll awaken, with pain in his head."

The prioress beckoned for Gregory. "You must carry him out and put him in a wagon, take him to his manor house. Use more men if necessary."

"Yes," said Brother Richard. "Get him off the property as quickly as you can."

"No, no, please, not that." Lady Chester grabbed the prioress's shoulder. "Do not have him hauled out like a common criminal. It will cause even greater scandal. You have lodging rooms here, don't you? Let him stay here tonight; let us both stay here. We will leave as soon as he awakens. He must walk out of Dartford. It will be in the morning, I promise you."

The prioress shook her head.

Lady Chester said, "He is much upset . . . because of our son." Her voice broke. "He still grieves his death, a year later. What my lord said and did here tonight—he was not himself. It was the wine. I beg you not to have him hauled out. Think of the consequences."

There was an angry stir from the crowd of nuns in the room. Sister Rachel burst forward like an avenging archangel.

"Prioress Joan, he must not remain in this priory," she shouted. "This man's defilement must end *now*. He is evil. We saw evil here, in our chapter house. Both words and deeds." She gestured toward Sister Winifred, gasping for air, in the arms of Sister Agatha.

A murmur of agreement rippled through the group. Sister Eleanor looked especially tormented, trapped between her loathing of Lord Chester and her loyalty to the prioress.

Weeping, Lady Chester called out, "Christina, where are you? Help us. Please."

Sister Christina moved toward her mother. Her face was filled with torment. She stopped in the middle of the floor, her hands trembling at her sides.

Brother Edmund helped his gasping sister to the door. "No matter what is decided about Lord Chester, Sister Winifred needs treatment in the infirmary," he said. "With your permission, Prioress?"

She nodded, and brother and sister left.

Brother Richard cleared his throat. "Prioress, much damage has been done here. I fear what will happen if he remains, even for one night."

Lady Chester wept harder, crouched next to her husband.

Prioress Joan frowned at the sight of the senseless Lord Chester. We all waited for her decision.

"Gregory," she said to the porter. "Have Lord Chester carried to our guest lodging rooms. They are not well prepared, but he and Lady Chester will have to make do. Then lock the cloister doors so there can be no reentry."

She turned to face us, her head held high. "This is my judgement. We are still a religious house, bound to hospitality if it is requested, by chapter rules. We will return our sacred objects—our reliquary and book and other possessions—to the church and library. We will hold Mass for All Souls' Day. We will still honour the departed as Brides of Christ, as our vows compel. We will continue."

Brother Richard scowled, but he said nothing. Doubts and fears registered on the faces of the other nuns. But we all bowed to the will of the prioress.

Sister Eleanor said loudly, "Come, you've heard what we must do. Lift up our holy treasures."

Sister Rachel hurried to the reliquary. "I will cleanse it myself," she said, her voice breaking. "I will try to remove the defilement."

A group of senior nuns picked up the other objects on the table. Gregory and his men moved toward Lord Chester, to carry him out.

I left the chapter house with Sister Christina. I had seen enough tonight to understand what had brought her to Dartford with such fierce commitment, why she'd sworn never to leave.

At the requiem Mass that night a grave Brother Phillip said a few special words on All Souls' Day, though they were not as inspiring as Brother Richard's, it must be said. The Mass was so late that not much time elapsed before the bells rang again, compelling us to Matins at midnight.

Afterward, climbing the stairs to our dormitory, I tried to express my sympathy for Sister Christina. I didn't want her to misinterpret my silence for any sort of censure. Her parents' offences were not hers.

"Sister Christina," I began, "in your life before Dartford, it must have—"

She turned on me, anguished.

"Do not ask me anything. I beg you, Sister Joanna. Do not speak of my family—of my father. I can't say a word about him. You of all people must understand that he must never be spoken of."

"Of course, Sister."

When we had changed into our shifts and were lying in bed, Sister Agatha stuck her head in. "Sister Winifred will sleep in the infirmary tonight. She is not well at all. Brother Edmund will remain with her and look after her."

She looked at me and shuddered, her plump jowls shaking. "Nothing like this has ever happened at Dartford Priory before. *Nothing.* I can't imagine what was—"

"Good night, Sister Agatha," said Sister Christina brusquely, and turned her face to the wall.

I blew out the candle.

It took a long time to fall asleep. I'd feel myself sinking into a dream, but then, right at the brink, I'd jerk awake, and stir, restless, in my bed. I couldn't quiet my mind. I kept hearing the music we played, seeing the reliquary hand on the table, flinching at the profane shouts of Lord Chester.

When the bells rang just before dawn for Lauds, my limbs felt heavy and my head throbbed. I glanced over at Sister Christina, sitting on the edge of her pallet as she pulled her habit on over her head, her movements just as sluggish.

Filing down the stairs to our church, I noticed the other sisters looked worn, too, even haggard. No one had slept well at Dartford. Sister Rachel looked as if she'd aged ten years in a single night.

I was waiting my turn, with Sister Christina, at the back of the line, to bow and take our place in the church, when a long scream rippled through the passageway. This was no animal facing slaughter. I heard a woman, a terrified woman.

Sister Christina froze. "That is my mother," she said.

I grabbed her and we ran together, past the cloister garden, to the door leading to the front of the priory.

"Gregory!" I shouted, pounding at the door. "Let us in. Unlock the door."

In no time, Prioress Joan was there, with Sister Eleanor and Sister Agatha, and, five steps behind, Brother Richard.

"Get back to the church," the prioress ordered Sister Christina and me.

"But she says it's her mother," I protested.

The door swung open. Gregory stood there, ashen-faced. Sister Christina and I pushed past him and ran to the guest lodgings. They were to the west, at the end of the passageway, at the opposite end from the prioress's chamber.

We'd almost reached it when Lady Chester staggered out of the doorway. Wearing the same black dress as she had the night before, she came toward us, feeling the wall as if she'd turned blind and must cling to the bricks to keep from falling. She fell into her daughter's arms.

"Don't go in that room, Sister Joanna—stop!" shouted Prioress Joan behind me.

I didn't stop. I disobeyed, yet again. I don't know what drove me down that passageway, past Lady Chester, into the lodgings rooms. It was as if there were an answer I needed inside the rooms, and I would perish if I didn't get it.

The second door, leading to the bedchamber, was ajar, and I ran inside.

I saw him at once. Lord Chester sat up partway in the bed. He, too, still wore his black clothes, his mourning wear for Queen Jane, but they were drenched in blood. The headboard and the wall behind him were spattered with it. The left side of Lord Chester's head had been crushed. He had no left eye. It was just blood and bone and tissue. The right eye bulged in a fixed expression of sad surprise.

On the floor, next to the bed, lay the reliquary of Dartford Priory, in pieces. The fragments were also drenched in blood. A clump of Lord Chester's brown hair was tangled in the two outstretched fingers of the reliquary hand.

28

I was the only novice in the tapestry room the following afternoon. I sat in front of the loom and wove in the white and light blue threads. Sister Helen and I worked in silence, just the two of us. Sister Christina was comforting her devastated mother in the *locutorium*, and Sister Winifred was still in the infirmary. I had no idea of Sister Agatha's whereabouts.

I had to carry on with my duties today, until the arrival of the men.

During those first few minutes, after the discovery of the body, there was a great deal of crying and shouting. Prioress Joan and Brother Richard had dashed in after me and then retreated, aghast. The prioress had ordered the room sealed and guarded.

"There is a murderer loose in the priory!" Sister Agatha screeched in the passageway, hysterical. "The servants must search the priory. The man could still be anywhere."

Brother Richard said, "You fool, he was killed hours ago. Do you think a murderer would strike and then linger here? He's long gone."

He whirled to confront Gregory.

"Did you lock all the doors last night?" he asked.

"Of course I did," said Gregory, insulted. "That is my chief duty, to ensure that the priory is enclosed. No one could get into these guest rooms from outside of the priory—or from the cloister area, either. That door was locked, both sides, right after we carried Lord Chester to his bed, just as the prioress ordered. No one could get in, and no one could get out. I would swear to it before the king himself."

"The windows?" asked Sister Eleanor.

Gregory shook his head. "I've checked them all. They are closed and secured."

Sister Agatha whispered, "You're not suggesting Lady Chester . . . ?"

"Do you believe she begged us to let him sleep here so she could murder him?" Brother Richard demanded.

"Silence yourselves!" shouted the prioress. "There will be no more speculation, or gossip, in this priory. We will alert the Bishop of Rochester immediately; this is a matter for the church courts."

"The church courts?" repeated Brother Richard, incredulous. "This is a murder of a peer of the realm! And we may face the Star Chamber for it, if not the Tower."

I couldn't help but flinch.

"You're wrong, Brother Richard," said the prioress. "This crime was committed on church property. It is not a matter for the king's court."

Brother Richard shook his fists in a rage of frustration. "Listen to me, you must, for once, *listen* to the president and steward of your priory. I pleaded with you not to invite Lord Chester to Dartford, and you disregarded me. Last night I asked you to have him removed from our grounds, and again you showed disdain for my advice. But now, Prioress, it is more than just your pride at stake. It is the future of the priory, our very lives. Will you hear me out?"

Her lips trembled with emotion. And then, the prioress nodded.

Brother Richard took a breath. "If we attempt to make this a church investigation, and repel all outsiders, we will be destroyed. This crime will give our enemies an excuse to say monasteries are riddled with vice and crime and lies. That we operate in secret. But neither should we make ourselves vulnerable to the Star Chamber. Heretics eager for our dissolution rule there. No, we must open the priory to the men who investigate such crimes as their living. We must raise a hue and cry for the coroner and abide by his judgement in how to investigate and proceed."

"The coroner?" Prioress Joan was uncertain. "Where is such a person found? I don't want to send to London. This can't become a London matter."

"You said that Dartford is under the jurisdiction of the Bishop of Rochester. That city is not a far distance, within a day's ride, and quite large enough that it would have a coroner. Those are the men with experience in murder, in holding an inquiry, in examining a corpse. If we send out the hue and cry now, he should be here tomorrow."

Prioress Joan looked back at the bedchamber, apprehensive, as if expecting that Lord Chester, with his crushed head, would lurch out of the room.

"Then let it be done," she said dully. "Gregory, send a trustworthy man to Rochester with a message by fastest horse. Have the men search every inch of the grounds, to seek evidence of an intruder."

She turned to face us, in a frightened cluster. "Until the inquiry begins, I want all of you to carry on with your usual work. Just be sure that no one is alone anywhere in the priory. We must stay in groups, or at least in pairs."

We dispersed. After I'd helped to clean the refectory, I made my way to the infirmary, to check on the condition of Sister Winifred. She was in a sorry state: curled up on a pallet, lying on her side, her knees pulled up. It was the position of someone in a deep sleep, but when I drew close, I could see her eyes were open. "Sister Winifred," I said. "Are you all right?" She shuddered and did not answer me.

I turned to Brother Edmund, alarmed. "Can you help her?"

"Time and prayer will help her," he answered, his back to me. The friar was at his distilling apparatus, feeding a handful of herbs into the mouth of the mechanism, placed on a long table.

"Then is there anything I can do—right now? Fetch some food? *Anything?*"

He shook his head. I came around the table and got my first look at Brother Edmund's face. New lines of exhaustion creased around his eyes and the corners of his mouth. I doubted he'd slept a minute.

I lowered my voice to a faint whisper: "Does she know of Lord Chester's murder?"

"No, I don't want to tell her yet." He grimaced. "Oh, this is a terrible, terrible tragedy."

"You grieve for Lord Chester?" I wondered.

Brother Edmund nodded. "He was a brutal man, dissolute and cruel, but he was one of God's creatures. And now I have to live with my sin without his forgiveness."

"Sin?"

"Anger," he said bleakly. "It has haunted me since I was a boy. I have prayed, I have struggled . . . His voice trailed away. "I should have found a peaceable remedy last night. I'll always regret this lapse."

"Brother Edmund, you must not berate yourself, please," I said.

The lines softened around his eyes. "You are very kind, Sister Joanna."

"Kind?" I was taken aback. "No one ascribes that quality to me."

"Then no one has been paying much attention," he said.

His distilling apparatus hissed and spat. Brother Edmund turned to cope with the problem, and I slipped out of the infirmary. I was unused to compliments. My mother's way was to correct, not to praise. The only two people to proclaim virtues in me were Prioress Elizabeth and, many years before, my cousin Margaret. Both of them were dead and buried.

The next day, there was a flurry of activity in the late morning. The coroner had arrived already, I heard. In the mid-afternoon, in obedience to my order, I went to the tapestry room. I sat at the loom and did my work. It was so quiet there, just Sister Helen and me, weaving and tapping the pedals. There was much ugliness and violence in the world, and now it had crawled into our priory. We must do what we could to create beauty.

But the peaceful silence also allowed me to reflect on what had happened. Before long I was filled with uneasiness. The crown, assuredly dangerous, was hidden here at the priory. Lord Chester had bragged that he knew our secrets: *"No one knows better than me the secrets of Dartford Priory."* Hours later he was murdered with vicious strength. For the first time I wondered if Lord Chester had been killed to protect the crown. But who here besides myself knew of its existence and its powers—and would take such swift action if the crown were threatened?

"Sis—Sis—Sis—"

The low, raspy stutter was a shock. I looked at Sister Helen. It was hard to believe, but the nun who had said nothing since her brother was hanged in chains at Tyburn now tried to speak to me. She seemed desperate to speak to me. Though it was a cool day, her face gleamed with perspiration.

"Sister . . . Joanna?" she managed to get out.

"What is it?"

"Must t-t-t-tell you."

The door opened, and Sister Agatha bustled in. She beckoned for me, her face pink with excited nerves.

"You're needed now," she said.

"Where?" I asked.

"In the prioress's chamber," she said. "The men arrived from Rochester two hours ago, and they want to question *you*."

A cold wave of fear rippled through me.

"Why?" I asked.

"Because you are one of the few who saw Lord Chester dead."

I turned to look at Sister Helen, but her mouth was closed tight. She shook her head, very slightly, and she rubbed her arm, as if it hurt her.

I followed my novice mistress out of the cloister area and back to the front of the priory.

"Why did you say 'men,' not 'man'?" I asked.

"The coroner has brought two others with him, because of the seriousness of the crime. An old man and a young one."

To be interrogated by men reminded me of the Tower. I bitterly hated the prospect. It was important that they not learn of my months of imprisonment in the Tower; I prayed that the prioress had not told them. It would shed doubt on my character and lead to questions about why I had been allowed to come back. The last thing Bishop Gardiner would want would be for me to be drawn into a murder investigation.

Sister Agatha ushered me inside but then did not stay. She took a place on the bench, next to a grim Sister Eleanor and an even grimmer Brother Richard. The door shut between us.

Prioress Joan sat tall at her table, and three men clustered by the window. The one who stood out most immediately was a tall, stooped man wearing long, full black robes, not unlike a physician's. There was a string around his neck, attached to a mask that hung just beneath his chin. I guessed him the coroner. A second man spoke to him in a low voice; he was grey-haired and heavyset. The third man looked out the window, his hands clasped behind his back.

Prioress Joan pointed at the chair across from her, and I sat down, consumed with dread.

The grey-haired man looked me over. He had an open, kind face, like a grandfather. "This is the novice, Joanna Stafford?"

"Sister Joanna," corrected the prioress.

The man at the window turned around. He was in his twenties, with light-brown hair. The afternoon sun was bright in his face; it revealed a faint red mark on his forehead, a months' old wound that was hardening to scar.

It was Geoffrey Scovill.

29

Leaning on his cane, the grey-haired man said, "Sister Joanna, I am Justice Edmund Campion. I am the justice of the peace of the city of Rochester. Coroner Hancock requested my involvement, due to the sensitivity of this inquiry. We have certain questions for you to answer today. After I am finished with my questions, you will write out a statement. I've been told you are able to read and write. Is that true?"

"Yes, Master Campion," I said.

I looked at Geoffrey, waited for him to give some sign he recognised me. He did not. He showed a polite, expectant face.

Campion followed my gaze to Geoffrey. "This is Master Scovill, a constable in Rochester. He has a fine mind and a strong pair of legs"—he rattled his cane—"and so I've borrowed him from the chief constable for the length of the investigation."

"Yes, I see," I said.

Geoffrey bowed, his expression blank.

Campion continued, "Now, Sister Joanna, I will ask you about what you saw, this morning, in the guest lodging room. Lord Chester's body was, unfortunately, moved, as was the murder weapon—"

The coroner groaned and held his temple in his bony right hand.

"This makes our proceedings a bit difficult, you see," continued Campion. "We are forced to re-create the circumstances of the death through careful questioning."

He broke off and turned to the prioress. "It is quite cold in this room, Prioress. You have no means of making a fire?"

Prioress Joan raised her eyebrows. "This is a religious house, not a palace. Our winter warming house, our *calefactorium,* is south of the chapter house. If you wish it, we can have a fire lit now and you can be escorted there."

I noticed the prioress did not mention that the infirmary, too, had a fire lit for warmth.

Justice Campion tightened his grip on his cane. "Never mind." He turned back to me. "Let's continue. I'd be most gratified if you would answer our questions in every detail."

I told the men what I could remember: Lord Chester's position in bed was of great interest to them, as was the exact placement of the reliquary pieces. The coroner sat in a chair and questioned me about the colour and texture of the blood, and, though it made me squeamish, I did my best to describe it. He wrote my answers on a sheet of parchment paper. Campion smiled at me, pleased every time I came up with a new detail. "Ah, very good," he'd exclaim. Geoffrey did nothing but listen.

"What was the humour of his intact eye?" demanded the coroner.

I shook my head, unsure what he meant.

"Was it melancholic, phlegmatic, sanguine, or choleric?" he asked.

I thought back to the expression in that eye. I had formed an impression when I saw it, but now it was hard to articulate. "It was closest to melancholic," I said finally.

"Not choleric—he was not angry or fearful?" the coroner asked, his thick greying eyebrows twitching in concentration.

"No," I said. "He was . . . surprised. But not shocked."

For the first time, Geoffrey spoke.

"As would be the case if Lord Chester died while looking at someone he knew?"

Yes, it was the same voice. He was the same man: Geoffrey Scovill.

I shook my head. "I do not wish to speculate, sir," I said in the same polite tone.

Justice Campion smiled. "Ah, but we *require* you to speculate, Sister Joanna. You have an acute eye. You have given us the most detailed descriptions of his lordship so far." He turned to the prioress. "I commend you for having such an observant and intelligent young woman in your priory."

Prioress Joan said nothing.

"I was taken aback to see such large quarters for guests in the priory, since you are so adamant about keeping out the world," mused Justice Campion.

The prioress answered, "The point of the *domus hospitum*—"

"The what?" The older man squinted at her.

"A house of hospitality," spoke up Geoffrey.

So Geoffrey Scovill knew Latin. I had not realised.

The prioress explained that special permission was given for certain guests. Widows longing for spiritual comfort had boarded here. Also, in times of war, a local noble might make request that his wife and daughter stay in the guests' rooms of the priory. When Henry the Fifth led his army to France, the rooms had been full.

Nodding, Justice Campion thought for a moment, then his attention turned back to me. "So please, Sister, your thoughts. You must have formed an idea."

I swallowed. "Sir?"

He walked across the room, poking the floor with his cane. "Lord Chester comes to the requiem feast. He eats and drinks a great deal, so much so that he loses consciousness and is taken to the front of the priory. I remain surprised that he would be served so much wine that he would lose himself completely."

Eager to defend Dartford, I said, "He came to the priory drunk."

"Did he? How do you know that? No one else made note of that."

"I smelled it on his breath."

Justice Campion's eyebrows shot up. "I see." He glanced over at Geoffrey. "Tell us about Sister Winifred. He attacked her?"

I winced. "Yes."

"And so Brother Edmund, who is in fact her own older brother, defended her by striking Lord Chester so hard he fell to the floor?"

I nodded.

"And Brother Richard?"

I exchanged a look of confusion with the prioress.

"What do you want to know about him?" asked the prioress.

"Brother Richard himself said that he did not desire Lord Chester's presence, that he resisted the idea for the feast. That he did not consider it seemly."

Shifting in her chair, the prioress admitted, "That's true."

"So both of these friars, here at Dartford Priory for a month, felt some form of hostility toward Lord Chester."

Prioress Joan said, "Your inquiry is misguided. These are friars. They would not commit such an act."

"But Brother Edmund did commit an act of violence against Lord Chester, just hours before he was killed," Justice Campion said, his voice hardening. "And last night he was in the infirmary, not in the friars' lodgings, which is a separate building."

In a panic, I jumped to my feet. "He wouldn't do such a terrible thing as murder," I cried. "It's impossible. Brother Edmund is a good, kind person, a true man of God. He helps people."

A thick silence filled the room. The coroner stopped writing, and the three men looked at one another. Justice Campion nodded at Geoffrey Scovill, and the younger man hurried out of the prioress's chamber.

"Someone killed Lord Chester, and it was a most terrible act, I agree," said Justice Campion. He had resumed his grandfatherly manner, but I no longer felt at ease with him. "I think we can all agree that the murderer was someone who harboured great hatred for him."

"That is without a doubt," muttered Coroner Hancock.

"Certainly this was *not* a thief wandering the countryside," Justice Campion said. "A thief would have taken the rings off his fingers—they are worth a fortune—and there would have been more noise. Lady Chester slept in the room next to his, and she heard nothing. The doors were closed between them and the walls are thick, but still, she would have heard her husband had there been a prolonged struggle."

The prioress said, "But Lord Chester was killed in his sleep."

"I don't think so, Prioress. Sister Joanna's description is of a man sitting up in the bed at the moment of the attack. He did not get up or try to evade his attacker. I think someone entered the room and communicated with Lord Chester in such a way that his lordship was not in fear of his life initially. And then he was struck hard by a man of some strength."

"He had enemies at court," insisted the prioress.

Justice Campion nodded. "Yes, I am sure he did. A violent death, committed within these walls, would also taint the priory, the whole monastic way of life. On my way to Dartford from Rochester I suspected a crazed reformer, eager to cast such a taint on the old ways."

He paused and shook his head. "To kill him here, though, first the murderer would have to know that Lord Chester stayed in the guest lodging rooms. That was a spontaneous decision, made after the feast. How would an outsider know of it, and then . . . know where to find the rooms? There is the problem of how he entered a locked and guarded priory. No one should have been able to gain entry to the guest bedchamber, from the cloister or the outside. And, finally, we have the reliquary."

A chill rippled through me.

"I find it interesting that Lord Chester was killed with the reliquary, the most sacred possession you have. And the one that he had groped, in order to taunt all of the sisters, at the feast? Do you not agree that the choice of weapon is significant?"

Campion paced across the room, his cane thumping on the floor.

"But how did the reliquary make its way from the church to the front of the priory? Someone removed it from the church after the last service of Matins, after midnight, and then carried it to the lodging rooms. Your porter seems a steady man, and he has sworn that the door between the front of the priory and the cloistered area was locked. Is he the only one with a key?"

"I have my own key," the prioress said.

The coroner and justice of the peace exchanged a quick look.

"Where was it last night?" asked Justice Campion.

"In my room, I sleep separately from the sisters. It was there this morning, Justice Campion. And no one crept into my room and took it, let me assure you. I am a very light sleeper."

"And you did not leave your bedchamber between Matins and Lauds?" he asked, his voice devoid of emotion.

"I have already told you twice that I did not." I heard the rapid *click, click, click* of the prioress fingering her pomander ball.

Justice Campion stopped pacing and looked out the window. "Do you have any building plans, made at the time of the priory's construction? I must learn how the murderer was able to move around the building. It is almost two centuries old. There could be doors or windows or even passageways, not readily visible, that he was able to use."

I went rigid in my chair. *The secret room.*

Prioress Joan said, "I have never seen any such plans."

"They must exist, Prioress."

I heard raised voices outside the prioress's chamber. The door flung open, and Geoffrey Scovill strode in carrying a box, with an irate Brother Richard on his heels.

"You have no right—no right to do that!" shouted the friar.

"What's this?" asked Justice Campion.

Geoffrey grinned. "He's all a-fluster because I found this next to his pallet in the friars' quarters during my search." He pulled a slim book out of the box and held it up in the air.

I recognised it at once: *From Caractacus to Athelstan.*

Brother Richard reached for the book, and Geoffrey, taller than the friar, held it up high, over his head, with a laugh. Justice Campion smiled, and the coroner looked up from his writing with a snicker. With athletic ease, Geoffrey tossed the book to the justice of the peace.

Justice Campion leafed through the book. "It seems harmless."

Prioress Joan sighed. "None of the books should be removed from the Dartford library. Brother Richard knows that."

Brother Richard's face was beet-red. He seemed to be avoiding my gaze, though I couldn't tell if it was general embarrassment.

Geoffrey said, "Other than that, I found a quill and ink pot and parchment, but not letters. There's quite a nice chess set. And a fine trunk filled with religious books. For the other friar, Brother Edmund, nothing at all. Not a single possession."

Justice Campion handed the book to the prioress and then turned to Brother Richard. "Since you have joined us again, Brother, you can perhaps add to the discussion. We were trying to determine how the reliquary made its way from the church to the guest lodging rooms, even though the doors were locked."

"I have no idea," Brother Richard said. "This priory is quite secure. It obeys all the rules of enclosure. I know that the sisters do not leave without written permission."

"Are you completely certain of that?" asked Geoffrey.

I did not look at Geoffrey or anyone else.

Prioress Joan said icily, "There was an incident, this past spring, concerning a member of this priory, who left without permission, through a kitchen window, to attend to a family member. The matter is behind us—and has nothing to do with Lord Chester's visit whatsoever."

"Attend to a family member?" asked Justice Campion.

"Yes, and the window in question can no longer be opened," she said. "It has been sealed."

Justice Campion asked nothing more about it. He returned to last night's requiem feast, probing for every detail remembered, every bit of conversation. Prioress Joan and Brother Richard answered the questions. I kept my eyes down until the quick, sharp thud of my heart had slowed.

It was only then that I looked up at Geoffrey. I caught him staring at me, and not with the face of blank courtesy he'd shown thus far. There was a baffled, hurt expression in his eyes, the same as I saw in the Tower, after I'd insulted him before the Duke of Norfolk. I ached to explain all to him, but it was impossible.

Campion was inquiring about the tapestry again. "So he asked you, all of you who were in the room, 'How could you know?' when he looked at that tapestry, the one woven by the sisters last year."

"That is correct," said Brother Richard.

"What was he referring to?"

Brother Richard and the prioress looked at each other; they both shrugged. "He was very drunk, I fear," said the prioress.

"And that was the last thing he said before he collapsed?"

"No," I said. "He said one thing more."

All eyes turned to me. Campion, justice of the peace, beamed as he said, "Ah, our novice, our most attentive novice. And what were the last words of Lord Chester?"

"He said, 'How could you know? How could you know about her?'"

Geoffrey said, "About Sister Winifred?"

"No, he was looking at the tapestry when he said that." I realised one thing more. "He was looking at the figure of the girl in the middle of the tapestry."

The coroner spoke up. "He was not of right mind due to excessive wine."

"Most likely," said Justice Campion, "but the tapestry should be seen. Is that possible, Prioress?"

"It has not yet been taken down from the wall of the chapter house," she answered.

"Geoffrey, why don't you do that now?" asked the older man. "Could someone escort him to the chapter house?"

I said quickly, "I will."

Justice Campion squinted at me. "Yes, I suppose I am finished with you, Sister Joanna. For now."

I turned to Geoffrey, "Master Scovill, if you will follow me?"

He bowed, a flicker of excitement in his eyes. "I appreciate your assistance."

And with that, I led Geoffrey Scovill out of the room.

30

We'd made it only a short distance down the passageway when Sister Eleanor called out to me, "Halt, Sister Joanna."

She hurried to catch up to us.

"Prioress asked me to accompany you." She looked Geoffrey up and down, barely concealing her distaste. Fighting a smile, Geoffrey bowed to her.

Sister Eleanor now led the way to the chapter house. I followed a respectful distance, with Geoffrey right behind me. I could feel his breath on the back of my head. His steps were loud on the stone floor.

When we reached the open passageway running along the cloister garden, I no longer heard those steps. I turned to see why. Geoffrey stood next to a column, staring at our garden. The sunlight flickered on the delicate leaves of the quince trees and the neatly tended herbs that flowered in autumn.

"This is so beautiful," he said. "I've never seen the like."

"Master Scovill, if you please?" Sister Eleanor snapped. "We are very busy at the priory."

I edged into the chapter house, reluctant to return to this room. But all signs of the feast had been removed, except for the tapestry. There were no tables, no candlesticks, no cloths or silver. The stench of meat had evaporated. Geoffrey walked in just as slowly as I did, his eyes tracking every inch, as if he was re-creating the evening's mayhem.

Indifferent to his need to concentrate, Sister Eleanor said, "Master Scovill, how much longer will you and the other men from Rochester be here at the priory?"

Geoffrey was now taking in the details of the tapestry. Without looking away from it, he explained, "The coroner is bound to hold an inquest within three days of arriving on the scene of a suspicious death. A jury of twelve local men must hear the evidence, must decide if murder has been committed. A coroner may indict a suspect, and if the jury agrees, a justice of the peace may then bind that accused person over for trial."

Only two days remained before the inquiry would need to take place, I realised.

"This tapestry is based on a story?" Geoffrey asked.

"It's a story taken from ancient Greece," answered Sister Eleanor. "The tale of Daphne, the nymph. She was turned into a tree by her father, a river god."

"Why did he turn her into a tree?"

Sister Eleanor laughed scornfully. "I hardly think this is based on something that really happened, Master Scovill."

"I understand that, Sister," he said, still patient. "But there could be deeper meaning to these figures." He pointed at the figure of Daphne. "She looks frightened to me." He turned to examine the three hunters to the left of Daphne. "Is she meant to be frightened of them?"

"I have no idea," Sister Eleanor said.

"There is more of a story to this," I said. "I heard that a couple of days ago."

Geoffrey turned to me. "From whom?"

Too late, I remembered who it had been. "Brother Edmund," I muttered.

Geoffrey nodded. "Ah, of course. Brother Edmund."

I did not like the way he said it. "Why do you not speak to him then?" I asked. "You will soon see what kind of person he is."

"We shall be speaking to Brother Edmund, be assured. He is last on our list."

Sister Eleanor murmured, "Actually, now that you make mention of it, there is something about this tapestry." She squinted hard. "The girl, Daphne, she looks like someone I've seen. But I can't think of who."

"Do you use models for the figures in your tapestries?" asked Geoffrey.

She shook her head.

"Sister Agatha also said she looked familiar," I recalled.

Geoffrey brightened. "Sister Eleanor, please go and find this Sister Agatha and bring her here."

She looked at me, unsure.

Geoffrey waved his hand. "Sister Joanna will be fine. I may have more questions about the tapestry for her to answer, so she must remain. Please make haste. As you said, we are all busy people."

In a moment she was gone and we were, finally, alone.

I cleared my throat and said, "I am pleased to see that you are healthy and well." How awkward it came out.

Geoffrey said cautiously, "And you, Sister Joanna." He paused. "The last time I saw you, you did not look at all healthy and well."

"That's true. But all is mended."

He asked, "How did you manage that?"

"I was cleared of all suspicion and released to Dartford," I said.

"How fortunate."

I did not know what else to say. I'd arranged for this opportunity, to speak to Geoffrey, and now I'd turned mute.

He was the one who broke the silence.

"They don't know I was held two nights in the Tower," Geoffrey said in a low voice. "Sir William Kingston checked my name on the rolls of constabulary office for Rochester—the records were in London—and that, along with my sworn statement, was enough. I was never officially arrested. So when he released me, I went home and told the chief constable I'd stayed at a London inn. I feared for many weeks that someone would come, that a letter would be sent. It never happened."

"I see."

He bit his lip. "I would appreciate it if you would not expose my involvement in your case. It could ruin me."

"But you nearly exposed that I was the one who left Dartford without permission," I pointed out, still angry.

"I have a duty to perform here," Geoffrey said. "My loyalty is to Justice Campion, to assist with this inquiry. I owe him a very great deal."

"Oh?"

Geoffrey looked uncomfortable but continued. "He pays most of my monthly wages from his own private accounts. The job of constable is unpaid—I don't know if you are aware of that. The chief constable of Rochester is a man of means. But I am not. If it weren't for Master Campion, I certainly could not hold this position."

There was the sound of women talking outside, in the passageway. I thought it was Sister Eleanor, returning with Sister Agatha, but the chatter died away.

"Geoffrey, I have something to say," I began.

His eyes widened at my use of his name.

"What I said about you, in the Tower, when you were brought in—it wasn't true." There, at last I had managed it. But Geoffrey still looked dissatisfied.

"Then why did you say it?" he asked.

"The Duke of Norfolk—you don't know him as I do. I couldn't speak up for you; it would have set him off."

Geoffrey narrowed his eyes. "But you spoke up for Brother Edmund—there was no impediment to that."

"There are far different circumstances," I protested.

"What is he doing in the middle of a priory? That's what I want to find out," Geoffrey said. "My understanding is that nuns are supposed to be kept very separate from friars and monks."

"We don't pray together or work together or eat together," I said.

"Or sleep together?"

Fast as a whip, my hand shot out. The cracking sound of a slap rang out across the chapter house. I stared at my reddened palm, horrified.

Geoffrey held his cheek. "I wager I deserved that." He laughed. "For a religious house, you all hand out a fair number of blows."

Before I could respond, Sister Eleanor led in a nervous, flustered Sister Agatha.

"I don't know how I can be of assistance," protested the novice mistress.

Geoffrey pointed at the tapestry. "Who is that girl?"

Sister Agatha looked confused. "Daphne. The girl from the fable. She was turned into a tree by her father to save her."

"Save her from what?" Geoffrey asked.

She pointed at the three hunters. "Them. The men who were

hunting her." She glanced at me and lowered her voice. "We do not discuss why."

"And the girl was modelled on someone real?" he asked.

"Oh, no," said Sister Agatha. "We don't work that way."

"But you and Sister Eleanor have both said she looks familiar," he pressed.

Sister Agatha looked at the beautiful blonde girl in the tapestry, her legs winding into a trunk, her arms sprouting leaves. "I didn't see it when we were weaving the tapestry, but now, these months later, when I look at her, I see . . . Sister Beatrice."

"Yes," Sister Eleanor gasped. "That's it."

His voice hard, Geoffrey said, "Who is Sister Beatrice?"

"She left the priory in 1535," said Sister Agatha. "When the king's commissioners came, they brought us all together. They said anyone younger than twenty-five years of age must be released. No one was. Then the commissioners asked if anyone wanted to leave. They said that question was being posed at every priory and abbey, and Sister Beatrice came forward. She was a novice, and she said she wanted to go. She didn't give any reasons. Once she—"

"That's enough," Sister Eleanor hissed.

"Did Sister Beatrice know Lord Chester?"

"Of course not," said Sister Eleanor.

"Where is she now?" asked Geoffrey.

"I don't know. With her family, I assume. They had a home near Canterbury."

Sister Agatha gave a cry and pointed, not at the girl this time but at the corner of the tapestry, where the head of the old river god peered out of the weeds. "Do you know who that looks like? Prioress Elizabeth."

"Who?" asked Geoffrey.

"Our former prioress, who died last month," said Sister Eleanor. "But that's ludicrous. She was my aunt, and I should know that . . . Her voice trailed away. I peered at the figure. And suddenly, to my shock, I saw it: white hair, hooked nose, large blue eyes. There was no denying it: the river god resembled Prioress Elizabeth Croessner.

"Who is in charge of the tapestries?" asked Geoffrey.

We all looked at one another.

Reluctantly, Sister Eleanor said, "Sister Helen. She plans the designs and personally weaves the faces of the figures. I will fetch her and bring her here, although she—"

Geoffrey broke in. "No, you will take me to her now."

"That would not be appropriate, Master Scovill."

"We were told we would have all your cooperation, Sister," he said. "I don't want any of you to speak to her about this before I do. Where is she right now?"

Sister Eleanor said, "The tapestry room."

"And is that far?"

She shook her head.

"Then let's go."

It was past the usual hour in the tapestry room. We didn't do our work after the natural light had gone. Loom work by candlelight ruins eyes; moreover, the light makes it impossible to consistently match colours. But the bells still hadn't rung for prayers, most likely because these men were here, asking their questions, occupying the prioress. And so Sister Helen must have remained. This was the room, after all, that she felt safest in.

Indeed, Sister Helen was alone, behind the loom, when we all walked in. She stood up, confused, her hands full of the exquisite silk and woolen thread bundles we sent for from Brussels.

"Sister Helen, I have questions for you about the tapestry hung at the requiem feast," Geoffrey said.

She moaned—an awful, guttural noise—and backed into the corner, dropping all of her threads.

Sister Eleanor moved in first. "Don't be alarmed, Sister. Please. It will be fine."

Sister Helen bent over, clutching her chest.

"She's sick," shouted Sister Agatha, as Sister Helen toppled to the floor. "Get Brother Edmund," Sister Eleanor ordered the novice mistress.

I knelt next to her, as Sister Helen writhed in pain. She panted, her eyes wild with fear as she looked at Sister Eleanor and me. After what seemed like an eternity but was probably just a minute, she grew quiet and her eyes slid shut. I placed her head in my lap, stroked her damp forehead. "Oh, Sister Helen," I said, tearful. There was no response.

Brother Edmund ran into the room. He felt her wrists and her throat, and then pulled up her eyelids. Geoffrey watched him from the doorway, wary.

"We must take her to the infirmary," the friar said. "She must be carried."

"I'll help you," Geoffrey announced. The two of them took their measure of each other, and Brother Edmund nodded. "Thank you, sir," he said.

They carried her together, each man gripping an opposite end of the long table they lifted her on to. It was a most upsetting sight, the conveying of a deathly ill Sister Helen through the passageways. The sisters cried out and crossed themselves as we passed, and many of them gathered in the infirmary, to be near her. Some of them said they'd noticed Sister Helen earlier, agitated, not herself, moving around the priory. Brother Edmund finally had to plead for quiet because their talk was too distracting. From her corner, Sister Winifred watched all, distraught.

It was proposed that a few of us would assist in the nursing of Sister Helen and Sister Winifred through the night. My time would be two hours after midnight prayers. "The youngest are the strongest and can best endure having little sleep," Sister Agatha decided.

When I shuffled into the refectory for the evening meal, I was surprised to see Sister Christina at the novices' table. "My mother has been taken home," she explained.

"How is she?" I asked.

Sister Christina shook her head. "She's lost. My father's will has been hers for thirty years."

"And how are you?" I laid my hand on her shoulder. It was rigid, like a stone.

"I turn to God for all answers," she said fiercely. "He must guide us through."

At the end of the meal Sister Agatha sidled up to us. "Is it true a deputation from London came, to talk to your mother and to the justice of the peace?"

Sister Christina nodded, reluctant. "Yes, they came from the court, from the king's council, after getting word of my father's death."

"And did they seek to take control of the investigation—is it true there is a quarrel?"

"I did not follow it, my concern was prayer and my mother's lamentable condition," Sister Christina snapped, and Sister Agatha scuttled away.

After the last prayers of the night, Sister Christina and I climbed the steps to the dormitories. I thought I'd lie down in my habit, try to rest for a short time, so I'd be of more use to Brother Edmund.

When I stretched out, on top of my blanket, something poked my belly. I pulled down the blanket. A sheet of paper had been folded and sealed and placed there.

I broke the seal as Sister Christina busied herself on the opposite side, preparing for sleep. There was one sentence scrawled across the top: "Seek out the Howard tapestry." It was not signed.

I refolded the parchment and slipped it under my pillow, my pulses racing. Should I give it to Justice Campion? At first that seemed the best plan, but then I turned against it. If the person who wrote it wanted the information to go directly to the investigators, then why give it to me? No, this was placed in *my* bed. There had to be a good reason.

My instincts told me it was Sister Helen. The message was about a tapestry. She'd tried to speak to me earlier in the day, but we had been interrupted. The other sisters saw her moving around the priory, in agitation. She must have secured parchment and quill, written this message, and then placed it in my bed.

It was not welcome. I did not like to see the name "Howard" or be told to seek out an old tapestry, presumably woven at Dartford and then sold to this family. How was such a search to be accomplished? And if found, what could it tell me?

My mind went round and round until Sister Rachel shook my shoulder. "Wake up, it's your turn to go to the infirmary," she said. I didn't tell her I hadn't slept a minute. I followed her downstairs, clutching the paper in my sleeve.

"This isn't necessary," Brother Edmund said when I arrived. "They're both quiet, so there's no aid needed. You should rest."

I insisted on staying, until at last Brother Edmund relented. My mind was so weary, I had to seek answers from the friar, who was so learned and perceptive and often understood human nature better than I.

As soon as Sister Rachel had gone to her own bed, I produced the paper.

"Who wrote this?" he asked.

"I don't know, but I think it was Sister Helen." We both glanced at her slack face; she could tell us nothing.

I waited for Brother Edmund to comment, to explain the message to me. His face was preternaturally still in the candlelight.

"What do you think it means?" I finally asked.

"I don't know," Brother Edmund said, "but I think it possible that Sister Helen observed a great many things here, things that other people did not realise she observed."

Such as the existence of a hidden crown? I thought, my throat tightening. Lord Chester bragged of knowing a secret, and he was murdered. Sister Helen also possessed some sort of knowledge of something that had happened in the priory and may have relayed it through her design of a tapestry. Something that involved a novice named Sister Beatrice and our own dead Prioress Elizabeth. But now Sister Helen lay senseless.

I said no more to Brother Edmund. I couldn't confide in him any further; it might have been a mistake to have said as much as I had.

We worked in silence. The friar moved back and forth between the two women in his care, while I prepared linens and ground herbs for poultices. He sat in a chair next to Sister Winifred, his elbow propped on the bed. After a few moments his shoulders drooped. He slowly sagged onto the bed, his head resting next to her thin shoulder. He was definitely asleep.

I lit a small candle and ran down the passageway. I must do what I could before he woke.

With all that was going on in the priory, I prayed that locking the library door would have been forgot. For once, my hopes were answered. I pushed open the door and made my way straight to the section that once had contained the book that could reveal all to me.

It was there. *From Caractacus to Athelstan* stood on the shelf, sticking out half an inch farther than any of its neighbours, as if it had been replaced in haste.

I hurried to the last chapter, where I had left off two weeks before.

Athelstan brought many other smaller kings and lords under submission to him and built a great kingdom. He established new laws in England. He honoured his family, his half sisters and half brothers. His sisters were the most beautiful princesses in all of Christendom. Hugh the Great, Duke of the Franks and Count of Paris, sought the hand of Eadhild, the fairest of all of the sisters. Duke Hugh was a Capet, and his son would become the King of France and father to the race of French kings that had continued on in an unbroken line for centuries.

To make an alliance with Athelstan and become the husband of Eadhild, Hugh Capet made over fine gifts to Athelstan. He had in his possession the relics of Charlemagne, for he was direct descended from that great Christian ruler. He awarded to Athelstan a sword and a spear and chalices and a sacred crown.

There were those who refused to pay Athelstan tribute and bow to his fierce will. They said they would die before becoming "under-king" to England. An alliance formed of three such kings to destroy Athelstan. The Viking king Olaf Guthfrithsson, King Constantine of Scotland, and King Owain the Bold of Wales marched in 937 to meet Athelstan. The morning of the battle of Brunanburh, Athelstan put on his head the crown given to him by Hugh Capet and led his army of soldiers with their shields onto the field. Athelstan was vastly outnumbered. But he was not afraid.

It was a battle great, lamentable and horrible. Athelstan led his men in battle as no king had ever done. He was a magnificent force, unstoppable by any opposing army or alliance or armies and showing no mercy. At the end of the battle, he emerged victorious. It is said that rivers of blood never soaked the ground as deeply as they did at Brunanburh. The corpses were so numerous that the black raven, the eagle, the hawk, and the wolf feasted for many days.

Thus did Athelstan become the first man to rule over one kingdom of England, Wales, and Scotland. There now reigned one king.

The crown. It had to be the same one. The crown came from France, a gift from a king who fathered a race of kings. It was worn by a young English king into a battle that should have been lost but was won. A battle that united our island as never before, because of the implacable, unstoppable Athelstan. And then, for reasons I couldn't fathom, the king's crown was taken to France and buried in the ground in Limoges, near the Aquitaine.

I picked up the candle, burning low. Dawn would be coming, and I needed to be in the infirmary when the bells rang summoning us to first prayers.

Outside, in the passageway, it was cold and very dark. Morning wasn't as close as I had thought; it was still the thickest part of night.

I hadn't walked more than a few yards when the trail of a dank breeze stirred the air. I hadn't experienced anything like it inside the priory. The cloister garden was too far away to cause this sort of wind. There were no windows on the passageway.

I stopped and waited. The air had grown thick and still again. And yet there was something else in the passageway. I held up my candle and turned this way and that. No sign of a person—my candle would have revealed the figure of a man or woman. It was a watchfulness. All alone in the passageway of Dartford, I felt myself watched.

Anyone who might have possessed some knowledge of the secrets of Dartford had been struck down. Minutes earlier, I'd read enough to piece together the role of King Athelstan in possessing a crown with powers. He had won a battle that all expected him to lose. Was it because he wore the crown on his head?

I heard something. Not words, not a step on the stone floor. The sound was like breathing, but not air from a warm, mortal body. I felt myself in the presence of a stern, relentless judgement.

The strange shifting breeze crawled through the air again. It was the priory itself. It was stirring to life all around me. The crown of Athelstan moved within the stones and mortar, rippling toward me.

At that very instant, my candle went out, as if extinguished by a breath not my own.

I bolted down the passageway as fast as I'd ever run in my life. I rounded the corner, my arms flailing in blind, terrible panic. I slammed hard into what felt like a person.

I screamed, but only for a few seconds. A large, strong hand clamped tight over my mouth and silenced me.

31

It was only after Brother Edmund had wrapped me in blankets and given me ale to drink that I could put a sentence together.

After he had run into me in the passageway, he'd lifted me up, kicking and weeping, and carried me to the infirmary. I'd waited there while he searched the dark passageway, armed with a long stick from the infirmary.

"I didn't find anyone, Sister Joanna," he said. "Now tell me exactly what you saw."

I shook my head. "I didn't see a person," I said. "I heard what sounded like . . . breathing."

"Where was it coming from?"

I couldn't answer. Now that I was in the infirmary, looked after by Brother Edmund, I feared nothing so much as for him to think me mad.

"Sister Joanna?"

I couldn't meet his gaze. "It seemed as if the walls were breathing. As if the priory were . . . alive."

He didn't laugh or show alarm. "How long since you last slept?" he asked.

"God's servants don't require sleep," I murmured.

"To best serve God, we require sleep and food and drink," he said firmly. "I have known strong men to imagine fearful things when they are severely weakened. Now I want you to lie down on the pallet next to Sister Winifred's."

"Not here," I said, alarmed.

"You must. I can't enter the dormitories, so I'm unable to escort you, but I don't want you walking around the priory alone again." He steered me to a pallet. "You'll get no more than an hour sleep, but you need it. I'll wake you for Lauds."

Brother Edmund was right. I was exhausted. I fell asleep less than a minute after I stretched out on the pallet. The last thing in my mind was a question: *Why hadn't Brother Edmund asked me why I left the infirmary in the first place?* But then sleep pulled me down, and I puzzled over it no more.

True to his word, the friar woke me for Lauds. I hadn't heard the bells. I went through the motions of our morning routine, heavy with tiredness and confusion. In the midmorning, I glanced outside the kitchen window and was startled to see Geoffrey Scovill walking alongside the barn, with Justice Campion stomping behind him, pointing at things with his cane.

Sister Agatha materialised next to me. "They've been here for hours," she whispered. "The coroner met with Lady Chester. He's questioning the prioress again; then they say they will go through all of the servants and get statements."

As much as I hated to think any of our servants a murderer, I was relieved to see their suspicion move away from Brother Edmund or Brother Richard. By the end of the following day, they would hold their inquiry.

"Does the girl in the tapestry really look like Sister Beatrice?" I asked.

Sister Agatha nodded. "Oh, yes."

"Why did she leave the priory?"

She looked around to make sure no one was listening, and then delivered up the history of Sister Beatrice to me. The onetime novice was the youngest child of a large family, her father a merchant. A few months after her father died, her mother had sent her to Dartford. "She never had a good word to say about her mother," Sister Agatha whispered. "They quarrelled all the time; the mother was hard-hearted, she told me. Prioress Elizabeth tried to be patient with her; she said that Sister Beatrice had spirit and that it should not be crushed but moulded. She was a beautiful girl—she loved music the most."

I smiled. "She sounds like someone I would have liked to know."

"But then when the king's commissioners came, it was a grievous embarrassment that she stepped forward and said she wanted to leave us. We were so surprised. She hadn't been the easiest novice, but no one expected that."

"And what happened? She left, just like that? What must her mother have said about it?"

Sister Agatha thought for a moment. "I don't know," she said finally. "The next day she was gone. We never heard another word about her." She craned her neck to look out the window. "Until now."

I finished my work in the kitchen; I sang the offices and ate dinner with the others. I attempted to carry on, with normalcy. But all day, growing inside me, was a sick dread. It grew worse when I went to the infirmary and was told Brother Edmund was in the prioress's chamber, being questioned again. Sister Winifred was out of her bed, but wringing her hands, disconsolate.

"Where is he?" she pleaded with Sister Rachel. "Why would he need to go to the prioress's chamber?" Because of her fragile state, we had decided to keep Lord Chester's murder from Sister Winifred, but it necessitated so many small falsehoods and evasions, I regretted the choice.

I took Sister Winifred's cold hands in mine. "It will be fine, Sister. Don't distress yourself, please."

"Yes, don't distress yourself," said a voice behind us.

"Oh, I've missed you," Sister Winifred cried, throwing herself into Brother Edmund's arms. He patted her back and shoulders, and then smiled at me. His large brown eyes gleamed with calm.

Waves of relief washed through me.

After he'd calmed Sister Winifred, he turned to me and said, "Sister Joanna, I would like to show you something."

I followed him to his apothecary cabinet. Brother Edmund took a handful of dark leaves from a box on the wall and sprinkled them in the bowl. He leaned over the fire and demonstrated how close the bowl needed to be to the flames.

"It's important," he said, "that the leaves not incinerate."

I drew close to him, so close that the heat from the fire made my fingers tingle. "Why," I whispered, "are you showing me this now? She's not having a fit."

"Sister Joanna, I need you to pay attention and to remember."

"But why?" I repeated. "*You* are the one who administers the remedy. Why would I need to do it?"

The church bells rang, and I was forced to leave the infirmary without getting an answer. The end of the day arrived without any more developments. And the next day we saw nothing of the trio from Rochester. It seemed that all suspicion had passed over the friars and the others who lived here. Perhaps they had found the man who killed Lord Chester and had not yet informed us.

Just after dinner I returned to the infirmary to help Brother Edmund with his patients. Sister Rachel was attending Sister Helen, who was still unconscious. I said a Rosary with Sister Winifred while Brother Edmund prepared a poultice for her.

There was an outcry behind us. "Brother Edmund, hurry!" called out Sister Rachel.

Sister Helen's eyes were still closed, but she gasped for breath. There was a terrible wet rattle in her throat; she could not seem to draw in any air. Her fingers twitched as if she were trying to fight for it. Brother Edmund opened her mouth and pressed down her tongue; afterward, he rubbed her arms.

Within minutes, a dozen sisters had come in to gather around her. We formed a chain, holding hands as we prayed. The prioress joined us, her clear voice the loudest of all. I could feel the love we all harboured for Sister Helen pulsing in the air. It seemed that together, tapping into such a force, we could save Sister Helen. One heart and one soul seeking God.

But that day God willed otherwise.

Brother Edmund stepped back. "It's over," he told Prioress Joan.

I burst into tears, as did some of the others. The prioress called out, "Sisters, listen to me. Listen. Remember what Saint Dominic said on his deathbed: 'Weep not, for I will be of more use to you in heaven.' Sister Helen will be in heaven, and she will do God's work just as beautifully there as she did here. She will find true peace." The prioress closed her eyes, and her lips moved in a silent personal prayer.

I drew comfort from her words. Sister Helen had been a remarkable presence at Dartford; we had all been fond of her, protective of her. But no one could say that, after the horrible execution of her brother, she had been at peace.

There was a strange hissing noise next to me. It was Sister Rachel. "What are *you* doing here?" she seethed.

I turned, shocked, to see whom she referred to.

On the other side of Sister Rachel, Geoffrey Scovill stood in the doorway to the infirmary. Gregory, the porter, hovered behind him, unhappy.

There were other shocked sounds as the sisters realised his presence. Prioress Joan opened her eyes. "Master Scovill, you cannot enter the cloistered part of the priory without my express permission," she said. "And to come here, at such a time? It is not fit."

Sister Rachel could not contain herself. She pointed a finger at Geoffrey. "It was you who killed Sister Helen—you frightened her to death."

A few other sisters took up her accusation. "He did this to her!" someone agreed.

"No," I protested, "he didn't."

Geoffrey shot me a quick glance and then took a step inside the infirmary. He had something in his hand. "I am sorry to disturb you, and I deeply regret the passing of Sister Helen," he said sombrely. "But, Prioress, I come here on urgent legal business."

He held up his paper. "I am here to bring Brother Edmund Sommerville to the coroner's inquest in the village of Dartford. Twelve men have been summoned to hear evidence in the murder of Lord Chester. An indictment has been prepared for Brother Edmund, and the jury will decide whether to confirm it."

"No! No!" cried the sisters of the priory, who now formed a protective circle around the friar.

But Brother Edmund wouldn't allow it. He gently pushed his way through the sisters and walked to Geoffrey, his head high.

"I am innocent of this crime but ready to obey the law," he said.

Geoffrey reached into his pocket and removed something. To my horror, he was binding Brother Edmund's wrists.

"What is happening?" called out Sister Winifred, in a panic. "What did that man say? *Edmund?* Where are you taking him?"

Brother Edmund sent one sad look to his sister, and then turned to all of us and said, simply, "Good-bye."

In a moment he was gone.

Sister Agatha went to Sister Winifred and tried to calm her. I could not move or speak. It was as if my mind refused to accept what had just happened.

After a few minutes, Gregory, the porter, returned. He also held a piece of paper. It bore a large red seal.

"This just came from London," he said, and handed it to Prioress Joan.

With a frown, she broke the seal. I could see it was a short letter. She read it while we watched. The only sound was Sister Winifred, crying in the corner, in Sister Agatha's arms.

All the colour drained from the face of the prioress.

"What does it say?" asked Sister Rachel.

The prioress looked at her, and then at all of us.

"The letter is from Thomas Cromwell, the Lord Privy Seal and Vice Regent," she said. "Because of Lord Chester's murder, Dartford Priory is the scandal of the kingdom and must be newly examined for error. The king's chief commissioners, Layton and Legh, are changing their schedule of visitations to come here now, instead of in the spring. They should arrive in Dartford within three weeks' time."

PART THREE

32

This leech was different than the others. The dark-brown creature that the barber chose for Sister Winifred's face was thinner and livelier than the three he'd already applied to her forearms. It squirmed in the air when the barber plucked it from his water jar and calmed only when it attached to her left cheek, near her ear.

It bit her. I could always tell when the leeches bit because Sister Winifred's eyes would widen and her lips would part. I was leeched three times myself, as a child, and I remembered that stinging twinge, followed by a spread of numbness.

I leaned forward to catch Sister Winifred's gaze. I prayed that this leech would draw out the ill humours from her blood. But as I watched, her eyes glazed over; the dullness returned.

Two weeks earlier, the jury of inquiry in Dartford took an hour to decide it was Brother Edmund who must stand trial for the killing of Lord Chester. Coroner Hancock, Justice Campion, and Geoffrey Scovill took him directly back to Rochester, to gaol—we did not see him again. Brother Edmund would stand trial in Rochester when the winter session of the Courts of Assize opened. I overheard a distraught Brother Richard tell the prioress that he had never heard of a murder trial where the accused went free. All murder defendants were found guilty—and all were hanged or burned.

I sat by Sister Winifred's bed when she heard the judgement of the coroner's jury. She understood; she thanked the prioress. But then the melancholia truly consumed her. She went from speaking very little to not at all. It reminded all of Sister Helen. However, our tapestry mistress had been very much a part of the bustle of the priory. Sister Winifred, on the other hand, didn't want to get out of bed, and she didn't want to eat. Despite our best efforts, she'd shrunk alarmingly since Geoffrey Scovill had taken Brother Edmund away. Her cheeks grew more sunken; her ribs seemed to arch from her body. Soon there would be nothing left.

The suffering of Sister Winifred was but an extreme case of how we all felt. Dread of Cromwell's commissioners hung in the air of the priory, mingling with grief over the death of Sister Helen and revulsion over the horror of Lord Chester's murder. It was so unbearable an atmosphere that two of our servants left Dartford, even though work was scarce. The parents of the girls who learned lessons at the priory withdrew them from attending, and that was especially painful for me. Ours was the only school for females in northwest Kent.

When the leech had drunk its fill, it trembled, and the barber returned it to his second jar, to swim with the others that had fed off her. He examined Sister Winifred. "I don't see any stirring of the spirit," he announced. "Shall we try another one, Prioress? I could do three more leeches for the agreed fee."

"No, that's sufficient," said Prioress Joan. "We may still see improvement later today, or tomorrow, correct?"

"It's possible," said the barber in a tone suggesting otherwise.

After he'd left, Sister Rachel spoke up. She had resumed her duties in the infirmary, with my assistance whenever possible. "Prioress, it costs a great deal, but there is a physician in London who treats the insane. He cuts holes in the skull and sees startling improvement. We could send for him."

"Sister Winifred is not insane," I said hotly.

Sister Rachel frowned at my rudeness. I knew it was best for me to assume silence, but I simply couldn't. "If Brother Edmund were to return," I said, "that would bring her back to us, not cutting holes in her head."

The prioress said, "It is too soon to take that particular action, Sister Rachel, but I will bear it in mind, thank you. For now, we will continue with our nursing. Tender care and prayer will prevail, I believe."

Sister Rachel nodded.

The prioress turned to me: "Fetch a bowl of broth. Get as much into her as you can."

"Yes, Prioress," I said. I hurried for the door.

"And Sister Joanna?"

Something in the prioress's tone made me freeze. "Yes?"

"We will meet in chapter house in one hour's time to discuss the various infractions committed by our members in the last month. It has been too long since correction."

"Yes, Prioress."

As I waited in the kitchen for the cook to heat the broth, I chafed at the prospect of chapter discipline. It wasn't because I was unquestionably the one who would be receiving the most of it. We had seen death inside these walls, both natural and unnatural, and one of our own had been imprisoned—wrongfully. We faced imminent dissolution. What could be served by a round of chastising?

But it was no use fretting. Whatever the prioress willed would, of course, be done.

I peeked inside the pot strung up above the fire; the broth did not yet bubble. Restless, I paced around the kitchen until my eyes fell on a poignant sight: the rag doll of Martha Westerly's, carefully propped next to a box of herbs on a shelf.

"Why would Martha leave her doll behind?" I wondered aloud. The cook, busy chopping vegetables, paused in her labour. We looked at each other, both struck with sadness at the thought of the Westerly children.

"Or did she give it to you?" I asked, curious.

"John found the doll and brought it to me," the cook said, resuming her chopping.

"John, the stable hand?"

She nodded.

I walked over to the cook and gently tapped her hand, to stop her from chopping. "When did John find the doll?" I asked.

She thought for a moment. "Sister, he gave it to me the day the men came from Rochester." She lowered her voice. "He had to stand guard that morning, outside of the room where Lord Chester's dead body lay."

I was taken aback. The Westerly children had nothing to do with the murder of Lord Chester. Connecting the two, even through the finding of a doll, upset me. I'd heard that the day after Brother Edmund was taken away, the Westerlys' father appeared at the priory to claim his wife's body, and showned anger when told she'd been buried already in the priory graveyard. Word had been sent to his house in town the night of her death, but no one had responded, so the sisters took initiative. It was an honour for a servant to be buried there, but Master Westerly didn't see it that way. He left uttering curses and refused to answer inquiry about the safety of his children beyond that it was no one's business but his.

The broth bubbled and popped behind me, on the fire. The cook ladled some into a bowl, and I bore it on a tray to the infirmary.

Something about the doll bothered me. At first, I couldn't sort it out. I sat next to the listless Sister Winifred, preparing to feed her, when it struck me.

"What if they saw something?" I asked aloud.

Sister Rachel, measuring out some healing potions, jumped. Purple liquid spilled onto her table.

"Sister Joanna, see what you've done?" she scolded. "What are you talking about? Who saw what?"

"Can you feed Sister Winifred?" I scrambled for the door. "I'm sorry, but it's very important."

Without waiting for a reply, I raced back to the kitchen and persuaded the cook to let me borrow the doll.

It was a sullen November day, and I ran to the stables without a cloak. But I didn't care. For the first time in weeks, purpose sang in my veins. I'd felt weary and defeated ever since Brother Edmund had been taken and, more than anything, was preoccupied with Sister Winifred's decline. I'd learned not one thing more about the Athelstan crown, and since that terrifying night when I'd felt the priory breathing around me, I had never again sensed its mystical powers. Most of the time I despaired, feeling I would never find the crown, nor puzzle through the identity of Lord Chester's killer. My father would never be freed from the Tower.

But now, just the possibility of discovering something that would help the priory made my feet fly over the damp, cold ground.

I found John pitching dirty straw out of a stall at the end of the barn. My questions plainly made him wary.

"Why do you want to know how I found it?" he asked. "What does the doll matter to anyone?"

"Please think," I begged.

Avoiding my eyes, he muttered, "I don't know, it was a while back."

"John, listen, I know it sounds trivial, but it's not. The doll matters."

"Who would it matter to?" he asked.

"Well, to all of us here at Dartford, but most of all, to Brother Edmund."

John put down his pitchfork. "Brother Edmund mended my arm . . . he kept the porter from dismissing me," he said. "By the Virgin, I'll do anything for him."

"Then tell me exactly when you found the doll—and where."

"All right, Sister. That morning, ye know the porter ordered me and Harry, the head farmhand, to stand guard outside the guest bedchamber, to keep anyone from viewing the corpse. After a time, I looked down the passageway, to the end, and I saw something small and white lying there. It was the doll. Looked like it had been dropped. The maids came by, and I asked them about it. They got all angry; they said the doll wasn't there the day before. They swore they'd done a good job sweeping and cleaning and they wouldn't have missed it. So I just stuffed it in my jerkin and gave it to the cook later."

"Didn't you think it strange?" I asked.

"What, Sister?"

"The doll was not there the day before, but appeared that morning?"

John threw up his hands. "I just thought the maids missed it. I didn't want to get no one in trouble, especially since the men from Rochester came right after. Everyone was scared of them."

I took a deep breath. "I don't think the maids missed it, John."

He looked truly bewildered. "What are ye saying, mistress?"

"Do you know where the Westerly house is in the village?" I asked.

"Aye. I've lived in Dartford all my life."

"And their father, you know him?"

He made a face. "Stephen Westerly is not an easy man, I've not had many dealings, but yes, I know him."

I patted his arm, excited. "John, prepare two horses. I have to go back to the priory. But I'll return as soon as possible."

33

When I ran through the entranceway to the chapter house, all the sisters were in place. They sat on the stone benches, their heads bowed. Sister Rachel stood at the lectern, finishing the reading from the Martyrology.

The prioress and Sister Eleanor, loyal *circator*, standing near the lectern, turned and stared at me.

"Forgive me, Prioress," I said, out of breath. "But something has happened. I think it is quite possible that—"

"Take your place next to Sister Christina," interrupted the prioress.

"But I need to tell you—"

"*Silence, novice!*" Her thundering voice echoed off the stone walls.

I sat next to Sister Christina. She noticed the rag doll still in my hand and shook her head in disbelief, as if I'd gone mad, just like Sister Winifred.

The prioress gestured to Sister Eleanor. "You may begin," she said.

And so it began, the list of chapter infractions. One sister was observed smiling in Matins, obviously distracted when she should be singing the office; another sister slept through midnight prayers; a third shirked her cleaning duties to spend more time in study. The acts of penance were proclaimed by the prioress and accepted with humility by the offenders.

It all felt unreal to me. I knew that our priory was built on rules, all of them created many years ago by spiritual men and women much wiser than I. And religious houses depended on strict adherence to such rules. But we existed in a time when following rules would not save us from destruction. Did no one see this but me?

Sister Eleanor cleared her throat meaningfully. "And now," she said, "I come to the case of Sister Joanna."

I walked to the prioress and knelt before her on the stone floor. No one else had ever done that in chapter correction. I heard a rippling of unease around me.

"I plead with you, Prioress, to be allowed to speak," I said. "After that, I will hear what Sister Eleanor has to say and gladly accept all punishment for every instance in which I've broken rules of the order."

The prioress said, reluctantly, "Very well."

But now I wasn't sure how to begin. "I love this priory," I finally blurted.

The prioress and Sister Eleanor looked at each other, startled.

"I know I have committed sins here, large and small, and I don't deserve your forgiveness," I continued. "I don't deserve God's forgiveness. But this place, this priory, is a sanctuary of light and beauty and purity in the darkness."

My voice broke; I willed it to stop.

"I want so much to serve you, Prioress, to be your humble servant in protecting Dartford from all of our enemies."

The wariness in the eyes of our prioress softened, just a little.

"Today I learned something. It may be small; it may be insignificant. Or it may be very important. It concerns the Westerly children, the same Westerly children whom I failed in the hour of their mother's death. I know something about the children that I realise I should have told you before, but I did not think to do so. Which is that the children were able to move around this priory, day and night, with great subtlety. Were they not innocent children, one could say with deviousness. I found them in the infirmary one night, and I have no idea how they were able to get there, unnoticed."

Sister Eleanor fidgetted; I could tell they were unsure why I was relaying this now.

I took a deep breath. "I believe that the children did not leave the grounds of Dartford when their mother died. I think they hid somewhere for at least a day. The night Lord Chester was killed, they may have at some point been in the passageway outside, in the front part of the priory. The children could have seen or heard something . . . or someone."

"Why do you think this?" demanded the prioress.

I held up the doll and explained that it had been found the morning of the murder, near the guest bedchamber, in a place that had been swept the day before.

"If I find the Westerly children, I can ask them what happened," I said. "They will tell me the truth, I am sure of it. And what I learn could help clear Brother Edmund of suspicion."

The prioress shook her head. "It is not our place to gather facts about a crime," she said. "A judgement was made by a jury of men. As difficult as it is to accept, we must abide by their decision."

"But they did *not* have all the facts!" In spite of myself, my voice rose.

The prioress stepped forward and reached for my hands, to pull me to my feet. "We all saw Brother Edmund as a true man of God when he served here. And we grieve the melancholia of Sister Winifred, caused by his imprisonment. But this is God's will moving before us, in ways we simply can't understand. One thing you have not yet learned, Sister Joanna, is to accept God's will."

She was correct. I could not give up.

"*Verum est notus per fides quod causa,*" I cried out, desperate.

The prioress stared at me, shocked.

"Truth is known through faith and reason," I said quickly, for the benefit of those not proficient in Latin. "We are a priory—we worship divine truth. Saint Thomas said faith and reason complement each other: they do not contradict. And he said that the intellect must seek out facts to support reason. May I please be permitted to find the Westerly children, to gather those facts?"

The prioress managed to ask, "Just how would you proceed?"

"I will go with John, our trusted stable hand, to the village, to the house where the children's father lives. There's been no sign of them since the day of the murder. But Stephen Westerly did return to Dartford from London, and the children must be with him."

The prioress clapped her hands three times. "Again, you would break the rule of enclosure? Have you learned nothing at all?"

A voice rang out behind me, from the stone benches. Sister Agatha said, "May I be permitted to accompany Sister Joanna, to ensure all is done properly in gathering these facts?" Sister Agatha came to stand with me. "Prioress, I will be with her every minute. You have the authority to approve our leaving for a short time."

The prioress went silent. I could hardly breathe.

"Very well," she said at last. "Sister Joanna and Sister Agatha have my permission to go to the village, with John, our good servant, as guide and protector. But you *must* return by nightfall, whether you've found the children or not. And we shall list your correction at the next chapter."

I turned to Sister Agatha. "Thank you," I said.

Once we'd reached the stable, the travel plans changed. The fastest way to the village would be riding priory horses, but Sister Agatha, I learned, had not ridden a horse in almost twenty years. Today was not the day for a lesson. John hitched a wagon to the two horses, and we took our places in the back. The village was so close that it wouldn't cause too much of a delay.

John shook the reins, and we rumbled up the priory lane.

Sitting beside me, Sister Agatha pulled nervously on the few hairs that sprouted from her chin. It occurred to me she probably had not left the grounds of Dartford since she had arrived as a novice.

"Why did you come forward?" I asked her.

"This is my home, Sister Joanna. The king's commissioners will be here soon. Perhaps they will order us to be dissolved—and, yes, perhaps that is God's will. But if there's anything we can do to help ourselves, we must attempt it. If we can prove that Brother Edmund did not commit this terrible sin, it might prevent our closure."

I reached out and hugged her.

"Thank you," I whispered.

She hugged me back, making a little clucking noise.

I hadn't passed through Dartford since last autumn, when my father brought me to the priory. Rumbling up High Street, past the shops and inns, the storefronts for carpenters, bakers, fishmongers, and tailors, I was newly impressed by how clean and well ordered a town it was. Though Dartford was by no means small—I'd heard almost a thousand people lived here—many of the townsfolk seemed to know one another. They called across High Street with a smile;

two stout women, one of them holding a parcel of fish, laughed in front of the parish church, Holy Trinity.

There were no smiles for us. A few people waved at John, sitting in front, flicking the horses on, but Sister Agatha and I drew uneasy stares. Some townsfolk stopped in their tracks to watch our wagon go by. John turned around and said apologetically, "It's because of the death of Lord Chester. They talk of nothing else, the townsfolk." The scrutiny unnerved Sister Agatha. When we passed the rabbit warren, a crowd of men scowled at us and she gripped my arm so tight I could feel her sharp nails through my habit and cloak.

In the centre of Dartford, in the middle of High Street, stood a cross. Nearby was the large market building. Crowds of people streamed out, carrying bags of grain or buckets of fish. One well-dressed woman proudly touted a box of cheeses. John turned the wagon at the corner just past the market and, after passing a block of half-timbered homes, turned again.

The narrow street we ventured down was not as fair as the others. The homes looked less solid. A few sported thatched roofs, even though that was discouraged in town dwellings, for fear of fire. A flock of emaciated chickens scattered before our wagon wheels. Two men walked away from us, down the street. I saw no sign of the children.

I tapped John on the shoulder. "How much farther to Master Westerly's house?"

John pointed at the house at the end of the street. "It's that one. He lives on the top floor."

"Why don't you stop and tie up the wagon, John? We'll walk the rest of the way." I had the idea to come upon the house gradually.

While John attended to the horses on the side of the street, Sister Agatha and I approached the house. It was two storeys tall and timber framed. The roof was steeply pitched, with a wide chimney on the side. At least the children would be warm this winter.

The door to the house was shut tight; there was no one out front.

The two men who'd been walking ahead had stopped. They stared at us, their eyes crawling up and down our nuns' habits and caps. I hoped they would keep their distance, at least until we were inside the Westerly house.

But no. My heart dropped as the men doubled back toward us.

One of them had a thick black beard; the other was younger and red-haired.

"Sisters, what are ye doing in town?" asked the bearded man. "Is all not well at the priory?"

Sister Agatha recoiled from him, frightened.

"We know ye're not supposed to go out and about," said the red-haired man.

Out of the corner of my eye I saw another two men bearing down on us from across the street.

"Have they come to kill ye, Tom?" shouted one of the newcomers.

Our stable hand, John, had reached Sister Agatha and me. "Stay behind me," he muttered. "These are ruffians."

The man who'd shouted his insult strained to get around John. He had watery eyes and a thick, sneering mouth. "Ye killed Lord Chester, didn't ye? Bashed in his brains while he slept under yer roof."

"Show some respect," demanded Tom, the black-bearded man.

"Why should I?" retorted the watery-eyed man. His companion snickered.

John called out bravely: "Do not interfere with the sisters. They come here on important priory business. If ye insult them, ye will be sorry indeed."

I tapped John's arm. "Don't fight them, there are too many," I whispered. "We must calm them with words instead. Let me attempt it."

Sister Agatha said to me, "They are common varlets; you cannot address them directly, Sister Joanna."

The watery-eyed man howled, "Hear me, Sister, I don't barge into your priory and call you an ugly doxy, so I'll thank you not to come on my street and call me a common varlet."

With a curse, Tom, the bearded man, pushed his way forward. The next thing I saw was a fist flying. Grunts and laughter filled the air.

I glanced up at the Westerly house—no sign of anyone home. But we needed a refuge from the melee. I grabbed Sister Agatha with one hand and John with the other and shouted, "The house!"

But before we made it a single step, a stream of cold water hit my arm.

I turned and saw that the men who'd been fighting now swayed in confusion, dripping water. A tall young man gripped a large wooden bucket—he was the one who'd drenched them.

"Men, do I beat you on the heads, right now, and drag you to your beadle?" he bellowed. "Or will you get off this street *now*?"

It was hard for me to believe, but the man was Geoffrey Scovill.

Grumbling, the townsfolk dispersed.

Geoffrey tossed the bucket onto the street and turned to me with a crooked smile.

"Ah, Sister Joanna," he said, "what would you do without me?"

34

"But what are you doing here?" I asked Geoffrey Scovill.

He laughed. "What am I doing here? What are *you* doing out of your priory, in the middle of town, and not the most respectable part of it, either?"

Sister Agatha said haughtily, "We are not required to inform you of our business, Master Scovill."

He bowed to us. "Well, then, I will be on my way."

"Wait!" Sister Agatha said in a panic. "You can't leave us now, with only John to protect us. Those men could return."

Geoffrey stood there, arms folded. His blue eyes danced as he waited.

I sighed. "Sister Agatha, we have to explain our purpose to him." Over her protests, I quickly told Geoffrey how I'd learned of the doll, where it was found, and when, and what the implications were. He listened closely.

"So now you're personally going to interview possible witnesses to a serious crime?" he asked. "Why didn't you send word to Justice Campion or the coroner? Or to me?"

Sister Agatha said, "We knew you had all made your judgement."

I studied Geoffrey's face.

"You're *not* sure the right man was arrested, either," I guessed. "That's why you've returned to Dartford. You're continuing to investigate, too."

Geoffrey said quickly, "I knew nothing of these Westerly children—that's not why I'm here. But since we have collided, I suggest that I accompany you into the house and lead the questioning."

"I will ask the questions," I insisted.

Geoffrey laughed again. "I know that if I give you an order, you'll not obey it, Sister Joanna. So I can only suggest some form of cooperation?"

"Very well." I turned to John. "I think it's best you stay here and watch over the horses."

Sister Agatha and I moved to the front door of the house. She gave me a strange sidelong glance, which I ignored.

We knocked, hard. It took a couple of moments for the door to open, and then only partway. A sharp-faced teenage girl, in a soiled apron, peered out, suspicious.

"Were ye part of the fighting on the street?" she asked. "We don't want no trouble."

Geoffrey pushed the door open. "I am the parish constable of Rochester. We have some questions, not for you but for the Westerly family."

"Are they at home?" I asked her.

"Aye, some of them are." She beckoned us inside, grudgingly. It was a dim room, not very tidy, smelling of onions.

The ceiling creaked above. I looked up, my heart racing.

The girl nodded. "The woman's home, with the daughters."

Sister Agatha and I stared at her. "What woman?" I whispered.

The girl swiftly backed away, twisting her apron in her hands. "I don't want no trouble," she repeated. She pointed at the worn set of stairs on the side of the room. "It's that way."

We went up the stairs, single file, Geoffrey leading. He knocked on the door at the top of the stairs and said loudly, "We need to speak to the Westerly family."

I heard a faint rustling on the other side of the door, but no one answered.

I whispered to Geoffrey, "What if the children go out the windows?"

He nodded—then pushed against the door with his right shoulder. It had been locked, but the lock was a poor one and it broke easily.

I pushed my way around Geoffrey, to be the first. It appeared empty of people. It was a cleaner room than downstairs, with light streaming in through the back windows. A row of stools lined one wall; the other end contained a long wooden table. It opened into a kitchen.

"Sister Joanna!"

Martha Westerly flew to me like a small bird. I had her in my arms, felt her thick hair and smelled her skin. I held her so tight I feared I'd crush her bones.

"What is your name?" Geoffrey asked someone.

I turned to see whom he spoke to. A slim, dark-haired woman stood in the corner, next to the kitchen. She was a little older than me, and wore an apron, cleaner than the one worn by the girl downstairs. She would have been pretty but for the red scar next to her left ear—and the look of terror in her eyes. She had flattened herself against the wall, as if we were a trio of killers.

"I am Catherine Westerly," she said. Her voice was low and rather rough. Her chest rose and fell; she was actually panting in fear.

"How are you related to Master Stephen Westerly?" I asked.

"I am his wife."

"Impossible," said Sister Agatha. "His wife died less than a month ago, at Dartford Priory."

The woman stirred from the wall. "I am his second wife," she said, a touch defiantly. "All was done legally. The banns were read."

"It's true, Sister Joanna," said a voice from the doorway.

It was Ethel, wearing a clean dress—and a face puffy with misery. Behind her was the bedroom, with straw pallets on the floor.

"My father has married this woman." Ethel shot Catherine Westerly a look of resentment. Instead of reacting in anger or offence, Ethel's stepmother bit her lip and looked down.

Sister Agatha cleared her throat. "We are glad to see that you are safe, children, though the circumstances are . . . irregular. We've come to ask you a few questions."

Catherine Westerly said quickly, "What about? Shouldn't my husband be here? He's out for the day, with Harold."

"The questions are for the children," I said. I set Martha down and beckoned to Sister Agatha, who carried the sack. She nodded and pulled out the doll.

Martha screamed, "Lucinda! You found Lucinda!" She grabbed the doll and danced in a circle.

Ethel looked at me, confused.

"You came all this way to bring her the doll?"

"Do you know where we found it?" I countered.

Ethel shook her head.

"In the passageway, outside of the guest bedchamber where Lord and Lady Chester slept on All Souls' Day."

Faster than I'd ever seen anyone go in my life, Ethel streaked for the bedroom door. She was just an inch from its open window when Geoffrey grabbed her by the waist and pulled her down.

We placed Ethel and Martha, both of them frightened, on two stools. Plainly something had happened they did not want to tell us.

"We won't punish you," Geoffrey repeated. "We just want to know what you saw and heard that night. It's very important."

"We weren't in that part of the priory—we don't know anything," Ethel said.

"Girls, listen to me, I know you were upset because I wasn't there to comfort you right after your mother died," I said. Martha nodded, and her eyes filled with tears. "And I should have come looking for you before today, or someone should have. I've sorely disappointed you. But some strange and frightening things have happened at Dartford Priory. You are young, but you should know this."

I had their full attention now.

"I need to protect the priory, the place where your mother worked since she was fifteen years old. But I can't do it without your help. Will you help me?"

Little Martha looked at her sister pleadingly.

Ethel groaned and said, "All right, Sister Joanna."

She took a deep breath and began.

"After no one could find you, we ran away and hid in the friars' brewery. There's a little room no one goes in. It was cold, and it smelled bad, but we were safe there. We didn't want to leave the priory just yet. The next day, everyone was running about, getting ready for the feast; we weren't noticed. We had places all over the priory we liked to go to, where no one saw us."

I opened my mouth to ask more about their secret hiding places, but Geoffrey tapped my arm gently.

Ethel went on: "We overheard the sisters and servants talking about the feast, and we knew that most people didn't even want that man at Dartford. It wasn't right he be there. And then, afterward, we heard some of the sisters crying. We knew that Lord Chester said very bad things about the priory—that it would be closed down soon. And he hurt one of the novices. We heard it was you, Sister Joanna."

I shook my head. "It was Sister Winifred."

Ethel hung her head, and I knew the next part of her story did not come easily. "We don't have much money, Sister. We heard that Lord Chester wore very fine rings when he came to the feast. And then he fell down drunk and had to be carried to the front rooms . . ." Her voice trailed away.

Geoffrey said, very softly, "You thought you'd sneak into his room and take one of the rings?"

Martha began to cry again. "We're so sorry." I stroked her soft little arm, trying to soothe her.

"How did you get to the front of the priory, when the doors were all locked?" Geoffrey asked.

"Through a window," Ethel said.

"But we checked all the windows and—" I poked Geoffrey this time. I didn't want to use up the goodwill we'd built by challenging them on the windows.

"What time was it?" I asked.

"I don't know," said Ethel. "It was a long time after last prayers. We'd slept for most of the afternoon, so we weren't tired. We knew where the guest rooms were, so we went there as quietly as we could. We opened the door off the passageway just a crack and—" She jumped in her chair as if she were reliving some shock.

"What?" Geoffrey asked in a low, urgent voice.

"There were two doors. Left and right. A woman was going through the door to the bedchamber on the right."

My stomach turned over.

"Do you have an idea who it was?" Geoffrey asked.

"No, sir." She shook her head violently. "It was dark."

"Did she wear a habit? Was it a sister?"

"I just couldn't tell. It was a . . . a glimpse. She went through the door and shut it behind her. But I saw that what she wore was long and dark."

Dominican habits were white, so it couldn't have been a nun. Unless the woman wore a cloak over it.

Geoffrey leaned in, closer. "Young or old? How quickly did the person move?"

"Quickly, sir. But I just couldn't say how old the woman was."

I couldn't hold back any longer. "Did you see anything more?"

She shook her head. "We went back out into the passageway."

I grimaced in disappointment. But Geoffrey's eyes stayed locked on her face. "There is something else?" he prompted, calm as ever. I don't know how he managed such patience.

"We heard voices. Two people. One voice was definitely a woman's."

"Did you hear what they were talking about?"

"No, sir," said Ethel. "They spoke for a moment or so. Low voices. Then the man said, 'No.' He wasn't shouting or angry. Just the one word. But then, there was this strange thumping noise from the room. We heard it at least four times. *Thump, thump, thump, thump.*"

A chill clawed at my spine. The children had heard Lord Chester being murdered.

"It was so strange, we ran away," Ethel said. "We went back to the friars' brewery house, and the next morning we walked to town. Father came back the next night."

Sister Agatha grabbed my arm and shook it. "It was a woman in his room," she said, excited. "Not Brother Edmund."

Yes, but which woman? I wondered.

We both looked at Geoffrey Scovill. He was deep in thought.

"What happens now?" I asked him.

"I will report to Constable Campion and Coroner Hancock what I've heard here—what happens after that, I can't be sure," he said carefully.

Sister Agatha pressed to leave at once, to return to the priory, but Geoffrey said he needed to speak to Catherine Westerly for a few more minutes, with the children not listening. He persuaded a reluctant Sister Agatha to occupy the girls, and beckoned for me to help him with their stepmother.

Catherine Westerly regarded the two of us with hard, wary eyes. "What do you want from me?"

"Before you married the children's father, where did you live?" Geoffrey asked. "Did you say it was Southwark?"

"Why?"

"Because I think that before you married, you worked for a bawd."

Catherine Westerly covered her face with both hands and turned away from us, toward the wall. "Go away, go away," she moaned.

I was shocked. I'd never been in the same room as a harlot before.

"I'm not asking you this to shame you," Geoffrey said, his manner gentle. "I saw how terrified you were when we came in, as if you were in hiding. Also, that scar on your face is one that the bawds give to whores who've disobeyed. Did Master Westerly settle up for you when he took you to Dartford?"

She shook her head slightly, her face still covered. "He tried and tried, but he couldn't earn enough money to pay off my debt. He knew his wife was dying, so we went into hiding in London. We *are* married—that is true. I have the papers."

Geoffrey nodded. "I believe you, Mistress Westerly. I only bring up this delicate subject because the children will need to be interviewed again, officially, and I fear that you will not remain in Dartford."

She shrugged. "It's up to my husband where we live."

"Very well," Geoffrey said. "I will come back and speak to him as soon as I can." He touched my elbow. "Now we can go."

We were halfway to the door when the girls flew into my arms. Martha had a lock around my waist. "Don't leave us here, Sister Joanna," she begged.

Ethel's eyes filled with tears. "I want to go to the priory, to be with you and the sisters," she whispered. "I'm old enough to work. Take me."

My throat tightened; I couldn't speak. I glanced at Catherine Westerly, who'd heard everything.

"Yes, the children hate me," she said flatly, and straightened her shoulders. "They blame me for the neglect of their mother the last year of her life. But I shall do my duty and care for them the best I know how. Perhaps, in time, they will come to like me."

Geoffrey turned to me: "Come, we'll talk outside."

I kissed the girls good-bye one more time and followed Geoffrey out the door.

"I can't let the children be raised by a harlot—it's a crime," I whispered to him, brokenly, as we walked down the steps.

"Working for a bawd may be a sin, but it's not a crime," he said. "Those brothels are licensed. In fact, I've heard tell the Bishop of Winchester is the landlord for most of the Southwark brothels."

Stephen Gardiner owned the land that brothels were built on? I put that from my mind. Unthinkable.

"What of the children's souls?" I demanded. "They require moral guidance, not just food and a bed."

We were outside the house. Sister Agatha was right: it was late. We hadn't much time to get back to the priory.

Geoffrey said, "She appears to be penitent and desire a new life. Westerly must love her very much to make her his wife and risk so much on her behalf."

I shuddered. "*Love* her? How could he love such a person? His poor dead wife, Lettice, the mother of his children, was a kind woman, a good Christian."

Geoffrey looked up at the second floor of the house, as if he expected to see the faces of the Westerly children. No one looked back. "We can't always help whom we love," he said in a strange voice.

Sister Agatha shouted from the wagon. "What are you waiting for? We must get back to the priory, Sister."

"Yes, let's depart, Sister Joanna," Geoffrey said, and steered me to the wagon. "My horse is in town, near the market. Why don't you take me there, and then I'll escort you? I should have a word with your prioress about what we've learned."

Sister Agatha said, "Couldn't you walk to the market?"

Her rudeness surprised me. "Sister, we should not begrudge this." I turned to Geoffrey. "Please, come with us."

It was an uncomfortable ride to the market, with Sister Agatha puffed up with disapproval. As soon as Geoffrey leaped out of the wagon to mount his own horse, I leaned over to ask, "Why are you angry with Geoffrey Scovill? He has assisted us today."

"Sister Joanna, there is a certain familiarity between the two of you that, as your novice mistress, I must correct you on," she said, in her most pompous and scolding tone. "When you converse with him, it appears that you are well acquainted with each other, though I don't see how that's possible. It is most certainly inappropriate."

I could feel my cheeks redden. "Yes, Sister Agatha," I said, as meekly as I could manage.

We rode the rest of the way to Dartford Priory in silence, Geoffrey trotting ahead. The sun had never appeared that day. It was the kind of damp November afternoon in which the grey gradually darkens until all trace of light is finally extinguished. I don't know if it was the grimness of the day, or my nervousness about being late to the priory, but I didn't feel as much joy as I'd expected over obtaining proof that Brother Edmund was innocent. The discovery that a woman may have killed Lord Chester with such vicious fury unsettled me.

A bleak dusk gripped the countryside as John turned the wagon into the lane leading to Dartford Priory. When we rounded the curve, I saw a ball of orange light glowing in the distance. It made me uneasy; I couldn't imagine its cause. Two torches burning at our gatehouse wouldn't illuminate the grounds like that.

Geoffrey kicked the sides of his horse and galloped the rest of the way—he would arrive well ahead of us.

Once we'd neared the gatehouse, I could see a bonfire freshly lit in front of the priory, with two of our servants tending it. Prioress Joan, Brother Richard, and Gregory clustered around three men I did not know. Geoffrey had leaped off his horse to talk to them.

Sister Agatha said, "This can't possibly be because of us, can it?"

"No, the sun just set a few moments ago," I said.

We rumbled through the gatehouse arch. As soon as the wagon came to a halt, I scrambled out the back and ran toward Geoffrey.

He turned away from the others to speak to me.

"Did you tell Prioress Joan what the children said?" I asked.

"Not yet," he said, running his hands through his hair.

"But she must know that a woman's voice was heard, that it was a woman that night."

"It's already known," Geoffrey said.

"But . . . but . . . how?" I stammered.

"The priory received word from these men that today Lady Chester threw herself out the window of her manor. She left a note asking for forgiveness for her crime. It would appear that she killed her own husband and now she's killed herself."

35

At my mother's insistence, I had a tutor when I was young who schooled me in mathematics as well as Greek, Latin, literature, and philosophy. He was an excellent teacher, and I mourned when we could no longer find the money to pay him and he left Stafford Castle. I learned from him how to do complicated sums, and I remember well the feeling of solving one, of hearing a click in my mind as everything fell into place. I heard that same click when Geoffrey Scovill told me that Lady Chester had killed her husband.

And yet, a moment later, a new uneasiness formed. Lord Chester had been a vile husband; I did not doubt that. His behaviour toward her at the requiem feast had been execrable. It was hard to believe she'd slept through a murder in the next room. But I'd heard the screams of Lady Chester that morning and seen her stumble down the passageway, blind with panic and horror after the body had been found. Was she such a good play actress? And what of the reliquary—how had she obtained it from the church? This revelation answered some questions, but it created new ones.

Geoffrey had returned to the bonfire. "Prioress, this is very important," he said loudly. "Did any member of the house leave the priory this afternoon, besides Sister Agatha and Sister Joanna?"

"No," the prioress said.

"Are you sure?" He turned to the porter.

"I was in the front part of the priory all afternoon, Master Scovill," Gregory said. "The cloister door was kept locked the whole time, and no one but the prioress went in and out."

Geoffrey nodded, and hurried to his horse.

"Wait." I ran to him, but he was already mounted and shaking the reins. "You harbour doubts?"

"Not of Lady Chester taking her own life," he said. "Her servants saw her standing in the window and then leap out. The letter left in her room was definitive."

"But there's something," I insisted. "Tell me."

The bonfire reflecting in Geoffrey's eyes lent him a strange visage. "I've never been certain that Lord Chester was murdered solely because of what occurred at the feast."

"What do you mean?"

"Remember what he himself said that night: 'I *know* you have secrets. No one knows better than I do about the secrets of Dartford Priory.'"

I shuddered; it was so odd to hear the words of Lord Chester, words I'd repeated to myself, come from Geoffrey's lips. "You think that he was killed because of the secrets he knew?" I asked.

He straightened his jerkin. "At present, my theories are not important. I must be off to Rochester. The coroner and justice of the peace must be told of Lady Chester's suicide immediately."

"Tonight?" I asked, alarmed. "Is it safe to ride that distance after dark? What of robbers on the road?"

Geoffrey bent down from his saddle with a smile and said: "Don't you want Brother Edmund freed as soon as possible? I thought that was more important to you than anything else."

Before I could say a word to that, he straightened up and rode away.

That evening I detected a ripple of hope in the refectory and the passageways of the priory. Soon all of England would know that it was not a friar, not a member of a religious order, who'd killed a noble guest under our roof. When the king's commissioners arrived to examine Dartford, we'd be free of that stain on our honour.

There was, of course, one person in the priory directly affected by Lady Chester's suicide. I wasn't with Sister Christina when she was informed and did not see her for a number of hours, but after last prayers, when I came to novice quarters, I found her there and greatly changed. Her determination and her sense of intelligent conviction were gone. She looked completely lost. Frail.

"Do you need anything?" I asked. "I feel I should do something for you, Sister Christina. You've had a tremendous shock. Should I fetch Sister Agatha?"

"No, please don't." Her voice was scratchy. "I don't want Sister Agatha with her questions, or Sister Rachel with her potions, or the prioress with her prayers. The only person I can bear to have near me is you, Sister Joanna. I know that if I ask you to be silent here, you will respect my wishes, won't you?"

"Of course."

And not another word was said.

Late the next day, Sister Christina's uncle, the Bishop of Dover, arrived. He had not come to the priory after the murder of his older brother, but the suicide of his sister-in-law brought him to Dartford. Sister Christina spent several hours talking to him in the *locutorium* and emerged from it less lost, though still subdued. I honestly couldn't imagine how she would cope with the horror of a murdered father and a mother who took her own life. Lady Chester could not be buried in consecrated ground.

But it was Sister Winifred who worried me the most. The morning after I went to town I made my usual stop at the infirmary and found her tossing, restless, in her bed. Her forehead felt warm; two red spots flared in her cheeks.

Sister Rachel said nervously, "This is what I've been fearing. She has contracted infection and does not possess the strength—or the will—to throw it off."

"What can I do?"

"I'm preparing an application of comfrey; you can assist me," she said. "Although you most likely should keep your distance from Sister Winifred."

"I never take ill; please let me nurse her," I pleaded.

She sighed. "Very well, but if we lose you both, the prioress will be most grieved."

I received permission to spend all my hours in the infirmary, except for time spent observing the Dominican offices. Yet my nursing made no difference. The comfrey did not bring her relief, nor did the remedy Brother Edmund taught me. In the night Sister Winifred started a wet cough. Every time I heard it, my body tensed.

The next morning, cooling her brow with a dampened cloth, I couldn't deny my fears any longer. Sister Winifred might very well die. For the tenth time, I wondered if it would strengthen her to learn that Lady Chester had admitted to killing her husband, that Brother Edmund was innocent of crime. Sister Rachel and I had discussed it the day before, but the manner of Lady Chester's own death was so upsetting, and, without the certainty of Brother Edmund's return, she felt the news would only further confuse Sister Winifred.

She coughed, and it was such a deep one, she shuddered with pain. "May the Virgin heal and protect you, Sister Winifred," I whispered. She turned her head toward me. Her eyes widened, and her lips parted. "Edmund," she groaned.

"Yes, I know, I miss him as well," I said, patting her delicate throat with the cloth.

"I am here, Sister," said a familiar voice behind me.

My heart leaped—it was Brother Edmund.

With a strength I wouldn't have thought possible, Sister Winifred sat up. She stretched out trembling arms. "Oh, God has heard me."

With his usual swift, deft movements, Brother Edmund lowered Sister Winifred onto her bed while feeling her forehead. "Yes, I am here and I shall care for you now," he said. "Calm yourself." My heart leaped with a fierce joy.

But then I saw his face.

Brother Edmund had aged ten years in less than a month. Wrinkles creased his face; deep violet shadows sagged under his exhausted eyes. Worst of all, he was sweating. It was November, but his face was as damp as if it were the hottest day in July.

I caught his sleeve, horrified. "You're ill, too, Brother Edmund."

"No, I'm not."

"But it's obvious you are," I persisted. "What can I do?"

Brother Edmund shook his head. "Nothing. You're not an apothecary or a barber, and you're certainly not a physician, Sister Joanna. You have no knowledge of illness."

I could barely see, for my eyes swam with tears. It was ridiculous to react this way, but I couldn't help it.

Brother Edmund did not notice my tears. He was too busy searching through his cabinet of supplies for the right herbs for Sister

Winifred. He'd made a fresh poultice and applied it by the time Sister Rachel returned.

She, too, expressed joy at his return, followed by dismay over his appearance.

"I'm telling you both, I am *not* ill," he snapped. "Now please, let me concentrate on healing Sister Winifred."

Sister Rachel, deeply offended, swept out of the infirmary. I remembered the tactful way that Brother Edmund had dealt with his arrival at Dartford in October, how he'd made sure to smooth the transition of replacing her as the chief healer of the priory. It was like he'd become a different man.

But was this so surprising? I thought of where he'd been for the past three weeks: in gaol, accused of murder. No one knew better than I the harsh effects of imprisonment, on body and soul. I determined not to be dismayed by any other affronts.

Under his devoted and skilful care, Sister Winifred improved remarkably. The dullness had gone from her eyes, and she took every drop of broth I spooned her. While she ate, Brother Edmund sat on a stool on the other side, never taking his eyes from her.

"I thank you, Sister Joanna, for caring for Sister Winifred," he said quietly.

This was the voice of the Brother Edmund I'd missed. His face still shone with sweat, but I said nothing more about his appearance. I did not want to irritate him anew.

"Did Geoffrey Scovill bring you to Dartford?" I asked.

He frowned. "No, Justice Campion released me. I haven't seen Scovill since the coroner's inquest. Why do you ask?"

"No reason," I muttered, and helped Sister Winifred with her broth.

A short time later, the bells rang, and I hurried to church, eager to say my prayers of gratitude for the return of Brother Edmund. But in the passageway, just outside the entranceway, Sister Agatha pulled me aside. "They're here," she whispered.

"Who?"

"The king's commissioners, Richard Layton and Thomas Legh." Her lips curled with distaste. "They're staying at an inn in Dartford, with a large party of men. Tomorrow morning they will officially arrive and begin the questioning of the prioress. Thank the good Lord that Brother Edmund was released ahead of their arrival."

My heart pounded. "What will happen now?" I asked.

"No one knows." She pulled at her chin. "As the prioress said, it is all in God's hands now."

I doubt that anyone slept soundly in the priory that night. In the darkness I could hear Sister Christina shifting and turning, this way and that, and I knew that sleep eluded her as well. As soon as I learned of the commissioners' ruling, their plans for the priory, I would write another letter to Bishop Gardiner and leave it at the leper hospital. I'd written a second letter two weeks ago, telling him only of Lord Chester's murder and Brother Edmund's arrest, nothing more. Seeing the lilies and the crown above the entranceway and atop the columns of the chapter house wasn't something that advanced my search. Nor was reading the story of King Athelstan and learning that he had worn into battle a crown given to him by Hugh Capet. The bishop already knew that very well, I was sure. I wasn't here to learn the secrets of the crown, only to find it.

If the commissioners ordered us dissolved tomorrow, how long before we were expelled from the priory and the walls torn down? It could be some poor workman, paid a day's wage for his labours, who knocked down a wall and discovered the hidden crown. What would be unleashed in that moment?

And how would Bishop Gardiner punish my poor father for my failure? I saw him again in the Tower torture room, the scar disfiguring his face, the anger and fear warring in his eyes at the sight of me. And then the pain as he was racked.

A sob escaped my throat. On the other side of the room, Sister Christina turned over again. Perhaps I'd disturbed her, or perhaps her restless torment had nothing to do with me. Two unhappy novices, waiting for the night to be over.

"Sister Christina, are you not well?" I whispered.

She didn't answer at first, and I thought her asleep after all. But then she said, "I was thinking of Christina."

"You reflect on your situation?" I asked.

"Not me. Another Christina. I was not named for her, I am sure, and yet because we have the same name I often think of her."

"Was she English?"

"No, no, she was born in Lieges, hundreds of years ago. I read about her in one of the books in the Dartford library when I was a postulant. I have never been able to get her out of my mind since."

"Tell me," I said, curious.

"She was the youngest of three sisters. Their parents died, and Christina, who was a young girl, was set to watch the animals all day. She was alone and thought of God all day while tending the beasts. She became ill and died, and her sisters had her body laid out in church. During Mass, she came to life again and flew like a bird to the rafters of the church."

"How can that be?"

"It was God's work. She explained to her sisters when she came down from the rafters. She had been taken to a place of fire and torment, where men screamed all around her, and she felt tremendous pity for them. After that she was taken to a place of even greater pain and unimaginable sufferings. Then Christina went to a throne room that was very peaceful and beautiful, and God spoke to her and explained all. The first place was purgatory, the second was hell, and now she was in heaven. God gave her a choice. She could stay with Him, or she could go back into the mortal world and endure the sufferings of a mortal in an immortal body, and by doing, she could deliver the men she pitied from purgatory. Christina chose to return to her body. And so from that time on she sought out the greatest pain she could find."

"And she didn't feel any of it?" I asked.

"Oh, but she did, Sister Joanna; she did. She walked into fires set in people's homes, and she crawled into the hot ovens for making bread, and she jumped into cauldrons of boiling water, and Christina felt *everything.* Her own suffering was extreme, but her flesh was untouched. Her skin did not show any marks or blisters. She was always completely uninjured."

After a moment, I said, "But that must have been so frightening to behold."

"Yes, her sisters were greatly disturbed, and they kept her bound with ropes and even chains to protect her from herself. They didn't understand." Sister Christina went silent. When she spoke again, her words were slow and syrupy, and I knew she was on the verge of sleep. "Later, they realised she was holy. The whole countryside heard about her. She became a . . . preacher . . . and . . ."

In a short time, I heard heavy breathing.

Telling the story had calmed Sister Christina, but it did not do the same for me. What a frightening tale. It took a very long time for me to fall asleep, and then it seemed I had snatched only a few moments when the first bells rang for Lauds.

I noticed that the prioress attended Lauds and Prime but not Terce. She must already be in the hands of the commissioners. I had heard they worked quickly.

In Terce, I said my prayers with such ferocity that a few of the other sisters turned to look at me. But honouring Christ in our daily offices made me feel that I was helping to strengthen our priory; it was the only structure I had in my life. If Dartford was destroyed, I honestly did not know how I would survive.

When Terce was over, I hurried to the south passageway. Brother Edmund might require my help in the infirmary.

I'd got as far as the cloister garden when Gregory, the porter, called my name. The sun was out; it was one of those late-autumn mornings that glowed with wistful promise. The leaves had fallen from the quince trees, but their branches glistened. It was as if the trees sent out a dare: warm us enough to restore us to glory, and let us forestall winter and the death it brings.

"Sister Joanna!" Gregory shouted, from across the garden. "Come with me now."

When I'd reached him, he said, "You're wanted in the *locutorium*."

I backed away from him, shaking my head. "I have no visitors; you are mistaken."

"The king's commissioners request you," he said impatiently. "They have questions for you specifically."

I'd known this, somehow, through those exhausting slivers of dreams, the despair of the night. As much as I struggled to stay out of the centre of the investigations, the grasp of the interrogators, I couldn't.

I followed Gregory to the door leading to the front of the priory. He unlocked it and went through first, but a second later, he cursed.

The ugly words, so foreign to a religious house, quivered in the air.

Gregory charged down the passageway to the prioress's chamber. "What are you doing?" he shouted at two men coming out of the room, covered with dust and dirt. I heard banging noises within and more voices. There must have been six men inside her room.

The king's men weren't waiting for any formal dissolution of the priory. They were taking apart the prioress's office today—right now.

"Stand back," one of the men warned Gregory. "We have our orders."

"You can't destroy the priory like this, without process," I cried.

"We're just working in this one room," a man said. "For now."

A young man's voice sounded from farther down. "Bring her in here, you fool." With a start, I realised he was addressing our porter.

Red-faced with anger, Gregory led me down the long passageway to the *locutorium,* halfway to the guest bedchambers. The young man, who had a face like a ferret, roughly grabbed me by the arm and pushed me inside.

I'd been in the *locutorium* before. My first week back at Dartford, I'd checked every inch for a sign of the hidden crown, and twice since. Nothing. It was a long room, simply furnished: a set of chairs and a table on one side and a long wooden bench on the other. This was the room set aside for outsiders—family and trusted friends—to meet with the sisters of Dartford. The nuns always sat on the bench, to drive home their decision to forsake all comfort, and the guests occupied the chairs. This morning, on the bench, sat our two friars: Brother Richard, stone-faced, and Brother Edmund, looking even more exhausted than the day before.

Brother Richard beckoned, and I took a place between them. My limbs felt heavy and my mind dull; I was paying dearly for my lack of sleep.

We had company, though, and I'd need sharpness of mind. Two men fussed in the corner, next to the window. They were about the same age—nearing forty—and wore long, rich furs and medallion chains. Their attention was on the two chalice cups displayed on the table. The taller man held up one of the cups to the light and turned it, admiringly.

The other one, balding and stout, glanced over at the three of us and said, "Shall we begin?"

With a nod, his companion replaced the cup. "We shall."

The tall man approached us with a smile. "I am Thomas Legh, a lawyer in the service of His Majesty. This is Richard Layton, a churchman and a clerk to the Privy Council. You know why we are here?"

"To examine us," said Brother Richard.

"Yes, very good, Brother. Very to the point."

Layton took the chair opposite and scrutinised us.

Brother Edmund shifted on the bench next to me. A slight acrid smell came off him; I recognised it as sweat. The poor man. Why would he not admit to me his illness?

Legh said, "I think it best to tell you something of us first. Of our background. At the very end of 1534, Thomas Cromwell declared he would form a commission to examine the monasteries—only to reform and purify, you understand—and we stepped forward to volunteer. We would perform visitations and put forward the questions. We would learn and report back whether all of the rules were being followed, if vows had been broken, if there were financial or moral laxeity."

As Legh droned on about the great honour of being chosen to persecute those who'd chosen a religious life, I struggled for alertness. I studied the wall to my right. A large bookshelf was carved into the wall, but it was empty of books. I thought I remembered seeing books there, but now it was empty. My eyes strayed upward, and above the shelf, carved into the wall, I saw those dread symbols of our priory: the lilies and the crown. They truly were everywhere. Here the crown stood in front, not sheltered by the flowers of the Dominican Order.

"We made special request to examine the abbeys and priories of the North, where we have familiarity with the land and the people," Legh was saying. "Across the entire country, the monasteries were most revered in the North. We visited one hundred twenty-one religious houses in less than four months." He took a dramatic pause. "And in those houses we found a level of corruption, waste, idleness, and neglect that was not to be believed."

Brother Edmund looked down. I watched him dig his right thumb into the palm of his left hand.

I, too, found it difficult to look at the faces of these two men. They were destroyers. Rumours abounded of their own greed, of how they plundered the abbeys that they bullied into submission. But there was no mistaking the gleam of fanaticism in their eyes. They actually believed themselves to be serving God's will. I felt an impulse to rise from my bench, to take each of them by the hand and lead them around Dartford Priory, to meet and speak to the sisters. I would show Legh and Layton where we prayed, where we sang and slept, tell them stories of the sisters' sacrifices and quest for union with a higher power. How hard we all tried to follow the rules of our order. At the end of such a visitation, could they still hate and despise us so?

Layton took the lead part from his fellow commissioner: "Shall we call you 'Brother' or 'Friar'?"

Brother Richard said, "'Friar' is more correct, but we are accustomed to 'Brother.' It is a term of respect for any man who has taken religious vows."

Layton's lip curled at the word *respect.* "Very well, Brother. We did not have the honour of investigating Dartford Priory or of your Dominican friary in Cambridge previous to this, but I attended the university as a young man, and I keep up with what is happening there." He leaned forward. "Your prior admitted to buggery *and* thievery, on a level that was so abominable that the whole friary was dissolved forthwith."

Brother Richard said in a careful voice, "Neither Brother Edmund nor myself was found guilty of any violations of chapter order, so there is no relevance to the proceedings here."

Legh grunted. "Spoken like a lawyer: you've missed your calling, Brother Richard. Then let us turn our attention to Dartford Priory, where there have been very strange proceedings, indeed."

"Very strange," echoed Layton.

Brother Richard said, "In reference to the death of Lord Chester, I assume you have been acquainted with the facts? That no member of the priory was guilty?"

Legh waved his hand. "Yes, we know all about the murder. That is not the focus of our investigation today. Did you think it was?"

My heart skipped. Brother Edmund stirred again on the bench. He was having such a difficult time keeping still.

"No," said Legh, "I have summoned the three of you, out of the hearing of your prioress, to find out exactly what Bishop Stephen Gardiner said to you at the Tower of London on October 12, and the true reason you have been sent to Dartford Priory."

36

I looked down at the hands folded in my lap. I'd learned a few things about concealing emotions since my face had given away too much in the Tower. I fought my exhaustion and struggled to keep my breath regular and my face calm.

"You don't deny that Bishop Gardiner dispatched you here?" asked Legh.

"Of course not," said Brother Richard matter-of-factly. "There were vacancies here at Dartford that could be filled by only a Dominican friar; we were most fortunate to be chosen by the Bishop of Winchester for the positions and to come under his protection." His voice carried the silken promise of a threat.

Legh and Layton exchanged a glance. They were the men of Cromwell, the enemy of Gardiner. I felt as if I were on a chessboard, two sets of opposing pawns sent forward by their ruthless kings.

"The bishop said you would be president and steward of the priory, and Brother Edmund here would supervise the infirmaries?" Legh asked.

"Correct."

"And what else did he tell you about Dartford? Remember that if you lie to us, the penalties are very grave."

Brother Edmund leaned forward to answer: "He charged us to be a credit to the Dominican Order."

Layton's eyes flashed in anger and he opened his mouth to say something, but there was a sharp rapping at the door.

The ferret-faced man peered in and said, "The prioress is giving us some difficulty, sir."

"What sort?" snapped Legh.

"She demands to know what we are looking for her in her chamber, why we are removing the carpet and damaging the walls."

Again, I focused on my lap.

Layton said, "I can never accustom myself to the arrogance of these people. Tell her to stop interfering with the king's business. We will speak to her again shortly."

"With pleasure, sir."

"And has any progress yet been made in that room?" Layton asked.

"No, sir." The man left.

"She probably wonders what we are looking for," said Layton. He turned to us, with a chilling smile. "What do you think we could possibly seek in the prioress's chamber? Any ideas?"

Silence filled the room.

Legh said, "You've have never been told of a relic or other object of sacred value that was placed in Dartford Priory by its founder, Edward the Third?"

I felt as if I would vomit from fear. Cromwell's men knew of the existence of the Athelstan crown, just as Gardiner had feared. Perhaps they had recently confirmed it was hidden at Dartford. Or they had only a vague suspicion, and the murder of Lord Chester had given them the perfect excuse to force their way in and search.

It was Brother Richard who answered. "Bishop Gardiner never spoke of such a thing to me, no."

Both Brother Edmund and I shook our heads.

Layton tapped his fellow commissioner's arm. "We'll not get anything from them."

Legh glared at us. "It would appear Gardiner chose his people well. There's just that one remaining matter, then." He glanced at Layton, who nodded, as if giving permission.

With a slow smile, Legh said, "I would like to explore in more depth the history of Sister Joanna, the novice who spent an interesting interlude in the Tower."

I looked up, into the face of Legh, who stood directly over me.

"Yes, sir?" I said as calmly as I could.

"Do you know I met Lady Margaret Bulmer at the house of her sister, the Countess of Westmoreland? She was a very beautiful woman." His face twisted into a leer. "No one could understand why she chose old John Bulmer for a husband. But then a woman's heart is the greatest mystery of all, eh, Richard?"

Layton shuddered with distaste. "I don't have the slightest interest in understanding a woman's heart."

Legh focused on me once again. "Women understand each other, though, don't they? Especially women who are related by birth. You felt a strong bond to your cousin, didn't you, Sister Joanna?"

I said, "We were close as children, yes."

"Oh, I'd say that closeness extended beyond childhood. After all, you broke the rule of enclosure to go to London for her burning at Smithfield. I'm told you had a Thomas Becket medal you wished to bury with her. Which would be touching, if we were not speaking of one of the leaders of the rebellion against His Majesty. She was a traitor of the very worst order."

I managed to stay silent—the efforts to bait me were so obvious, I would not allow myself to be crudely manipulated.

"You were charged with interference with king's justice, along with your father, and bound over to the Tower. Questioned by the Duke of Norfolk personally, who recommended further interrogation. But that is when it all gets rather . . ." He paused, as if searching for the right word.

"Murky?" offered Layton.

"Yes. That's the perfect word for it. *Murky*. You were held for four months, questioned by Bishop Gardiner, and then rapidly released." He slapped his thigh. "How rare is that? To be released from the Tower? And not only that, to be sent back to Dartford Priory, with these two friars, as if nothing were wrong. The order was cosigned by Gardiner and Norfolk. I saw it with my own eyes in the office of Sir William Kingston."

I couldn't stop myself from shuddering at the sound of Kingston's name.

"Oh, yes, Sister Joanna, we made a stop at the Tower on the way to Dartford." Legh, who noticed my revulsion, smiled. "That is the reason for our preeminence among the king's commissioners. Our attention to detail. Now, Sister Joanna, you will tell us why Bishop Gardiner had you released and restored here."

"Because he found me innocent of crime and worthy of redemption," I said.

"A supporter of rebels against the king's majesty?" shouted Layton. "A member of a family grossly tainted by high treason? A novice who violated the rules of her order? And you dare to say you are worthy of redemption. You, Joanna Stafford, are the opposite of worthy."

Brother Richard called out, "That's enough! You will not abuse her any further."

Layton said, "Friar, you have no authority here."

"And you exceed your authority, sir," said Brother Richard. "This is not a treason trial of Joanna Stafford, nor a tribunal before a Dominican prelate. If report were made of these proceedings, it would not reflect well on you."

I was astounded that Brother Richard would go so far to defend me.

Layton tugged on Legh's furred sleeve, "Ah, but we have the other path to take." He turned on me. "It is within our charge to investigate the chastity and moral soundness of those professed to Dartford, both nun and novice."

On this front, I had nothing to worry about at all. Relieved, I said, "Yes, sir?"

He shuffled through his papers, until he caught sight of something that refreshed his memory. "And so, Sister Joanna, I ask you about the man Geoffrey Scovill."

It was too unexpected. I could not help but flinch.

Layton's eyes sparkled.

"You will now tell us about the young man who was arrested with you at Smithfield. I understand he was freed almost immediately because he was innocent of any treasonous intent—he merely sought to protect you when the king's guard repelled you from the flames. But I'd like to know how a novice aroused this protective instinct, how you had even made the acquaintance of a man in London."

I felt dizzy. Now Brother Edmund and Brother Richard would learn that I'd concealed knowing Geoffrey Scovill before I came to Dartford—and they would wonder why.

"H-he was a member of a large crowd at Smithfield, and he . . . came to my aid," I stammered. "There is nothing more to know."

"You had not know him before that day?"

"No," I said.

"And you have not seen him since?"

I had to protect Geoffrey's secret.

Mother Mary, forgive me.

"No," I repeated.

But Layton was not satisfied. He sensed something was amiss. "Brother Richard and Brother Edmund," he said, "do either of you know one Geoffrey Scovill? I understand he is a parish constable of Rochester. That is not far from here."

Now it would all be over. *Just say it and let's be done with it,* I thought.

But Brother Richard said in a clear, calm voice, "No, sir."

And Brother Edmund shook his head.

Legh made a disgusted noise. "We've wasted enough time. We must pursue the other course of action. That shall satisfy."

And with that Layton and Legh swept out of the *locutorium* and left us sitting on our long, hard bench.

I could feel Brother Richard's furious glare before I'd even turned to look at him.

"Do you know what you've done?" he said between gritted teeth. "That falsehood could destroy you—and the two of us with you."

"Why did *you* lie?" I asked. But he stormed out of the room without answering.

I turned to Brother Edmund. "Let me explain this to you," I pleaded.

Brother Edmund was on his feet, too, backing away from me. His eyes were clouded with pain and confusion.

"I do not judge you," he muttered. "We are all of us frail and subject to sin."

Desperate, I grabbed his arm. "Listen, Brother, I beg you."

He pulled away. "I must go to Sister Winifred—she needs me." He followed Brother Richard out the door.

I was alone.

Richard Layton and Thomas Legh left Dartford Priory with all of their men at sundown. I expected an announcement at Vespers, or a special meeting to be called in the chapter house. We'd be closed soon; I had no doubt of it. The tearing apart of the prioress's chamber was just the first step.

Knowing full well I'd not be welcome there, I decided to go to the infirmary anyway, before the last prayers. I could hear Sister

Winifred's soft, musical voice as soon as I walked in. The cough and the fever were both receding. She sat up, talking to Brother Edmund, who was grinding herbs in a set of bowls.

"Sister Joanna!" she sang out in welcome. "I haven't seen you since morning. Do you know I shall be able to return to the dormitory soon?"

Brother Edmund did not turn from his bowls.

"Your recovery is God's work," I said.

"There is better news than that," she said. "We are not to be dissolved. Sister Rachel was just here to inform us."

I was stunned. "Did she say why?"

Brother Edmund said, "Actually, they are postponing a decision until the spring, the original time of the commissioners' visitation. That is when they'll be back."

My heart leaped with relief that Brother Edmund spoke to me, but this development was confusing. Why would they wait?

Sister Winifred said, "What is wrong, Sister? You don't seem very happy tonight. And neither does my Brother Edmund. Is there anything I can do to help?"

Brother Edmund turned away from me, his shoulders hunched. Tension filled every corner of the infirmary.

I bent down to kiss Sister Winifred's cheek, now as cool as mine. "I must go to the dormitory to see to Sister Christina," I said quietly. "God give you a good night."

I paused, hoping to hear something from Brother Edmund, but there was only silence. I left the room as quickly as possible. I didn't want Sister Winifred to see me weep.

The next day, after morning Mass, I tucked the letter I'd written to Bishop Gardiner in the sleeve of my cloak and climbed the hill to the cluster of tall trees.

The warm reprieve of yesterday was gone. There was a bright briskness in the air; the ground was hard. Winter was inexorable. And now that the leaves had fallen off all of the trees, the leper hospital looked more exposed than ever. But not so forlorn. Somehow, in the frigid, sunny morning, those same crumbling walls assumed a certain dignity.

I removed the panel and slipped in my letter. It was the most important one yet. Bishop Gardiner must know of the commissioners' pointed questions hinting at knowledge of the crown, their fruitless dismantling of the prioress's office, and their promised return come spring.

I was almost to the archway when I heard a snap behind me, like a foot on a dry twig. Out of the corner of my eye I saw a shadow leap back.

Someone else was in the ruins.

I did not start; I did not betray that I'd seen or heard anything. I climbed back to the fringe of trees atop the hill. I was certain that hiding in the ruins was the person Gardiner had arranged to pick up my letters and send them to France.

And today I would discover who that was.

I found a place to wait, just behind the tallest, thickest tree. I could still see the leper hospital, but in my black cloak I'd be hidden from view.

As I waited, it occurred to me that the timing of this was disturbing. How would the stranger who took my letters know that today I'd have a fresh one, not on the appointed day—every fortnight—but an irregular one prompted by yesterday's visit by the commissioners? Unless it was someone familiar with the doings of Dartford. This couldn't be a villager, paid for his troubles.

I saw the shadow again in the leper hospital—it was moving. Nervous, I gripped the rough trunk.

Through the gaping window I glimpsed the flash of a dark cloak over a long, white robe. This was a nun, or a friar.

My mind spun. Brother Richard. It had to be him. He was so close to Bishop Gardiner; of course he'd been told why I'd been sent back to Dartford. I'd felt him gnawing at the edges of my mission since I came here.

But then the person who conveyed my messages to Gardiner appeared in the doorway of the leper hospital.

And standing there, with my sealed letter in his hand, was Brother Edmund.

37

When Brother Edmund had almost reached the top of the hill, I stepped out from behind the tree to show myself. My head was full of shocked and angry words, but in the end all I could manage to utter was one.

"Deceiver," I said.

Brother Edmund threw up an arm in front of his face, as if I had hit him. He stumbled back down the hill and nearly fell. When he'd righted himself and lowered his arm, his face flooded red with shame.

"How much do you know, Brother?" I demanded.

"Nothing," he choked. "I don't break your seals. My instructions from Bishop Gardiner were to take your letters from the secret place in the window and arrange for them to be couriered to Paris with all speed. I receive and send parcels all the time because I am an apothecary; no one questions it."

"And you have no idea why I was sent here?" My voice rose in disbelief.

"It's true," he insisted. "The bishop said that I was never to ask, that it would be dangerous to know. I am just the means of communication."

I shook my head. "But why would you do this for Gardiner?"

Brother Edmund's lower lip trembled. "That I can't tell you."

I was so angry, I literally danced up and down on the cold ground.

"You can't tell me—is *that* what you just said?" I shouted. "But do you want to know why *I* do it? Why I spy on the sisters of Dartford? Do you, Brother Edmund?"

He did not answer me. He looked truly ill. But I could no longer restrain myself. "He tortured my father to induce me to come here and work for him. Did your esteemed Bishop Gardiner supply you with that fact?"

Brother Edmund's mouth fell open. "By the Holy Virgin, that cannot be possible."

"He was racked in the Tower, right in front of me, with Gardiner giving the orders!" Tears of rage filled my eyes. "The bishop forced me to come back here, where I was not wanted. You heard from the commissioners how I was arrested at Smithfield and imprisoned. Bishop Gardiner pressured the priory to take me. My father is still in the Tower. I am here to find something at Dartford, something hidden for a very long time. If I ultimately fail, God alone knows what will happen to my father . . . and to me."

Brother Edmund whispered, "What does he seek, Sister Joanna, that he would go to such terrible lengths to secure it?"

I said, "If he had wanted *you* to know, he would have told you." Brother Edmund flinched, and I felt a twinge of regret over my cruelty.

Neither of us spoke. Two red-breasted birds landed on the front wall of the leper hospital and began calling out, singing a cheerful duet. I was seized with an urge to throw something at the birds—a rock, a tree branch, anything to smash their joyfulness. It was terrible, to feel such murderous anger.

"What of Brother Richard?" I asked. "Why was *he* sent to Dartford?"

"I'm not sure," said Brother Edmund. "We don't speak of it, not . . . directly. But I believe Gardiner placed him here to protect the priory while you investigate."

"And in return he gets his own monastery someday—he'll finally make prior?" I asked bitterly.

"Actually, I don't require that level of quid pro quo," said a voice behind us.

Brother Richard emerged from the bank of trees.

"I followed you, Sister Joanna," he said, not the least embarrassed. "I thought in a time of crisis, more aggressive action needed to be taken." He brushed the dusty brown leaves off the shoulders of his friar's robes as he walked toward us. "I've had quite enough of skulking in the trees, thank you."

Neither Brother Edmund nor I could find words.

"You are as perceptive as always, Brother Edmund," he continued. "Bishop Gardiner instructed me to protect Dartford Priory and, as much as possible, to protect Sister Joanna during her investigation. Which has proved quite challenging at certain junctures." He sighed deeply.

Brother Edmund said, "But what is the crisis, Brother? Cromwell's commissioners left without ordering our dissolution."

Brother Richard kicked the ground. "It's hard, isn't it? Winter is upon us. It wouldn't be so easy to take down a priory such as Dartford, as mighty as a castle, in such a season, particularly if there must be digging beneath. That scope of necessary destruction must wait until spring, when the ground softens."

"Is there no way to avoid such a fate?" I asked.

He laughed humourlessly. "There is, indeed. I believe the prioress has brokered some sort of arrangement with Layton and Legh. They have told her what they seek, and she intends to find it for them."

"She told you this?" Brother Edmund asked.

"Of course not. Part deduction, part listening at the door. There is a reprieve on the priory until spring. If she produces the desired object, they spare Dartford. If she does not, they tear it apart, brick by brick."

"No, no, no," I moaned.

"But if the commissioners were not able to find it thus far, nor Sister Joanna, how will *she* manage it?" asked Brother Edmund.

"The prioress cannot be underestimated," he said sombrely. "Oh, this woman. How she plagues me." He rubbed his temples, weary. "She is the most dangerous combination: a person who possesses terrible judgement and tremendous cleverness, in equal measure. She believes that if she gives Layton and Legh what they want, it will save the priory."

"Save it?" I cried. "That is why the priory was built: to *conceal* it. If she uncovers it without understanding its power . . ." My voice trailed away as Brother Richard's eyes bored into me.

"It would, of course, assist me immeasurably if I knew what everyone was searching for," Brother Richard said. "Gardiner would not tell me."

Now both friars looked at me, with grave expectation.

"But that is the very thing I can't tell anyone," I cried. "I promised someone, a very great personage, I would never breathe a word of the secret of Dartford Priory. I only told Bishop Gardiner under duress. At the end, his instructions were specific—that I was to say nothing to the friars."

Brother Richard turned away, anguished.

"Brother, he keeps us divided out of suspicion," said Brother Edmund gently. "If we could work together, we would stand a greater chance of success, but Bishop Gardiner fears it too much—the strength and unity of purpose that come with knowledge. This object must possess such powers that he does not trust us with it. He has Sister Joanna in such a grip of fear of him, it is only she whom he trusts. And even she is kept in half ignorance."

Brother Richard nodded. He turned his face up to the November sun and shut his eyes, as if in meditation. In the harsh light, I saw grey hairs I'd not noticed before.

"Bishop Gardiner is wrong," he said, his eyes still closed. Brother Edmund and I looked at each other, startled.

"The savage politics of the court have soured his judgement of humanity." Brother Richard opened his eyes. "There's very little time left. It is not a matter of saving our homes, our habits of living. These monasteries are all just bricks and mortar and glass. What has been torn asunder can be rebuilt. Those who were cast out can be summoned again. Saint Dominic walked among the people barefoot to preach the word of God; he slept on the ground at night and ate next to nothing. No, what is being destroyed is the soul of England. The darkest forces are gaining in strength, fostering ignorance and pain and destruction. All that has been created here, in our island kingdom, all of the labour and wisdom and beauty of our holy church, it stands in the gravest peril."

My heart pounded in my chest. Yes, if all were made right, Brother Richard should lead other Dominicans in service of God. He possessed a true gift, the gift of inspiration.

"Bishop Gardiner believes there is something in Dartford Priory," he continued, "something that, in the right hands, could halt the destruction of the monasteries."

"But how?" asked Brother Edmund.

"We can't know that unless we know what it is. You realise its existence is why we were sent here. That is why the commissioners came, with the pretext of Lord Chester's murder. We three must join in trust now; we must work together to achieve the end that the bishop himself desires above all other things. No one has been able to stop Henry Tudor thus far. Sister Elizabeth Barton, the nun of Kent, prophesied against the king's divorce and was hanged for it. Cardinal Fisher and Sir Thomas More refused to swear the Oath of Supremacy to the king, and they were executed. They died martyrs, revered throughout Christendom, but it did not slow the king's determination to rule over the church. Others refused and were tortured and killed, those poor abbots and monks and priests. And it mattered not a whit. The entire North of England rose in rebellion, calling for the restoration of the monasteries and the saints' days, to protest the prominence of Cromwell, and their army was crushed. Their leaders horribly killed."

I thought of my cousin Margaret, and my whole body ached.

"But I can't find it," I whispered. "I've tried and tried. I can't."

"Let us help you," Brother Edmund said. "Sister Joanna, won't you tell us what it is, so we can help you?"

His plea moved me. Brother Richard's words stirred me. But I could not tell them of the Athelstan crown. I could not take such a risk. It was not simply for my own safety—it was my father's life. I wished I could make them both understand.

A painful silence filled the air. The birds had stopped their singing; there was only the whisper of the wind in the trees. My bones were chilled.

Brother Edmund cleared his throat. "We have been away from the priory a long time. I think we should return."

"We shall, Brother, but give me a few minutes more," said Brother Richard. "I came here vowing to help Bishop Gardiner in his quest. We know Sister Joanna has been guided by love of her father and fear for his life."

I started, in surprise. I had not thought him capable of such understanding.

Brother Richard nodded. "Yes, Sister Joanna, I grieve that you were handled so roughly in the Tower. These desperate times have brought out the worst in Bishop Gardiner. Although that excuse has been made for savage methods since time immemorial."

"But I thank you for your words," I said.

He turned to Brother Edmund. "And now—what of you? Why did Gardiner select you? I must know that, at least."

Brother Edmund winced. "It was not to my better instincts the bishop appealed, as with you," he said angrily. "It was more along the lines of Sister Joanna's experience."

"This is the time to disclose it," said Brother Richard. His words were calm but carried a hint of command.

A haunted look came over Brother Edmund's face. "You spoke of the Oath of Supremacy before. Of those who refused to take it and embraced martyrdom instead. I did not want to take it, to forsake the Holy Father and swear allegiance first to King Henry the Eighth, a man obsessed with lust for his wife's handmaiden." He bit his lip. "And yet, I was afraid. I prayed for courage, but it eluded me. I'd heard about the Charterhouse monks. I could not face the reality of a full execution for high treason. Of being hanged and taken down while still alive, of then being slit open and my intestines and organs removed before my eyes as I experienced the most intense pain."

I swayed on the hill with the horror of what he depicted. To be hanged, drawn, and quartered—yes, it was the most terrifying death of all.

"That was when I first took it," Brother Edmund said in a voice so faint I could hardly hear him.

"Took what?" asked Brother Richard.

"The red flower of India."

Brother Richard gasped. "No, Brother, no."

I had no idea what he was talking about. How could a person "take" a flower?

Brother Edmund said, "Do you remember, Sister Joanna, when I was nursing Lettice Westerly, and I gave her something for the pain? I told you then."

It took only a moment to recall that eerie name. "The stones of immortality?"

He nodded. "A certain red flower of the East has a powerful effect on the mind. Many apothecaries and physicians know that, but they use it rarely because it is so difficult to know how much is the correct dose for each patient. Just slightly too much of it will kill. I give it only when the patient is sure to die soon anyway."

"So you risk death each time you take it yourself?" I asked, aghast.

"No, no, I consume it in a different form: in a tincture, using proportions taught me by a travelling monk, Brother Mark, who learned it in Germany. He told me to use it sparingly to calm the nerves and ease the suffering of the soul."

He swallowed. This was a very hard story for Brother Edmund to tell.

"I was so tormented by my cowardice over the Oath of Supremacy, I took my first dose the day that the king's men arrived to administer it. And Brother Mark was right. It did ease my suffering. I felt quite calm. I hardly minded swearing the oath at all. But I did not want to face what I had done. I was warned to take it sparingly, but I took more the very next day."

He laughed, a high-pitched, ragged, frightening sound. Brother Richard patted his shoulder, but he swung away. "I cannot accept your sympathy," he insisted. "I am cursed with this, bedevilled. And have been for three years."

"So why do you keep taking it?" I asked.

"*I have no choice!*" Brother Edmund cried. "If I try to pull away, if I cease taking it completely, I become sick, nauseated, agitated—eaten up with fears. And the nightmares. Oh, you cannot imagine the nightmares it inflicts when you try to break free."

"That is what you are enduring now," I said. Now I understood his radically changed appearance and behaviour.

He nodded. "I hid a small amount in my cowl the day that Geoffrey Scovill took me to gaol in Rochester. But it ran out, and I began to suffer the torment of *addictus*."

"How did Bishop Gardiner find out about you?" asked Brother Richard.

"I receive my drug in parcels from Venetian traders; everyone does. There are secret sufferers at monasteries all over Europe. Physicians, too."

Brother Richard said solemnly, "I'd heard rumours of this."

"Bishop Gardiner has many contacts on the Continent, and I believe he paid someone in Venice to learn who received the red flower here, in England. When he came to our abbey, he already knew. At first I denied it, but it was easy for him to get the truth from me." Brother Edmund's eyes glittered. "He told me I was to accompany you to Dartford Priory, Brother Richard, to serve as apothecary and help you in any way you saw fit. But then we received those new separate letters, remember? The orders had changed. We must report to the Tower of London and accompany Sister Joanna Stafford to Dartford. And I must take her letters from the place at the leper hospital and courier them to France without opening them or telling you anything about it. If I refused to go to Dartford or failed in my mission, I'd be put out on the road with the other displaced friars, but he would also make public my weakness. I'd be damned forever."

"Oh, Brother Edmund, I am so sorry," I said.

"I realised something in that gaol cell." His voice broke. "I would rather be dead than go back to the pain of *addictus*. I will not order any more of it—ever. I will pray that God eases my torment, but if He does not, I accept my punishment and shall willingly die."

His tears turned to sobs. Brother Edmund covered his face with shaking hands and hunched over, abandoning himself to despair.

Hearing him weep, realising all that he had suffered, I felt the devouring flames of a new rage. Brother Richard was correct. We faced opposing forces of tremendous ruthlessness. So many lives had been destroyed by the king's quest for absolute power: over his wives, over his people, both noble and common, and now over the church. My uncle the Duke of Buckingham, my cousin Margaret—both had met terrible ends. Now my father rotted in the Tower of London. The king's saintly wife of two decades, Katherine of Aragon, died abandoned; God only knew what fate awaited the recalcitrant Princess Mary. The parade of martyrs to Henry the Eighth stretched very long.

"Brother Edmund," I said. "I have something to tell you."

He lowered his hands and looked at me, his face a ruin of grief.

"What Bishop Gardiner seeks, what King Henry and Thomas Cromwell seek, is an object known as the Athelstan crown."

The brothers sank to their knees in prayer of gratitude.

I told them everything on that hill above the hospital of the lepers. About Athelstan wearing a precious crown into a historic battle, how the crown was at some point sent to France. How over the centuries it was buried, discovered, hidden again, revealed, and finally delivered unto England. I shared with them what I'd read of the deaths of King Richard the Lionhearted and the Black Prince and Prince Arthur Tudor, each an untimely death after encountering the crown in some way. I relayed the story of Arthur coming to Dartford Priory with his bride, Katherine of Aragon, and his mother, Queen Elizabeth. I described the carvings I'd seen of the crown and the lilies throughout Dartford, but that without the last letter of Prioress Elizabeth Croessner, I'd been unable to determine where the crown was hidden, despite all my searching.

Brother Edmund was riveted by my words. But he seemed puzzled, too.

"I've read a little of Athelstan and know him to be an important early king," he said. "But why would a crown from a French monarch, given to win a bride, mean so much to him? Why would he wear it into the battle of Brunanburh? And how could it assume such tremendous powers centuries after his death? How would it halt the dissolution?"

The same questions had plagued me, and we stared at each other, frustrated.

He took a deep breath. "Tell me everything you know of how the crown came to Athelstan."

"The crown was one of the relics that Hugh Capet inherited," I said.

Brother Edmund grabbed my arm. "Relics?" he said. "Of which saint?"

"The book didn't specify."

"And from whom did Hugh Capet inherit them?" he persisted. His grip was so tight my arm burned.

Then I remembered. "Oh, yes, the relics came down from Charlemagne. Hugh Capet was descended from Charlemagne."

For a minute I thought Brother Edmund had frozen. He did not move, did not even blink. Brother Richard reached out and shook him. "Is the sickness upon you?" he asked. "Brother, speak to us."

The deluge came. It was tears, mixed with laughter, uncontrolled. For the first time, I was frightened of Brother Edmund. "Calm yourself," I begged. "Please."

Brother Edmund charged halfway up the hill, then whipped around to race back to us. "Don't you know?" he demanded, a crazed light dancing in his eyes. "Can't you put it together?"

"No," I said. "Tell us."

"Charlemagne lived in the eighth century. He brought the conversion of thousands of souls to the true church. He founded cathedrals, universities, monasteries, shrines. He had the will and the power and the devotion to collect and preserve the most sacred relics of the newfound Catholic Church. Don't you know whose crown he possessed?"

"*Ce n'est pas possible*," cried Brother Richard. He crossed himself.

"Tell me," I implored. "I don't know."

Brother Edmund said, "It was the crown of Christ himself, worn at his crucifixion. That is one of the relics Charlemagne is believed to have had. The crown of thorns."

38

The argument began on the hill overlooking the leper hospital and continued in the priory library later that night, where we three gathered again. Brother Richard came up with an excuse for the prioress: a request had arrived from Bishop Gardiner for research urgently needed. "She was suspicious, but she does not dare to gainsay Gardiner," he said.

Not yet, I thought.

Now, sitting at a table covered with books and priory documents, Brother Richard and Brother Edmund quarrelled, as only two highly educated Dominican friars could, over a point of religious history. Did the crown bestowed on King Athelstan once rest on the precious head of Christ?

"The crown of thorns is housed in the Sainte-Chapelle in Paris, heavily guarded," Brother Richard said wearily. "It has never been in England. It was kept in the Holy Lands, until the crusader King Baldwin of Constantinople obtained it in the thirteenth century and sold it to Louis the Ninth."

"But haven't you ever wondered at Baldwin's unveiling Christ's crown of thorns just when he had fallen into dangerous debt to the Venetians?" asked Brother Edmund. "Louis paid one hundred thirty-five thousand livres for it and cleared Baldwin's debts."

I squirmed, uncomfortable with the image of a holy object being bought and paid for by earthly kings.

"Remember, this sale was made after the *third* crusade," Brother Edmund continued. Talking about history pumped life into him; his illness, his torments, receded. "For centuries all manner of relics and sacred objects had been discovered in the Holy Lands and brought to Europe by crusaders. A steady stream of them came west. At the end of all this, the crown of thorns appears on the international market?"

"Then you're saying that Louis the Ninth—the revered Saint Louis—and all of the French kings since, have been fools," countered Brother Richard. "Don't forget it was two Dominican friars who escorted the crown to Paris. Say what you will about the monarchs of Europe, but a Dominican friar could never be duped. And yet you persist in thinking the crown was part of a dowry, in the tenth century, to win an obscure English princess?"

"Stop, please!" I begged, waving my hands in their impassioned faces. "I'm so confused."

Brother Edmund and Brother Richard both smiled sheepishly. "Forgive us, Sister Joanna, we could debate such matters all night," said Brother Edmund. "Let us start at the beginning."

Brother Richard stood up. "Agreed. And the beginning is . . . Golgotha." He took down a book of scripture and searched for a passage. Translating from Latin, Brother Richard said, "Then Pilate took Jesus, and had him scourged. And the soldiers plaited a crown of thorns, and put it on His head, and they put on Him a purple robe, and said, 'Hail, King of the Jews!' and they smote Him with their hands. Then came Jesus forth, wearing the crown of thorns, and the purple robe. And Pilate said, 'Behold the man.'"

Brother Richard said quietly, "The crown of thorns has always represented something very profound to me, about suffering and humiliation, yes, but also about how we must all experience pain to find transcendence."

Brother Edmund nodded. "The cross that Jesus was crucified on, the nails that pierced his body, the crown of thorns, the scroll that said, 'King of the Jews,' the spear that a Roman used to pierce his side—these are the relics of the Passion. After His crucifixion, they were preserved in Jerusalem by His followers, and nothing happened for a few hundred years. But then Rome became Christian, and Saint Helen travelled to Jerusalem."

"Saint Helen, the mother of the first Christian emperor?" I asked.

"Yes, very good, Sister," exclaimed Brother Edmund. I learned how Helen went to Jerusalem in A.D. 326, to collect evidence of His life. She located the true cross, in pieces, and oversaw the building of a church to house it. In the next centuries, other relics of the Passion were discovered, and Christians travelled to the Holy Land to view them.

The sighting of the crown of thorns was first written about in the sixth century, Brother Richard explained. By that time, the unscrupulous activities had begun: the thefts of relics, the ransacking of crypts. Even the smallest part of a minor saint's body—a fingernail, a lock of hair—was thought to have healing powers.

"Shrines were built everywhere for the pilgrims who came to make vows, to be healed . . . and to give up their coins," said Brother Edmund with a grimace. "And then in the eighth century came Charlemagne, the first sovereign of a truly Christian empire of the West. He was a very devout—and very wealthy—collector of relics. To me, it makes a great deal of sense that along with the nails of the cross and the spear and all of the other relics of the Passion, Charlemagne secured the crown of thorns. And so it passed down to his descendant, the first Capet."

Brother Richard tapped the table with his fingers. "There is another explanation."

The two friars stared at each other, and then Brother Edmund nodded, as if he read the other's mind. "The distribution."

Irritated, I said, "Brothers, please?"

"Forgive us again, Sister," said Brother Edmund. "It is possible that *both* the crown that Hugh gave to Athelstan and the one residing in Paris today are holy."

"How?"

"It is said that seventy thorns adorned the branches of the crown Jesus wore. There are reports that they were not all kept together, that the crown was at some point broken up and the thorns distributed."

"But who would commit such a violation?" I asked, aghast.

Brother Richard answered, "The world of relics has always been shaded with darkness. Humans are frail creatures, subject to pride and greed."

I recoiled at his cynicism. "Perhaps in the past, in times of ignorance to God's truths, some mistakes were made," I said. "But not today, surely. No one would misrepresent the validity of the relics at the shrines of England."

A sad, heavy silence settled over the library. Neither friar met my gaze.

"No—that can't be true," I cried. "You cannot say that lies are told in our monasteries today. That's *impossible*."

Brother Edmund sat down and leaned across the table. "Sister Joanna, you are a strong young woman. You must hold on to your faith through what I am about to tell you." He took a deep breath. "At Hailes Abbey, in Gloucestershire, there is a phial of blood—it has been on display since the thirteenth century, purporting to be the blood of Christ."

"Yes, of course I know of it, my cousins Margaret Bulmer and the Duchess of Norfolk made a pilgrimage there many years ago," I said. "You aren't trying to say that . . ."

The words died in my throat. I could see Margaret, by the fire, telling me, awed, about the spiritual beauty she'd found at her pilgrimages.

"The monks used pig's blood," said Brother Richard flatly. "There had been rumours, but then last year they admitted it, under pressure. There are similar incidents, at other monasteries."

If I had learned one thing in my life, it was the frailty of man. And yet this latest disillusionment hit me with brutish strength. I rose to my feet, as the friars watched.

I said, "If that is indeed true—and I cannot believe you would be so cruel as to tell me this unless you were certain—than what is the point of our struggle to save the monasteries, to stop Cromwell from destroying our way of life, if everything is built on lies?"

Brother Edmund jumped to his feet and clasped my hands in his palms. "It is *not* all lies. There is some small corruption in the religious houses of England, yes. Why do you think these commissioners have been able to make reports that justify dissolving the abbeys? If anyone looks long enough, they can find error. But there is also dedication and true spirituality."

"We are on a journey that has brought us to Dartford, Sister Joanna," said Brother Richard. "For wisdom, for truth, for justice . . . for God. You were forced into this part of it, as was Brother Edmund, but I think you also believe in the journey."

I bowed my head. A memory sprang to mind, of we sisters of Dartford, in a circle, praying and weeping together as one of our own, poor mute Sister Helen, died. How we helped one another and supported one another through all hardships—and amid the harsh yet beautiful, mysterious, and transcendent power of our faith.

"Yes," I said, looking up. "I believe."

Brother Edmund's face flooded with relief.

"Then let us turn our attention to the Athelstan crown," he said. "We agree that the Saxeon ruler was presented with a crown that was once, in some form, the crown of thorns?"

Brother Richard nodded, convinced.

"Now the crown of Jesus has no inherent powers that I have read about, beyond being revered. Therefore, the dangerous aspects of coming into contact with it—the suspected deaths of King Richard, the Black Prince, and Prince Arthur—must have come later, in the time of Athelstan. That king somehow oversaw its transformation. But it must have become so powerful or so uncontrollable that it was hidden away, and the need for secrecy became profound."

A memory stirred. "Lord Chester spoke of the secrets of Dartford Priory the night he died."

Brother Richard inhaled sharply. "Yes, he did. Could it be possible that such a debauched man had knowledge of the crown?"

"At one point, Geoffrey Scovill believed His Lordship's death had something to do with knowledge of a priory secret," I said.

The friars both scowled at the mention of Geoffrey's name, and I took that opportunity to tell them the story of our odd friendship: how Geoffrey protected me from harm at Smithfield, was imprisoned for it, and asked me not to reveal his stint in the Tower to the investigators he worked with.

"Despite his having assisted you, I have no fondness for Master Scovill," huffed Brother Richard. "And yet . . . it's true that there are aspects of Lord Chester's behaviour at the feast—some of the words he said—that also puzzle me."

"Such as the tapestry," said Brother Edmund thoughtfully. "The way he reacted to it was so strange. As if there was a message that Sister Helen had woven into it that only Lord Chester understood."

Brother Richard said, "Then you believe Sister Helen knew of the crown's existence at Dartford and was trying to convey it to the world through her designs of the tapestries?"

I clapped my mouth with my hand. "The note!" I cried. Brother Edmund drew back. "Oh, yes," he said.

"What note?" Brother Richard asked.

"I found a note slipped into my bed that said, 'Seek out the Howard tapestries.' I believe it was put there by Sister Helen shortly before she collapsed. Do you think that the tapestries now owned by the Howards could contain clues?"

"What of the tapestry that is unfinished?" asked Brother Richard. "Could that help us?"

I shook my head. "There are no finished faces to look at. Sister Helen died before she reached that stage in the work."

Brother Edmund agreed. He explained that he, too, had examined the newest tapestry and found nothing in its story or its figures that seemed to have deeper meaning.

"If only we could see that Howard tapestry now," I said, frustrated.

Brother Richard furiously dove into his pile of ledgers and scrolls. "I know that a record exists of the Dartford tapestries sold over the years," he muttered. It took him a minute to find the right ledger, his finger racing down a list. "Here it is," he said. "Large tapestry, Greek myth, sold to the Duke of Norfolk . . . 1533 . . . for a wedding gift to the Duke and Duchess of Richmond . . . to hang in Wardour Castle, Wiltshire, jointure property of the Duchess of Richmond."

"Any description of the tapestry itself, beyond 'Greek myth'?" asked Brother Edmund, eagerly.

"I'm afraid not."

They turned to me. "This was well before you came to Dartford, Sister Joanna, but do you remember hearing anything of this tapestry?" asked Brother Richard.

"No," I said regretfully. "But the Duchess of Richmond should be able to describe it to me."

Brother Richard looked at me, askance. "Why should she do that for you?"

"Because she is my cousin once removed," I said. "Before she married, the Duchess of Richmond was Mary Howard, the daughter of the Duke and Duchess of Norfolk. I am related to the duchess." I remembered well the pretty red-haired girl who had come to

Stafford Castle with her mother—and with Margaret and Charles Howard—ten years ago. I'd seen her a few times afterward; Mary always favoured her Stafford relations.

"I'll write her a letter tomorrow," I promised. "The Duke of Richmond died last year, but if Wardour is her jointure property, she may reside there now. I will ask for as many details as possible."

Brother Richard smiled. "Ah, your connections are never to be underestimated."

I shrugged. Pointed mention of my Stafford background always embarrassed me.

Brother Edmund rubbed his temples, more troubled than ever. "Finding the crown is essential, but is only half of our quest. We need to understand its power. To do that, I must learn more of its history, why it was so important to King Athelstan. I am thinking of what Bishop Gardiner said to Sister Joanna. 'It is more than a relic. It is a blessing, and it is a curse.' I wish I was knowledgeable about Athelstan's reign."

"Is there a library you could use, that would have books and documents on that period?" I asked.

Brother Edmund stared at me, and his face lit up with the same strange fire I'd seen on the hill overlooking the leper hospital. "I am a fool," he said in a strangled voice. He leaped to a wall of books, grabbing one so ferociously I thought he would rip off the cover.

It was a book listing the abbeys and priories of England. Brother Edmund quickly found the page he sought and jabbed a page with a trembling finger. At the top it said, "Malmesbury Abbey, founded A.D. 675." I saw a list of names following, of the prior and resident monks—it was a large establishment—and a description of the abbey's possessions.

Brother Edmund pointed at a paragraph. "Look," he gasped.

I read aloud: "The abbey also contains the tomb of King Athelstan of the Saxeons, who requested he be buried there in the year 940. Documents of his fifteen-year reign are preserved there."

"His tomb!" I cried. "Where is Malmesbury?"

"The northern tip of Wiltshire," said Brother Edmund. "Not much more than a week's journey from here."

"But are you well enough to travel?" asked Brother Richard.

"Oh, yes. I just need another two days to nurse Sister Winifred, to be sure she is safely recovered. Then I ride to Malmesbury."

"I can easily explain your absence," said Brother Richard. "Bishop Gardiner gave me a copy of his seal in case of a crisis. He anticipated I might need to generate a document, an order coming from him."

Brother Edmund peered at him. "You will falsify documents?"

"Like all good Dominicans, I am a pragmatist," said Brother Richard. "As president and steward of Dartford Priory, I can authorise departures for limited periods of time."

"This is an excellent plan," said Brother Edmund. They smiled at each other.

It was then that I spoke. "Brothers, it *is* an excellent plan," I said. "Except for one thing."

The friars had forgot I was in the room. Now both turned to me, surprised.

"What's that?" asked Brother Edmund.

"I am going with you," I said.

39

It was too early in the year to snow. Whether I lived at Stafford Castle in the midlands or Dartford Priory in the South of England, I'd rarely seen flakes fall before Christmas. But on the road to Wiltshire, on the sixth day, when we drew close to our destination, the air chilled and the sky swelled and turned darkest grey. The flakes slanted down on us, just a whisper of snow at first, then thicker. Last winter had been the coldest one in living memory; the Thames froze solid, and the wealthy took to the ice in enormous sleighs. This winter threatened to be just as frigid.

Ahead of me, Brother Edmund turned in his saddle, concerned, as the snowflakes rested on his hat. I smiled at him, trying to reassure. Did he think, after all we had endured, both separately and together, that snow would trouble me? He did not smile back but pulled on the reins and kicked his horse, to ride farther ahead.

Brother Edmund had not wanted me to come. Nor had Brother Richard. They'd argued against it, furiously. It would be much harder to explain my needing to leave Dartford Priory than it would be to explain Brother Edmund's. There was the danger of a long journey on the open road. And, of course, the impropriety of a friar travelling with a novice.

"You'll endanger the entire venture," said Brother Richard in his most forbidding voice. "Sister Joanna, I must insist that you remain here, and let Brother Edmund travel to Malmesbury Abbey alone."

"Then I will leave Dartford by myself and travel there separately," I said. "I've gone without permission before. I'm perfectly capable of doing it again."

The friars stared at me, too shocked to speak.

"I realise that I may be disciplined or even turned out when I return to the priory," I said. "But what does that matter? We shall be doomed by spring, one way or another. With my 'connections,' as you put it, Brother Richard, we should be able to gain admittance to Wardour Castle and see the Howard tapestry for ourselves. Then we can ride to the abbey, which is also in Wiltshire, and learn everything there is to know of King Athelstan. I was sent here to find the crown, to do everything in my power to find it, and I *will* do so."

Having been given no choice, the friars made arrangements. Brother Richard produced a document supposedly written by Bishop Stephen Gardiner, bearing his seal, requesting the presence of Brother Edmund and myself in London.

Prioress Joan agreed without asking any questions at all. She produced the necessary licences for us to be gone for longer than a few hours.

I should have seen it as a blessing, but her new complaisance worried me. Standing in front of the priory, giving us her blessing as we mounted the priory's best horses, Prioress Joan stared past me, over my shoulder, at the grounds. I realised that since Cromwell's commissioners left she had rarely looked me in the eye.

Would she write her own letter to Bishop Gardiner and thus learn he had no knowledge of this trip? I speculated. But there was nothing I could do about it, no way to stop her. Brother Richard said he intended to observe her; I could only hope he was up to the challenge of outwitting the formidable prioress of Dartford.

My fellow novices came out to say good-bye. Sister Winifred's health had improved dramatically. The day before, she'd returned to the novice dormitory and resumed her duties. Now I feared more for Sister Christina, so grim and silent, and so lacking in colour. I told myself that she and Sister Winifred would be all right in my absence, that they had each other, after all.

Brother Edmund and I waved good-bye and headed up the lane, toward the road. As soon as we were out of sight of the priory building, we both hurriedly removed our habits. Underneath I wore the plain dress I'd had when I came from the Tower to Dartford; Brother Edmund wore the clothes of a country gentleman. It was my idea to do this. After seeing what a fuss Sister Agatha and I raised when we rode through the village in our habits, I doubted we would even reach the gates of London if dressed in the garb of our order.

We were not Brother Edmund and Sister Joanna any longer. We were siblings, travelling the country on urgent family business.

The shedding of clothes alarmed John, our stable hand. He'd eagerly agreed to accompany us to London because of his devotion to Brother Edmund. But the poor man came close to panic when we told him we were setting out on an incognito mission—not to London, but to Wiltshire.

"We need you to care for the horses, John, to see they're fed and watered and kept safe," said Brother Edmund. Left unspoken was that we also required the appearance of a servant, or else we would look too odd—and be too vulnerable to thievery.

"And we'll still be back at Dartford in a fortnight?" asked John. "My wife is with child, Brother."

"Yes, John, I know that," he said gently. "It may be longer than a fortnight, but not more than three weeks, I promise you."

John's eyes widened at that. For a moment I feared he would break away from us and gallop back to the priory. He'd tell the prioress everything and our mission would be over before we'd reached the main road.

But John did not break away. He fell into line. And on the journey he proved invaluable, not only caring for the horses but provisioning food when our supplies of bread and salted fish ran out, and riding ahead to secure lodgings at the inns along the way.

After we left the outskirts of London we took the wide road that cut west through the whole of England, all the way to Wales. We rode by low-lying woods, interspersed with vast open fields stripped of harvest and fenced-in sheep farms. Small knots of men and women cut wheat stubble to mix with hay for the winter fodder. Every so often we'd pass through a market town; many had small churches, and whenever time allowed, we stopped for a quick prayer. The largest towns boasted inns for travellers. I'd never been inside an inn before. When I'd journeyed in the past, with my family, we'd always stayed overnight with our relations, in their manor houses or castles. Some of the inns were comfortable; others were mean, loud, and dirty. It never mattered to me. I was always exhausted after a day of riding on the sporadically maintained road, and would fall onto my bed, asleep in seconds.

It troubled me that Brother Edmund spoke so little. Sometimes I feared it was because he was still angry with me for insisting on joining him. But at other times I wondered if all of his strength—of body and mind—must go toward his battle with his demon. I remembered that when he first confessed to his weakness, he said the nightmares were agony. One glance at his face each morning—ashen and damp with sweat—proved that was still the case. The hours of hard riding through the cold countryside always seemed to brace and revive him. He was most like his old self at the end of the day.

One evening, while we shared supper, I learned of the complexity of his feelings for Bishop Gardiner.

"When I heard that the bishop was personally coming to Cambridge, on the eve of our dissolution, I was most excited," Brother Edmund admitted.

"But why?"

"His is the most brilliant mind to emerge from Cambridge in the last fifty years."

I was taken aback. "But Brother Edmund, he was the one who supplied the legal framework for the king's divorce from Katherine of Aragon."

"Yes, he did, no doubt to ingratiate himself with King Henry. And he succeeded. But no one knew in the late 1520s how far the king was prepared to go, his real intentions toward overturning the true religion. The king, the nobility, the commons, many were desperate for a male heir for the kingdom—or else we'd become nothing more than a dowry land of Princess Mary's when she married a foreign king."

I shook my head, frustrated. "Why does no one think Mary could rule this country in her own right?"

Brother Edmund thought for a moment. "A queen who rules alone? But could a woman be strong enough to rule this fractious, violent kingdom?" He saw my expression. "Forgive me, Sister Joanna. I did not mean to offend you."

"I do forgive you—you speak as an Englishman, and that is, of course, no surprise, since you are one."

He laughed. "And you speak as someone who is half Spanish." He thought for a moment. "Yes, Katherine of Aragon believed absolutely in her daughter's right to be heir to the throne, as did her

Spanish nephew, Charles. And Emperor Charles controls the pope. So our king could not get his divorce from the Holy Father. He had to break free from Rome and grant himself a divorce as the head of the Church in England."

"Which Gardiner assisted in," I reminded Brother Edmund.

"The bishop tried to prevent this, the dissolution of the monasteries."

"So he has told me," I said bitterly.

"But Sister Joanna, he did make a brave effort; he published a paper in 1532, an argument in defence of the religious structure of England. It was called 'The Answer of the Ordinaries.' It nearly cost him everything."

I stared at Brother Edmund. "What do you mean?"

"Gardiner was considered by everyone to be next in line, when Warham died, to be named Archbishop of Canterbury. But because of that paper, he angered the king and lost his position as chief secretary. Thomas Cranmer was made archbishop instead; he is Cromwell's trusted ally. They are now both closer to the king, who once called Gardiner 'my right hand.'"

It took me a moment to absorb everything said. "So Gardiner is undoubtedly a supporter of the true faith," I said.

I saw a shadow cross Brother Edmund's face.

"There is something else?" I asked.

He nodded. "Cardinal Wolsey handpicked Gardiner to serve him, as he did Thomas Cromwell. But when the cardinal fell, Gardiner abandoned him utterly, refused to help him. Cromwell, it is said, shed tears for his master. Not Gardiner, though he owed him just as much."

I remembered the strange tone of Gardiner's voice when he spoke of Cardinal Wolsey in the Tower of London. "We are enmeshed with a most treacherous man," I said, looking down at the scratched wooden table. I had a thought and looked up. "You haven't told me. When Gardiner arrived at Cambridge, how did he treat *you*?" I asked.

Brother Edmund's face darkened. "I hoped I was going to receive a position in the bishop's employ, that he'd perhaps recognised my own scholarly efforts. But Gardiner only wanted me to assist Brother

Richard, and then to assist you. He has little respect for me, because of my weakness."

I reached out, timidly, and patted his arm. It was rigid to the touch.

"Brother Edmund, you must persevere. It has been more than a fortnight since you returned to Dartford, correct? Your suffering may end soon."

He nodded without speaking. I hoped the next morning, when we met by the horses, he would not look so ravaged by nightmares and discomfort. But my prayers were not answered. Brother Edmund's face was ashen again. We set out on our journey, and the dusting of snowflakes did little to ease his misery.

John appeared at the top of the road and trotted toward us. "I've found the road to Wardour Castle," he shouted.

Brother Edmund and I nudged our horses to follow John. Soon we would be at the home of my second cousin, Mary Howard Fitzroy.

Although I had not seen her since she was thirteen, I'd heard much report of her. Mary's beauty and wit made her the pride of her father, the Duke of Norfolk. He cherished her almost as much as his heir, the Earl of Surrey. A brilliant marriage had been expected for Mary, and indeed, she was just fifteen when she wed Henry Fitzroy, also fifteen and a royal bastard. The Duke of Richmond was the son of King Henry and Bessie Blount, a lady-in-waiting to Queen Katherine. There had been rumours for years that the king sought a legal means to make the Duke of Richmond his successor. It proved moot, for the young duke died, last year, of lung rot, and left my cousin a young widow.

The road to her property, Wardour Castle, was not much more than a trail. The snow had stopped, but the ground was still wet, and we rode slowly, careful of our horses.

The sun had poked through the clouds when we first glimpsed the castle, in the centre of a clearing, a lake glittering far behind. It was a white stone structure with turrets and towers, small triangular windows, and prominent battlements. As we rode closer, I saw it was not of square design, like Dartford Priory, but a massive hexagon.

A wide, dry ditch surrounded the castle. To reach the front doors, we'd have to cross a drawbridge, which, thankfully, was down today.

But the portcullis, the metal grate with sharp points that barricaded the doors, was also down, barring entry.

We found a man asleep in the gatehouse, and Brother Edmund roused him.

"I am Joanna Stafford, kin to the dowager duchess, and will be presented to her today," I informed him.

The man looked at me with the same sullen expression I'd seen on many people's faces along the way, whether they were farmers or innkeepers. I waited for him to tell me the dowager duchess was not at home. Wardour did not look occupied. In which case, I would still insist on leaving a letter for the lady of the castle. The rules of hospitality meant one would be received by someone—a steward or a housemaid—and given something to drink. That would be our chance to tour the main rooms and look for the Dartford tapestry.

Without a word, the man led us to the drawbridge. A towheaded boy appeared to take the horses. John fell back, to remain with them.

We walked across the drawbridge. It was very old; the wood crumbled a bit under my feet. Brother Edmund winced when he too stepped on a weakened strip of wood. In the harsh sunlight he looked unquestionably ill: brown eyes burning in a gaunt face.

Someone inside must have seen us approach, for the portcullis in front of the doors rose. The rusty old chains creaked as they hauled up the heavy metal grate.

The double doors swung open and a sharp-faced woman appeared.

"She is kin to the dowager duchess," the man growled and retreated.

The woman looked us over, suspicious; after all, we weren't dressed like noble folk. She wore a finer gown than I did.

I gave her my name as I pushed my way inside. It was important not to ask permission. Brother Edmund followed me over the threshold, and as she got a closer look at him, the woman's caution edged into trepidation. In another second, she'd call for some menservants.

I snapped, "I'm surprised my cousin employs such a rude servant."

Her head swivelled back toward me. She sank into a grudging curtsy, and then led us into the heart of the castle. I wasn't sure where she was taking us but tried to appear assured.

We passed through galleries and a large courtyard, then up the stone staircase. It opened into an enormous hall, built for feasts and dances, for occasions of state. At the other end of the hall a fire roared in a fireplace tall enough for the tallest man to stand in. In front of the fire were chairs and a table. A lone figure, a woman dressed in black, sat in a chair. The servant hurried over to say something to her, then retreated to the corner.

The room was so large, it took some time to cross. Our shoes clacked on the smooth floor. As we neared the fireplace, my heart began to jerk in a quick, painful rhythm. The woman by the fire looked very familiar.

As impossible as it was, the woman looked like my cousin Margaret. I had seen her burn at Smithfield, six months ago. But the bright red-gold hair peeking under her French hood, the long oval face, the slim figure, were exactly like her.

She watched us cross the hall, turning a goblet in her hand. Once we'd reached her, I reminded myself that this woman was too young to be Margaret. It was Mary Howard Fitzroy, grown into the image of her beautiful aunt.

I pulled down the hood of my cloak, to better show myself, and sank into the curtsy a dowager duchess was due. "Your Grace," I said.

"Cousin Joanna?" she said wonderingly. "What are you doing here?"

"We are journeying through Wiltshire, and I wanted to stop and visit you," I said smoothly, using the explanation we'd worked out ahead of time. "This is Edmund Sommerville, who assists me."

He bowed before her.

She was still confused. "But aren't you a nun, Joanna? What happened? Was your priory dissolved?"

"No, Dartford still stands. We are traveling to another abbey, on business of the Dominican Order."

"Are you? That seems to me very odd." Her eyes went back and forth between the two of us, and then lingered on me. "I heard about you, actually. My mother wrote to me that you were in some sort of trouble."

I tried to deflect. "Just a bit, cousin."

But Mary would not let it drop. "She'd heard you were confined in the Tower of London, and you gave my father a difficult time."

Brother Edmund tensed beside me. The fire popped; a log sizzled madly.

I took a chance and said, simply, "Well, cousin, that is true."

To my surprise, she smiled. It was not Margaret's smile; it was knowing, almost wicked. With a shiver, I was reminded of no other but the Duke of Norfolk.

"Huzzah, Joanna," she giggled. She gestured toward a bottle of wine on the table. "Let me call for more goblets. We will drink a toast to you. I so rarely have anyone to drink with. I despise my neighbours, and I haven't sunk so far down I'd drink with servants."

She beckoned, and the sharp-faced woman reappeared from the shadows with two goblets. I had no desire for wine, but it would be rude to refuse. We three raised our goblets to each other and drank. The wine was rich tasting and potent.

"So you do not like it here?" I asked, curious. "Why then do you stay?"

"This is my only property; it was my jointure according to the marriage contract," she answered. "All of my husband's lands and homes and monies returned to the king."

Brother Edmund said, "But that is unfair and not even legal."

My cousin Mary threw back her head and laughed. "How entertaining you are, Master Sommerville." It took her a long time to stop laughing. I wondered how much wine she'd had to drink so far that day. "My loving father-in-law, the king, said the marriage was not entirely valid because it was not consummated. Of course it was not consummated at his command. His son's health was too delicate for any 'marital excess,' as the king phrased it, until he turned eighteen. Which he never did." She raised a goblet. "And so here I am, a virgin widow with one crumbling castle in the middle of Wiltshire."

"But what of your parents?" I asked quickly. I was uncomfortable with the topic of women's virginity being discussed in front of Brother Edmund.

"My mother spends all her time dictating letters, primarily to Cromwell, listing her grievances against my father and describing his cruelties. I'm told the Lord Privy Seal finds the correspondence of the Duchess of Norfolk a terrible burden. As for the duke, I stay out of his reach, since he talks of arranging for me a second grand marriage." She rested her head against the back of her chair. "I'd rather stay here."

I did not know what to say. I took another sip of wine; my head swam from it. I put the goblet down. Brother Edmund shifted in his chair.

"Cousin Mary," I said, "I've heard that you were given one of the tapestries of Dartford, as a wedding gift, to be displayed here at Wardour. We'd be most interested in seeing it."

She frowned at me for a few seconds and then shook her head. "We had it in this room at first, but then moved it to my husband's bedchamber. That room is locked to me." She rolled her eyes. "Even when he was alive, it was locked to me."

Brother Edmund and I exchanged a quick look.

"Cousin, it would mean a great deal to us to see it," I said.

"I'm sorry, Joanna. It can't be done. More wine?"

How obedient she was, how she conformed to their wishes, her father, the Duke of Norfolk, and her father-in-law, the king.

I held up a hand. "No, Cousin Mary. I don't want any more wine. There has been enough wine here for today. I say it's time you call for your servants to find the key to the door. This is *your* house, is it not? And you are half Stafford. Staffords have spirit."

Her cheeks reddened. I could see that I'd pushed her quite far. But with a practised little shrug, she rose to her feet, called for her lady-in-waiting, and gave the order.

Indeed, there was little of the resistance from servants that she'd feared. Soon enough we were upstairs, pushing past her sour-faced lady-in-waiting and into the bedchamber of the dead Duke of Richmond. It was large and lavishly furnished. I'd never seen such an elabourately carved headboard. Gleefully, Mary jumped onto the bed. "At last!" she laughed. Her French hood came off and her long, thick red-gold hair tumbled down her back.

Brother Edmund veered away from the bed. He strode over to the long far wall, where three tapestries hung.

Dartford's tapestry was in the middle. It had all the features of our workmanship: the wide variety of colour, the fine detail, and the group of mythic figures.

This tapestry featured two women and a man. A woman stood

among an explosion of grain fields and fruits and fine vegetables. She held the hand of a younger woman, a beauty, who pointed down, toward the far end of the tapestry, where a handsome bearded man surged up from a dark cavern. None of the three looked like anyone I had ever seen at Dartford Priory.

"Do you know this story?" I asked.

Brother Edmund nodded. "It's Persephone."

My cousin Mary spoke up from behind us. "Yes, the bride of the underworld," she said. "A fitting companion for me now, don't you think?" She laughed as she struggled to sit up. "My brother of Surrey adored this tapestry, as did my husband. They were educated together, you know. Yes, my brother loves this tapestry more than the other Dartford one, at Norfolk House."

"The Howards own *another* Dartford tapestry?" I asked.

"Yes, the Lambeth one is older than this and larger, too." Mary had finally slipped off the bed.

Brother Edmund asked eagerly, "Do you remember what story it tells?"

She squinted into the distance as if she were trying to conjure the tapestry in her thoughts. "I know that it shows a group of sisters, dancing sisters."

"Are they nuns?" I asked, trying to keep my voice calm.

"No, I'm sure they aren't. "She moved forward and ran her fingers along the edge of the tapestry. "I prefer this one, my own. One day, Persephone"—she pointed at the beautiful girl in the tapestry's centre—"was out gathering flowers, and the god of the underworld, Hades, saw her and was smitten and opened up a chasm in the ground to pull her down. We won't linger on what happened then, for I *am* still a maid." Mary giggled. "Her mother, Demeter, the goddess of the harvest, searched the earth for her, and went to Zeus, the leader of all the gods, to demand to know what happened to her daughter."

Brother Edmund picked up the story. "Zeus knew the truth, of course. But Hades was his younger brother, so he could not take Persephone away from him entirely. Zeus worked out an arrangement, that for six months of the year, Persephone would live with her mother and the other six with Hades, her husband. When mother and daughter were reunited, the sun was warm and the plants grew tall.

When she was pulled down again, the plants all died and the cold came, for Demeter always grieved her daughter's absence, and her defilement by Hades. That is how the ancient Greeks explained the rise and fall of the seasons."

My cousin Mary clapped her hands, as delighted as a child. "You tell it almost as well as my brother, Surrey, and he's a poet. You are most erudite. Please stay with me for a few days at least—I'd so enjoy your company."

Brother Edmund flushed. Perhaps he'd never been praised by a beautiful young woman before. I felt a strange twinge.

Mary's eyes were on me, and she smiled mischievously.

"What will happen to you, Joanna, if the priories are all dissolved?" she asked. "Will you cease being a nun altogether?"

"I haven't given it any thought," I said.

She said, "I suppose I should tell you that both my brother and I follow the teachings of religious reform. The king wished it."

Stricken with disappointment, I said, "You know why I was sent to the Tower, don't you, Cousin? In May I went to Smithfield."

She bowed her head. "Poor Aunt Margaret. Yes, you were the only one brave enough to do that, you and your father." She raised her head, curious. "Where is your father now?"

"He pays the price of someone who acts according to conscience, not according to ambition," I snapped at her.

Mary's eyes flashed. "It's easy for you to pronounce judgement, Joanna. You don't attend court, you hide away at Stafford Castle or in your priory; you don't know what it is like to be in the presence of the king. How angry he becomes, just like that"—she snapped her fingers—"when he is defied. No, you don't have any idea how fearsome he can be."

"That's where you're wrong," I cried. "I know better than anyone how fearsome it is in the presence of King Henry."

As both Mary and Brother Edmund turned to look at me, shocked, I bit my lip, furious with myself. I couldn't believe I had revealed so much.

I swung toward the door. "We will leave now," I said.

"But you've just arrived," she protested, looking at Brother Edmund.

"I'm sorry," I said firmly.

"Where are you going?" she pouted.

"Malmesbury Abbey," I said. Brother Edmund winced. Again, I'd said too much.

"That's far from here, and the roads are not good," she said. "You can't possibly reach it before sundown."

"We will find an inn halfway between."

"An *inn*?" she exclaimed, shocked. "What an idea." She looked Brother Edmund up and down, and another of those mischievous smiles lit up her face. "But then, who am I to interfere in your plans, Cousin Joanna?"

Now I was as embarrassed as Brother Edmund.

She walked us through the castle, her lady-in-waiting shadowing us. At the front entrance she called to another servant, "Send for Luke, at once." She said to us: "You must have a guide to Malmesbury; this boy of mine knows the roads very well."

"But we may not return this way," said Brother Edmund.

"He can find his way back from anywhere," she said.

When the boy appeared, I recognised him as the towheaded lad who'd taken our horses. "Luke, do you know the way to Malmesbury Abbey?" she called out.

"Aye, Your Grace," he said, fingering a lock of his hair as if he were a serf of the manor.

"Then be of service to these people," she ordered. "Take a swift horse."

We said our good-byes. Mary watched us from her doorway as we mounted the horses, now followed by both John and Luke. I waved to her one last time, and we started off. I could hear the creaking noise of the chains of the descending portcullis as it crashed back down on the drawbridge.

I pulled up my horse close to Brother Edmund's.

"So what did you make of the tapestry?" I asked.

"There are similarities to the other one, from the requiem feast. A young woman falls prey to a man and is saved, at least in part, by an older person, a family figure."

"What could that have to do with the Athelstan crown?" I was careful to keep my voice low.

"I'm not sure," he said.

"Do you think the other Dartford tapestry, at Lambeth, would tell us more? The one with all of the sisters? Perhaps that is the one Sister Helen intended for me to see. It would seem much more relevant to the priory. Stopping here, to view this one, seems not to have borne fruit."

Brother Edmund thought for a moment. "Do not be certain of that. I think that in choosing these stories, Sister Helen was trying to say something about an ongoing struggle she knew of at the priory, between earthly desires and salvation, perhaps between good and evil itself."

I shivered, but it was not because of the cold.

40

We reached the town of Amesbury after sundown. My cousin had been correct about travelling difficulties; we moved slowly through Wiltshire until we reached a main road running between London and Exeter. Amesbury, with its parish church and small market, was on that road, and it boasted a fine inn for travellers, Luke said.

Brother Edmund and I trudged inside the establishment. It was surprisingly large and had a high, whitewashed ceiling. The owner greeted us at the door, with a worried expression.

"My name is Edmund Sommerville; my sister and I seek lodgings," said Brother Edmund. "We will require two rooms, and stabling for our horses and barn quarters for two male servants. We are ready to pay your rates."

"Oh, I'm so sorry, sir, we have only one room left in the inn."

This was a surprise. We'd had no trouble securing separate rooms at any inn thus far, since it was not a popular time of year for travel.

"There is still a Benedictine abbey in our town, although I hate to turn away business," said the innkeeper. "They are good monks, committed to hospitality. You could send one of your servants to see if they have rooms to spare."

Brother Edmund shook his head. It had been decided before we left that we could not stay in any religious houses, for fear that we would in some accidental fashion reveal ourselves.

"Ah, you do not favour the old ways. I am sorry I suggested that," the innkeeper said, flustered.

Brother Edmund sighed. "Do not be troubled. I am willing to pay you extra; do you truly have but one room?"

The innkeeper picked at his hands. "I wish I could oblige you.

We have a large party here tonight. Brother and sister have shared a room before; the quarters are spacious, and I can have an extra pallet brought in."

I nudged Brother Edmund. "We can't go back on the road. We can make do with one room."

"Very well," he said.

Relieved, the innkeeper said, "We serve hot meals right through the archway—it's no tavern, so it would be a proper environment for your sister. At no cost to you, allow us to serve hot fish pie and ale."

That did sound a great deal more tempting than a hunk of cold bread from our saddle.

The side room, set with a half-dozen wooden tables, was as pleasant as promised. A fresh fire blazed. Within minutes we were devouring the steaming hot pies. A servant set down mugs of cold ale.

"Not the same sort of drink as served by the dowager duchess, though, is it?" Brother Edmund asked, smiling.

I shrugged. "It tastes fine."

Brother Edmund regarded me thoughtfully over the table.

"What is it?" I asked.

"I find it remarkable, your temperament, Sister Joanna. At the priory, and now during our arduous travel, you have not once complained of any hardship or inconvenience."

"Do not we all forsake comforts and worldly pomp when we adopt a religious life?" I asked.

"Yes. However, having met your kin, it is all the more singular to me, the way you conduct yourself."

I felt a glow of pleasure.

"I thought you admired the dowager duchess," I said shyly.

He smiled and said, "She is not the sort of woman a Dominican friar would admire."

"Does a friar admire any woman?"

He opened his mouth, then closed it. Brother Edmund, to my amazement, looked embarrassed.

There was a commotion in the entrance area, followed by the sounds of men's voices. A moment later, we were joined by the most extraordinary group. A dozen men found places to sit, each of them wearing the robes of a monk or a friar. But not of the same order.

They were Benedictines mostly, but I also saw two Franciscans and an Augustinian. The only order noticeably missing was our own, the Dominicans.

The most unusual-looking one of them was a Cistercian monk. Wearing a white habit and black scapular, the man had pale skin, light-blue eyes, and a fringe of white hair, though he could not have been more than thirty-five years of age. With a shock I realised he must be an albino.

The Cistercian sat at a table nearest to us. Brother Edmund could not take his eyes off the group.

"I bid you greetings on this fair evening." His voice was mellifluous. "I am Brother Oswald."

Seeing that Brother Edmund was struck dumb by this party of monastics, I said, "Greetings, Brother. We are Joanna and Edmund Sommerville, traveling from Kent on family business."

He smiled. "It is a pleasure to meet such a fine couple. How long have you been married?"

"We are not married," Brother Edmund said. "She is my younger sister."

Brother Oswald's eyes flicked back and forth, no doubt noticing our complete lack of resemblance. "Ah, very good," he said, in the same sweet voice. He took a long draught of the ale put before him. "Brothers, are we not fortunate? Is God not smiling on us? First to hear Mass at a blessed church, then to return to this inn and partake of a generous meal, and now to meet kind strangers, a brother and sister also on the road of travel."

The rest of the men looked over at us and smiled, with great friendliness.

"What is your destination?" asked Brother Edmund.

Brother Oswald smiled. "Divine truth," he said.

"Amen, Brother, amen," shouted the other men in the room.

"We have a spiritual destination," said Brother Oswald. "We travel this country, looking for it. We are no longer able to seek it in the abbeys. You see, our homes have all been dissolved by the king's command. We were forced to leave. But that is no impediment. No, no, no. We have come together—drawn together is another way to describe it—to travel as one. Someday we will find the answer to how best to serve God, how best to live the rest of our days here on earth. We will yet perceive His intentions in allowing the dissolution of the religious orders of England."

Brother Edmund looked down at the table; his thin shoulders quivered. I feared he would lose control of himself in front of all.

"May I ask a question?" I asked, quickly.

"Of course, Mistress Sommerville."

I winced. It was shameful to deceive a man like Brother Oswald with false names. But I pushed on. "Do you go from church to church, travelling through England, seeking enlightenment through prayer?"

"We attend Mass whenever possible," he answered. "But we also look for God in the forests, in the fields, in the marketplaces, in any place where His wisdom could be found. We have come here, to Amesbury, to make a pilgrimage to an ancient site. It is one of the oldest places on earth. Have you heard of it? Of Stonehenge?"

I tensed in my seat. "Is it nearby?"

"Oh, yes. I believe this inn chiefly houses those who've come to look upon it."

As a child I'd heard terrifying tales of Stonehenge, that it was a temple built by a race of Irish giants, many centuries ago. "But isn't that a place of druid worship?" I asked.

"We open our minds and our hearts to any sign of God, Mistress Sommerville, and we have heard that God sometimes speaks to the faithful at dawn at Stonehenge."

Brother Edmund looked up. "At dawn?" he asked, his voice thick.

Brother Oswald studied Brother Edmund. The Cistercian's pale-blue eyes lingered on his hat, as if he detected the tonsured head beneath it.

"Do you want to join our morning pilgrimage?" he asked gently. "It is walking distance from here. We will leave shortly before sunrise."

"Oh, no, we are not worthy to accompany you," Brother Edmund said.

Brother Oswald smiled. "All are worthy, in God's love," he said. "And although I have just met you here tonight, I feel strongly that you and your kind sister are meant to come with us."

Brother Edmund looked at me. "If you wish it, we will go," I said. He nodded, grateful.

We made arrangements to meet Brother Oswald and the others before dawn. Most had paid for rooms, but Brother Oswald and two others would sleep on the ground in the stables, he explained. It was what he desired; Brother Oswald, a true Cistercian, had not slept in a bed since taking his vows as a teenager.

Brother Edmund and I climbed the stairs to our one room. I opened the door. It was a large space. The innkeeper had, as promised, placed a pallet on the floor, opposite the bed, heaped with blankets. There was even a fire.

Brother Edmund hesitated at the door. "I feel more strongly than ever that this is not fit," he said. "I can sleep in the stables, with Brother Oswald, and John and Luke."

"But look at all this space," I protested. "I cannot take it all for myself."

After a long, uncomfortable silence, he said, "Very well. But we must hang a blanket beside the bed, to give you greater privacy."

Brother Edmund was able to rig a blanket to shield us from each other. I pulled down the blanket atop my bed and crawled under. Fully concealed, I undid my skirt and bodice and put them on top of the blanket. I wore only my shift.

I couldn't hear anything in the room but the crackling of the fire.

"Good night, Brother Edmund," I said nervously.

There was silence for a long time. I had begun to think he'd fallen asleep when I heard Brother Edmund's voice. "Good night, Sister Joanna."

The dream did not come at once; I was so tired that oblivion claimed me for a time. But then I found myself on a field. It was delightfully warm. I saw flowers everywhere, of all colours. I plucked them and put them in my basket. One patch of red flowers was particularly beautiful, and I reached down to make my selection.

A white hand seized my wrist and I went down, down through the wet ground. A tunnel formed, and I hurtled through it. I screamed, yet I knew that no one could hear me.

I found myself in a cave, sitting up, my arms hugging my knees. Water dripped into a dark pool. I heard footsteps in the cave and began to breathe rapidly. I did not see anyone approach, but suddenly a man knelt next to me. He smiled, trying to calm me. "Nothing bad will happen to you now, Sister Joanna," he said.

"You know my name?" I asked.

He nodded.

I felt very weak and lay down on the floor of the cave, the water dripping faster into the pool next to my head. I closed my eyes. I knew something was about to happen to me. I did not want to see it. But I did not want to get up, either.

I felt soft breezes, delicate puffs, shiver across my body. There were no hands on me, just the breezes. They caressed me, tickled me with achingly long strokes. The water dripped even faster into the pool; it was becoming a waterfall. I heard short, gasping, panting breaths, but not a man's; they were the sounds a woman might make. My limbs burned and tingled.

With a start, I woke up. The coolness, the caressing breezes were gone. I was tangled up in my blanket, sweaty with confusion.

An enormous wave of shame washed over me. I had had a sinful dream. I turned toward the mullioned window next to the bed. The moon was high. It was still the middle of the night.

I was tired, and yet I was seized with a great restlessness. I began to wonder if Brother Edmund was asleep. If he wasn't, I needed to talk to him. It was selfish of me, and terribly wrong, but I craved reassurance from him that I was not a terrible person. I sat up in the bed. My hand shook as I reached up to pull back the blanket he had erected next to my bed.

I moved the blanket aside, just a few inches, and peeked out. Moonlight flooded the room. I could see the pallet clearly on the other side of the room. It was empty. Brother Edmund was gone.

I slumped back down in the bed. He must have left for the stables after all. I felt confused and a bit angry that he had done this after our discussion. But I was also oddly relieved.

Within minutes I fell asleep again.

It was easy to waken before dawn; I was accustomed to it from my time at the priory. I dressed and found my way downstairs.

The monks and friars milled about in the courtyard outside the inn. Brother Edmund talked to two Benedictines. I spotted John and Luke to the side, with our horses gathered.

Brother Edmund made his way over to me. I expected him to say something about his disappearance from the room.

"This pilgrimage should not take long," he said in a cool, impersonal tone. "We will walk with the brothers to Stonehenge, and then go our own way, on horseback. We should make it to Malmesbury Abbey well before sundown."

I nodded, and waited. He still said nothing about the night before. I noticed that he did not look as ill as the other mornings. The nightmares had not ravaged him.

He leaned down to say something else, quietly. "I will walk with the brothers, but you should ride one of the horses."

I recoiled. "Did they ask you to tell me to separate myself?"

"No."

My throat tightened. "Do you want me to walk apart from you?"

"It might be best," he said.

"If we are going to make a pilgrimage to this ancient place, then I will travel as a pilgrim does, which is on foot," I said angrily.

He started to say something, but I brushed him aside. I strode up to Brother Oswald. "I thank you for your invitation. Whenever you are ready, I am prepared to walk."

We set out through the dark, silent town of Amesbury. A Franciscan monk led the way, carrying a thick candle. Our shoes made crunching noises on the frozen ground.

I purposefully walked far apart from Brother Edmund, I felt so angry with him. Every time he neared me, I strode faster, or started a conversation with a friendly friar. After the third approach, he seemed to give up and fell back.

We settled onto a path out of town, walking in single file, singing hymns. The white clouds of our breath hovered in the air.

The path travelled a series of small, low hills. A faint light crawled higher up the eastern horizon. I peered behind me, to the end of the line of religious men. Brother Edmund was halfway back. Luke and John were at the very end, with the horses.

The Franciscan carrying the candle paused at the top of a hill, then turned around to us and dramatically blew out his candle. A reddish glow pulsed in the sky.

"Hurry," someone shouted. We started running, to get to the top of the hill the Franciscan stood on. We were no longer in single file.

Once we'd reached him, we stood shoulder to shoulder, all equals.

From the top of the hill, I saw atop the next one a rough, broken circle of enormously tall stone slabs of the same height, surrounding a handful of other, smaller slabs. It was the strangest thing I'd ever beheld. Yet it was familiar, too. Like a fragment of a dream I'd had years ago, coming to life on this undulating plain.

As we walked together to the stone slabs, the sun rose over the hill far behind Stonehenge. Suddenly, where there had been light-grey stone on dark soil, I saw blinding contrasts. Gold shimmered on black. Shadows leaped everywhere.

The monk closest to me laughed at the sight of the shadows. He was a Benedictine, stout, with wide-set brown eyes and a greying beard. Tears coursed down his cheeks. I had not spoken to him yet that morning, had not known he existed before last night. Yet we smiled at each other as if we were lifelong friends. I held out my hand, and he took it. His rough fingers scratched my palm. We walked the rest of the way together.

As I approached the outer circle of stones, I trembled. I was filled with the conviction that everything I'd done in my life, every decision, every word spoken, had led me to this hill, on this morning.

Some of the monks and friars paced around the stones; some prayed on their knees; some stood in the centre, their palms stretched upward. I saw Brother Edmund turn in a circle, slowly, looking at the slabs. Brother Oswald knelt near him, chanting.

I walked between two outer slabs, three times the height of any man, to enter the circle. The giant stones in the middle were twisted, more misshapen, almost as if they were hurt. It came over me how protective the outer stones were in their circle. It resembled the priory, how we sisters cared for one another. The sick or the hurt or the infirm moved into the centre, and the stronger ones made a chain, to heal and comfort. Our lives, our commitment, were celebrated here. We mattered.

I knelt on the ground. The rising sun bathed my face. I began to pray. I had not got very far when I felt a foot nudge my knee. It was Brother Edmund, his mouth twisted.

"We need to leave," he said.

"Now? So soon?"

"There are no answers here," he said. "Just enormous stones hauled up a hill by pagans, centuries ago."

"And Brother Oswald?" I glanced over at the chanting Cistercian.

"He won't learn anything here, certainly not why God has allowed the dissolution of the monasteries." The friar's voice was harsh. "The only way we can help him, help all of these poor lost men, is by finding the means to stop Cromwell."

Brother Edmund reached down and pulled me to my feet, his grip surprisingly strong. He trotted to the horses, never letting go of me. When we passed a large thicket, I walked too close and a branch raked my arm.

"You don't need to drag me," I snapped. "That hurt."

"Did I just hear you lodge a complaint, Sister Joanna?" he asked. "Well, one memorable thing did occur this morning, after all."

I tore myself away from Brother Edmund. "What is *wrong* with you?"

"Forgive me, I should not speak so. I just feel tremendous pain for these blameless men. And pity. On the way to the stones, Brother Oswald told me they have pooled the money of their pensions. They don't intend to use it to live on for the years to come, or to pay for bookings to Europe, to seek out abbeys that will take them in. They refuse to leave their country, and they are spending all the pension money *now*, on this senseless wandering across England."

"Are you certain that they are the senseless ones, and not us?" I asked.

He winced. "No, I'm not."

We walked in silence for a few minutes. Brother Edmund and I took one last look back at the monks, still praying and chanting and milling around Stonehenge. I mourned that I would never set eyes on them again.

"They could yet find enlightenment today," I said, thinking of my own revelation while standing within the stones. "You cannot see into another man's prayers."

Brother Edmund's lips tightened. "We must get to Malmesbury Abbey."

We mounted the waiting horses and rode away.

Our direction was northwest. Luke was a great help—my cousin was right, he did know the land. He guided our journey, as we threaded through the barren farms and the cattle fields, going slowly because the roads were so narrow and poorly maintained. It did not seem possible that a large abbey, the burial place of a great king, would be found tucked away in this simple country. Brother Edmund kept looking up at the sun, as it reached its highest point, and then began its western descent. He spoke very little, except to say no whenever John or Luke suggested a rest.

In the middle of the afternoon, I finally prevailed. "The horses must be fed. I want to get there as quickly as you do, but the animals will falter without food and water, and we don't have a second string."

While the horses rested and I shared bread and apples with John and Luke, Brother Edmund stood apart from the rest of us, his fingers laced behind his back, staring at the trees along the side of the road. I could tell from the wary fashion that Luke glanced over at him how much he feared Brother Edmund.

I took the last apple and marched over to the friar.

"Please, Sister, don't ask it of me—I can't eat anything today," he muttered. I spotted a bead of sweat rolling down his brow, despite the cold. His affliction was worse than ever.

Suddenly, he pointed at a thicket of trees, far off the road, and scrambled toward them.

"What is it, Brother?" I called. "Please, stop. Wait for me."

He just ran faster, and I followed, frightened.

Behind the trees was a stone ruin. Only the foundation remained, and half of one wall. But at the far end of the square foundation rose a strange cross. It had a circle in the middle, the points of the cross extending just beyond. Faint markings ran up the base. It stood about four feet tall, with a centre that was low to the ground—the cross seemed to be sinking into the earth.

"This could be seven hundred years old," he said to me, excited.

"What language is that?" I pointed at the markings.

"I'm not sure—Celtic, perhaps," he said. He reached out and caressed the cross, reverently, and began praying.

When we returned to the others, he asked Luke whether he'd seen any such others in the countryside.

"Aye, sir," he said. "This be the oldest part of England."

"'Oldest'?" the friar repeated sharply. "In what way?"

Luke shrugged, uncomfortable. "It's just what people say, sir. This road we're on, Kingsway, it was built many, many years ago. My grandfather called it 'Alfred's Road.'"

Brother Edmund and I exchanged a look, and he strode to his horse.

"Come—let us be off again," he called out, his brown eyes blazing.

John and Luke exchanged their own worried looks as they trudged to their horses. I tried my best to pretend to the men that all was well.

Sundown drew near. The day should have been getting colder. But instead, as we rode north, going as quickly as the road allowed, the air grew milder. It was unnerving. I did not share Brother Edmund's affliction, the part that made him sweat, so what reason could there be for this? Then I noticed John loosen his outer clothing as well.

It was as if something rose up from within the earth to warm us.

At a crossroads, Luke lifted up in his saddle. "Malmesbury ahead," he called. A flat hill stood against the western horizon. Atop it, a wall ran around a tight cluster of roofs. This was far more than a market town.

I heard a rushing noise. To the left ran a river, tumbling over smooth rocks. It curved around the city on the hill. An ancient stone bridge crossed the river. The river split, the other arm encircling Malmesbury. Then the road made its ascent, climbing up to a town that was almost an island between the rivers.

"Look—do you think that's it?" asked Brother Edmund, pointing at the largest building atop the hill. I saw towers and a long slanted roof.

"But that's as big as a cathedral," I said, awed.

He kicked his horse to clatter over the bridge. "Where is the abbey?" I heard Brother Edmund shout to a man walking on the side of the bridge.

"The north end of town, sir," the man said, fingering his cap.

Brother Edmund surged ahead, at a full gallop through the gates of Malmesbury. My horse was exhausted—I did not want to whip her to go fast up a hill, so I trotted behind with John and Luke.

When we reached the main part of town, I could see him ahead. Brother Edmund slowed and jumped off his horse, so quickly he stumbled and then righted himself. He ran to a high brick wall on the right of the street and then froze, like a statue.

"No!" I heard him scream, as if he'd been run through.

By the time I'd reached him, Brother Edmund was openly weeping. A small crowd gathered: two women, an old man, and a boy, all concerned for the distraught stranger.

I ran to Brother Edmund. "In the name of the Saviour, what is it?" I pleaded.

"Malmesbury has been destroyed," he choked.

I peered through the archway. A long and magnificent abbey stretched behind the wall, with sweeping towers and columns, but its enormous spire lay on the ground, leaving a gaping hole in the structure. It looked as if the front of the abbey were being taken down, piece by piece. A mountain of bricks lay next to it. Two carts were piled with bricks. A hole had been dug nearby.

"We've come too late," said Brother Edmund.

41

One of the women in the crowd nudged me. "But the abbey has not been destroyed, mistress," she said.

Brother Edmund heard her. "What do you mean? Isn't this the work of the king's commissioners?"

"No, sir," she said. "The commissioners have come to make a report, but they've not yet dissolved our abbey. The spire collapsed in a terrible storm many years ago, before I was born. They are finally taking down all the damaged parts; they don't have the money to make repairs. But in the back section, the abbey is intact. There's a prior, and monks, and all of our memorials." She paused. "Can't you hear the singing?"

"I don't hear anything," Brother Edmund said, despondent.

The woman pleaded with everyone to be quiet. That's when we heard, from behind the wall, a beautiful sound. The lilting harmony of many voices, proudly singing the offices of Vespers.

The woman turned to Brother Edmund. "Be of good cheer, sir," she said. The others also moved forward to comfort him. "We still have our fine monks here," said the old man. "You will not be disappointed with Malmesbury Abbey." I had not seen such compassion from strangers for a long time. Nor had Brother Edmund; he was greatly touched.

"Oh, thank you, good Christian people, thank you," said Brother Edmund, and made the sign of the cross. He walked through the archway and onto the abbey green.

I hurriedly gave John and Luke some coins and told them to find supper and to provision the horses. "See if there is an inn here, in town, and return in three hours," I said.

"But it will be night by then," said John. "What will we do if there isn't an inn?"

I didn't answer. I turned to follow Brother Edmund, striding across the green. The fallen bricks were hard to see in the dwindling light. I fell over one and hurt my right knee. I could feel the spreading warmth of blood but ignored the pain.

"Wait for me, Brother!" I said.

He'd made it to the open doorway, on the side of the abbey, and hesitated. The second I reached him, he quietly removed his hat, revealing his tonsure. "I won't play a false part here, before God," he said.

"We don't know this prior, if we can trust him," I warned.

Brother Edmund closed his eyes and listened to the song, as it echoed from deep within the abbey. "Isn't it beautiful, Sister Joanna?" he said. "Don't you feel as if we're coming home?"

"It is good to hear the offices again," I said carefully. There was something about this elegant, half-ravaged abbey that disturbed me.

"I wish I could make confession while I am here," he said, peering inside. "It has been too long, and my sins are great."

"Surely not, Brother Edmund."

He reached out to grip the abbey wall, as if he needed it to strengthen him. "I have something to say to you, Sister Joanna."

"Yes?"

Looking away, at the side of the door, he said, "I wanted to lie with you last night. I have never been with a woman in my entire life, but in that room I felt great temptation. I have to say this before we go inside the abbey."

I looked at the side of his thin, sensitive face.

"That is why I left the room and why I treated you so coldly this morning," he continued, haltingly. "Which was unfair. You did nothing wrong. I am a very weak man—you and I both know this. Yet it is your faith and your belief in me that have sustained me these many weeks. I pledge to you, with my life, that I will never violate your trust."

Words swelled in my throat. He seemed to be waiting for me to say something. But I couldn't speak.

The song of the Vespers reached a crescendo inside: "*Come, let us sing to the Lord, our God . . .*"

Brother Edmund turned to look at me, his eyes both proud and sad. "Shall we go in now, Sister?" he asked.

"Yes, Brother."

The singing led us to the Benedictine monks of Malmesbury. We passed through the wrecked portions of the abbey to the back section, which was intact. Their church was large and old. The columns, the pews, resembled those of other places of worship. The apse rose in a pointed arch, filled with stained glass of exquisite beauty. The flickering of the candles danced off the many faces in the glass.

Brother Edmund and I waited, respectfully, at the back of the church, for Vespers to be finished.

The prior spotted us. He stepped down from the apse and walked down the nave to meet us.

Brother Edmund did not move. He did not shrink away. But I was afraid. What would the prior make of a man with a tonsured head who did not wear a monk's or friar's habit, and was accompanied by a woman?

The prior, a tall man with striking green eyes and high cheekbones, about forty years of age, stopped a few feet from us. He raised his hands to heaven in exultation.

"You have come!" he cried. "God be praised, you have come."

Brother Edmund started, confused. "Do you know us?" he asked the prior.

"We all of us know you; we see you every day," answered the prior.

I edged closer to Brother Edmund. This was all wrong.

"Prior, we have never been to this abbey in our lives," said Brother Edmund gravely.

He smiled. "I am Prior Roger Frampton, and I welcome you to the place where you've been expected, and on this very night."

The prior turned and beckoned, to lead us up the aisle, to the apse of the church. There were about twenty monks seated in their boxes. They broke into joyful smiles as we passed, as if we were prodigal children returned. It frightened me even more; I stayed close to Brother Edmund. As we passed the first box, I saw a single monk, a thin, greying man, who did not smile but glared at us with fear and distrust.

Prior Roger beckoned to a panel of stained glass, to the far left. It was centuries old. There were two stark figures side by side: a man and a woman. The man was blonde, his hair cut in an unmistakable tonsure; the woman, shorter, had long dark hair. At both of their feet glittered a golden crown.

Brother Edmund and I looked at each other, dumbfounded. Our coming to Malmesbury had been foretold, and immortalised in blessed glass.

"Then you know why we are here?" I managed to ask.

The prior nodded. "You are here to serve *him*." He lifted up both hands, to honour the largest figure, in the central panel of glass. The man wore golden armour, a red cape hanging off his broad shoulders, and wielded a shield and a sword. Long flaxeen hair hung to his shoulders. His face was young and strikingly handsome, but unsmiling. He had one foot raised, as if he were about to step out of the glass window and stride into the church.

"King Athelstan," I breathed.

"Athelstan the Glorious, the first king of all England and our abbey's benefactor." The prior's voice rang out across the church; a wave of fervent murmurs answered him. "Strong and fearless, yet wise and fair in all his actions. A man of the greatest purity."

"His tomb is here, in the abbey?" asked Brother Edmund.

The prior nodded. "I will take you to him."

He lit a candle himself and led us down a winding stone staircase off the side of the church. It opened to a hall and we moved toward a heavy rounded archway. I wondered if we were below the altar of the church.

The prior lit candles as we walked into the plain stone room. He ushered us to stand before the massive carved figure of Athelstan. It was a majestic memorial, yet stark, unadorned. The king was stretched out on a rectangular block, facing upward, wearing long robes and a simple crown. I felt as if I were plunged into the soul of a lost Saxeon kingdom.

Prior Roger knelt before the tomb, and we took places on either side of him. The floor was worn, from the humble knees of so many other people prostrating themselves. At the corner of the monument was carved ATHELSTAN, 895 TO 939, ANNO DOMINI.

He recited: "Holy King Athelstan, renowned through the whole world, whose esteem flourishes and whose honour endures everywhere, whom God set as king over the English, sustained by the foundation of the throne, and as leader of earthly forces."

Something stirred in the air. I glanced over my shoulder. I had the impression of a man entering the room. But I saw no one. My right knee throbbed from my fall on the green; I prayed I would not bleed on the floor.

I turned back to the marble figure of the king and tried to find my prayer, but I was distracted by an oppressive sense of being watched, and not with kindness but with judgement. I remembered being in the passageway off the cloister of Dartford and running in terror from this same feeling. I peered up at the carved face of Athelstan, his face sterner than in the stained glass. This was a king who, when still very young, forced his own brother into a boat with no sail, no food or water, and cast him out into the sea.

The prior crossed himself and rose to his feet. We did likewise.

I ached to escape from this room, but Brother Edmund did not appear disturbed by any presence. He scanned the tomb with great interest. "I have studied history my whole life, but I know little of this king. I have no explanation for why I am so unfamiliar with his reign. Did he have a queen, a family?"

"Oh, no," said the prior with a shudder, as if such an idea were distasteful. "Athelstan never knew the touch of woman. He dedicated himself to God."

"Did he take vows?" asked Brother Edmund. "Was the king a monk?"

"No, he was something else. Something not seen before his ascension or since his death. A king of utter purity." The prior smiled. "We have many documents honouring him in our library, which is undamaged. The writings of William of Malmesbury, our esteemed historian, are collected there." He ran his hand along the corner of the monument. "I fear though that in our country, history is written by the conquerors. Few come to visit the library any more. Since the family of Alfred, Edward, and Athelstan died out, no truly English king has held the throne. They have all carried the blood of the foreign conquerors, the Normans and the Plantagenets." He paused again. "Sometimes I think a mist was sent out by Athelstan to obscure his memory, to help protect his sacred relics from the touch of those who have proven unworthy, who would misuse them."

Brother Edmund and I both tensed.

"Do you speak of his crown?" I asked.

The prior's green eyes glittered in the candlelight. "Yes."

I looked over at Brother Edmund, questioningly. He nodded.

I took a step toward the prior. "My name is Sister Joanna Stafford; I am a novice at the Dominican Order in Dartford Priory. This is Brother Edmund Sommerville, a friar at Dartford. We believe King Athelstan's crown to be hidden at our priory, since the time of its foundation. We've travelled here to learn more about the king and his crown, to better understand its powers."

Prior Roger nodded, as if this were exactly what he expected to hear. "Come with me."

Brother Edmund touched my elbow, gently, and I followed him and the prior back up the stairs. We walked down a long passageway to the prior's own chamber.

I expected him to offer us chairs. But instead he went to a bookshelf in the corner and reached up, to a place in the upper right-hand corner. He pushed, hard. There was a sliding noise. The bookshelf eased back to reveal a narrow, secret place.

I covered my mouth with my hands. This was precisely the sort of thing I had been hunting for at Dartford, without luck, for weeks. At first my pulse raced, exultant. When I returned to my own priory, I would search the walls in the prioress's chamber for a similar point of entry. But then I remembered how Cromwell's men had pounded on all of the walls in that room, torn up the floor. They'd suspected an entranceway was there, yet found nothing.

The prior beckoned for us to follow. "Bring the candle," he said.

We slid inside the space, Brother Edmund carrying the source of light. Almost immediately it led down a steep set of stairs.

"Was this place created to hide the relics of Athelstan?" Brother Edmund asked as we descended.

"No," said the prior. "It leads to our dark house. We moved the relics into it later."

"What is a 'dark house'?" I asked.

"A place of punishment for those who have sinned against the order so greatly they must be set apart for a period of time," the prior said.

"A prison cell?" asked Brother Edmund, shocked.

We'd reached the bottom of the steps.

"Of a sort. There were monks who, judged guilty by their priors, spent years down here, in chains." The prior turned back to us, reassuringly. "We do not use it this way, and haven't for many, many years, even before the Holy Father send out an edict discouraging their usage in 1420. But many of the monasteries and abbeys of England were built with them, rooms or whole chambers underground. After the edict, most filled in their rooms. We, of course, told the commissioners who came two years ago that we had had ours filled in. We showed him the original entrance, from another part of the abbey. The door opened to nothing but a wall of dirt. This entrance, from the prior's chamber, was constructed in secret."

The prior began to lead us down a narrow passageway. The floor was dirt.

Brother Edmund asked, "Did the king's commissioners specifically seek the relics of Athelstan? Did they ask about the crown?"

"Oh, yes. We were pressed to tell them, several times. They have somehow discovered that the crown exists and suspect it has great powers, but they don't know where it is hidden. The king's commissioners, Layton and Legh, made visitations, and their men searched every inch of the abbey. And Bishop Gardiner himself has made inquiry."

"Gardiner was here?" My voice rose in alarm.

A monk stepped in front of us; he had been listening in the darkness. He was the grey, nervous one from the front of the church.

"Why do you ask?" he demanded, pointing straight at me. "What do you know of our sworn enemy, Stephen Gardiner?"

42

A tense silence filled the passageway leading to the dark house.

Prior Roger said, "This is Brother Timothy. He is a brilliant monk of many questions." The prior's tone was patient. He turned back to us. "Bishop Gardiner was a friend of the former prior's. He came to Malmesbury many times. Sometimes it was to seek guidance from God on how to navigate through the difficulty of the king's divorce. But sometimes it was to ask for details about the relics of Athelstan, and particularly the crown. Neither my predecessor nor myself nor any other man here has ever told the bishop the truth about the crown. We would happily die the full death of a traitor, torn limb from limb before the mob, before we would tell him where to find the crown of Athelstan."

"Why?" I whispered.

Brother Timothy said, "Because it is a greater risk for Gardiner to have the crown than for anyone else."

"We don't know that for certain," chided the prior.

Brother Timothy took a step closer to me, studying my face. "With all my heart, I feel we should not tell this female anything more," he said.

"Their coming here, both of them—their quest—was foretold," the prior said.

"Oh, yes, by Brother Eilmar." The monk rubbed his hands, agitated. He turned to us. "Four hundred years ago, Eilmar had a series of visions. One was of a man and woman who'd come on the eve of the distribution; he drew them over and over. The design was taken up and made into the stained glass that you saw in our church. But he had other visions, too; oh, yes. Brother Eilmar was convinced he could fly and fashioned himself wings. One day he strapped on his wings and jumped from a tower—and broke both his legs. Our good monk said afterward that his only fault was in not fashioning himself a tail!"

The prior laid his hand on Brother Timothy's arm. "You know that to be the chosen vessel for great visions can be disturbing as well as transporting."

Brother Timothy glared at us. "But Prior, they could be spies from Gardiner. They're Dominicans, and I've heard the bishop favours Dominicans for his most devious tasks. The risk is enormous. We could be delivering the most valuable relics in all of England—and knowledge of the crown itself—into the hands of the devil, to the Protestants!"

Prior Roger said sternly, "Bishop Gardiner is no Protestant. You forget yourself."

I had never before heard that word—"Protestant"—but I could see Brother Edmund had, and he shook his head, vehemently.

Brother Timothy cried, "Their numbers grow stronger every day. And look what evil they do—in the North, the poor starve because the monks have all been killed or driven out of their monasteries after the Pilgrimage of Grace. There is no one to give alms to the destitute and starving; the sick have nowhere to go since the monks' infirmaries were all torn down. Cromwell says there will be new hospitals and almshouses in places where the monks' abbeys once served that purpose, but not a single one has been raised. Not one. They destroy, the king's men, but they do not build!"

It was at that moment Brother Edmund spoke.

"We have not come here because of a vision or a prophecy," he said. "But we have come, nonetheless. We know that the crown of Athelstan has a power that men seek. The king's commissioners look for it in Dartford Priory, as well, and yes, Bishop Gardiner looks for it. He is frantic to find it. But he did not send us here today."

I stood frozen. I could not believe Brother Edmund was telling them so much.

"I swear to you, upon my eternal soul, that I will not give the crown to anyone who could possibly use it to harm the faithful." Brother Edmund's voice shook. "I will do nothing that will endanger our blessed monasteries."

The prior nodded, as if satisfied. But Brother Timothy turned on me, his face filled with loathing.

"She will deceive us," he insisted. "I know it in my soul. She is a creature of our enemies. And she already knows enough to betray all. Haven't we all been taught of the wicked frailty of woman? Their own Thomas Aquinas said the female is defective and misbegot."

Brother Edmund moved toward me, protectively. But I stepped in front of him, to confront my accuser.

"I am a sworn servant of God, equal in dedication to you," I told Brother Timothy. "I've seen wickedness and defect and frailty in men who practise all forms of religion, greater than in the actions of *any* woman."

Brother Timothy threw himself at the feet of his prior. "I plead with you not to tell her!" he begged. His Benedictine habit slid off one shoulder and I could see the deep red grooves on his back, some of them scabbed. This was a monk who mortified himself with knotted cords.

Prior Roger held up his hand, to bring matters to a halt. Brother Timothy got to his feet. With those disturbing green eyes, the prior examined my face. I shivered under his gaze. But I did not flinch.

The prior closed his eyes; his lips moved in prayer.

"Prior, what is your will?" pleaded Brother Timothy.

The prior opened his eyes and said, "We will take both of them to the room."

Brother Timothy bowed his head in agonised submission.

In just a few minutes more, a door was opened on this dark passageway, and I blinked in shock. Laid out on a velvet cloth were objects of blinding beauty and magnificence. There was a long golden sword, a spear, a jewelled crucifix, and a goblet.

"These were sent from France, by the father of the first Capet king?" whispered Brother Edmund, mesmerised.

"Yes," said the prior. "They were objects he inherited as the direct descendant of Charlemagne. He sent them to win the hand of Athelstan's beautiful sister, but even more important, to forge an alliance with the man they called the English Charlemagne."

Brother Edmund moved toward the sword. "Is this the . . . ?"

"Sword of Emperor Constantine, the first Christian emperor of Rome? Yes."

Brother Edmund crossed himself, in awe.

Four monks shuffled into the room. They stood against the wall, murmuring prayers.

The prior greeted them and said to us, "Tonight is the first part of the distribution. The faithful here will take the relics from Malmesbury and hide them, separately."

The prior opened a small trunk and removed a parchment with but a few sentences written on it. I could see from its colour and delicacy that it was extremely old.

"It is time you heard this," said the prior.

Brother Edmund and I would finally learn the secret. My heart hammered so loudly I felt sure everyone could hear. But all attention was on Prior Roger.

He read aloud: "The crown of Christ Athelstan wore. If your blood be royal and your soul be pure, wear the crown and rule the land. For the worthy, there is victory. For the pretender, there is death."

"This was proclaimed by Athelstan?" Brother Edward asked. The prior nodded.

My mind raced as I absorbed the words of the parchment.

"But what makes a man pure enough, or worthy enough?" I asked.

The prior only shook his head. "No one knows."

"And if he is deemed worthy, and wears it, then he cannot be defeated? By anyone or anything?"

A tense silence filled the room. "That is what is believed," said the prior.

"Is it truly the crown of thorns, which Jesus wore?" Brother Edmund whispered.

The prior made the sign of the cross; the others followed. "The crown that was given to the king contained a dozen thorns embedded in crystal, and those thorns were said to be taken from the crown Christ wore at Golgotha. Athelstan had it blessed by the Archbishop of Canterbury before he wore it on the field of the battle of Brunanburh. Before his death he bequeathed it to the abbey, along with his other most precious relics. Special instructions were given to the prior, and handed down." He hesitated. "But the very next King of England came to Malmesbury and begged us to hide the crown from all. He feared that it would lead to great confusion and chaos in the land, that any man bearing the slightest royal blood would lay claim to it, to usurp the throne. His request was granted. Occasionally, the other relics were shown to those who could be trusted. But all too soon, that became a very small number. There were attempts at theft."

The prior looked at us proudly. "And so we took action. In the twelfth century, the Prior of Malmesbury made a bequest of some smaller relics and important documents to Exeter Cathedral. At the time it was proclaimed that we had given up all we had. Everything you see here became a secret from that time onward. We no longer allowed anyone outside of the abbey to have knowledge of Athelstan's relics."

"When was the crown separated from the rest and sent to France?" I asked.

"It was removed from Malmesbury well before the transfer to Exeter. After the battle of Hastings, all here agreed it must be removed. We could not risk the danger of foreign rulers laying claim to it."

"Who was it who took it away?"

"A female descendant of one of the brothers of Athelstan." The prior glanced at me. "We are not sure of her name. As you know, Athelstan had no direct descendants. The woman took it and left England; she said she would return it to the land of Charlemagne. The abbey never heard from her again."

I said, "Do you know that it was dug up, in the South of France, and then seized by Richard the Lionhearted? And that he may have very well died because of it? He tried to wear the crown. That has to be it. As did Edward, the Black Prince, and Arthur Tudor. They all died because of their desire for the crown and to control its powers."

The prior nodded, solemnly. "We heard report from a brother who had been to Rome and assumed as much. I'm afraid the rumours of the crown's existence have haunted the Holy City as well as England. When the Black Prince brought it back and his father the king built Dartford Priory, we believe that other members of the royal family learned of it. No one knows who, or how much knowledge they possessed. But Prince Arthur, our king's older brother, must have heard the stories and gone to Dartford to try it for himself."

And Arthur brought his bride, Katherine of Aragon, with him, I thought. She witnessed the power of the crown and was frightened that it could be used to harm her daughter, the Lady Mary. That is why she asked me to profess at Dartford, to protect the princess from the crown's dark reach.

Brother Edmund asked, "If you knew it was kept at Dartford, why didn't you go to claim it?"

The prior shook his head. "God's will sent it there, and has kept it safe from human transgression. We could not meddle."

"And you have no idea where it could be hidden within the priory?" My voice rose, desperate.

"I am sorry," he said. "I have told you all I know."

After a moment, Brother Edmund asked, "What did you mean, this is the *first* distribution?"

"We cannot allow the body of our king to fall into the hands of heretics. After Easter, we must do what we are called upon to do."

I shivered. The body of King Athelstan, dead for five centuries, would be disinterred and buried in some secret place.

Brother Edmund had another question. "Prior, why did you say that Bishop Gardiner, of all men, should not obtain the crown?"

The prior shuddered. "Because it is possible the bishop will try to wear it himself and rule the land."

"But he's not royalty," I protested.

From behind us, Brother Timothy said, "The bloodline does not have to be legitimate issue. King Athelstan was the son of a concubine."

Brother Edmund shook his head. "What are you trying to say?"

"Do you not know Bishop Gardiner's background?" asked the prior. "It's true he does not speak of it openly, but I thought it known in certain circles."

Dread growing inside me, I asked, "His background?"

"He comes from a merchant family, doesn't he?" asked Brother Edmund. "Didn't Gardiner's father trade in cloth, and earn enough to send his son to study law at Cambridge? That is my understanding."

"The royal strain comes through Gardiner's mother," said Brother

Timothy. "She was Helen, the bastard daughter of Jasper Tudor, uncle to Henry the Seventh. Jasper carried the royal blood of France, through his mother, Queen Katherine of Valois, the widow of Henry the Fifth."

Brother Edmund said, "So Bishop Gardiner is cousin to His Majesty on his father's side." Once again I heard that voice, ferocious in its intensity, in my Tower cell: "*I serve the House of Tudor!*"

The prior cleared his throat. "And now, we have a certain ceremony to perform. These relics have been our sacred trust for many generations, and tonight they will be separated and made safe from the heretical agents of Thomas Cromwell. Brother Edmund and Sister Joanna, I will give you my blessing, should you wish it."

We received the blessing of the Prior of Malmesbury. I admit I did not hear his words; I was so stunned by everything I'd seen and heard.

When Brother Edmund and I stepped onto the wide, dark abbey green, the wind was up. Feathery wisps of clouds rushed across a sky heaving with stars. Luke and John hovered at the entranceway on the street, waiting for us.

"Brother Edmund," I said, "I must ask you, what did you mean with the promise you gave to the prior, about never giving the crown to anyone who would possibly use it for harm?"

Brother Edmund peered down at me. "It was fully meant. Surely you agree."

I clenched my hands. "You know I was sent to Dartford to find the crown and to tell Bishop Gardiner its location. I have no love for the bishop, but he promised me that it would be used to save the monasteries, not destroy them."

Brother Edmund's voice was very quiet. "And how would he do that?"

"I don't know," I cried. "In the Tower of London, he refused to explain. Perhaps if he possessed the crown, he could use it to prove to all of Christendom that relics are not just superstition. We know the crown has powers. Look at what happened to those who have tried to take it for themselves. Bishop Gardiner could threaten the king with the crown's powers, to force him to stop the dissolution."

He shook his head slowly.

I protested, "Brother, it is completely senseless that Bishop Gardiner would send me on a secret mission if the purpose was to hasten our doom. And my father is imprisoned in the Tower, as guarantor that I carry this out."

Brother Edmund said, "But you heard what the prior said. We can't be sure what Bishop Gardiner would do. We did not know the secret of the bishop's birth before. Athelstan said that the crown could be worn only by someone 'pure.' I fear that a man of the cloth with royal blood, someone of bastard descent like Gardiner, fits all the requirements perfectly. Now that we have learned this, we can't let the crown fall into his hands. Gardiner has betrayed so many people. The risk is too great."

I said nothing more as we walked toward the street. But I felt deathly cold. Not from the frigid night breeze that shivered through my hair and made my knee throb. No, it was the realisation that my intent and Brother Edmund's intent were no longer one and the same.

43

On the journey back to Dartford, Brother Edmund's health improved. He did not appear so ravaged in the morning; I did not see the sweats or the bursts of irritability. A new source of strength seemed to flow through him. I should have rejoiced to see it, but I found it ominous. We were elabourately polite with each other on the road, in the inns, during our shared meals. I longed to know his purpose when we returned to the priory, yet I feared knowing it, too. I never brought up the search for the crown.

But I thought about it every minute. I became convinced that Dartford, too, had rooms below ground—a "dark house"—and that the crown was hidden there. Based on the story of Prince Arthur's visit, the entrance to it had to be in one of the front rooms of the priory, not the cloistered section. The commissioner's men had already torn apart the prioress's chamber and found nothing. But that still left other rooms and passageways to examine.

I wondered if the second Howard tapestry created at Dartford Priory—the one of the sisters, hanging in Norfolk House, in Lambeth—would give me the final piece of information I needed to find the crown. Lambeth lay on the south side of the Thames, facing the city. It was not far from Dartford at all. And the Duke of Norfolk was earl marshal of the kingdom and owned so many houses that he was often not in London at all. His base of power was East Anglia. The chances were small he would be in residence at Norfolk House.

There was one problem, however. I did not want Brother Edmund to come with me.

The final morning, as we gave our horses water outside the last inn where we would stay, I said, "We should reach London by noontime, don't you think, Brother?"

He nodded as he checked the saddle on his horse. "Yes, and Dartford well before nightfall."

Struggling to keep my voice casual, I said, "I could make a short stop, in Lambeth. Perhaps John could accompany me, while you ride ahead to Dartford?"

"You wish to view the other tapestry?"

"Yes, I could take note of all I see and report to you, Brother." I, too, checked my saddle, grateful for an excuse not to meet his gaze. I waited for his reply, but there was only silence.

I mounted my horse and finally looked over at him. Brother Edmund stood by his mount, with eyes so sad I was flooded with remorse.

"Sister Joanna, I would like to come with you—to be of service to you," he said very quietly.

I focused on untangling my bridle. "As you wish," I said.

About an hour after we set out, the sky opened, and a freezing downpour forced us to seek shelter. Standing next to Brother Edmund, holding our horses' reins, shivering in the cold, I was tempted to speak openly to him, as I used to. It was not just about our divergent wishes for the crown. I thought of his admission to me, in the doorway of Malmesbury Abbey. There were things I wanted to say as well, and would—if only John were not standing near us. But John never left, and when the rain ceased, we started again for London.

We took a different route this time, straight through the heart of the city, since we planned the Lambeth stop. When we rode down Cheapside, Londoners crowded around us, so loud and boisterous, such a change from the country. It put me in mind of a sullen May day, and a cart filled with empty ale barrels that rumbled along, a market of spices, and a young urchin girl fleeing through the streets. The journey to Smithfield—the horror of Margaret's burning—was with me every day, but being on Cheapside made the memory burn bright and deep, like a branding.

Once we'd crossed the Thames and made it to Lambeth, the noise died away. There were a few boatbuilding yards, but otherwise it was marshland, rising to cold, barren fields, and then, in the distance, wooded hills. Tucked among the woods were a handful of grand manor houses. John made inquiry as to Norfolk House's location.

"I'm told to go to Paradise Street," he said when he rejoined us.

Brother Edmund gave me a long look, and together we found our way to Paradise.

In truth, all we needed to do was join the queue. There was a parade of people—all of them young and well dressed—headed for a particular manor house on the street. On horseback, in fashionable wagons, even in litters—they laughed and shouted to one another as they hurried up Paradise Street. We heard "Howard" on their lips. As I rode down the long, well-maintained drive, I could see that Norfolk House was large and distinguished, flanked by groves of trees, their branches bare.

"This could work to our advantage," I reassured Brother Edmund. "If the Howards are entertaining, if there is a large gathering, we may be able to slip in and out, unnoticed."

"But doesn't this mean the duke himself is here?" asked the friar, worried.

"He's not a man who enjoys large gatherings; he thinks everyone in the world far beneath him," I said. "And he's more than sixty years old. No, this is the notion of some younger member of the family—it's a very large clan."

He gave me a sceptical look but nudged his horse to follow me down the drive to Norfolk House.

We left the horses with John and, as inconspicuously as possible, followed a group of young people in through the front doors. As I'd hoped, the entrance hall was jammed with guests, all of whom seemed to know one another.

"You should smile," I whispered to Brother Edmund. "You look too grim for a party."

Brother Edmund said dryly, "Many things have been asked of me since I left Dartford Priory, but to be jovial in the home of the Duke of Norfolk? That request is the one I'm unable to meet."

I burst out laughing—and felt a hand tug on my sleeve.

A plump and pretty auburn-haired girl, short in stature, no more than fourteen years old, said, "Welcome to Norfolk House. And what will you be tonight? A nun or a lady?"

My mouth fell open.

"Don't look so scared," she giggled. "Don't you know why you're here?"

"We're here for the party," said Brother Edmund.

"But what part will you play for the masque?" she said. "My cousin of Surrey was explicit with his announcements. You can choose to remain yourself, a lady and gentleman"—her eyes swept doubtfully over our plain, travel-rumpled clothing—"or you can wear a religious costume. We have *so* many." She turned to Brother Edmund and smiled, a single dimple deepening in her right cheek. "You'd look perfect as a monk, sir!"

We stared at the girl, astounded. And then it was Brother Edmund's turn to laugh. His shoulders shook; I thought he would weep from it. I began to worry when a few heads turned to see who was making such noise.

The girl's cheeks turned pink. "Are you laughing at *me*?" she quavered.

"No, no, no," Brother Edmund gasped. "I would not do that." He took a deep breath and composed himself. "I would very much like to be a monk, mistress—what is your name?"

She dropped a curtsy. "Catherine Howard, sir. I live here."

Brother Edmund bowed. "I am honoured to meet a member of the family."

She giggled again. "Oh, don't be. I am not an important one." She pointed to the doors on the other side of the hall. "That's where you get the costumes. First we dance, and then my cousin of Surrey has a masque written to perform. And there's much wine for all."

With a final, kind little wave, she moved on to the next guests.

I whispered to Brother Edmund, "What could be better? We costume ourselves and find the tapestry. We'll be out of here soon."

We separated and went to the rooms set aside for changing. I took off my winter cloak and donned a black nun's habit over my skirt and bodice. It gave me pause; I felt as if I were mocking our traditions and values. A servant handed me a mask for the upper part of my face, and I tied it on, around my black hair. I dropped the borrowed veil over my hair.

I moved into another antechamber, where the guests were lining up. Musicians played a jaunty tune within the great hall. More than half of the people wore the habits of a monk or nun. I saw three bishops, too, and even a scarlet-red cardinal of the church.

At the entranceway stood a page dressed in the ducal livery of the Howards: his crest boasted a red, long-tailed lion on a gold background. He had a scroll in his hands. After listening to what one gentleman said, he glanced at the scroll, turned, and shouted into the hall, "Sir Henry Lisle!"

I drew back. The guests were being announced—something we must avoid. I searched the antechamber for Brother Edmund but could not find him at first in a sea of laughing friars and monks.

I moved among the guests, my pulses racing, until I found him. Taller and thinner than most of the other men, he now wore a Benedictine's habit, much like those worn by the monks of Malmesbury. He had exchanged his travelling hat for a large monk's cap atop his blonde hair, covering his tonsure. His brown eyes gleamed behind the mask.

"We cannot be announced under our own names," I whispered to him. "But we can't use a false name, either. It wouldn't be on the list."

Brother Edmund looked to the entranceway. "The tapestry could be in there," he said. "If I could just gain entry for five minutes, that's all that's needed."

No clear solution presented itself. We stood aside, while others moved forward, to be announced. Soon we would be conspicuous for not entering the party.

A short nun hurried by us, auburn hair rippling down her back below the veil. I recognised her.

"Mistress Howard?" I asked. An idea sprang into my mind.

She looked us over and broke into applause. "The costumes suit you both so well."

I smiled at her as warmly as I could manage. "I am acquainted with your cousin of Surrey. In fact, I've just visited his sister, the dowager duchess of Richmond. But I wish to surprise him, you see. I would rather *not* be announced. Is there a way to manage it?"

Her eyes widened. "All Howards love a surprise," she said, and thought a moment. "Come with me!"

Catherine Howard led us out of the antechamber, to a narrow passageway running alongside the great hall. "Do you see the doors?" she asked. "One of them opens directly into the great hall."

"How will we know which one?" Brother Edmund asked.

"Look at the carving over the door. The lion is in front of the ivy," she said.

"What?" he asked, puzzled.

"Ah—the crest," I jumped in. "The Howard crest is a golden lion and ivy."

"You know our family well," she said, pleased. "Most of the time, the ivy is in front of the lion. But atop that door, the lion is in front. That's how I remember which door to use."

She winked conspiratorially and melted back into the crowd.

It didn't take long to find the door and join the party under way in the great hall of Norfolk House. There must have been sixty people gathered, and almost all of them danced.

My eyes darted around the room. There were tapestries hanging on opposite walls. The long one on our side of the hall was of an exquisite garden—but I could tell other hands than those of Dartford nuns had stitched it. "It must be on the other side," I told Brother Edmund.

A sea of people twirled and bowed and jumped between the tapestries and us on the wall. Everyone danced, except for two older women and the servants circulating with wine.

"We have to find a way over there," Brother Edmund said.

There was a call for attention from the head of the hall. A stage had been erected between two huge candelabras. In the centre of the stage stood an athletic young man, about twenty-one years of age, dressed like a bishop but without a cap or mask. He had a proud, handsome face and short-cropped red-gold hair.

"Is it the Earl of Surrey?" asked Brother Edmund.

"Yes," I said distractedly, for a memory stirred. "And he is the image of his grandfather—and my uncle—the Duke of Buckingham." In Surrey, I could see my uncle, the duke, dashing about his beautiful homes and gardens, organising the fantastic parties he loved so much. There was a certain justice to this—the Duke of Norfolk despised his wife and her family, but both of his cherished children were entirely Stafford in looks.

"Fine people, before the masque begins, we shall have an allemande!" the young Earl of Surrey shouted. The crowd roared with approval. The musicians raised their instruments.

Everyone rushed to select partners and their places for the dance—except for Brother Edmund and me.

"Dancing would be one way to get across the room," I pointed out.

"Excellent idea, but for one problem," he said. "I do not dance."

"I know it is unseemly, Brother, but doesn't the occasion call for it?"

He bit his lip. "It isn't that. I would dance if I could, Sister. I don't know how."

I was surprised. I'd thought dancing lessons part of every child's life.

"I've been intended for the monastery since I was eight years old," he said apologetically.

The Earl of Surrey clapped his hands again, surveying the hall. "Excellent, form your lines." My heart sank as his roving attention settled on Brother Edmund and myself off to the side.

"Friends, I have assembled the finest musicians in the land, after the king himself," he called to us, smiling. "Why will you not dance?"

I held up Brother Edmund's hand, grateful for my mask. "We are pleased and happy to take our places, my lord," I said loudly. I led Brother Edmund to the front of the line, next to Surrey's stage. "Just follow what I do," I whispered right before we had to part and take our places.

"That's the right spirit, my fine brunette," said the earl said with a flourish and a bow. "And now, before we dance, let me bring out the guests of honour. For there is an excellent reason we don the habits of the monastery and the nunnery today. One of their champions has returned to our shores."

A door next to the stage opened, and two older men appeared.

They were Thomas Howard, third Duke of Norfolk, and Stephen Gardiner, Bishop of Winchester.

44

Brother Edmund and I stood, frozen, just inches from the stage. I could hear the creak of the three wooden steps as first Norfolk and then Gardiner climbed them. What was the Bishop of Winchester doing back in England? Had he already learned I was not at Dartford Priory, and neither was Brother Edmund?

"Thomas, this is flattering to be sure, but not a fit occasion," I heard Gardiner say in his low, mild voice.

"Oh, come, Bishop, take it in the right spirit," cried the Earl of Surrey. "My father has missed your presence greatly. We all have—and hope you will stay with us and not return to France too soon."

Surrey turned to the musicians' gallery. "Play for my father the duke and the mighty Bishop of Winchester!" he commanded.

And it began.

The allemande is a simple dance. If the earl had called for a galliard, we would have been doomed. No, the allemande is a procession, down a line, with each couple holding hands across the centre and moving sideways. Every three steps comes a halt, a hop, and a kick; then the line resumes. As the dancers reach the end of the line, they recombine on opposite sides.

Because Brother Edmund had no idea what to do, he did not stop after three steps, he crashed into a fellow dancer, a man who flinched with an "Oomph!" and looked over, angry. I glanced back at the stage; the three men talked among themselves and did not notice Brother Edmund's gaffe.

But the next time, Brother Edmund did stop at three steps and the time after that, he even hopped and kicked. He was picking up the dance quickly, his love of music no doubt helping him.

I turned my attention to the tapestries, hanging on the wall behind Brother Edmund's head. He could not see without twisting around, and with the demands of the dance, that was impossible.

Yes, one of the tapestries was from Dartford. All the tell-tale signs of our workmanship were present. And it was the longest one I had ever seen; it must have taken at least two years to construct. There was a group of female figures depicted, and yes, they danced. But ironically, with all of the people dancing and kicking and shifting before me, I could not make much sense of it. There seemed no story here, no myth plucked from ancient Greece. Seven young women cavorted in a line. There might have been something frenzied to their dance, something almost angry to the way they moved their arms upward, towards the heavens woven at the top of the tapestry.

Brother Edmund and I made it to the end of the hall. I pulled him forward, then turned him, so he would face the side of the hall bearing the tapestry. "Tell me what you see," I cried over the music. "It means nothing to me."

We began our dance back toward the direction of the stage. By now Brother Edmund knew the dance. His eyes were glued to the tapestry; I prayed he would decipher its meaning.

I was halfway across the room when it happened. Brother Edmund, staring at the tapestry on the wall, gave a cry so loud our neighbouring dancers heard. Just then the third step was supposed to take place, but he stood there, rooted to the floor, and the man to his side kicked so high that he and Brother Edmund collided and both stumbled. Brother Edmund did not fall. But the costume monk's cap dropped off his head and revealed his tonsure.

"What's this?" mocked his neighbour. "Don't you think you take the disguise a bit far, sir?" His laugh died as he realised the true oddness of Brother Edmund having the tonsured head of a friar.

The musicians played on, oblivious. Brother Edmund frantically scrambled on the floor, to find the cap. Heads were turning all the way up the line, to the stage itself. I spotted it and dived to the floor to retrieve his silk cap, and, with trembling fingers, toss it to Brother Edmund. My throw fell short. It dropped to the floor between us.

"Hold!"

The Duke of Norfolk sprang off the stage. His son, confused, gave the musicians the signal to stop playing. The duke reached us in seconds. Everyone stared and whispered.

"What mummery is this?" roared the duke. "What true man of the monastery would dance in disguise?"

Brother Edmund removed his mask and bowed to the Duke of Norfolk.

"Bring him to me, Your Grace." The voice of the Bishop of Winchester rang out across the floor.

"Do you know this man?" asked the duke, incredulous.

"Just do it!" spat Gardiner.

I stared at the floor; I could not look in the direction of the bishop.

Brother Edmund calmly followed the duke. He pretended I was not there. I was still in costume—unknown. I realised he ignored me to protect me.

The duke pushed him forward, to hasten his walk to the stage. They were almost there when the duke came to a complete halt.

Ever so slowly, he turned around and walked back to the centre of the room. He looked down at the cap, still crumpled in the middle of the dance floor, and then up at me, the closest person to it and Brother Edmund's apparent partner.

"Turn around," he growled.

I did so, and felt his rough soldier's hands on the ties of the mask as he ripped it off my head.

I will never forget the expression on the duke's face after he turned me around to get a look at me. No man had ever been so stunned as Norfolk at the moment of recognition.

I stepped into the custody of the duke once more. I turned to face the stage: Brother Edmund's face was a story of sorrow. Bishop Gardiner, standing next to him, had turned red. His fists were clenched at his sides.

I tried not to panic, to show fear. I had learned long ago it was paramount not to expose weakness to these two men.

And so it ends, I thought as I walked to the stage. We could offer no possible explanation for our presence here. Probably, within the next day, I would be back in the Tower. My deepest regret was pulling Brother Edmund down with me. I wished I had listened to him and to Brother Richard and not insisted on going to Wardour Castle, to Malmesbury, and now here. "You are an impetuous girl!" I heard my mother say, exasperated.

Bishop Gardiner came down the steps, with Brother Edmund.

"Where shall we take them?" he asked the duke.

Before Norfolk could answer, there was a stirring at the other end of the room, at the entranceway. The Howard family page ran into the room, flustered.

"Your Grace, she is here!"

"Who?" Norfolk growled.

"The Lady Mary!"

Everyone bowed and curtsied as one when the king's oldest daughter swept into Norfolk House, followed by two maids.

I had not seen Mary Tudor since she was three years old and I was eight, at Christmas festivities at Greenwich. Now she was past twenty, and shorter than I expected, not much taller than young Catherine Howard, but thinner and dressed all in black. A jewelled crucifix dangled from her neck. I felt awe but also great protectiveness. Her mother, Queen Katherine, had wanted me to help her, all those years ago.

Despite her small size, Mary Tudor moved with a dignity that no other woman in the room possessed. She was too sombre to be called pretty, although there was a definite loveliness to her; the princess's skin was luminous, purest white. Dark eyebrows delicately arched above her piercing hazel eyes. She took in every detail of the room, all of the costumed guests. I saw her mouth tighten in disapproval.

In a clear, deep voice, she said, "I came here because I heard that Bishop Gardiner had landed and was to be honoured by the Howards, and I could not wait to see him again. I must say, the manner in which he is honoured surprises me. I had not thought it time for parties. I have been much preoccupied with mourning my stepmother, good Queen Jane." She crossed herself. "And the mocking of the religious faithful cannot be pleasing to my friend the bishop."

"It is not meant as mockery, my lady," protested the Earl of Surrey.

The duke scowled at him. "I apologise, Lady Mary."

"You spoil your children, Your Grace," she said. "You are a most indulgent father." But she did not scold; there was wistfulness to her words. She had been reconciled to him after her mother died, but I could not imagine King Henry was an indulgent father.

Bishop Gardiner stepped forward, and, to my surprise, he went down on one knee before Mary Tudor. "Please forgive what you see here tonight—and accept my heartfelt gratitude that you would seek me out," he said fervently. "My eyes rejoice to see you, Lady Mary."

He kissed her hand, and I could see a bond existed between them. I remembered what I'd heard at Malmesbury—that Gardiner was a cousin to the royal family through an illegitimate strain—and wondered if Lady Mary was aware of their blood tie.

Then it was the turn of the Duke of Norfolk to kiss her hand, with a reverence I'd never seen him show anyone. Yes, she was the heroine and hope of their party. Although deemed illegitimate by the king, she could yet be restored to the succession. If the king did not marry again, she would be second in line after an infant boy.

Gardiner peered at me out of the corner of his eye. In a moment an order would be given, and Brother Edmund and I would be swept out of her sight—to be dealt with later.

This was my only chance.

I made a deep curtsy, not one seen in the English courts, but the sort of curtsy that was practised in the castles of Castile, where my mother was raised. As was Katherine of Aragon.

"Dona Maria, es un honour estar en su presencia," I said.

She drew back in surprise. *"Senorita, habla el español muy bien."*

"Dona Maria, yo hablo la lengua de mi madre, Lady Isabella Stafford."

She trembled, and for a moment, I thought Lady Mary would collapse. A violet vein quivered on the side of her pure white throat.

"You are Joanna Stafford!" she gasped. "I have wanted to meet you for so long. Maria de Salinas told me you attended on my mother. I wanted to find you, but Maria died before you could be located." She turned to the Duke of Norfolk, eagerly. "Is there some place I could speak to her privately, here in your house?"

"Of course," the duke said, between gritted teeth. "Follow me."

I saw him send Gardiner a look, his head extending ever so slightly in Brother Edmund's direction. They meant to get their hands on him now, at least.

"Lady Mary," I said swiftly, "allow me to present a friend of mine, Brother Edmund."

"You are a man of the monasteries—truly? This is no disguise?" she asked, a radiant smile transforming her delicate face to beauty.

Brother Edmund bowed, with great dignity.

"Then come with us, please." She turned to the Duke of Norfolk. "Lead the way, Your Grace," she ordered. He had no choice but to do so.

Soon we were all upstairs. The Lady Mary walked the entire way with her arm linked with mine, as if we were already the closest of friends. It was a tremendous honour to walk next to a king's daughter, not behind. My heart pounded as I tried to decide how much to reveal to her.

In the dim, quiet parlour facing the lawns of Norfolk House, Lady Mary asked me about the last weeks of her mother, at Kimbolton Castle. We stood close to each other, by the window, watching the guests streaming out of Norfolk House. Apparently the party had been cut short. There would be no masque tonight. While the rich young aristocrats mounted their horses and rode away, I re-created that cold, lonely house off the fens and her mother's brave death. Tears spilled down the Lady Mary's cheeks, and she fingered her crucifix as she listened. Norfolk, Gardiner, and Brother Edmund stood silently, a discreet distance away. After I described how the queen made it to dawn, to hear the last Mass, and then faded into death, I bowed my head. No one spoke for a moment.

Lady Mary said, "I know that you came as replacement for your mother, but the service you rendered my mother, the queen, will always be cherished by me. I reward those who have shown my mother a kindness. Tell me how I can begin to repay you."

I shot a look at Brother Edmund. I was still not sure what to say—if only he and I could consult with each other. But it was not possible.

"Do you live at court now?" she asked. "I have never seen you there, Mistress Joanna."

"No, my lady, I took novice vows after the queen's death."

She drew back, confused. "So this is not a costume?" she asked, examining my nun's habit.

"It *is* a costume," I said haltingly. "I am a member of the Dominican Order at Dartford Priory."

"Ah, Dartford," she said, smiling. "My mother spoke of the Dominican Order to me. She admired them, I know. In Spain, they are honoured above all."

I took a deep breath. "Lady Mary, I professed at Dartford because your mother asked it of me."

Tears filled her eyes again. "Truly, you are a woman dearer to me than any other living. Ask anything of me, anything, Sister Joanna, and I will grant it."

I could feel the men tense on the other side of the room. I took a step closer to the Lady Mary. "I ask not for myself but for my father, Sir Richard Stafford, who is in the Tower of London. He is charged with interfering with the king's justice in the matter of the execution of my cousin, Lady Margaret Bulmer."

She looked at me with regret. "I can do nothing for a prisoner in the Tower. I cannot gainsay my father's commands."

"But he is imprisoned on the authority of the Duke of Norfolk and Bishop Gardiner," I said. "Not the king."

She turned on them. "Is this true? Bishop, why would you do this? Is this man considered dangerous—is he a traitor to His Majesty?"

Gardiner looked at her, torn with emotion. Finally, he said, in a strained voice, "No, he is not. He sought to shorten the suffering of a family member who burned at Smithfield, but that is all. The crime does not meet the definition of treason."

"Then you will see he is released?" she asked. "Do you have the authority?"

Gardiner and Norfolk exchanged a look.

"Why do you hesitate?" she asked, anger rising in her voice.

Gardiner bowed. "I will see to it. Stafford will be released by the end of the week."

"I am glad," she said, and then turned back to me. "Isn't there anything else you need?"

"I only need to return to Dartford Priory, with Brother Edmund, in *safety*." I placed an emphasis on the last word no one in the room could mistake. "I ask for your blessing, Lady Mary."

She took my hands in hers and squeezed them. "You have a friend for life. My mother, the queen, cherished a Dominican blessing; shall I say it to you?"

Brother Edmund and I knelt before her and closed our eyes.

She recited softly: "May God the Father bless us. May God the Father heal us. May God the Holy Spirit enlighten us, And give us eyes to see with, ears to hear with, hands to do the work of God with. Amen."

I got to my feet, and made a final Spanish curtsy. "*Gracias a Dios y la Virgen*," I said.

She smiled and her eyes glistened again with tears.

"I know you must wish now to have conversation with the Duke of Norfolk and Bishop Gardiner," I said, quickly backing toward the door, for no one could turn their back on royalty. "And so we will take our leave."

"Only if you promise to write to me, and often," she said.

"It would be an honour." I was close to the door now, Brother Edmund beside me.

He opened the door for me. I took one last look at Lady Mary, and then at Bishop Gardiner. His light hazel eyes were fixed on me, but with an expression I could not read.

And so we were out of the room—and, moments later, out of Norfolk House. Night had fallen.

John almost wept with relief when we appeared at the stables. "Everyone else left but there was no sign of ye—I did not know what to do."

"Could you get us to Dartford, John?" Brother Edmund asked. "Do you know the roads well enough?"

"Aye, I can do it," he said. "I miss my wife so much, Brother. I'd do anything to get back to her tonight."

As we trotted up the drive, to Paradise Street, I said to Brother Edmund, "Will Gardiner release my father?"

"He must. He gave his word to the princess."

"And what about us? Are we safe from Gardiner?"

He turned in his saddle, to peer at Norfolk House again. "For a short time," he said. "Perhaps just tonight. He will endeavour to learn why we were at Norfolk House and what we are doing out of the priory."

A realisation came to me. "If my father is released, I am no longer constrained by Gardiner."

"Yes," said Brother Edmund. "You need not search for the crown any longer."

I felt a rush of anger. "Do you think it is only because of the threat to my father that I try to learn about the crown and find it in the priory? I wish to save the monasteries as much as you."

Brother Edmund reached out, awkwardly, across the horses. His fingers grazed my arm. John was riding ahead of us, fast; we would have to cease talking if we hoped to pick up speed.

"I honour your commitment," he said. "Truly I do."

"Then we shall continue—together?" I demanded. "And when we return, we will do all we can, use all that we have learned?"

He nodded.

"Brother, what did you see in the tapestry inside Norfolk House?" I asked. "Something disturbed you greatly. What is the story of the sisters?"

"I believe them to be the Pleiades," said Brother Edmund.

"Who are they?" I asked. "What is the significance of the dance?"

Brother Edmund said quietly, "They are dancing for someone."

"Who?"

He opened his mouth, then shut it.

"Brother, it seemed to me they were frenzied in their movements, perhaps even angry. You must tell me: Who were they dancing for?" I demanded, my voice rising. Could it be possible that Brother Edmund was withholding information from me, after what we had just been through at Norfolk House?

Finally, he answered me. "They were dancing for their father, Sister Joanna."

What was sinister about that? Confused, I looked over at him. Even in the darkness on the road out of Lambeth, I could see in Brother Edmund's eyes the flicker of fear.

And he whipped his horse, something I'd never seen him do before, to ride faster down the road to Dartford Priory.

45

"Something is wrong," I said to Brother Edmund.

After more than two weeks away, I did not know what to expect at Dartford. Exhausted and stiff from the cold, we turned off the road onto the priory trail. It was past midnight; Dartford would be closed up and locked for the night.

But as we rode around the bend where the priory first comes into view, a torch flickered at the gatehouse. Beyond, the priory door hung open, even though it was a frigid night. A man stood in the doorway, holding a lantern. It was Gregory, the porter.

We jumped off our horses and ran to the arched entrance.

"Gregory, what's happening?" I asked.

He stepped down the stairs, not in greeting but with his arms stretched out, as if to bar us.

"Stay back," he said.

"Why?" asked Brother Edmund.

"It's the bailiff who ordered it. He told me no one could go inside until he's found help in London. He promised to return by midnight."

My stomach clenched.

"Why is help needed?" I asked.

"The prioress has been missing for two days," he said. Now that we were much closer, I could see Gregory's eyes were hollow with exhaustion. "We have searched everywhere. She's disappeared. Then, this afternoon, Sister Christina and Brother Richard went missing, too." Gregory's voice broke into hysteria. "They're vanishing one by one. This priory is cursed. That's what they say in town, and God's blood, they're right!"

Brother Edmund moved one step closer to the agitated porter. "Gregory, you *must* let us in. We may be able to find them."

"No." Gregory came down, so that he stood face-to-face with Brother Edmund. "The bailiff said no one else comes in, without his approval."

I moved forward to try to persuade him. "We won't go into the cloistered area. We only want to look in the front rooms. We may—"

Gregory pushed me back. "I won't do it."

"Don't lay hands on her," Brother Edmund said angrily. Our porter turned on him, and before I knew it, he'd struck Brother Edmund.

As they grappled on the steps, I darted around them and slipped inside.

"Wait for me, I beg you," Brother Edmund called after me. "It's too dangerous for you to go alone."

"Stop, Sister Joanna!" bellowed Gregory.

I didn't stop.

I ran as fast as I could, past the statue of the Virgin Mary, through the entranceway hall, and then I turned. I wouldn't search for a door to underground rooms in the prioress's chamber, I knew it couldn't be there or Cromwell's men would have found it.

I snatched a taper from the wall and ran into the guest bedchamber. I felt all the walls, every corner, jabbing at shelves and cracks the way Prior Roger had pushed on the wall in Malmesbury.

Nothing.

I was burning with frustration. It had to be here. There had to be a way down. I didn't have time to push and pull and bang against every inch of the wall. Even if Brother Edmund were able to get the better of Gregory, the bailiff would arrive soon with his men.

I needed a sign to tell me where the door was, just as the lion and ivy carvings over the door at Norfolk House revealed it to be the one leading into the great hall.

It hit me, with such force I gave a loud cry.

Young Catherine Howard said: *"Most of the time, the ivy is in front of the lion. But atop that door, the lion is in front. That's how I remember which door to use."*

All over Dartford Priory, I'd seen the carvings of a crown and lilies. Always the crown was behind the symbol of the Dominican Order. Except for one place. The room where outsiders were allowed to sit with sisters—or with the prioress herself. In the *locutorium.*

I could hear men shouting outside the priory as I scrambled into the room where I'd sat with Brother Edmund and Brother Richard and been questioned by commissioners Layton and Legh.

I had only minutes before they'd find me.

I went to the half-empty bookcase directly under the carving of the crown in front of the lily. I ran my hands up the shelves. I pushed against the sides hard, searching for something that opened, something that slid.

On the top shelf, it gave way. There was a *click*. I pushed hard, and the bookshelf eased open several inches.

My taper held high, I stepped into the opening, and then closed the shelf behind me.

It was a narrow opening behind the shelf. No more than two feet wide. And very dirty. This was not the well-kept passageway of Malmesbury. My candle alighted on a pile of rotting crumbs. It was a yellow cake. With a start, I realised it was one of the soul cakes gathered by the Westerly children. This was how they moved around Dartford Priory so stealthily.

I came to a set of rickety stairs and descended.

At the bottom was a wider passageway, not much more than a tunnel. I followed it, scanning the walls for another sign of the crown.

I heard a woman's voice. Someone was talking down here. Perhaps I'd find the prioress . . . and Brother Richard. Obviously, they had located this entranceway, too, but I couldn't understand why they'd remained down here so long. Didn't they know Gregory and the others would sound the alarm?

The dirty tunnel met with a wider passageway. Its walls were lined with bricks. The woman's voice was a bit louder. I didn't hear anyone else; who was she talking to? The voice died away. I kept walking.

When I rounded the end of the passageway, I saw three things in sequence.

A man in blood-soaked friar's robes lay on the ground, very still. A woman was tied up in ropes and gagged, sitting on a short barrel against the wall. Next to her stood my fellow novice, Sister Christina. She was half-turned away from me and held a long knife in her right hand.

I stood there for a while before Sister Christina noticed me. I could not move; I could not speak. I was struck motionless, dumb, by the tableau before me.

I realised the man was Brother Richard. His eyes were open. He was most definitely dead.

Prioress Joan saw me. She shook her head, very slightly. That movement made Sister Christina turn around quickly.

"Sister Joanna," she said in a hoarse voice. And then louder, with her usual vigour, "Sister Joanna."

"What is happening?" I asked. "I don't understand."

"I had to do this," she said, very earnest. "You must understand, I had to. The prioress found the door in the *locutorium;* she came down here, to the tunnels. She was looking for it, the crown. I came at her from behind with this"—she brandished her knife—"and I tied her up."

"Is the crown here—now?" I asked, my eyes scanning the floor.

Sister Christina laughed, and the sound of it brought me into the reality of what was happening. I had been too shocked and confused until that moment. With my eyes I could see Brother Richard was dead and the prioress was in ropes and gagged—and Sister Christina was free with a knife. But I could not accept what it meant.

But the laughter, the bitter, angry laughter, made me understand, finally, that Sister Christina was a murderess. And she was, most likely, within the next few minutes, going to attempt to murder me.

"The crown! The crown! The crown!" she shouted, mockingly. "Is that all that matters to you, even now? It's all that mattered to her"—she swung her knife at the prioress—"and to Brother Richard. He came looking for her, but he wanted to find the crown, too. Instead, he found *me.*"

"You imprisoned the prioress two days ago?" I asked, trying to calm her.

"Yes, and it caused me no regret to do so," she said. "If it weren't for her, none of it would have happened, Sister Joanna. She invited my father to the priory. She defiled our chapter house with his presence."

"Your father?"

"I killed him," she said defiantly. "God will not punish me for it. He was a despoiler—a demon. He was not human. Did you know that?"

I did not dare to bring up her mother. But a shiver of torment crossed Sister Christina's face. "I didn't kill my mother. I went to her that day, using the tunnels. I've known about them since the day Prioress Elizabeth died. But the Westerly children must have found out how to get to them, too, and I knew that if you found the children that day and spoke to them, all could be discovered. They'd finally know how someone would get from the cloister to the guest bedchamber, and that it was I who killed him. I had to be the one to tell my mother; I wanted to explain myself." Sister Christina began to weep. "She went mad when I told her why I'd done it. She said that it was her fault, and that she had failed me. After I left, she wrote that letter and took her own life to remove any suspicion from me."

Sister Christina slammed her other hand against the wall, inches from the prioress's head. The prioress shrank back from the novice's rage.

I tried again to calm Sister Christina. "The tunnels go far?"

"They go all the way to the barns," she said. "There was a foolish prioress, a hundred years ago, who feared someone would try to take the crown by force. She had workmen dig another tunnel and connect it to the dark-house passageway. They added another entrance, from a hidden door in the passageway just outside the church. That way, she thought, if the priory were set upon, they could smuggle out the crown and themselves. She swore all the workmen to silence. But someone didn't stay silent."

There was a noise behind her, at the end of the passageway. A man's voice said, "That was how Lord Chester found out about the tunnels."

Sister Christina sprang away from the wall, waving her knife with a snarl.

And Geoffrey Scovill stepped around the corner.

With a quick darting of the eyes, he took in my position and the prioress's. But mostly he stared at Sister Christina. He held a long stick at his side; I recognised it as a baton.

"Lord Chester found a way to send a message to a young novice named Sister Beatrice he'd seen at the priory. He lured her down here. He seduced an innocent girl, a lonely, confused girl."

Sister Christina screamed, *"How do you know that?"*

"Because I found Sister Beatrice, and she told me how to find the entrances to the tunnels," he said. "I finally forced the old porter, Jacob, to tell me where she was hiding."

I started. That was why we ran across Geoffrey in town that day—he was searching for Jacob.

"When the commissioners came, Sister Beatrice said she wanted to leave. The prioress had no choice but to allow it. Jacob took her to the house of her mother. She was sick twice on the way. When he returned to the priory, he told Prioress Elizabeth about her vomiting, and she realised Sister Beatrice was with child. The prioress was horrified, and she went to the family house. The mother had already driven out her daughter, called her a whore. The prioress and Jacob found her living in the forest, half dead, and hid her in a small farm far from here. The prioress gave her an income for all her expenses. Sister Beatrice had to hide from Lord Chester, you see. If he knew of the pregnancy, he'd have taken the child. Her baby was born before its time; it never drew breath. But she still wanted to hide. She was so afraid of Lord Chester."

Geoffrey took a step closer to Sister Christina.

"You know why she was afraid of him, don't you? The last time she met him down here, he was drunk and told her something evil. Something about you."

Sister Christina waved the knife at him and screamed, "Stop!"

Geoffrey edged closer.

"Your father meddled with you, didn't he, Sister Christina?"

I winced. "No," I groaned. But no one noticed, for Sister Christina screamed. Bent over and screamed, like a rabid beast.

Geoffrey took two steps toward her. "You found out about Sister Beatrice in the letter that Prioress Elizabeth wrote to her successor. Sister Beatrice left a few months before you came to Dartford. But you must have heard or suspected something, or you wouldn't have stolen the letter. The prioress had banned Lord Chester from the priory and wanted to make sure the next head of the priory did the same. She wrote in the letter about the tunnels, too. That's how you discovered them."

Sister Christina stared at him, her chest heaving.

"What your father did to you was a crime against nature, Sister

Christina. It is not to be wondered that you went mad yourself. But it is not an excuse for taking lives. You must now put down your knife and come with me."

She straightened up, eyes blazing, and ran back to the prioress. "No," she said with a terrible smile. "If you try to touch me, I will slit her throat."

The prioress's eyes bulged in terror.

I moved toward Sister Christina.

"Please," I begged. "Please. Do as Geoffrey says."

"Sister Joanna, do not forsake me," she said. "You must help me escape."

"You know I can't do that," I whispered.

"But you are the one who understands. The only one. I know that what happened to me, happened to you. I could tell, after all the time that we've been at Dartford together. Your father violated you."

I shuddered, revolted.

"No," I said.

"Don't lie to me now," she screeched.

"I am not lying. I love my father. He is a good, loving father. *He* would never do that to me."

Her face contorted with that terrible rage that had killed two people. Sister Christina threw her knife down and rushed toward me, her hands out like claws.

I backed against the wall. She was on me in seconds. She grabbed my throat and banged my head against the bricks with all her strength. I felt a sharp, terrible, hot pain in the back of my head.

The passageway under Dartford Priory slid down and went black.

46

Greenwich Palace, June 1527

The first thing that George Boleyn said to me was "Mistress Stafford, I am certain that you'd look better in French fashion."

He'd come into the queen's rooms with my second cousin, the king. I had been presented formally to Queen Katherine as her new maid of honour. I was sixteen years old. It was one of the proudest moments of my mother's life. All of her frustrated hopes would now be fulfilled, through my service. My rise in court would bring her back into the orbit of the queen.

Katherine of Aragon was gracious, dignified, and warm. I already felt comfortable in these rooms, inhabited by the woman who was my mother's age and had my mother's Spanish accent. Her sombre dress and tasteful decor also reminded me of my mother. The other ladies welcomed me; one girl, not much older, offered to show me the rituals she performed for the queen after supper.

"We will take good care of your daughter; I know she is your jewel," the queen said to my mother.

"No, no, Your Highness," my mother said quickly. "It is now up to her to take care of *you*."

They smiled at each other. The strength of the friendship, forged in the Spanish court, was undamaged by the last six years of exile. All was understood.

Queen Katherine turned to me. "I understand you are skilled at needlework. We will sew together—I have a batch of shirts for His Majesty that require finishing stitches."

I curtsied. "I would be honoured, madame."

The queen smiled again, and then signalled for her Spanish

confessor. Through all the years in England—marriages to two royal brothers; the birth of a daughter, Mary; and the sad procession of stillbirths and miscarriages—she had always clung to the service of a Spanish confessor.

The short, stout figure of the queen moved to her private chapel, followed by the confessor.

My mother was tactful and did not wish to hover over me. She had old friends to visit. "I will be back in an hour to say good-bye to you and the queen," she told me. "Acquaint yourself with the other maids while the queen is in chapel."

She had been gone only ten minutes when the king appeared.

There was a flurry of activity in the hall, a page appeared, and then King Henry himself strode into the room, followed by a half-dozen other men. I had not been in his presence since I was a young child.

We all sank into deep curtsies. I stared down at the floor, coming up slowly.

"Where is the queen?" His voice was surprisingly high-pitched.

"Sire, she is making confession," said Lady Maude Parr, the queen's lady-in-waiting, a tall and dignified woman.

He made an impatient noise; it unsettled me. I still did not look up.

I don't know exactly which man said it—it wasn't Boleyn—but someone, a courtier, said, "The queen has a new maid of honour?" By asking that, he called attention to me, made me stand out from the two dozen other women, young and old, and by doing so changed my life.

I could feel all eyes turn toward me. My heart hammering, I looked up.

King Henry the Eighth was the tallest man I'd ever seen. Taller than my father or his brothers. He had red hair, just starting to thin at his temples; small blue eyes; and an immaculately trimmed beard that was more golden than red. He looked younger than his age, thirty-six. That day he wore purple and a shower of jewels: huge rings and two medallions, layered on each other. I knew that royalty alone could don purple, but I hadn't expected him to wear it about the court on an ordinary day. Later it would become clear that this was *not* an ordinary day, and there was a reason he wanted to wrap himself in the colour royal for what he meant to do. But no one knew anything of that yet.

"Your Highness," I murmured, and made another curtsy.

"This is Mistress Joanna Stafford," said Lady Parr, an edge of nervousness in her voice.

He looked me up and down.

I hated my kirtle passionately at that moment. It was a costly one, made of burgundy brocade, carefully selected to flatter my colouring. It had a low, square, Spanish-style neck, exposing the tops of my breasts, something I'd assiduously avoided at home, and so was quite unused to. I felt undressed before these much older men.

The king showed no lechery. That is the truth. I'd been warned about his lustful nature, not just by my mother but also every adult at Stafford Castle. He'd bred a bastard by one lady-in-waiting and seduced several others, including one of my Stafford aunts, Catherine of Fitzwalter.

I think there are two kinds of females, those who resent it when a lustful man does not leer at them and those who are relieved. I was very much in the second category.

The king merely nodded at me and then gestured toward a young man in his party. He said something to him that I couldn't hear, then turned and left.

The young man sidled up to Lady Parr and said: "I am to take her to my sister."

Lady Parr grimaced. "There is another lady who serves the queen, and you will meet her," she said, very reluctantly. "This gentleman will escort you; he is Sir George Boleyn."

The man bowed with a showy, mocking flourish. I was taken aback, and confused. If the lady served the queen, why wasn't she here? But I did not see any other choice but to follow him.

Boleyn was somewhere between twenty-five and thirty and very dark, with huge black eyes. He wore an expensive doublet in a fashion I hadn't seen before, tightly fitted. He was of medium height and very slim.

Fashion meant a great deal to him. After criticising my clothes, he pointed out the styles worn by other ladies as we walked through a long gallery. His tone was instructional. I said almost nothing during our walk; I had taken an intense dislike to him.

He showed me into a large room off the gallery, sparsely furnished and flooded with light. The queen's rooms had been dark, verging on musty. These were airy, with decorative touches I'd never seen before: coloured ribbons strung along the window casements and a gaily embroidered cushion on a chair.

A young woman stood by the window. She closely resembled George Boleyn—black eyes and hair and very slim—and looked to be his age. It occurred to me they might be twins.

"Who is this?" she asked, unsmiling. She had a slight French accent.

"The new maid of honour, the Stafford girl," he said. "Remember? She's the one the queen insisted on."

I shot him a furious look.

The woman laughed, a low, throaty laugh. "She doesn't like you, George."

"No, she doesn't." He sounded gleeful.

She smoothed her skirts as she walked toward me. I had to admit she was graceful. They both were, but in a way that was strangely mannered. As if they were always on display, and revelled in it.

"I am Anne Boleyn," she said simply.

"And you also serve the queen?" I asked.

Her enormous black eyes danced with a joke I didn't understand. "For now," she said. George Boleyn burst out laughing.

I turned on him. "Take me back to the queen's apartments," I said.

"What spirit she has," said Anne.

"Yes, I know. And she has a good figure. Don't you like her, Sister?"

She looked at me for a moment and then wrinkled her nose. "No."

This was going too far.

"I don't know why I am here, but I insist on going back," I fumed. "I have been appointed to serve the queen."

They laughed again at their private joke.

"I don't think she understands a thing," George Boleyn said.

"The Staffords have botched it. Of course, they live so far from court and are in complete disgrace. They don't know anything."

"Do not insult my family, sir," I said. "We are one of the oldest in the land. Before today I had never heard the name 'Boleyn.'"

I did not know it, but I had thrown down a gauntlet before dangerous people. I meant that I had not been informed who the Boleyns were, but they took it as an insult against the prestige of their name. The mood in the room shifted from mockery to something more malignant. I started toward the door, to get away from them, when a page hurried in. I almost collided with him.

"The king," he said, breathless.

George Boleyn took me by the arm—I thought to lead me out of the room, out of the way of the king, who for some reason was stopping here. But in the next moment I was in a tiny alcove off to the side of the room, separated by a heavy curtain.

A hand clamped over my mouth. "Don't say a word," George Boleyn breathed into my ear.

I tried to pull away, but he wrapped his other arm around me and pressed me close to him. He was strong.

The voices in the other room made me stop struggling. One of them was the king's.

"Confession," he groaned, as if in agony. "I was ready—I was completely and utterly ready, Nan. But she's making confession."

"That won't last long," said Anne Boleyn, soothingly.

"I'm not sure that it should be done today."

"You promised," she said, much more sharply. "And it's dangerous to keep delaying. There are so many rumours; you've said the worst thing that could happen was if she sent a message to her nephew, the emperor. *You* have to tell her, and you have to get her to agree. No messages."

I could not believe this young woman spoke to the King of England in this way.

"Eighteen years of marriage—it's not a simple matter," he groaned. "I was ready when I went in before, but now . . ."

"By nightfall it will be done and behind you, think of that."

There were a few seconds of silence, and then in a voice full of pleading, he said, "Would you let me—?"

"No, no, no," she laughed.

"*Please,* Nan. Please."

There was silence, and then the softest moan.

At the sound of that moan, George Boleyn stirred. His left hand remained rigidly clamped over my mouth; the other began to move over me. His hand cupped my breast. I pulled away, horrified. Again he whispered, faint but with a new, terrifying roughness, "If you make a sound, it will be the end of you."

And then he put his hand down my dress.

How many minutes passed? I don't know. It could have been five. Or fifteen. Or much longer. But George Boleyn stopped the instant that the king and his sister stopped. The king said something, she answered, then there was moving around, and someone else came into the room. In another minute it was completely silent. Everyone left.

George Boleyn gathered together his hose, which had become loosened from his doublet, and rearranged his codpiece.

"And now, Mistress Stafford," he said with a laugh, "I will take you back to the queen's apartments."

When he'd dragged me into the room his sister and the king had just left, he said, "You will tell no one what just occurred. If you do, I will deny it. I am the favourite of the king; he will believe *me.* Or he will fear that his conversation with my sister will be made public. That could never be allowed. Your parents will be punished; you and your family will be shunned forever. You'll never, ever get anyone to marry you." He pressed his lips to my ear. "This will just be our secret. And who knows? You may come to like me. After today, I think I should be the one to take your maidenhead. Don't you agree?"

The gallery was a blur on the way back. I had a hard time walking; George Boleyn had to hold me up a few times, to keep me from falling. I don't know if anyone noticed my state. If they did, they didn't inquire.

When we were outside the queen's apartments, my mother appeared. "Where did you go? Did you have the queen's or Lady Parr's permission?" She looked at me more closely. "What's wrong, Joanna?"

I shook my head, numbly. I turned around. George Boleyn had gone. I am not sure she ever noticed him.

"The king is speaking with the queen privately," she said. She spoke about the friends she had seen, but she was agitated. She would look at me, worried, then peer inside the queen's chamber, worried for some other reason.

The king appeared, suddenly, and his waiting courtiers and pages reassembled around him, like barnacles to a ship.

His face was red and furious. For such a tall, powerful man to look like that, so enraged, it was terrifying. My mother actually flattened herself against the wall as he strode past.

We heard the queen then. A wounded sob.

My mother ran inside the rooms right after Lady Parr and the other senior ladies; I should have gone with her. I was a servant to the queen, after all. But I didn't move.

She reappeared in a few minutes, her face drained of colour. "It's unbelievable," she said. "Unbelievable. He told the queen he wants an annulment, that they have never been truly married. *Madre de Dios.*"

The queen was still sobbing. But she was soon to be drowned out. There was a louder noise, a hysterical scream.

It was mine. And it lasted as long as it took my mother to hurry me out of the royal palace of Henry the Eighth.

PART
FOUR

47

Dartford Priory, January 1538

It was grey for a very long time. A soft, insulating, peaceful grey. It was as if I were being rowed from Dartford to London on the Thames again, cocooned in morning mist. I remember when I sat in the boat and looked over the sides, into the water, I never once saw a bottom to the river. It was always an opaque liquid chalk.

I heard voices in spurts. There was my name: "Sister Joanna." Occasionally, just "Joanna." I didn't want to speak. I turned from them, stubborn. I wanted only to float in the soothing grey.

But after a time, a garden emerged, a familiar one. It was Stafford Castle, the gardens, one of my favourite places. This was no nightmare; I didn't feel the need to run or hide. No, the gardens welcomed me. I could smell the flowers and hear the birds calling and feel the insects' teasing wings.

Someone wept, though, and it was ruining the garden. I looked around to see who it was. No one.

"Please, Sister Joanna," a woman wept. "Please."

There was no help for it. I'd have to leave the garden. I couldn't let the weeping go on—that would be selfish, remiss. I tried to go in the direction of the weeping, but my legs wouldn't move. I reached up, with all my strength. The vibrant flowers and warm sun left me; greyness returned. The crying grew louder, and I finally knew who it was: Sister Winifred.

I opened my eyes, at last. I was lying on a bed, and Sister Winifred's blonde head was next to me, pressed facedown as she wept.

I reached for her; it was much harder than I expected. My fingers moved only a few inches. But she felt the movement. Her head shot up.

"Sister Joanna!" she cried. "Oh, thank the Virgin."

"Don't upset yourself—it's bad for your health." My voice sounded terrible, like a croaking bird.

Sister Winifred laughed, joyful. "Brother Edmund, Brother Edmund," she cried out.

And then he was there. His bony, tender hands were feeling my wrists and my throat. He lifted my eyelids and peered into my eyes. I peered back. He looked tired, but much like himself. His eyes were not the serene yet dull brown that I now knew was the product of a dangerous flower. They were full of aching concern.

"I greet you, Brother Edmund," I said.

He smiled. "And I greet you, Sister Joanna."

It rushed over me then, the fear and the horror in the tunnels under the priory. I shrank away and immediately felt a burning pain in the back of my head.

"No, Sister Christina, no!" I was frantic.

"It's all right, it's all right," Brother Edmund said quickly. "Sister Christina is gone. She can't hurt you. Don't move, Sister Joanna."

"My head," I groaned.

"You have been dealt a serious head wound," he said. "We had the barber here as well, and a physician came from London yesterday."

I stared at him. "Yesterday? How . . . how long have I been asleep?"

"You have been unable to speak or move for several weeks," he said quietly.

Sister Winifred took my hand and held it tightly. "It was thought you would die," she said.

I looked at her, at her loving face. And then at Brother Edmund, who was checking the bandages on my head. I could hear the crackling of a high fire in the infirmary fireplace. It was full winter now.

"I won't die?" I asked.

"You won't," Brother Edmund said firmly. "You will recover, though it may take some time."

I tightened my grip on Sister Winifred's hand. "My father," I said.

They exchanged a quick look. Brother Edmund leaned down and said, "We have not yet found him."

"But he was to be freed!" I cried. "Bishop Gardiner promised the princess."

"He was freed three days after we went to Lambeth. We know it for certain. Geoffrey Scovill rode to London and confirmed it."

I stared at him, confused. Finally, I said, "Then he must be at Stafford Castle."

"We wrote a letter, to your cousin, Sir Henry. He replied that he'd not seen your father, nor heard word. The letter came to the priory yesterday."

Salty tears burned in my eyes.

"Geoffrey Scovill is looking for him, Sister Joanna," he said. "And we know that when Master Scovill sets out to find someone, he succeeds. He is quite stubborn."

"Like me," I said.

"Yes," said Brother Edmund. "He is like you." Brother Edmund ducked his head and looked away.

The bells pealed. It was time for prayers. Sister Winifred looked at us, questioningly.

"Go, please," I said. "I want you to."

"Tell them of Sister Joanna," Brother Edmund said. "There can be prayers of thanks today."

When Sister Winifred left, I asked him about the crown.

He shook his head. "It's not to be found, either. There was a place for it, a room very much like the one at Malmesbury, but it was empty. I have searched the tunnels, every inch. Nothing."

"Sister Christina."

"Yes," he said. "When the men were taking her away, one of the things she screamed is that we would never find the crown. That she had sanctified it."

I swallowed. "Yes. Brother Edmund, her father's evil drove her mad. Sister Helen—she must have seen things no one else had and suspected that Sister Christina had murdered Lord Chester. But the tapestries—what did they mean?"

"The sisters dance for their father, Atlas, a god whom Zeus condemned to hold up the heavens on his shoulders. They mourn for him, but in some myths they blame him, too, for not protecting them from capture. The Pleiades all gave birth to children conceived from gods or demigods, sometimes through force. There's a version in which the sisters turn against their father. They hate him. In this tapestry, yes, their dance was angry."

I nodded. "That is why she wanted me to see the story, even though other nuns wove it long ago."

Now I had another frightening thought. "And what about Bishop Gardiner?"

"He returned to France after one week spent in London. He had been summoned by the king to hear in person his specifications for a new wife. Gardiner's charge is to negotiate with King Francis for a French princess."

"Poor princess." I shuddered. Something shifted in Brother Edmund's expression; I could see he had more to tell me. It would not be pleasant hearing.

"What is it, Brother?" I pressed him.

"Sister Christina has already been charged with murder and found guilty in the Courts of Assize." He hesitated.

"Tell me," I whispered.

"Sister Christina will be hanged," he said.

I took it in. I said nothing for a long while. And then I managed to whisper: "She would rather be burned."

The room was beginning to swim in front of my eyes. "Rest now," he said soothingly. "Don't think about Sister Christina, or the crown, or Bishop Gardiner. All will be well."

The greyness returned.

I began to recover. It took me two days before I could sit up without fainting. And my arms and legs were so weak and uncooperative—it was extraordinarily frustrating. Brother Edmund and Sister Winifred set up a regimen for me. Each day I endeavored to do more. To sit up, to reach with one hand and then the other. Finally, I could stand, but I couldn't walk. It was frightening how my legs collapsed under me.

I had visitors. Every time I was up to it, a different sister would come to sit with me, pray with me. Sister Agatha had to be reminded that it wasn't fair for her to take up all the visitor time.

Prioress Joan asked to see me with only Brother Edmund present. She sat by my bed, and her face was very serious and yet without a trace of anger or distrust.

"I think that if you had not come when you did, she would have ended my life," said the prioress. "Sister Christina meant to kill me—she told me several times she would. But it was very hard for her to kill a Prioress of Dartford. The training she received had had its effect, even on a girl who was mad. She hated me, yet she respected and feared me, too. She was praying for the strength to kill me when you appeared."

"And Brother Richard?" I asked.

The prioress's head sank. I could see how difficult this would be.

"Sister Christina sat next to me, with her knife pointed at my throat, while we listened to him come down the passageway. He kept calling out, 'Prioress? Prioress?' He sounded so worried for me. I wanted desperately to warn him. The sound of his voice, the way he called out for me, I can't seem to put it out of my mind. Every night I hear it, and every day I . . ." Her voice trailed away. After a long moment of silence, she continued. "When he came around the corner, she sprang on him. Brother Richard died quickly."

We all three fell silent, as we greatly mourned the loss of the brilliant Brother Richard.

She finally cleared her throat. "I wish to speak to you about the crown of Athelstan."

I tensed. A quick glance at Brother Edmund revealed he was not nervous about the subject. Yes, of course. They had already spoken, while I was senseless.

"Commissioners Legh and Layton told me they were certain you had been handpicked by Bishop Gardiner to search the priory for a relic called the Athelstan crown. They said there were rumours for many years of its existence, and Cromwell had them inquiring at all the monasteries, in particular Malmesbury Abbey, where King Athelstan was buried, but no one had found it. Certain reports of late led them to believe it was at Dartford. I was told that if I could find it, Dartford would not be suppressed—we would continue here. But they told me I must not directly confront you three and thus stir Gardiner to direct intervention. I must search with discretion. I was assured that the king would honour the ancient crown of a king."

I snorted in disbelief.

The prioress flushed, and then continued. "When Brother Richard said you were both recalled to London by orders of Bishop Gardiner, it sounded patently false. But I did not try to stop you, because I thought it would be easier to achieve my goal with just one agent of Gardiner in competition with me, not three. After many days of effort, and studying diagrams of other priories and monasteries, I realised there must be significance to the difference in the stone carvings over the bookcase in the *locutorium*, and was able to gain entry to the stairs. But I never found the correct room. Sister Christina seized me."

"Sister Christina found the crown," I said.

The prioress nodded. "She taunted me about it. She said she had removed it from the priory weeks earlier and sanctified it."

Sanctified. That word again.

"But how did she do that?" I asked.

"She told me she threw it in a fire and melted it. She broke it into pieces. Then she threw the pieces in the river."

I shuddered at the madness of Sister Christina.

"In truth, she was much more concerned with her father and his crimes against her and Sister Beatrice than with the crown. The greatest error of my life was agreeing to Lord Chester's coming to Dartford Priory. Prioress Elizabeth had forbade him from coming to the priory, but I didn't know why because I never read her letter. He meant to flaunt his power before his daughter, I think. What he did to her was a horrific crime against God and man." She shook her head. "She said her father became enraged when she said she wanted to take vows here, but she managed to send a letter to her uncle the Bishop of Dover and to enlist his support. She wanted to rebuild her life here, to try to forget the past and dedicate herself to God. Perhaps if Lord Chester had not come here, to the feast, she might have succeeded. I don't know. God is merciful. But when her father laid hands on the reliquary at our feast, something inside her snapped. There was no going back then."

The prioress straightened in her chair. "I have to find a way to live with this mistake, which has cost all of these lives. I shall ask for forgiveness and spiritual guidance every day that is left to me on earth."

I reached out to the prioress, I touched her hand. She looked at me, surprised—and then grateful.

"What happens to us now?" I asked.

She said simply, "Dartford Priory will be suppressed. I wrote to Cromwell and informed him of what happened, and he sent me a letter two weeks ago making it plain what must occur. I am surrendering the priory to the will of the king. There will be no persecutions or arrests. It will happen to us, the same thing that is happening to all the larger monasteries all over England. At least we will be spared another visit from Commissioners Legh and Layton. After Easter, we must all leave Dartford Priory. Pensions have been arranged."

The prioress leaned closer to me. "For our time remaining, we will conduct ourselves with dedication to Christ and with the dignity that comes from being members of the Dominican Order. I suggest to you what I am suggesting to all of the sisters. Give careful consideration to how you wish to live after Dartford is closed to you. Sister Joanna, you have options they do not. You are half Spanish, and the Dominican Order is very strong in Spain. You could travel there. I'd help you with the arrangements. You are not without means. There is your father's inheritance—"

I shook my head violently. "I am an Englishwoman."

She said, very gently, "You cannot become a nun here. It's not possible to perform the ceremony of final profession on the eve of our destruction. I sought permission, from our governing prelate, for you and Sister Winifred. I sent a letter the day after my rescue. I wanted to do that for you. Sister Joanna, you are the final novice to profess at Dartford. I wanted you to be the last nun. But it is too near the end of our days. My request was denied."

I clutched the edge of my bed. There had been so many tragedies, so many losses, and mysteries never to be understood. But this one struck me as the cruellest of blows. Was I to live out my life in this strange limbo, not a regular woman of the world but not a full nun?

"I wish to be alone," I said.

She nodded and quietly left, along with Brother Edmund. That night I wept without ceasing until finally I sank into a sodden, dreamless, dull sleep. It was all for nothing, the searching and the terror and the struggle. It was over.

The next week was very hard for me. I almost felt I was back in the Tower, that final period of listlessness, of hopeless stupor. To cheer me, Sister Agatha brought me a letter from the Lady Mary. The novice mistress was beside herself from excitement. I read it while she stood there, and then shared the gracious words of the king's daughter with her. It pleased her more than me. I would always revere the Lady Mary and be grateful to her, but right now she was part of a way of life that was dying. A life of grace and sacrifice and order, giving way to ugliness and confusion. The tragedy was too enormous.

Sister Winifred did her best to cheer me. She even begged me to make a life with her after Dartford closed.

"Brother Edmund says he will try to keep the infirmary open in the village, working as an apothecary, rather than a friar," she said. "There are those in the town who have pleaded with him to remain, to make the attempt. I will help him in the infirmary, and I will keep house for him, cook and clean. We'll find a house in town. I have not asked him yet, but I am sure he'd welcome you."

"No, I must be with my father," I said. "I know I can find him. When I am strong enough, I will purchase a horse and look for him myself."

"Yes, of course, Sister," she murmured, trying to hide her disappointment. "I understand."

Soon after that I learned about Sister Beatrice.

At first they hadn't told me; for some reason, they thought I would be too unnerved. But finally, it was revealed that Sister Beatrice had in a fashion returned to Dartford. The crimes of Sister Christina had so disturbed her, she wrote a letter to the prioress asking for an audience. During a very long discussion, it was agreed that she could come back as a lay sister for as long as Dartford existed. Other priories had them—women who performed mostly manual labour, freeing up the nuns and novices for religious study. Lay sisters wore different habits and slept with the servants, but were still required to obey the laws of chastity, obedience, and humility.

Sister Agatha asked me, rather nervously, if I wanted to meet her.

I shrugged. "I don't see why not."

The next morning, Sister Beatrice came to the infirmary. I had not slept well, and I was dreading a long confession from a penitent fallen woman.

She was taller than I'd expected, with hazel eyes and thick blonde hair pulled back tight under a cap. She slipped onto a stool and stared at me for so long I felt uncomfortable.

"So," she said, "I have heard you actually *like* tapestry work."

I laughed. "You don't?"

"I find it so dull, and I'm terrible at it. But I was bad at everything here, except for music. At chapter, my faults were doubly long as everyone else's. I'm sure I was the worst novice in the history of the Dominican Order."

"Then why did you return?" I asked.

"Prioress Elizabeth and the other nuns treated me better than anyone else in my life," she said. "Except for Geoffrey Scovill." To my amazement, she blushed as she said his name. She looked away until the blush receded.

"Geoffrey told me all about you," she muttered.

I should have minded this, but for some reason I didn't.

"He said you are a remarkable person," she continued.

"I'm not," I said, weary.

She bit her thumbnail; I could see that all her fingernails were torn to the quick. She'd shown me something of a sullen nature, but then it shifted into sadness. "Do you blame me, Sister Joanna?" she asked. "Is everything that happened here at the priory my fault?"

"No."

She nodded but still looked troubled.

"I think," I said slowly, "that for the rest of the time we have here, we should not blame one another or find fault with one another. It is very precious and beautiful, the life at Dartford Priory. We should cherish it until it is impossible to do so any longer."

She got up from her stool.

"You're mistaken about one thing, Sister Joanna. You *are* remarkable."

48

My recovery continued. With effort—and much patience from Brother Edmund—I was able to walk across the infirmary on a Monday afternoon. The next day, the prioress sent word that my presence was expected in church.

My spirits stirred. I believed what I'd told Sister Beatrice. For as long as I had left, I wanted to say the prayers, sing the songs, seek a holy union with Christ's love. With Sister Winifred on one side and Sister Agatha on the other, I walked to the church of Dartford. I knelt and performed our duties.

Although I could not yet move quickly, I made it to each and every office in the church that day and the next and the next. Making full confession filled me with relief and gratitude, freed me from some of my anguish. Brother Edmund proclaimed me well enough to sleep in the dormitory. I was glad to rest on my old pallet, though it made my heart twist to see the empty one against the opposite wall, where Sister Christina had slept.

The next day, I approached the prioress. "Would it be possible for us to finish Sister Helen's tapestry before Dartford is closed?" I asked.

She looked at me for a very long time.

"Yes," she said, "if you will lead all of the sisters in the work."

"I am not capable," I said, flustered.

"There is none more capable," she said firmly. "Sister Joanna, you are an extraordinarily talented novice. Learning, mastery of Latin, embroidery, music, mathematics, French and Spanish—your accomplishments in each area are outstanding." She paused. "I have not told you this yet because I thought it might bring you pain, but Prioress Elizabeth once told me that with your abilities and your family background, she expected you to make prioress at a young age. She once told me she thought you capable of brilliance."

I was surprised, saddened—and incredibly moved. "Thank you. I am very grateful to learn of her confidence in me. And yours."

I bowed and left to find Sister Winifred, who was ecstatic to learn that we would be sewing together again, at our loom.

The next morning, Sister Winifred and I reopened the tapestry room, closed since the death of Sister Helen. The loom and everything else was covered with dust. We worked hard to clean it, and then I went through the silks in the basket, still spilled open on the floor where it had landed the day Sister Helen collapsed.

Brother Edmund and I had discussed our various theories of the tapestries. It was clear now that Sister Helen never knew of the hidden crown. But she must have known of the tunnels beneath the priory, and she certainly was aware of the predatory lust of Lord Chester. The stories of Daphne and Persephone both revolved around innocent young girls who were attacked or brought down by a man, despite efforts to save them. In the Daphne tapestry, Sister Helen went very far in telling the world what happened at Dartford, by putting the face of the real Sister Beatrice into the threads, and placing Prioress Elizabeth in the river weeds as a parent trying to rescue her. After Lord Chester was murdered, Sister Helen must have guessed that Sister Christina had been the one responsible, and that explained Sister Helen's agitation. And she must have thought back to an older tapestry, the one depicting the Pleiades.

I found the original small drawing she had created for her last tapestry. It was made into a large cartoon and cut into vertical pieces. But the drawing revealed all.

"Yes," I cried to Sister Winifred. "I see it now." I began to assemble the colour schemes of thread and silk.

"Can we be of help, Sister Joanna?"

Standing in the doorway were Sister Agatha and Sister Rachel and, leaning on her cane, Sister Anne, our oldest member.

"I was a novice when this loom came to Dartford," said Sister Anne. "I think I remember the secrets of a good weave."

"But I can't instruct senior nuns; I am not worthy of that," I protested.

"Take your place, tapestry mistress," said Sister Agatha in her loud voice. She pointed to Sister Helen's stool, nearest the window. I swallowed, and sat, and began to distribute the work.

We made great progress that day, and on the next another two nuns appeared. They took their turns at the benches, to complete the last tapestry Dartford would produce before our suppression.

It was the second week of February, and we'd just finished our weaving for the day. I stretched my arms and, Sister Winifred by my side, walked down the passageway when I heard laughter ahead.

We looked at each other, intrigued.

The laughter came from the cloister garden. As we came around the end of the east passageway, we saw them, a half-dozen sisters, young and old. They were standing in the middle of the garden, their hands stretched up, toward the snow.

It was a blizzard such as I'd not seen in years. The flakes fell fast—the ground was completely covered and there were already three inches, at least, quivering on the branches of the quince trees.

I ran to join them. We kicked the snow; we twirled and bowed. I stretched out my tongue, to taste those huge, exquisite flakes sent down from God's heaven.

I closed my eyes and made a dancer's pirouette, from a long-ago lesson.

A hand shook my shoulder. "Sister Joanna!" said someone urgently.

My eyes flew open. A man walked toward me in the snow. It was Geoffrey Scovill, his head and clothes damp and creased with snow, his face reddened with cold.

"Sister Joanna," he said. A smile burst across his face. "I'd heard you were recovered but did not think I'd find you dancing quite yet."

"Geoffrey!" I shouted. I was so glad to see him. The other sisters stopped moving around; they were shy, self-conscious before this young man, even though he was the celebrated rescuer of the prioress and myself.

I moved toward him, aware that I should not be so familiar with a man but at that moment simply not caring.

"I am glad you are here," I said. Playfully, I tossed my handful of snow at him. It shivered and burst on his sleeve.

He laughed. I always liked the sound of his laugh, even when he annoyed me, which was often.

Someone else came up from behind him. It was Brother Edmund, and he looked unhappy. He disliked Geoffrey Scovill—I supposed that would never change.

I glanced back at Geoffrey; he was no longer laughing or even smiling. They exchanged a long look, but not of enmity. There was a shared knowledge of something.

"What is it?" I demanded.

"Your father is here," Geoffrey said.

I could not believe it for a few seconds. "Oh, Geoffrey, thank you, thank you," I said.

"It was not my doing; he'd almost made it to Dartford when I came upon him," Geoffrey said.

"So he was coming to me?"

Brother Edmund said, "Yes."

"Where is he?"

The two men exchanged another look. "He is in the infirmary," said Brother Edmund. "I will take you. First, you must know that—"

I was already running. I had been told not to run yet, but I ran anyway, forcing my weakened legs forward. I almost fell against a wall, but pushed myself off from it and kept going.

I came through the door, and there he was. Sitting up on the infirmary bed, where I had mended not long ago. My heart twisted to see his burned, scarred face.

Sister Rachel was giving him something to eat.

"Father," I said.

"Joanna, ah Joanna." His voice was weak. But he was alive.

Sister Rachel stepped back while I embraced my father. He was cold and, I could feel through his clothes, much thinner. The tears streamed down my cheeks as I held him and thanked God for bringing him to me. "My little girl," he whispered, stroking my hair, as he used to. "My little girl."

Something fell to the floor behind me with a clattering. I turned to look. A boy stood there, not four years old, with shining red-gold hair and a wide smile. He had grabbed a silver pan from the counter and had sent it crashing to the floor.

"Arthur, no," said my father. "Don't do that."

"Who is this boy?" I asked.

My father gripped my arm, tight.

"He is Arthur Bulmer. Margaret's son."

49

In a few minutes we were alone. My father requested it, and his tone was so insistent that all complied. Sister Winifred said she would take Arthur to the kitchen to see if Cook would make him something special to eat. Brother Edmund backed away, too, but not before preparing an herbal poultice for me to give my father. Geoffrey watched everything from the doorway, arms folded across his chest.

"I shall speak to you later, Master Scovill?" asked my father. Even now, severely weakened, his voice carried the authority of a Stafford.

"Of course, Sir Richard," Geoffrey said respectfully. He nodded to me and left with Brother Edmund.

"Drink, please," I said, handing him a steaming cup.

"In a moment, Joanna."

"No," I insisted. "Now." I smiled at him. "You are going to have to get used to my giving you orders on food and drink."

He looked at me, inquiringly.

"Dartford Priory will be suppressed in the spring," I said. "I should like to stay here until that time. Then I will join you wherever you think we should live."

He sipped his hot drink. The news did not give him as much happiness as I expected. Perhaps it was because he was so cold and tired.

"I must speak to you, Joanna. Please listen to everything I have to say. It will not be easy, this conversation. I think it will be the most difficult of my life."

My heart beating faster, I took a stool and sat next to him. He hovered on the edge of the infirmary bed, just above me, his hands on his knees.

"It's about Arthur," he said.

I nodded. Then it came to me. "You want him to live with us? Of course, Father. I want to help raise Margaret's son. I am only surprised her husband's family released him to you."

He closed his eyes. A moment passed. I heard the murmur of voices outside. One of them was Geoffrey's. He was staying close, as my father had requested.

My father opened his eyes again.

"Joanna, he is my son."

I was confused. "No, he is Margaret's. You just said so."

I could see my father's hands shaking on his knees.

"He is my son with Margaret."

"That's not possible," I said.

He closed his eyes again.

"You are not well, Father, or you would not say such a vile thing. I will call for Brother Edmund. He has remedies he can give you."

"No!" He grabbed my wrist. "Don't call for anyone. Hear me, daughter. You have no choice."

I went still. I had never disobeyed him in my life, but I felt a terrible pain, deep in my body.

"In the year 1533, in the summer, I went to London to see to the family property. Do you remember?" I did not speak or nod, and he continued. "I was out on the street when I saw her. It was Margaret. She had escaped from her husband the night before and had been walking through London, not knowing where to go or what to do."

My father paused. "I don't know how much you know of her first husband, William Cheyne. He was a foul man, riddled with vice. Norfolk should never have arranged the marriage. Cheyne got the French pox not long after he married her; she did her best to stay clear of him. But every once in a while, Cheyne would reclaim his wife. In 1533, Anne Boleyn was pregnant with the child everyone expected would be a prince. Norfolk was attending the king, and Cheyne was with him one day and ordered Margaret to accompany him, even though she'd hated the court all her life. That's the day the king got his first look at Margaret."

My father's face was full of loathing. He spoke faster than I'd ever known him to do. It was as if he felt compelled to tell me these terrible, sordid things.

"Henry had begun taking mistresses again, with the queen pregnant. Of course, when he laid eyes on Margaret, he had to have her. He told someone she was the most beautiful woman he'd ever seen. He knew she was the daughter of Buckingham, too. That must have added to the perversity of his attraction. He told Norfolk, always eager to play procurer, to fetch her to him. Norfolk was happy because it would mean someone loyal to the Howards would entertain the king, or so he assumed. Cheyne was ordered to deliver Margaret that night to the king's groomsman, who would take her to the king's bed."

I felt the sickness returning, my horror of the court.

"But she ran away," my father said simply. "She escaped her husband. She ran out of Hampton Court, where the royal family was in residence. She had absolutely nowhere to go. Her husband would, of course, look for her at their small house in London. Her sister the duchess would not be able to hold out against this sort of pressure. She had no money of her own to get across England to Stafford Castle. When I found her, she was half-starved and exhausted. She'd hidden in a church all night, she told me. I passed her on the street that morning. I couldn't believe it was she at first. She wept and begged me to help her.

"I brought her to my house, and I bribed the servants to help me hide her. Cheyne and Norfolk showed up later that afternoon, frantic, looking for her. I played innocent, said I had no idea she was even at court. Margaret and I thought the only way for her to be safe would be to travel far away, to the North of England, to seek refuge with her other sister, the Countess of Westmoreland. It would take an army to extract her from that castle, so close to the Scottish border and in the part of the country least friendly to the Tudors. I had a little money, and I raised more to pay for her travel."

My father stopped talking. He seemed to need to draw strength from somewhere to go on.

"We were both so very lonely. And unhappy. What happened was a sin; I am not saying it wasn't. It was adultery, twice over, and it was incest, too. But I won't lie to you, Joanna, and say I regretted it. Because that would be a terrible injustice to her memory. It lasted only one week, our time together. But Margaret was the love of my life."

He bowed his head and cried.

Something stirred in me then, besides the revulsion and the pain and the anger over the lies. I felt pity for my father and for Margaret.

"I could not escort her north; it would have raised too much suspicion with Norfolk to be gone that long. He suspected I knew something of Margaret's whereabouts. So I hired servants to escort her, and she went north. I never saw her again, until . . . Smithfield.

"I heard that she met Bulmer at her sister's castle shortly after she arrived, and went to live with him soon after. Then I heard she was having a child. I wondered. I became obsessed, really. I kept trying to get more information, without appearing too unseemly. When was the child expected? After he was born, the date of his birth indicated he could be mine. I couldn't bear it any longer; I wrote to her, demanding to know. I said if it were true, I was riding north, to claim them both, no matter what the cost.

"She wrote me back. She said the child was mine, and Bulmer knew—he knew everything. He loved her and accepted the situation. He would raise the son as his own. She said he was a fine man and she would live with him for the rest of her life, give him children of his own, along with the grown sons and daughters he had already. She said she would not agree to anything that could hurt my wife . . . and you. She never wanted you to know."

I nodded. Now I finally understood why, in her last letter, Margaret prayed daily for me to forgive her. And I also perceived the king's vicious hatred of my poor cousin, a woman who had fled to the North rather than bed him. And why Henry the Eighth had condemned her to burn to death before a pitiless mob.

"After I was freed from the Tower, I wanted to come to you, daughter, but first I had to find out about Arthur. It was not easy to travel there in the winter." He winced suddenly, and rubbed his arm. "I met with Bulmer's oldest son, Sir Ralph. If he had said Arthur's place was with the Bulmers, I would have accepted it. But he did not. He leaped at the offer for me to take Arthur."

"Does he know you are the true father?" I was aghast.

"No!" He recoiled. "But I think he has suspected the boy is not his father's. They asked to keep the baby daughter; his wife fancied her. Not Arthur. And the Bulmers do blame Margaret for taking an active role in the rebellion, rather than pushing her husband towards peace, as they say she should have."

"I thought that was Norfolk's lies."

He sighed heavily. "Like many other people of the North, Margaret opposed the religious reforms. But in her case, she harboured a personal loathing for the king and her brother-in-law, Norfolk. When all was lost, last February, Bulmer still tried to raise troops one last time, to engage Norfolk on the field. Bulmer pleaded guilty at his trial and tried to absolve her, but too many people heard her make statements that were damning to the king—and in support of the monasteries and the old ways."

I looked at my father, bleakly. "In support of me."

"There's more to it, Joanna." He looked deeply exhausted, but I knew my father. He was a stubborn man—in this, I was his daughter—and he would tell me what he needed to.

"Arthur is not like other children," he said miserably.

"What do you mean? He is a comely child, I saw him."

"He is almost four years old, and he does not speak more than a few words. He is not easy to deal with. Truthfully, he is the opposite of you at that age. I think the Bulmers were half gone out of their minds trying to raise him. And I have struggled as well."

"Father, he has been through a terrible ordeal, losing his mother and Bulmer, who surely acted as a parent to him. With love and patience, he will thrive."

Tears of relief filled my father's eyes. "Thank you, Joanna. Thank Christ and Saint Peter I was able to get here in time to talk to you."

"What do you mean?"

He clasped my hand in his. "I am not well, daughter."

"Don't say that," I cried. "You are not old."

He smiled. "It is not my age. I was wounded at Smithfield, and my time at the Tower weakened me. On the ride back down to Dartford, I fell sick. When I reached the priory property, I fell off my horse."

My father, one of the finest horsemen in all of England, had fallen off his mount? I was struck ice cold with fear.

He said, "I was unconscious and might have died in the snow had not Geoffrey Scovill come upon me. Arthur was sitting next to me, crying. He could not wake me. Master Scovill revived me, got me back up, and led me here. He knew you so well, I could not believe it. And he was at Smithfield . . . and saw us both there? Truly, it was divine providence that he should ride to Dartford today and save me."

"Listen, Father," I said. "Brother Edmund is a skilled healer, the best I have ever witnessed. He will help you. I will dedicate myself to your welfare, yours and Arthur's."

My father opened his arms. "Let me embrace you, Joanna."

We hugged each other for a very long time. And despite everything I'd heard, all that had shocked and hurt and even repulsed me, to be embraced by my father again was the answer to every prayer I'd had.

Later, I pulled Brother Edmund into a corner. "You must heal him," I said fiercely. "Promise me."

"I will use every skill I know, do everything I can," he answered. "You know that, Sister Joanna. But it would not be right to mislead you. And you are of an age and a strength to hear the truth. Your father's heart is damaged. The journey in winter down from the North of England almost killed him."

"Why did he do it?" I wailed. "Why did he not wait until spring?"

Brother Edmund said quietly: "He wanted to get here, to you, Sister Joanna, to speak to you before it was too late. And to bring you your cousin."

"Cousin?"

He looked at me. "Is not Arthur Bulmer your cousin?"

"Oh, yes." I took a deep breath. "Yes, he is."

I had five days with my father at Dartford. He remained in the infirmary, under the care of Brother Edmund and myself. Despite everything we did, he steadily weakened. There was a time when I would have refused to see it—that my father was dying. But Brother Edmund was right. I was now of an age and a strength to deal with the truth, no matter how painful. I myself raised the possibility of bringing up Arthur, of making a home with him after the suppression of Dartford, and my father nodded in gratitude.

"With you, Arthur will be safe," he gasped.

My father died on the evening of February 23, 1538. He had received last rites, and then drifted into sleep and did not wake.

Prioress Joan granted my request. He was buried in the Dartford graveyard on a hill halfway between the priory and the leper hospital. Many townsfolk requested burial there, longing to be near the nuns, to have prayers said for their souls wandering through purgatory as their bodies slowly turned to dust.

He was laid in the ground next to the grave of Brother Richard.

And for days in the priory church, special prayers were said for the departed soul of Sir Richard Stafford, youngest son of the second Duke of Buckingham, brother of the third Duke of Buckingham, and father of Sister Joanna, a novice in the Dominican Order.

50

There is little time for mourning or sadness or regret or anger or much of anything else when you are raising a small boy.

My father spoke the truth. Arthur *was* difficult. He understood what I said to him but spoke very little. He wanted to do nothing but explore: run, climb, uncover, yank, spill. He understood I was his family now, and cleaved to me, but he still ran wild and uncontrolled with me and with all of the other sisters. He calmed a little in the presence of Brother Edmund, but the worst place for Arthur was an infirmary, full of breakable objects and dangerous potions.

The person who was best with him was John. He set up games for Arthur in the stables, even some simple tasks. I felt wretched farming my half brother out to a stable hand while I couldn't be with him, but what choice did I have? I had to go to Mass and pray and lead the tapestry sessions; without these observances and duties, it was pointless to be here.

The prioress had made an enormous exception and allowed Arthur to sleep in the priory. Winifred moved into the nuns' quarters, and Arthur slept with me. He was different when he slept: his face was sweet, pure, gentle. I could see my father in him, and yes, Margaret, too. It gave me a feeling of connection to him, that this boy and I were joined by blood. During the day, when I struggled to raise him, I was not sure of my feelings for Arthur. The many moments of frustration tore at my patience. But at night, watching him sleep, so helpless, I knew that I loved him. I would die for him without hesitation.

On the third Tuesday of March, a windy day that threatened rain, I finished tapestry work a little late.

Sister Eleanor stuck her head in the door.

"You have a guest," she said, and was gone before I could ask who it was.

I went to the *locutorium*, the room that still made me deeply uncomfortable. I was relieved to find it empty. I continued my search of the front rooms of the priory but found only Gregory and the prioress herself, working in her cleaned-up and rehabilitated chamber.

It was time to check on Arthur, so I made my way to the barn. The mystery guest could wait; Sister Eleanor might even be mistaken. After all, who would visit me? I was alone in the world, except for poor Arthur. I tasted the bile of self-pity and fought it down. I mustn't give in to it.

I heard happy cries in the barn. A young woman's laugh and a man's voice, definitely, but not John's. I eased through the doors. Arthur stood on the edge of the top of a stall, his eyes sparkling. He threw fistfuls of straw at Geoffrey, who had donned a huge farmer's hat and clowned for the boy. Sitting there on a large box, watching, was Sister Beatrice, her face glowing with pleasure.

Geoffrey saw me, and the boyish foolery came to a halt. "Sister Joanna, I have to speak to you," he said, his manner respectful, almost formal. "It's important."

Again, the sourness rose within me. Was I never to know carefree, foolish laughter, to play? Why must Geoffrey take on such an official demeanour at the sight of me? Sister Beatrice gathered up Arthur. With a final smile at Geoffrey and a strange glance at me, she led the boy away. We were alone in the barn.

"I've come to tell you about Sister Christina," he said.

"She's dead."

He looked a little surprised at the way I hastened to it. "Yes, she is."

"You went to observe, of course," I said.

He cocked his head at me. "Why does that anger you?"

"It doesn't," I snapped. And then I did turn angry because I knew I was being unfair. Yet I couldn't help myself. "It's what you do, Geoffrey—observe the execution of women."

He stared at me, astounded.

"I'm sorry," I said. I sat down on the same box where Sister Beatrice had been moments before. "It's just so hard, to keep hearing things that are terrible, and seeing them with my own eyes, and yet knowing that soon enough, it will get even worse. The place I care about more than anything will be destroyed. I will no longer serve alongside the other sisters—I may never see them again. There's nothing to look forward to, just loss and more loss."

"There's Arthur."

I nodded. "Yes," I said wearily. "There's Arthur."

"Where will you go?"

I told him that my cousin Henry had answered my letter. Arthur and I could live at Stafford Castle with the family. There was not much enthusiasm in the letter, but I wouldn't have expected it. The Staffords were not affectionate with one another, but they closed ranks when called upon. We'd have a roof over our heads for life.

I took a deep breath. "Now tell me about Sister Christina."

"She was hanged at Tyburn. No one was there to represent her. The official of the court said a few words, and then they led her up to the platform. I'm told she had made no sense to anyone for weeks. Right before they hanged her, she said a prayer in Latin."

"It would have been the Dominican Prayer of Salvation," I whispered.

"At the end of her prayer, she looked out at the spectators. I'm afraid there was a large crowd of strangers; she'd become notorious. She recognised me and called out to me."

"What did she say?"

"She wanted me to tell *you* something."

I tensed with apprehension. "What?"

"She said, 'Tell Sister Joanna it's the fire on the hill.'"

I was silent for a long moment, and then the tears pricked at my eyes.

"You know what that means?" he asked.

I nodded. "You see, in a way, we understood each other; that is why her crimes are so especially troubling for me. I saw some of her spirit. She revealed more to me than to anyone, but not enough. If I had not been so blind and stupid, I could have helped her, and stopped her before all of the violence."

Geoffrey sat down next to me. The box creaked with the weight of both of us. "You can spend hours, days, weeks, years in the company of someone, and not fully understand the other person. Believe me, I know this. And you, you are not blind or stupid. You are the cleverest and bravest woman alive."

He put his arm around me, and I melted into the comforting strength of Geoffrey Scovill.

It happened so fast I lost my breath.

The closest thing to it was going underwater. I couldn't swim, but when I was a child I fell in a lake, and my father had me fished out in seconds. I remember that sense of tumbling down into something that was so powerful.

I should have recoiled from Geoffrey, yet I responded to his kisses. I behaved like anything but a priory novice. I pressed against him; I pulled on his hair; I sought out his lips, which were hard on mine, then soft, then hard again. I waited for the feeling of revulsion to seize me. It didn't.

I could feel his excitement, his passion, but his experience, too. He was practised in his caresses. I felt a pang, knowing that he had loved women before today.

I pulled away from him. We both sat there, stunned. Uncertain. It rose up in me then, the disappointment in my conduct. The sorrow over my lapse.

Geoffrey's rueful laugh interrupted my thoughts. "If only you knew how I was planning to lead up to this, the careful stages—nothing that would frighten you off. All would be done properly, with respect. And then we leap on each other? Ah, Joanna, nothing about us ever goes according to any sane plan."

I noticed he'd dropped "Sister." It gave me another pang.

He took my hand and held it carefully in his. "You didn't seem very enthusiastic about going to your family. I have to know what your idea is for your future."

"Nothing," I whispered. "There's nothing."

"Is it possible that your future could . . ." His voice trailed away. Geoffrey looked more nervous than I'd ever seen him, even when he was being rowed to the Tower of London.

"Don't say anything more," I pleaded. "I beg you."

He withdrew his hand and stood up.

"I was foolish to hope you could ever consider me," he said, his face reddening. "I am so far beneath you in rank. You're descended from royalty. I met your father. If you were to know *my* father . . ." His voice trailed away, and he shook his head.

"Is *that* what you think of me?" I demanded. "That I would reject a person for reasons of birth?"

Geoffrey said nothing.

"It is not that." Tears of frustration stung my eyes. "Oh, Geoffrey, it's what inhabits my soul. I took a vow to be a bride of Christ—that is what I wanted, the path I chose and worked toward. A commitment I made. If you don't understand that, then you don't understand me at all."

Geoffrey looked at me searchingly, a sad smile curving his lips. "No, I don't understand you, Joanna Stafford. And yet, the feeling I have for you is greater than for any woman I've ever known."

He made his way to the door of the barn and paused. "No matter what you decide, or where you go, I don't believe that can ever change."

The tears came fast. I rocked back and forth; loud, wrenching sobs filled the empty barn. I wept harder than any time since my father's death. I mourned my weaknesses at the same time as I regretted hurting Geoffrey. There was a part of me that wanted to run out of the barn, to find the road to Rochester, to ask him to take me. But I did not do it. Eventually, as my weeping subsided, I became aware of a new and strange feeling. It was, to my astonishment, relief. I was filled with anguish and yet I felt lighter, too.

It took a long time to realise why, but it finally came to me. I had responded to Geoffrey Scovill—although it was morally wrong, I had been able to do it. All these years, I'd been filled with shame and fear and disgust because of what George Boleyn had done to me when I was sixteen years old—and I'd recoiled from the prospect of any man touching me again. Sister Christina, even in her madness, had sensed that something happened to me. But Boleyn's defilement had not permanently damaged me, as I had thought for all these years. I knew something else at last, with certainty: I had not sought out Dartford Priory as a novice because of fear of man but because of hope for a spiritual life and true faith in Christ.

My tears spent, I rose to my feet and returned to my duties in the priory.

I dreamed that night, the most disturbing one I'd had since my imprisonment in the Tower. We women clung to each other, terrified. The axees were at the door, and we could hear the shouts. Smoke filled the room. I panicked and clawed for the window. Sister Christina tried to pull me back. Her fingers closed around my neck.

"No, Sister Christina, no—don't hurt me!" I screamed, hurtling out of sleep.

I lay in the dark, sweating and confused. My heart hammered so loud it rang in my ears.

"Jana?" said Arthur.

"I'm well, go back to sleep," I choked. I patted his plump little arm.

I took deep breaths and made a plan for tomorrow.

Sometimes the early spring throws up a day, a winsome day that thaws our bodies and souls. The sun shone warm and bright when, after morning prayers, I took Arthur by the hand and led him to the site of the ancient ruined nunnery on the hill.

In his other hand he had a long garden shovel. Arthur loved digging; a part of the barn was set aside for that activity after we discovered it would occupy him, happily, for long stretches.

"Look, Arthur, we can walk a square," I said. "Watch me." I found the stone foundation in the earth, where green shoots were just beginning to fight their way up out of the winter-scarred sod. I walked carefully, finding the rocks with my feet. Arthur happily followed.

I walked to the centre of the square of Saint Juliana, something I had not done with Sister Christina on All Hallows' Eve. Was this where they gathered, the nuns, when they immolated themselves? I looked down and noticed a place where the ground was fresh and torn.

I stared at it for a long time, while Arthur jumped and giggled and threw pebbles.

"Arthur," I finally said. "Give me your shovel."

He didn't understand, so I pulled it gently from his hand. "Dig," I said. "We dig."

We dug for at least a half hour. My back and hands ached from it. But Arthur never got tired. He was the one who tapped on the top of the box, then smiled at me, gleefully, as any boy would at the sight of buried treasure.

I pulled up the box from the earth. I started to open the lid, but I couldn't, my hands were shaking too much. "Open, Arthur," I said. "Open."

And he did. My little brother reached into the hole in the ground and opened the lid. I couldn't look down into the box because I was too terrified. I stared at Arthur's awestruck face.

I could see the jewels of the Athelstan crown reflected in his eyes.

I fought down my panic and prayed, out loud, seeking humble guidance and wisdom. I pointed my hands to heaven and begged for it, my eyes shut tight.

Arthur made a noise. I knew what had happened in the second it took for me to open my eyes.

Arthur wore the crown on his head.

"No!" I cried. "No, Arthur. *Oh, no.*"

I snatched it off his head—it was so heavy, how had he managed it?—and shoved it back into the box.

My weeping upset Arthur. He didn't understand it. I hugged him, desperate, crushing him with my terrified embrace.

"Are you all right, Arthur?" I asked over and over. But of course he didn't answer me. I dried his eyes and kissed his cheeks. A wobbly smile returned to his face.

"Everything will be all right, Arthur," I said. "Everything will be all right."

51

"A group of sisters have decided to live together after the suppression of Dartford Priory," said the prioress. "In other priories and abbeys, similar decisions have been made. Some of you will return to your families, but some shall pool your pensions and live in one house, a short journey from here, and attempt to follow Dominican rules for living. There won't be official enclosure, but you can, as much as possible, try to live out your ideals."

She was speaking to us in the chapter house, in the last official weeks of Dartford Priory's existence.

"Many of the largest abbeys and priories are submitting to the will of the king," she said. "By the end of this year, or possibly the next, I think it likely we shall all be suppressed."

I bowed my head.

"The fate of Dartford Priory has been decided," she said. "Several nobles and men of the court put in requests to receive the priory, and even one churchman. The Bishop of Dover expressed interest in Dartford." It was disgusting for a bishop to try to grab hold of a priory for personal gain, but it surprised no one that the brother of Lord Chester had made such a request. "I must tell you that the king has decided to grant Dartford to no other person. He is keeping it for himself. It will become royal property."

There were a few sobs in the room, from the stone benches. Even though we had all learned of it months ago, schooled ourselves to accept, this was still so deeply terrifying, the end of something that had lasted for centuries. King Henry the Eighth had personally stolen our home. And now we faced the prospect of a barren life devoid of the rich beauty of our faith.

The prioress said, "The friary is sending an almoner to dispense the pensions, since our abbey no longer has a president and steward."

The prioress lost her poise for a moment as the shadow of Brother Richard stretched across the room. She righted herself and went on. "Sister Joanna and her young cousin will ride to Stafford Castle next week. Brother Edmund and Sister Winifred will accompany them on this journey. When he returns, Brother Edmund will attempt to continue his work in the infirmary in the village, no longer as a Dominican friar but as an apothecary and healer."

Everyone made approving noises.

"And now," said the prioress, "we will not have chapter correction. We will instead go to the tapestry room, to see the work that has just been completed under the leadership of Sister Joanna."

The sisters slowly filed out of the chapter house and made their way to the tapestry room. We had hung our tapestry on the wall, for all to see. I proudly stood before it as they crowded in.

"The Greek myth that Sister Helen chose for her final tapestry was that of Icarus," I said. "Brother Edmund has shared with me the full story of the myth, and now I pass it to you."

On the side of the tapestry, an older man stood on the shore of a sea. "This is Daedalus, a talented craftsman. A cruel king imprisoned Daedalus and his son, Icarus, on the island of Crete. They were desperate to break free. They fashioned wings for themselves, to fly to freedom."

I pointed at the beautiful young man in the tapestry's centre, huge white wings springing from his back, soaring toward a pulsing sun, his hands stretched upward.

"Icarus was warned not to fly close to the sun, but it was so beautiful to him, he was drawn to it, to its greatness. He flew too high—" My voice broke. "He flew too high . . ." I simply could not continue. I looked out at the nuns and saw they, too, were fighting tears. We all knew why Sister Helen had picked this myth for the last tapestry of Dartford.

Sister Winifred surged forward. "Icarus's wings were melted and singed by the sun he flew towards, and he fell to the sea," she explained. I was so grateful for her help, for her strength. She continued: "But Sister Helen's intent was not to show Icarus falling and dying. She wanted to show the bravery of his ascent. And that is what Sister Joanna and the rest of us want to show you now."

We stood together, the nuns of Dartford, to celebrate the flight of Icarus. And then the bells pealed, and we filed into our church, to sing hymns and chant, to pray and honour God in all of His magnificent glory.

One week later, Brother Edmund, Sister Winifred, Arthur, and I gathered to leave. The brother and sister I'd grown so close to would return to Dartford for a short time, and then leave with the others. I'd never see the priory again.

I received the blessing of the prioress. She was accompanied by Sister Agatha, Sister Rachel, and Sister Anne. I'd asked the prioress not to have the entire community see me off, just a few nuns. I needed to ensure my departure would be as calm as possible; it upset Arthur to see me weep. Of course the prioress knew which nuns to select, which ones had touched my life most profoundly. For so long we'd been at cross-purposes, but now Prioress Joan and I understood each other perfectly.

Brother Edmund straightened the saddle on the grey palfrey once owned by Brother Richard. I'd learned that the day after we'd left for Malmesbury, Brother Richard had made his will and specified that all his belongings should go to Brother Edmund. He'd fully grasped the dangers he faced and taken all measures. It both deepened my respect for him and sharpened my grief over his death.

John would accompany us north. His wife had given birth to a daughter, and he had been hired as a servant by Brother Edmund after the priory closed. John had secured our belongings in all of the saddle packs, and we were about to mount our horses when there was a stir on the priory lane.

Sister Winifred's mouth fell open. "What is that?" she whispered.

Two horsemen approached, and behind them stretched something that looked like a small, low rectangular room, pulled in front and behind by other horses.

"It's a litter," I said. I'd not seen one in years.

We waited for the litter, this curtained platform for the old, the sick, or the wealthy to travel in. Brother Edmund shook his head, baffled. But I knew who was riding up the road, because he had come in my dreams so many times before today.

Once the party had reached us, a large white hand reached out and parted the curtains, and Stephen Gardiner, Bishop of Winchester, peered out.

He took in our packed horses and riding clothes.

"*Salve,*" he said pleasantly.

The prioress moved forward to greet him first, as was fitting.

"I came here for Easter Masses; I return to France tomorrow," he informed her. "I wanted very much to see Dartford Priory before . . . its next stage."

He moved toward the entranceway. "Yes, the statues of the kings," he murmured, pointing at Edward the Third and the Black Prince. "Cardinal Wolsey looked upon this; he came here in 1527, on his way to France, with a retinue of hundreds, but I was not with him. I had already gone on, to Rome." I shuddered involuntarily. What mission did he devote himself to in Rome on that occasion—arguments before the Holy Father to divorce the king from Katherine of Aragon? Or was he searching through documents stored at the Vatican to find proof of the powers of the crown of Athelstan?

His head tilted up, Bishop Gardiner studied the carvings over the door, the Ascension of the Virgin. His eyes widened, and I knew it was because he had detected the carved outline of the crown.

Arthur, bored, banged a toy against a rock on the side of the drive. Bishop Gardiner turned to look at him, and then at me with those light-hazel eyes.

"Ah, little Arthur Bulmer," he said.

Horrified that the bishop knew who he was, I scooped Arthur up in my arms.

The prioress said firmly: "Bishop Gardiner, I would be honoured to accompany you into the priory. There is much to show you. But first we should say good-bye to Sister Joanna and her party. They have a long journey ahead of them, to Stafford Castle."

The bishop took his measure of her.

"Prioress, where is Brother Richard buried?" he asked.

"That cemetery is on the hill to the west; it is between the priory and an abandoned building, a leper hospital," she said.

"I will go there now," he announced. "Sister Joanna will escort me."

Brother Edmund said, "I wish to accompany you as well, Bishop."

"No, Brother, that will not be necessary," said Gardiner dismissively. "Sister Joanna can do without you for a short time."

Brother Edmund's lips tightened. I lowered Arthur to the ground and whispered to the friar, "Take care of my cousin."

And I turned to the Bishop of Winchester, to lead him to the graves.

We walked in silence. I could feel the eyes of the others as we rounded the corner of the priory, some of them fearful, some confused, some no doubt impressed with the coming of a famous bishop to Dartford.

When we reached the grave of Brother Richard, Gardiner knelt to say a prayer. I veered to my father's grave, which I had visited the day before in order to place a few mementos. I wondered if the bishop felt any remorse at all for what he had done to these men, to all of us.

Bishop Gardiner finished his prayer and stood up. "Sister Joanna, I want you to know that I forgive you for failing me."

I couldn't believe it.

"I . . . failed . . . *you*?" I choked out.

"Dartford will be suppressed, as will Syon and Glastonbury and the rest of the great religious houses," he said harshly. "All are being torn down, distributed, liquidated by Cromwell's minions. Nine hundred years of spiritual beauty and dedication—destroyed. England's centres of prayer and learning, of civilisation and incalculable blessings. All made plunder for the royal treasury."

His eyes met mine for a fleeting instant; they brimmed with pain, with guilt, with regret.

In a thick voice, he said, "If we had been able to gain hold of the Athelstan crown, it could all have been stopped." He pointed at the graves of my father and Brother Richard. "Was the quest not worth some sacrifice and hardship?"

I was so angry I blurted the question that had tormented me since Malmesbury: "What would you have done with it if I'd found it for you? Would you have used the crown as a weapon in your private war with Cromwell? Or retained it for other purposes?"

He stared at me, a nerve quivering on the side of his throat, and then said, "Take me to the leper hospital."

I stalked ahead of him, tears of impotent rage rolling down

my cheeks. I pushed through the grove of trees, fragrant with new growth, and went down the hill.

I waited for him at the open door. A burst of yellow and white flowers lined the front wall, under the crumbling window where I had left my letters to him.

The bishop hovered just outside the ruins. He did not seem to want to enter. "I wonder," he said, "if years from now, people will walk among the ruins of our abbeys and wonder about those who lived within their walls."

I was startled that he would have a thought so like my own.

He took a step toward me, a fierce purpose in his eyes. "You have made a great champion of the Lady Mary. She keeps bringing you up in her letters to me, to everyone. It will not be easy, but we should be able to make you one of her ladies-in-waiting, and then you can be of great use to us. I think you should marry first; I have several well-trusted candidates in mind."

"No, no, no—stop," I cried, putting my hands over my ears.

"Your chastity will be honoured; it can be a marriage in name only," he said soothingly, as if that were what offended me most. "Marriage will put some distance between your vows as a novice and your service to the princess. You will arouse less suspicion if you carry a husband's name and title."

"Why would you go to such lengths to arrange this, to place me in her service?" I demanded. "You believe me to be a wretched failure."

He hesitated, and then admitted, "It is possible that the crown was destroyed by that accursed mad girl in the very first days you were back in the priory."

I winced at his description of Sister Christina.

The bishop studied me even more closely. "You are headstrong and difficult, yes, but the way you maneuvered yourself out of danger in Norfolk House . . . I had not seen the likes of it before. You are exceptional, Sister Joanna; I knew that before I ever came to your cell in the Tower. You cannot spend the rest of your life in Stafford Castle, an insignificant member of a fallen house. And I don't believe it is what you truly desire, either. Or why would you have left the family home to take vows in Dartford Priory at all? You wished a more meaningful role for yourself. A spiritual existence."

I swallowed. I had no answer to that.

"And then, while you were here, why did you go to such lengths to learn about the crown, about all that had happened in the priory? That was not what you were charged with. But you sought to learn all, to gain knowledge and experience." His voice was loud, almost thundering. I had never heard him speak this way—as if we were not in an abandoned hollow but a cathedral pulpit. "You wanted to infuse your life with meaning, Sister Joanna. And now, that need not end. It is just beginning. The forces that have massed against us are strong and devious. With my guidance, you can still serve God and the righteous cause of restoration of our faith."

"But not through political machinations," I insisted. "I have no interest in politics."

"No?" He circled me. "You went to Smithfield to pray for and to comfort your cousin, the rebel Lady Bulmer. You risked much for family feeling, but I have long been convinced it was more than that. You believed in what she believed—*and you do now.* If you will not become involved in our cause for your own sake, then do it for hers, for the memory of your cousin, who suffered and died at the stake."

I trembled. I couldn't deny the truth to his words, but to join forces with Bishop Gardiner, to bind myself to such a man, was dangerous. Dangerous to my soul, not just my flesh.

As if he could see into my thoughts and knew that I wavered, the bishop said, much more quietly, "I do not go about to prove myself a saint, yet I am not utterly a devil. Follow my lead, Sister."

Something rose up within me, stirred by the memory of my father stretched taut on the rack. I said, "And if I do not agree, what will you do to force me this time? Will you seize Arthur, imprison him, hurt him?"

Rage ignited in Gardiner's eyes. The mask of the flattering, persuasive, sincere bishop fell, revealing the cold-hearted, ruthless schemer.

"Bishop Gardiner, I will never again be your tool," I said.

I started up the hill. He leaped after me and grabbed my arm.

"I am not finished speaking to you, Sister Joanna."

I pulled my arm away. "My priory has been suppressed, Bishop. I am released as of today, and am no longer subject to church jurisdiction."

"How *dare* you address me in such a way?" he roared. "I am not some parish priest for you to shove aside, I'm a chosen adviser to the King of England. I was once his principal secretary, and I shall rule over his council again some day. Defy me, and you shall bitterly regret it, as shall all my enemies."

"Then take me now," I shouted back at him. "Return me to the Tower. Put me on your rack. Torture me—pull the levers yourself this time. But I will not live as your creature ever again, nor any other man's."

I turned and walked up the hill. I waited for him to grab hold of me, to force me. But he did not impede me. With all of the strength I possessed, I resisted the urge to turn around and look at the bishop one last time.

I pushed my way through the trees and hurried to rejoin the people who awaited me.

"Where is the bishop?" asked Prioress Joan, peering warily behind me.

"Bishop Gardiner is reflecting," I said, and turned to Brother Edmund. "Let's go. At once."

We mounted our horses, and I shook the reins, Arthur sitting on the saddle in front of me. The bells rang as we cleared the gatehouse. It must be time for the office of Sext. Everyone would file into the church, take their appointed places, begin the psalms and songs.

While making our way to the road, I heard the voice of Brother Richard: *"It is not a matter of saving our homes, our habits of living. These monasteries are all just stone and mortar and wood and glass. What has been torn asunder can be rebuilt. Those who were cast out can be summoned again. Saint Dominic walked among the people barefoot and penniless to preach the word of God. There is no reason we can't follow that wisdom in our search for meaning."*

52

By the end of the third day of travel, Brother Edmund was confident we were not being followed. Our explanation of a journey northwest to Stafford Castle was believed. And indeed, we would go there. But we'd stop somewhere very important along the way.

We found the Celtic cross in the ground, just a few hours south of Malmesbury Abbey. Brother Edmund and I examined it while Sister Winifred played with Arthur. It was a warm day, full of promise.

As I watched Brother Edmund study the writing on the cross, I thought it a shame that he had chosen not to become a priest and directly share his spiritual vision with the people. I knew it was not so much because he recoiled from the changes in religion ordered by King Henry, as difficult as they were, but because he felt himself too unworthy. Brother Edmund might never forgive himself for falling prey to the numbing powers of that tincture. I hoped that in time, after dedicating himself to helping the sick, the dying, and the poor, he would find some peace.

Thoughts of illness always triggered my deepest worry, one that nagged at me day and night.

"Arthur looks well, doesn't he?" I asked anxiously. "You don't see any signs?"

"No, and I don't think we ever will, not the kind you fear."

I stared at Brother Edmund, horrified.

"Yes. Of course. Arthur has royal blood. You think that someday it will be he who . . . who . . ." I couldn't put it into words.

"No, Sister Joanna. I don't expect that, either."

Then I understood.

"You don't believe in the crown's power or its curse. But, Brother Edmund, how could you say that? You have always been blessed with faith."

"I do still have faith," he said. "But I am also a man who knows healing and disease. And those three princes whom we suspect touched the crown, they could have been struck by ordinary fatal illnesses that kill men every day, no matter if they're royalty or blacksmiths."

I considered what he said. Part of me was desperate to agree, for Arthur's sake. But I remembered the night the walls came to life at Dartford Priory. Or when I shivered in the presence of an inexorable force in the abbey crypt. And I wasn't sure of anything.

Brother Edmund made a joyful sound. "I think I have it," he cried, of the words he had been struggling to translate on the Celtic cross. "It says, 'Without darkness, there can be no light.'"

We looked at each other for a moment, and then returned to the others, to continue on to Malmesbury.

Just as he had not been surprised when we first appeared in his half-ruined abbey, so Prior Roger Frampton greeted us calmly when we arrived a second time.

"The king will be buried with his most sacred possession," I said, my voice unsteady, as I held out the heavy box that contained the crown.

"I knew it, God in His mercy be praised," said the prior fervently. "I knew you would return to us in time."

Brother Edmund asked, "Was it foretold by Brother Eilmar?"

The prior smiled. "Not all is foretold. Sometimes it is what one feels in the heart and soul." His green eyes filled with tears.

The prior offered to allow us to witness the ceremony that he could now perform, the reunification of the king of all England with the crown he wore into historic battle. Then the long-dead Saxeon would be buried in a place of great secrecy.

But I had no desire to look upon the crown again. I saw flashes of it every day, and it quivered in my dreams every night. The pointed, swooping golden crown: simple, ancient, with gleaming crystals running along the rim, within which you could see the tiny dark speck of what might—or might not—be thorns plucked from a desert hill fifteen centuries ago. Nor did I want to be any nearer to the spirit of the king, to contemplate the wreckage caused by his irresistible challenge.

Outside the abbey, on the green, Arthur hopped over bricks

while Sister Winifred clapped and smiled. His heedless laugh made the rubble of Malmesbury less tragic, the king less ominous.

"How many more days do you think it will take to reach Stafford Castle?" asked Brother Edmund.

"Not that many," I said. I reached out to touch his arm.

"But Arthur and I will not be travelling to Stafford Castle, Brother Edmund."

He looked at me for a moment, and then his thin, sensitive, suffering face was suffused with joy.

"Shall we begin the journey back to Dartford now?" he asked.

I nodded. I did not know what I would do in the village after the priory was dissolved, or whom I would be with, or where I would find guidance. But my destiny lay there, not with my relations at Stafford Castle. Of that I was certain.

And so Brother Edmund and I gathered up Arthur and Sister Winifred, and left the beautiful, broken green of Malmesbury Abbey, to find the road over the river that would take us south once more.

ACKNOWLEDGEMENTS

I am grateful for the help and encouragement I received in writing this book.

It all began in 2005. For more than a year, I climbed the many steps leading to the apartment of novelist Rosemarie Santini, leader of a fiction workshop. It was Rosemarie who helped me through the painful beginnings. She steered me toward historical novels I'd never read before and to spiritual possibilities I'd not explored. Through the years that I researched *The Crown* and wrote—and rewrote—my chapters, I gained immeasurably from the wisdom of screenwriter and teacher Maxe Adams and from the guidance of novelist and teacher Russell Rowland. In Russell's Gotham Writer's Workshop fiction course, I received the encouragement and constructive feedback I needed to finish my novel. I thank my fellow students Rachel Andrews and Barbara Sachs, in particular, for going the distance. Instructors Greg Fallis and Brandi Reissenweber also taught rich lessons in the craft of fiction.

The Crown would not exist without my wonderful literary agent, Josh Getzler at Hannigan, Salky, Getzler Agency. Josh responded with enormous enthusiasm to my manuscript and has kept me informed, grounded, and sane ever since. I'll always think of him when Fourth of July comes around. I'm also grateful to Jesseca Salky at Hannigan, Salky, Getzler and Kate McLennan at Abner Stein. Of course, the real fireworks began when Trish Todd, the amazing editor in chief of Touchstone Books, bought my book. Trish's insightful and meticulous edit pushed my novel to the next level. She was a pleasure to work with at every turn, as were publisher Stacy Creamer, editorial director Sally Kim, senior editor Heather Lazare, senior publicist Jessica Roth, and editorial assistant Allegra Ben-Amotz. I also have a deep regard for Genevieve Pegg, senior commissioning editor of Orion Publishing Group, in England. I can't quite describe my emotions when I learned that Genevieve liked my book, except to say it made all the skipped vacations and five a.m. writing sessions very much worth it.

Many wonderful people helped me with my research of *The Crown*. First on the list is Mike Still, assistant museum manager of Dartford Borough Museum, in Dartford, Kent. He generously shared his knowledge with me and alerted me to the two books written about Dartford Priory by Peter Boreham, now curator at Medway Council in Rochester. I also wish to thank Sandie Brown, parish administrator of Malmesbury Abbey; historian Ron Bartholomew; Christopher Warleigh-Lack, curator of the Architectural Drawing Collection of Historic Royal Palaces; Emily Fildes, curatorial intern, Tower of London; and Jarbel Rodriguez, associate professor of mediaeval history at San Francisco State University. Sandra Font provided valuable assistance with my Spanish dialogue.

I spent many productive hours working on my novel at the New York Public Library's Stephen A. Schwarzman Building on Fifth Avenue. The Beaux Arts architecture and exquisite ceiling murals of the Rose Main Reading Room never failed to move me. I thank Jay Barksdale, study rooms liaison, for accepting my application to work in the Wertheim Study. An important source of inspiration in New York City was the Cloisters Museum and Gardens of the Metropolitan Museum of Art, in Fort Tryon Park. I thank the curatorial staff for their patience as I pestered them with questions or lingered in the chapter house, the tapestry rooms, or at the tomb effigy of Jean d'Alluye. I appreciate the wonderful list of suggested resources sent to me by Egle Zygas, senior press officer of the museum, primarily the books on sixteenth-century tapestries written by Thomas P. Campbell, now director of the Metropolitan Museum of Art.

The Tudor group on yahoo.com, led by the incomparable Lara Eakins, has been a cherished place of historical discussion and debate. My special gratitude goes to member Hans van Felius, who read my book and gave me notes. My dear friend Harriet Sharrard also read and shared her keen observations; my novel benefited from her knowledge of tapestries and embroidery. I'm grateful to Kurt Buker for his comments on sixteenth-century lute music and the Reverend William Collins for his stimulating theological discussions. I wish to thank other friends who gave me support during this journey: Meredith O'Donnell, Lorraine Glennon, Donna Bulseco, Ariel Foxman, Isabel Gonzalez, Nikki Ogunnaike, Megan Deem, Nicole Vecchiarelli, Natasha Wolfe, Erik Jackson, Joanna Bober, Marcia Lawther, Eilidh MacAskill, Catherine Hong, Faye Wright Penn, Elaine Devlin Beigelman and her husband Mark Beigelman, Patricia Burroughs, Tina Jordan, Megan Kelley Hall, Jim Sullivan, Evelyn Nunlee, Nina Burleigh, Anthony DeCurtis, Patty Keefe Durso, Tish Hamilton, Sandy and Brechin Morgan, Karen Park, Sulya Fenichel, Ilissa and David Sternlicht, Michele Koop, Kitty Sibille, Rhonda Riche, Beth Arky, Diane Salvatore, Jessica Branch, Toni Hope, Ellen Levine and all the members of 5150. Special thanks to Maggie Murphy, Lisa Arbetter, Alison Gwinn, and Daryl Chen at *Parade.*

And my family deserves my most profound gratitude: my mother and sister, and my husband and two children, Alexander and Nora. They were the ones who had to live with me while I anguished over my book. Without their acceptance, their love and their patience, I couldn't have finished it.

Finally, I pay tribute to the love of my artist father, Wally Bilyeau, who, if he were alive, would be sharing in my happiness over creating something of my very own.

BIBLIOGRAPHY

Bell, David, N. *What Nuns Read: Books & Libraries in Medieval English Nunneries*. Kalamazoo, MI: Cistercian Publications, 1995.

Bellamy, John. *Strange, Inhuman Deaths: Murder in Tudor England*. Westport, CT: Praeger, 2006.

Bernard, G. W. *The King's Reformation: Henry VIII and the Remaking of the English Church*. New Haven, CT: Yale University Press, 2005.

Boreham, Peter. *Chronicles of Dartford Priory: The History of the Priory of St. Mary and St. Margaret the Virgins of Dartford*. Bromley, Kent: Peter Boreham, 1999.

———. *Dartford's Royal Manor House Re-Discovered*. Dartford, Kent: DBC Public Relations, 1991.

Borgman, Erik. *Dominican Spirituality: An Exploration*. London: Continuum, 2000.

Campbell, Thomas P. *Henry VIII and the Art of Majesty: Tapestries at the Tudor Court*. New Haven and London: Yale University Press for the Paul Mellon Centre for Studies in British Art, 2007.

Cavallo, Adolfo Salvatore. *The Unicorn Tapestries at the Metropolitan Museum of Art*. New Haven, CT: Yale University Press, 1998.

Cranage, D. H. S., the Very Rev. *The Home of the Monk: An Account of English Monastic Life and Buildings in the Middle Ages*. Cambridge, UK: Cambridge University Press, 1926.

Cressy, David. *Birth, Marriage & Death: Ritual, Religion and the Life Cycle in Tudor and Stuart England*. New York: Oxford University Press, 1997.

Daybell, James. *Women Letter Writers in Tudor England*. Oxford: Oxford University Press, 2006.

Duffy, Eamon. *The Stripping of the Altars: Traditional Religion in England 1400–1580*. New Haven, CT: Yale University Press, 1992.

Ferguson, George. *Signs & Symbols in Christian Art*. New York: Oxford University Press, 1954.

Fraser, Antonia. *The Wives of Henry VIII*. New York: Alfred A. Knopf, 1992.

Gasquet, F. A. *English Monastic Life*. London: Methuen, 1904.

Hill, Paul. *The Age of Athelstan: Britain's Forgot History*. Stroud, Gloucestershire: History Press, 2008.

Jansen, Sharon L. *Dangerous Talk and Strange Behaviour: Women and Popular Resistance to the Reforms of King Henry VIII*. New York: St. Martin's Press, 1996.

Jessopp, Rev. Augustus. "Daily Life in a Medieval Monastery," *The Coming of the Friars and Other Historic Essays*. 1889; repr., Whitefish, MT: Kessenger Publishing, 2007.

Keyes, Sidney Kilworth. *Dartford: Some Historical Notes Written and Collected*. Dartford, Kent: Perry Son & Lack, 1933.

Kuhns, Elizabeth. *The Habit: A History of the Clothing of Catholic Nuns*. New York: Doubleday, 2003.

Lee, Paul. *Nunneries, Learning and Spirituality in Late Medieval English Society: The Dominican Priory of Dartford*. University of York: York Medieval Press, 2001.

The Life of Saint Teresa of Avila by Herself. London: Penguin Books, 1957.

Loades, David. *Mary Tudor: A Life*. Oxford: Blackwell Publishers, 1989.

Loomis, Laura Hibbard. "The Holy Relics of Charlemagne and King Athelstan: The Lances of Longinus and St. Mauricius." *Speculum, A Journal of Medieval Studies*. October 1950.

Luce, Major-General Sir Richard. *The History of the Abbey and Town of Malmesbury*. Wiltshire, England: Friends of Malmesbury Abbey, 1979.

Mattingly, Garrett. *Catherine of Aragon*. New York: Vintage Books, 1941.

McBrien, Richard P. *Lives of the Saints: From Mary and St. Francis of Assisi to John XXIII and Mother Teresa*. San Francisco: HarperSanFrancisco, 2003.

Moorhouse, Geoffrey. *The Last Divine Office: Henry VIII and the Dissolution of the Monasteries*. New York: BlueBridge, 2008.

———. The Pilgrimage of Grace: *The Rebellion That Shook Henry VIII's Throne*. London: Phoenix Books, 2002.

Muller, James Arthur. *Stephen Gardiner and the Tudor Reaction*. New York: Macmillan Company, 1926.

Neame, Alan. *The Holy Maid of Kent: The Life of Elizabeth Barton*, 1506–1534. London: Hodder and Stoughton, 1971.

Redworth, Glyn. *In Defence of the Church Catholic: Life of Stephen Gardiner*. London: Blackwell Publishers, 1990.

Ridley, Jasper. *A Brief History of the Tudor Age*. New York: Carroll & Graf Publishers, 1998.

———. *Henry VIII: The Politics of Tyranny.* New York: Fromm International, 1985.

Sharpe, J. A. *Crime in Early Modern England, 1550–1750.* London: Longman, 1984.

Sora, Steven. *Treasures from Heaven: Relics from Noah's Ark to the Shroud of Turin.* Hoboken, NJ: John Wiley & Sons, 2005.

Spearing, Elizabeth, ed. *Medieval Writings on Female Spirituality.* New York: Penguin Books, 2002.

Starkey, David. *The Reign of Henry VIII: Personalities and Politics.* London: Vintage, 2002.

———. *Six Wives: The Queens of Henry VIII.* New York: HarperCollins, 2003.

Tremlett, Giles. *Catherine of Aragon: The Spanish Queen of Henry VIII.* New York: Walker & Company, 2010.

Tuchman, Barbara. *A Distant Mirror: The Calamitous 14th Century.* New York: Ballantine Books, 1978.

Warnicke, Retha M. *The Marrying of Anne of Cleves: Royal Protocol of Tudor England.* Cambridge: Cambridge University Press, 2000.

———. *The Rise and Fall of Anne Boleyn: Family Politics at the Court of Henry VIII.* Cambridge: Cambridge University Press, 1989.

Warren, Nancy Bradley. *Spiritual Economies: Female Monasticism in Later Medieval England.* Philadelphia: University of Pennsylvania Press, 2001.

Weir, Alison. *Henry VIII: The King and His Court.* New York: Ballantine Books, 1991.

———. *The Lady in the Tower: The Fall of Anne Boleyn.* New York: Ballantine Books, 1992.

———. *The Wars of the Roses.* New York: Ballantine Books, 1995.